I0831839

ALSO BY MICHAEL BRIMBAU

Point Road
(2017)

❧

By the Naked Pear Tree:
The Trial of Lizzie Borden,
a Play in Verse
(2015)

❧

The Sadness I Take to Sea and Other Poems
(2014)

❧

Lizzie Borden, The Girl with the Pansy Pin
(2013 and 2021)

❧

PERCHANCE FREEDOM

Emily rowing the *Sphinx*'s dory.

PERCHANCE FREEDOM

BY

MICHAEL THOMAS BRIMBAU

PearTree Press
SMALL PRESS. JUICY READS.
Westport, MA

PearTree Press
Westport, MA, 02790
peartree-press.com

ISBN: 978-0-9819043-6-4

Printed in the United States of America on acid-free paper.

Book design by Stefani Koorey

For John Louis Miranda,
who taught me the value of a bag
of pumpkin seeds.

It is not light that we need, but fire; it is not the gentle shower, but thunder.
We need the storm, the whirlwind, and the earthquake.

Frederick Douglass

Chapter 1: Perchance Freedom

Above, a small wooden sign hung from a wrought iron brace. The script was applied against a charcoal background in a flaking, gold font and read *Daily Whaler*. The weathered placard dangled from a pair of rusty J-Hooks, where it swayed and squeaked to a gusty harbor breeze. From Buzzards Bay, a chilled wind tunneled up the Acushnet River and laundered a trenched, fingered shore of malodorous wharfs and gangplanked jetties. A sky of shadowy cotton released its rain and I had to ask myself, what am I doing here?

I held a clutched fist by my cheek but paused before knocking. Rainwater fell from a fractured roof soffit onto my face. I looked up toward the building's seaweed-colored gutters as a cool rainwater stream trickled down my forehead. A solitary drop came to rest and swell at the tip of my nose. It hung there, tickling. I wiped it away with the back of my hand. I glanced down at my dress and waistcoat and made certain I looked presentable. Though I was wearing my best boots, I couldn't help but notice that they were well-scuffed and worn. Even the laces were beginning to fray. What could one do? After all, they were the best pair I had. One of only two, I'm afraid to admit, and the others were in need of new soles. I straightened my hair, tucking a stray strand behind one ear. A jabbing finger nudged me from a behind.

"What are you waiting for? You don't need to knock. Just open the door and walk on in," I heard her remark.

"I'm not so sure I should…" I began to say.

"It's a place of business, not a private residence," came the complaint.

"No. What I mean is…"

"Hurry and open the door, Emmie. I'm getting wet."

Her command was not easily ignored. When Amy Chaloner instructed you to do something, you best get it done … even if you didn't know why. It was easier that way. Her persuasion was always compelling and never in doubt. After all, she is my best friend. If one cannot bear encouragement or motivation from a best friend, why have one at all?

"Well, here I go." I twisted the brass doorknob and pushed. Nothing happened. I pushed again. "It's locked," I declared, sheepishly.

"Oh, Emily. Get out of the way."

I heeded her warning. When she called me Emily instead of Emmie, I was certain she was in a tiff. I was stepping out of the way when she jostled by me and burst through as if there was no door there at all.

"You should really eat more vegetables," she trumpeted, marching past.

It was an old building cloaked in chalky red brick. I lingered at the granite stoop and hesitantly peered inside. Toward the back of the room were two large windows that drenched the room with needed light. The commercial view out the window was of New Bedford harbor and its watery haven of whaling ships. All the whaling vessels in the world must be here. In the distance across the harbor, one could barely discern the small bucolic town of Fairhaven through the forest of masts and roping spars. The crowded moorage reminded me of a bamboo forest by the shores of the Amazon in the Brazilian rain forest. If you are asking me when I've last been to a rain forest, I must declare that I never have. One does see these things in books, you must know. However, I prefer the green fields and stone wall corridors of the Westport countryside. After all … it's where I live.

To the rear and off to the left of the large room sat two handsome desks. They were constructed of white tiger oak and appeared to have grown out of the hardwood flooring beneath them, fashioned from the same timber. The light oak made the desks stand out against the contrasting dark walnut wainscoting that skirted the room. The upper walls were cucumber green. A man with a barbed nose and gold, wire-rimmed glasses sat at one of the desks writing. Above him was a stately portrait of our president, Abraham Lincoln, though the most impressive sight in the place was the presence of an enormous potbelly stove that sat in the center and commanded the room. It was the size of a lumbering walrus and adorned with embroidered silver trim and studded in pearly steel rivets. It was unlike any stove I ever laid eyes on.

"Well," cried Amy, "don't just stand there."

"I'm coming, I'm coming." I was reluctant to enter since I already had a job and no idea why I entertained Amy's career proposal. As I mentioned to you previously, she is very persuasive.

Amy tromped over, reached out, and clutched me by the hand. "You'll be happy you came," she declared, towing me inside.

"But, I already have a job," I argued.

She turned, grasped my arms, and lectured. "What you need is a career. And sewing other people's clothing is not a career, Emmie. As you know, Father is extremely grateful for all you have done for us. He went through all this trouble to speak to Uncle French about a position here at the paper and you should be grateful. Ultimately, it's for your own good."

"I'm always grateful to your father … and what do you mean, sewing is not a career?"

"It's just not," she growled, removing her straw hat. Yellow tresses tumbled onto her shoulders. "This salt air just leaves my hair in shambles," she lamented, running her fingers through the flowing locks. "And now rain. I must find a mirror. You wouldn't have a hairbrush, would you?"

"Sewing makes me a living," I explained, ignoring her inquiry.

"Sitting at home all day with needle and thread? My-oh-my. You call that a living?" Placing her hat back on her head, she flung her hair off her shoulders with the tips of her slender fingers. "You live a sheltered life, my dear."

"I love sewing. Makes me a good living. If it's not a career, what is it?"

"Drudgery, my dear girl. You are much too young for that."

"Young?" I shouted. "I'll be nineteen this June."

"Nonetheless. You need to advance yourself ... make your place in the world." She rolled her eyes as if the idea of advancement was hopeless. "To make a dent in life at the very least."

"A dent?"

"Yes, you know … let the world know you're alive, ready to find a place in society, challenge all benchmarks, break all the rules … splash your colors."

"Sounds like a bit much, wouldn't you say?"

"Oh, Emmie. I love you, but you are such an innocent."

"I beg your pardon."

"You have been living in that tiny town of Westport too long. You need airing … extract yourself from familiar surroundings."

"Familiarity grooms the soul and comforts the heart. That is what Grandmamma always preached."

"It also cultivates complacency and complacency propagates dreariness. It's time for you to see and experience the big places. Lay out your own yardstick and elbow tradition out of the way."

Amy's approach of the spoken word was always direct, rarely poignant, and, at times, constructively accusatory. Elbow tradition? How revolutionary is that? Who would we be as a people if not for tradition? Then again, perchance she is right. Perhaps I have been living a sheltered life. In retrospect, I suppose one person's tradition could be another's constraint. If not for change, life would become dreadfully tedious.

It has been a year since Grandmamma Charlotte White passed away and six months since Samuel, healed from his war wounds, returned to military service. As you may already know, Samuel is my suitor. And though we never entertained the discourse of matrimony, a muted assumption was one I harbored, since I can only speak for myself. Before leaving, Samuel begged that I wait for him. I must make clear that he never hinted to the impetus behind his request. Some things are understood and need no expressed interpretation. Must be marriage. Would you not say?

The year 1861 was a bad year for me and for the country … especially in the South and the civil unrest there. With hopes of Samuel and I being married unfixed, and Grandmamma's guidance no longer handy, life has left me in an unresolved hiatus, one awash in routine and a chronic rehearsal for what may never be.

I walked across the room, extended my arms, and tried warming my hands by the stove. I gave Amy's proposal serious consideration. Though it was late spring, the rainfall outdoors and the day itself was a chilly one. And, according to Amy, so were my prospects. I was thinking about how uncertain I had become about my place in life, when my contemplation was abruptly quelled.

"The fiwa has gone out, Miss," announced the man behind the desk.

"Oh," I uttered, dropping my embarrassed limbs by my side.

"Morning, Mister Hick," sung Amy.

Hick sprung from his chair. "Ah, Miss Chalonwa. What a pleasant supwise," he declared, in less than genuine tone. He spoke with a flustering speech impediment, an abridged vocabulary that omitted the letter "R." A newspaper clerk, Hick was a demure man with a slender face, a bulbous, polished head, and a clean-shaven, spiky chin. Not tall at all, he wore a scarf of woolly gray hair that embraced his cranium from ear to ear. Chunky, wire-rimmed glasses incessantly slithered down a bony nose. And although he almost certainly saw Amy and I enter, he behaved as if we suddenly materialized out of thin air.

"We are here to see Mister French about some urgent business," declared Amy.

"Mistwa Fwench is a busy man. I'm not showa he can see anyone wight now."

"He will see me," insisted Amy.

"He will, will he?" chanted the man, somewhat dubiously. With glasses perched over a hump below the bridge of his nose, he appeared more farcical than authoritative. "Do you have an appointment with Mistwa Fwench, one I am not pwivy to?" he inquired in an interrogating nasal timbre. He rubbed his hands together when he spoke as if he took pleasure in detaining us.

"Father has been here many times and he never needed an appointment," declared Amy.

"Ah, yes, how is Mistwa Chalonwa?"

"Fine. Now can you tell Mister French that Amy Chaloner and Emily White are here, please?"

"Do you have a fomwal summons … a solicitation in wighting, pewahaps?"

Amy marched over to the man's desk, found paper and pencil, and started to write. Hick glared her way, sunken eyes widened. The desk was his private domain and how dare this woman invade it. Addled and somewhat distressed, he irritably nudged his spectacles back up his nose and held out a shaky limb in Amy's direction, as if the dangling appendage contained the occult dynamic to stop her.

After she finished writing, Amy folded the paper and strutted up to the anxious clerk. Standing only inches away from the man's face, their noses nearly touching, she stood sure-footed and defiant. Hick took a rickety step back.

"There, you have it. Something in writing," she professed, handing him the note she clutched tightly between two fingers.

With a perturbed look, Hick reached out and snatched the paper from her hand.

"Now, please tell Mister French, Miss Emily White is here and that she has other urgent engagements and can be detained no longer." Amy walked away and ignored the man as if he had already left the room.

Hick cleared his throat as he warily read what she had written. "Why … yes, wight away, Miss Chalanwa," he acquiesced. Pulling a wrinkled handkerchief from his pocket, he wiped his brow and scurried up a staircase behind the desk. He studied the note carefully as he climbed, looking back at us with a stumbled gaze.

Once he was gone, I leaned over to Amy and whispered in her ear, "What did you write?"

"A formal declaration like he requested," she said, holding up her hand and carefully studying her fingers. "Did you know you can count how many loyal friends you have by the white spots that grow above your cuticles?" she casually remarked.

"Oh, Amy, I asked you a question. What did you write?"

"The note said: It is my unfortunate chore to sadly inform you that Cornelius Chaloner will be divesting his considerable pecuniary investments in the *Daily Whaler*, forthwith."

"Will he?"

"How should I know," she affirmed. "I know nothing of Father's financial affairs."

I chuckled, a hand over my mouth. "Why, Amy. You did not."

"Just a small white lie. You can't let others push you around, Emmie. Our request was a reasonable one. After all, we are not asking for an audience with the King of England. Ezra Hick likes to exercise his authority, or what little he thinks he has, and I have no time for such trivial nonsense."

"Ezra. Is that his name?"

"Yes, Ezra Hick."

"I think Mister Ezra Hick was only trying to do his job," I said. "Perhaps he was sternly instructed by your uncle to conduct himself as such?"

"Listen. One ought to devise measures to keep moving forward. You must resolve to push those with ill motives and lacking potential or agency out of your way. And Ezra Hick was in the way."

"Sounds rude."

"Must be done if you expect satisfaction."

Amy's determination always sparked a string of questions. Her boldness was such that I wish I could bottle it and utilize it myself. Her unconventional schemes always spun results—even if not always in her favor. She had a way to quickly usurp adversaries and circumstance. Of course, her striking beauty was very helpful and, at times, even intimidating. There was nothing you could ask Amy that she did not have a defense or explanation for. And though I was fearful, ask I did.

"Mister French is expecting us, is he not?"

"No. But he soon will," she confessed.

I should have known. Uncomfortable with Amy's antics, I decided it was time to leave. I hastily started for the door.

"Oh, no you don't," she prompted, clamping onto my arm. "We have come this far and we will see this through … together. Besides, it's raining. We may as well wait it out here. In the meantime, we can entertain ourselves."

I folded my arms tightly to my chest. "Oh, Amy, you're impossible at times."

"Don't worry. Father spoke to the editor earlier about giving you a job, and Uncle French acknowledged that there was an opening just for you."

Knowing Amy, I was not so sure she was telling me the entire truth—or any truth at all.

"What sort of work can he offer me? What can I possibly do? I have no knowledge of working for a newspaper."

"Of course, you do. I know of no one who has read as many books as you have. And you write wonderful letters. Every time I receive one, I spend minutes reading them."

"Minutes you say?"

"Hours even."

"You are joshing me. I admit, I write long letters, but they are not that long."

"No, they are not, but before I slit one of them open, I take out old Noah's dictionary and prepare for an evening of scholarly gratification."

I blushed. Amy rarely makes me blush. Oh sure, she has no trouble turning my face red with embarrassment, awe, boldness even, but seldom with a compliment. I fanned myself with my hand as Ezra Hick came skipping down the stairs, his spectacles bouncing on his nose. Behind him was another man carrying a stack of newspapers tied with twine.

"You may collect the west of the papwas this evening, Mistwa Bowque," said Hick, as the man walked out the front door. He slammed the door shut, shook his head, and directed his attention my way. "Yes ... Miss White, Mistwa Fwench is in his office. He will see you now." He prodded his specs back up his nose.

"Thank you, Mister Hick," said Amy, with a decisive snigger. "We'll keep you informed whether the newspaper has the funds to continue operations. Come along, Emmie."

I gave the clerk a timid smile before scurrying up the narrow stairway. Hick wiped the back of his neck with his handkerchief, sighed, and sat back down at his desk. Poor Ezra Hick. He looked so disheveled and worried.

"You were sort of curt with him, Amy. He seems like a nice man."

"Oh, he is. And there lies the trouble."

"What, being nice?"

"No," she quipped, "being a man."

At the top of the stairs, I discovered a series of labeled doors. To the right, Journalist, to the left, Circulation Room, down a small side hall, Advertising and Classified. We walked the entire length of the narrow corridor until we came to a door labeled, Rudolf French, Editor in Chief.

"Well, here we are," confirmed Amy.

"Editor in Chief?" I said, nervously.

"Yep. Rudolf French. He's a big friendly bear."

"I'm afraid of bears."

"You will love him. Ready?" She knocked on the door with one hand and held me hostage with the other.

"Enter," heralded a baritone roar.

With a puckered frown, I clasped her arm before going in. “What will I say?”

“Don’t worry. I’ll do all the talking.”

I buried my face in my hands and gulped. “That’s what I’m afraid of.”

Chapter 2: A Most Inspiring Vocation

Rudolf Remington French was a man flying many banners—gentleman farmer, un-ordained deacon, politician, and ship's captain. Although the ensign he loved flying most was that of Editor in Chief of the *Daily Whaler*, the oldest daily paper in town. He was revered as a dispatcher of information, an appointed sentinel to detail and fact—an illustrious observer of brute reality, a correspondent of good and evil, of deeds discharged by the guilty, the innocent, and bystander. His job was to collect direct knowledge, relay the story, and paint it all with wisdom and insight. Using the simple printed word was to Rudolf French an obsessive preoccupation.

He lived not far from the water in New Bedford. His Cape Cod bungalow sat between the Thayer and Judd Paraffin Works and the Hersom Soap Factory. Once a thriving residential neighborhood, it was now taken over by textile and industry. Still, it was close to his newspaper company and had a bird's-eye view of his summer cottage and farm across the harbor on Water Street, in the tiny village of Fairhaven.

Like my dear friend Samuel Cory, Mister French was also captain of his own yacht, the *Advocator*, a racing schooner that was docked nearby. It did not win many races but helped to make him commodore of the Pope Island Yacht Club.

Mister French was a large man and all of six feet. He had a round face and a gray, neatly-trimmed mustache under nickel-wired glasses, which he continually removed and wiped with his shirttail. His stance was that of a field cannon, with a decisive delivery and convincing sermon every time he opened his mouth. When he spoke, one listened. But then again, one had little choice. His gravelly inflection was always forwarded with a thrusting roar. He sat at a similar desk to the one Ezra Hick occupied, but twice as large. It was cluttered with newspapers from all over New England and included *The Providence Journal*, *Fall River Daily Evening News*, and *Boston*

Herald. Open in front of him was the latest edition of the *Daily Whaler*'s closest adversary, New Bedford's *Daily Mercury*.

"Ah, little Amy," he blared as we walked into his private office. "What a pleasant wonder."

Rudolf catapulted from his desk with gymnastic ease. I have never witnessed such a big man move so quickly and gracefully. In all of two seconds, he was standing by the door with Amy's hand in his.

She leaned over and gave the amicable giant a faint kiss on his portly cheek. "Uncle French. Wonderful to see you so chipper and healthy."

"My dear girl. If only it were so."

"Why Uncle, what is wrong?"

"The headlines my dear. It's all bad, nothing but bad."

"Well, haven't you always said, the only profitable news is bad news …"

"It's what sells papers my dear," he shouted, wagging a fist in the air. "If it were all good news, we would all cry with boredom." He laughed, wrapping his fingers around his girth, as if the laughter would spill out of his belly. Suddenly he became stern and dour. "How is old Cornelius?"

"Fine as ever."

"'Good, good," he said, with cheer. "Now who is this, if I may ask?"

"Emily White, sir." I was quick to announce.

"Yes, you remember. Father spoke to you about her."

"Not that I can remember," said Rudolf, rubbing his chin, his eyes toward the ceiling. "Well, that's of no importance. Nice to meet you Emily White," he said, shaking my hand. He had a peculiar way of shaking a woman's hand by grasping only the very tip of one's fingers. "Any relation to Wallace White … White Stables?"

"White Stables," I said with uncertainty.

"You know that rumpled establishment on the main road into New Bedford."

"No, I'm afraid not."

"Good, good. Old Wallace is a headstrong Yankee." He murmured and cleared his throat. "Not well liked."

I gave him an awkward squint. "I'm related to no one," I said. "I was an orphan. Grandmamma raised me and gave me her name." Though I had told him the truth, I was not about to explain that Grandmamma was not really my grandmother but Charlotte White, the woman who raised me.

"Well, my dear. We have something in common," he said with gnarly elation. "Mother died when I was three. I, too, was an orphan," he confessed.

"You had a father, did you not?"

"Blind and wed to a bottle," he alleged, raising a cheek and squinting an eye.

"Oh, I'm sorry, Mister French. I wasn't trying to pry. It must have been awful having no mother and a blind father."

"Oh, he could see when he wanted to," said Rudolf, arching his back and working his thumbs up and down the back of his suspenders. "All he needed to do was divorce the bottle."

I blushed.

"So, you see, young lady, it's not about who raised you but how we raise ourselves. Now look at Amy. She has lifted herself up and grown to be a catch for any wealthy businessman."

Amy delivered him a bashful smile. "Why thank you, Uncle.

His compliment was anything but honest, if not downright baffling. Amy never lifted herself up from anywhere. She had a very happy home life. Her father was wealthy and her mother loving. Not only was Mister French's observation reported with erroneous affirmation but comparing Amy with an orphan was just unfair. And though I make claim to being orphan, I would never consider myself a catch or an annuity simply to profit from the opposite sex. In all fairness to Mister French, I suppose he was just trying to be nice, and, I dare say, I would support his approach when it came to flattering Amy. It was easier that way and Rudolf French was no fool.

"Now tell me. What's all this about your father revoking investments in the paper? He has no investment. I have been after him for years to place his money in the *Daily Whaler*."

"Sorry about that," said Amy with some chagrin.

She lowered her head and pitched Rudolf a contrite demeanor, though I doubt her remorse held any sincere candor. I knew Amy well. She had her means and methods of making someone sorry they asked.

"Well, Uncle, it's that Mister Ezra Hick. He ties up my goat. It's always the same when I come here. He hands me every excuse in the world to why I can't see you."

"Oh, you must forgive old Ezra, my dear. He is only doing what he thinks is good for me and the paper. He's been with me since the forties when I came to the business, you know—a devoted employee. China has the Great Wall. I have Ezra Hick. And you, my dear, are one of the few to scale that wall."

Amy looked over and handed me an indulging grin. I gave her one of my own special gazes—one of dissatisfaction and irritability. Her expression turned puzzled.

"What's wrong, Emmie? Are you not feeling well?"

"You know perfectly well what is wrong. You left me to believe that your father made arrangements."

"Had to. It was the only way you would come."

"If I had known, I would not have come."

She leaned over and patted my hand. "Sure you would. You love me."

As always, she was right.

Rudolf French cleared his throat and interrupted. "Come girls, sit," he instructed, guiding us to a pair of chairs with outstretched arm.

"We will not be long," declared Amy, as she unruffled her dress and sat conceitedly.

Looking pretty and in control was of main concern, an impression of vital importance. Appearance and presentation was an integral appurtenance to a poised and determined temperament. Not much ever tousled Amy Chaloner's vivacity and charm. My exasperation over her antics was hardly considered or validated and, ultimately, the least of her worries—if she indeed ever had any. With the situation I found myself in, I conceded two choices: squirm with agitation or wallow in complacency. The election was mine to make. Since my only option was to allow Amy to be Amy, I selected the latter. After all, that is what friends are all about—to be yourself and allow your friend to express the same. Though I must confess to having to work at being myself when she was considered. As for Amy ... she was always self-ordained whether anyone liked it or not. What overture we may regard as venturesome, or somewhat impetuous, was ebulliently devoured by Amy and with enterprising resourcefulness. At the moment, her sunlight bleached my consternation, and I was left lending her the benefit of doubt. As if I had a choice? Time would tell if my grief would turn into glee as Amy vowed. At the moment, I would be content with a neutral outcome and one that would accommodate me with the least embarrassment or humiliation. To turn tail and walk out would only make matters worse.

"Now, little Amy, what can I do for you?"

"Oh nothing, Uncle." Amy got up and walked to a window and investigated the fisherman unloading their catch. "Just a social visit, sort of."

Rudolf French knew her well. He gave her a generous smile. "Social visit, eh?" He took a walking stick he kept by the side of the desk and rapped it three times on the floor.

"Oh look. There's a man walking the dock with a shoulder full of iron hoops," she observed. "I wonder what they're for."

"That must be Zoeth the cooper," replied Rudolf, all the time eying her and attempting to solve the puzzle she embraced.

Suddenly, Ezra Hick burst through the door, gasping for air. "Yes Mistwa Fwench. I heawd you knock. Is they'wa something you want?"

"Ezra. Get the ladies something to drink, will you? Lemonade perhaps, and a couple of glasses."

"Lemonade?" repeated Hick. "But whe'a will I …"

"I'm sure you can rustle some up. Now run along. Hop hop."

The little man scurried off. Amy looked over at me and grinned. She was conducting this performance and her actors were complying with her subliminal instructions.

"Come, sit, girl. Tell me. What's on your mind?" said Rudolf.

With one foot in front of the other, as if she was measuring the room or walking a plank, Amy returned and sat herself down. "How long have you known Father," she asked.

Rudolf procured a cigar from his desk, flung his portly frame back in his chair and gave the inquiry some thought. A subtle smile graced his face as the rolled tobacco danced on his lips.

"Well … let's see," he mumbled, juggling the wrinkled cigar from cheek to cheek. "The first time I met Cornelius we were both crew on the whaling vessel *Phoenix* out of Nantucket … oh, back in the late twenties. Your father was a common whaler and I a cabin boy. He was older than I was, but not by much. He took a liking to me."

"As a matter of fact, Father watched over you, isn't that right?"

"Yes, he did."

Rudolf slouched forward and searched his desk drawers for a matchstick. Finding one, he struck the sulfur-tipped twig along the arm of his chair and a tiny flame erupted in his hand. A stout Havana ignited as the old newspaperman puffed fervently, ejecting an orbicular pall of white smoke through plump, puckered lips. He held the cigar at arm's length, rolling it between his burly fingers, examining it as he pondered Amy's question.

"The older whale-men were hellions, you know, always trying to take advantage of greenhorns. And that was just what I was, a fifteen-year-old greenhorn, a kid out in the world ready to make his fortune, though, as a cabin boy, the only fortune to be had was experience and skill."

"Still, you must have made some money, Mister French," I declared.

He pointed my way with the nibbled tip of the moist, pulpy cigar. Through a plumage of charred tobacco, he offered me an emphatic grin as he pattered his tongue off the roof of his mouth, clacking out a reply.

"Young lady, there was little money to be made as a cabin boy on a whaler. He is the least paid of all the crew … and a captured crew at that, I may add. Shipping out on a whaling vessel is like seeing the world from prison whilst on holiday, all at once. We traveled far from home to countless lands and for years at a time. Once out at sea, there was little you could do about your fate. Oh, of course you could disembark at a foreign port. But the captain would not give you any money to return home. Once a man signed onto a whaling mission it was for the duration and he was only paid at the completion of the voyage."

Rudolf removed the cigar from his mouth, caressing the black leaf with his fingers as if it were a delicate flower. A fairly sad but serene smile emerged. "In the end, I was left with countless tales to tell and little in the way of cash." He waved an amicable reassuring finger. "But they were tales that would make a dormouse curl his furry tail into knots or permanently thwart a sap rabbit's twitching nose." He contently reclined in his chair. Lacing his fingers together he rested his hands behind his head and his feet up on the desk while the cigar danced in his mouth. "Of course, Amy has heard it all before," he said, staring up at the ceiling.

"I haven't," I said, jutting at the edge of my chair. "I love listening to sea stories." And that was the truth. Even the stench of a nauseous cigar smoke could not distance me from the storyteller when the yarn was one of nautical adventure on the open sea.

"The North Pacific, I was told," said Amy, prompting him to continue.

Rudolf had told his tale many times. And though Amy had heard them all, Rudolf loved telling them. I discovered that he was a marvelous raconteur. However, I was onto Amy's stratagem. Like a scrupulous hunter-trapper, she fed her unwary prey morsels of baited queries, ones he could not resist. And being a man of tales and writer of news stories, he could not refrain from reporting them over and over to whomever would listen.

"The Pacific was where most of the whales were going at the time," he continued. "The Atlantic was being fished out and much of Nantucket's fleet was heading west. Ah, we voyaged all over the Pacific, we did—the Sandwich Island, the Galapagos, up through the Aleutians."

"Tell us about the last voyage … the one on the *Phoenix*," implored Amy.

Enraptured, I gazed over at Rudolf, then at Amy, and back at Rudolf. I could not wait to hear what he had to tell. He loved telling. I loved listening. Rudolf French reminded me of Seabury Cory, Samuel's father. Perhaps because they were almost the same age or maybe owing to the fact that both men radiated an ambiance of wisdom and knowledge that only maturity could consign.

"Ah, yes, a sorrowful day, a sorrowful day indeed," he sighed. "We were moored north of Japan along the Russian coast, off a spit of land we called Elbow Island. That's in the Sea of Okhotsk, as you well know."

"Why of course," I said, but having no idea where the place was located or having ever heard of it.

"In the Sakhalin Gulf, if I remember," chimed Amy.

I was impressed that she was so acquainted with that part of the world.

Wherever it was. But then again, she had heard the story many times before and if she was brilliant at anything it was mimicking a parrot. Oh, please don't tell her I said that. As a matter of fact, I take it back. I should not sell my best friend short. She had a very capable mind. It was just that it was more of thespian awareness than scholarly ability. Amy had no trouble learning her lines. Knowledge was just a tool she employed when confabulating with those she wanted to pocket or who could supply her with something she wanted. In that respect she impressed everyone with her intellect and insight. And she did so without a murmur of dubiety. I know. It sounds boorish and rude to speak of her that way. But it was the truth and she had keen eye on how to get along in the society. Yes. Amy was a genius at it.

"It was cold, was it not, Uncle?"

"An awful icy abyss. As far from home as a soul can get."

"You said it was a sorrowful day, Mister French. You must not dwell on it if it pains you so," I advised. "What do you mean by an awful abyss?"

"Ah, yes." He stopped and pointed at me; one eye barely closed. "You sound like you would make an excellent reporter, young lady. It's not about the answers you receive but the questions you ask."

I looked at Amy and gave her my own exhibit of a smug simper.

"Now listen carefully, girls, and I will recount what happened."

He got up from his desk, took hold of an ivory flensing spear he used as a walking stick, and hobbled to the window. He peered out at the crumbling New Bedford whaling fleet, past the soft rain that melted down the wavy window glass, and out to his schooner moored at Fish Island, a couple hundred feet from shore.

"After a week of whaling we had anchored behind Elbow Island to shelter the ship from a blow." His tone suddenly became glum, almost funereal. "We dropped the hook in a flow of drift ice, in a patchwork of bergs that had blown in from the open sea and battered the shore. Overnight, the wind intensified. The ship dragged its anchor. The chain that held us to the bottom was the size of a strong man's arm and as rigid as an iron rod. Captain Perry called for another anchor to be dropped into the sea. We all scurried along the deck dragging a second anchor from the bowels of the ship. Before we could dispatch the mooring over the side, the *Phoenix* parted her main anchor line—sawed off by a rocky bottom. The old girl was washed up onto a stony reef of ledge and ice. That night, the whaler *Phoenix* broke up in less than a half hour."

"Oh, my," I gasped. "What did you do?"

"Let him tell us," motioned Amy, flapping a hand in my direction. With grimaced annoyance, I swatted it away. Rudolf sat back down waving his arms over the desk as if to paint a picture.

"I was thrown into the black water, on a black night, by the darkest of storms, and in one of the most starless, moonless of places on earth," he scowled. "I wallowed in the frigid breakers with nothing to hold onto but the oily foam on the tip of frosty waves, while broken crests washed over me. I paddled like the devil tying to keep my frozen body afloat. My hands had become claws and my legs congealed into frozen stubs. I was certain that I would soon have an audience with my maker. Prayer and contrition occupied my every thought as my head submerged and the bottom of the sea beckoned me. I was lost like the ship. Suddenly, a hand clutched me by the collar and plucked me from the broken sea and into a lifeboat's greasy bilge. It was then that I gazed up and into the face of Cornelius Chaloner."

"In fact, Father had saved your life more than once, if I remember how it was told to me."

"Yes, he did, and I his. Many times. Like the time Cornelius got his leg tangled in the main line as a harpooned whale dragged us along the sea ahead of the whaleboat."

"Oh my," I cried, fingers over my lips.

I have had my own adventure on Samuel Cory's schooner and was always appreciative of another's sea story. Rudolf had an arrested listener and he knew it.

"The loggerhead snapped right off at the base and Cornelius was hauled overboard. The whale towed him several hundred feet ahead of us along with the rampant whaleboat. We surged over the billowed waves with the quickness of a runaway stallion. Abruptly, the whale came to a standstill, flapping his tale like a huge fleshy hammer. Fool that I was, I immediately dove into the water and swam like a minnow after Cornelius. I took hold of the line and, hand over hand, pulled myself toward him as the giant fish swam off once again, dragging us both through the bubbling surf. Finally, I was able to seize your father by the foot and pull myself closer. Taking my knife from its sheath, I cut the line knotted around his leg just before the whale dove into deep water and could sever his limb at the knee."

"Why those are breathtaking tales, Mister French."

"Father told me that story many times," said Amy. "You both owe one another a lot."

"Yes, we do. An enormous amount." He flung his body back in his chair. "Now we are getting old, my girl. Gray and old."

The door behind us swung open and a somewhat wet Ezra Hick shuffled in with tray, glasses, and a pitcher of lemonade.

"Ah, Ezra, my good man. I knew you would pull through," boomed Rudolf.

"I went ov'a to you'wa house on Fwont Stweet and had some fwesh lemons squeezed. I'm afwaid I haven't any ice."

"That's fine Ezra, fine."

Hick stood there, dry-washing his hands, waiting for further instruction.

"That will be all, Ezra."

"Yes, Mistwa Fwench." The little man backed away and left.

"That man's a treasure," proclaimed Rudolf, pouring some drinks into glasses. "The man should have been a magician. Pulls through for me every time." He handed us both a glass. "Lemonade, girls?"

"Thank you."

"Yes, Uncle. This is great."

"Now, let's get down to business. What brings you here today, my girl?"

"I wanted to discuss a matter," she said. "One that will be appreciably beneficial."

"I see. Go on."

"Father needs a favor."

"Oh, Amy," I moaned, my head in my hands.

"He thinks you should employ Emily here."

"Hmm, yes, I see." He rubbed his chin.

"Oh, Mister French, we are so sorry," I blurted, jumping to my feet. "Amy was just …"

"Quiet, Emmie. I'm not finished."

"No, no, let the young lady speak, Amy. Now, what can you do, Miss White?"

"Do?"

"Let me put it another way. You can write and read, is that right?"

"Oh yes, sir."

"She writes marvelous poetry," exclaimed Amy. She reached into her purse. "I have an example of her writing here."

She handed Rudolf some letters.

"Are those mine?"

"Oh, don't worry, Emmie. No personal letters. Most of them contain poetry."

Rudolf took the letters and sorted one out. He held the envelope up and asked.

"May I, Miss White?"

"Why, yes, I suppose."

"You are applying for a position here at the paper, is that right?"

Amy glared a warning, an unequivocal admonishment not to betray her efforts thus far. Sapphire eyes sizzled, reflecting both enthusiasm and critical notice.

"I would feel privileged if you looked over my writings. But I must warn you. It's just casual and spontaneous scribble."

"Just down my alley," said Rudolf. "Scribble is a journalist's trade. Let's sample your literary palate, shall we?"

Unfolding one of the letters he started to read.

"Let us see. Dear Amy. Blah, blah, blah, yes, yes, excellent introduction ... been a little under the weather, et cetera ..." He continued. "I would like you to read my latest poem ... et cetera."

I sat quietly as this stranger read over my letter aloud.

"Here's one of your poems. Let's see— 'On a quivering night, in the bosom of the moon, I will cache my desire, and hide in my room, and with a telluric heart, I will render the sun, mask from its light this desire I have spun.'"

His eyes danced in his head as he navigated each inked line. He smiled, then chuckled, suddenly becoming pensive, then thoughtful. He peered up at me through the top of his wired spectacles, then back to the letter. He continued reading. He smiled once again. Taking off his glasses, he flung them onto the desk and, with a serene expression, sat back in his chair. He looked over at me for a stiff long minute.

Amy reached over and gripped my hand in anticipation. I, on the other hand, kept calm. This interview was not as important to me as it was to Amy. If I was not to get the job, then the matter was of little concern—just a pleasant visit with an interesting gentleman.

"Well, Uncle?"

"You are a very benevolent writer," he declared. "Your words are meticulously heartfelt, graceful. They dance right off the paper with almost baletic sway and you show punctilious ability."

"Thank you," I said, plainly.

"You see, Uncle. She can write." Amy leaned over to me and whispered. "What does punctilious mean."

"Fussy," I whispered back.

"Miss White, your writing displays a delicate soul. One much too clement for the news business."

"I beg your pardon, sir?" I was uncertain whether he was giving my writing critical applause or an insulting appraisal.

"You see, the news business is dirty work. It is full of thorny people and unscrupulous ruffians ... murder even. Your writing exposes a proclivity toward frangible vulnerability. And that is reasonable, considering the fairer sex. And in many respects a superb quality, I must admit, but a gratuitous obstruction when confronting the world's sully business."

"Come now, Uncle. You're not being fair."

Rudolf shook his head and threw up a hand. Amy acknowledged the gesture as a warning not to comment.

I sprung to my feet outraged. And when I did, no one in the room was more astounded than I was. "You are claiming that I have ability, but on the other hand too fragile?"

"Listen, young lady. In this business, though one must be tactful, he must do so with assertiveness and, at times, bluntness, get under people's skin, you see."

"And?"

"And, quite frankly, you are a woman and …"

"Oh, I see. I am a woman, am I? And women are different … not as capable … lacking wit or resilience—lesser beings." I became more furious than I can ever remember. "Come, Amy. I have more important affairs to tend to."

"Coming, Emmie," she capitulated, to my surprise.

"Wait, girls."

Rudolf French rose from his chair as Amy collected the letters from his desk.

"Let me finish," he begged.

I ignored him and started for the exit. He rapped his walking stick on the floor three times.

"I'm ready, Emmie. Sorry, Uncle. We'll talk later." Amy dropped and picked up letters as she scurried to catch up with me.

I continued for the door. When I swung it open, I abruptly came face to face with Ezra Hick. He looked content and clever, all the time sporting a pompous smirk. After the newspaperman rapped his stick, I could have guessed Hick would soon appear.

"Leaving so soon, ladies?" he said, his arms bracing the doorway and blocking our egress.

"Ezra, escort the young ladies back inside, will you please?"

Hick stretched out one arm to show us the way. We sauntered back over to our chairs by the editor's desk. Though I exhibited polite composure, I was still steaming.

"That will be all, Ezra."

The door closed softly. The handle latch engaged the door casing's strike plate and rang out like a snapping tree branch, echoing loudly across the room.

"We're back, Uncle," said Amy, with a demure simper.

Rudolf French must have been a dynamic and influential individual. Never have I seen Amy rattled or cow down for any man. For the first time ever, I was the lion and she the lamb. She sat back down while I held my ground, my arms folded by my chest. Rudolf plopped his six-foot frame back in his chair and stared at me. Silence ruled the moment. Amy juggled the letters. She dropped one under her chair. The lull in the room rumbled in my head. The sound it made was muffled muteness, a vacuum of noise begging cacophony, not unlike what one would hear at a burial ground in the dead of night or the hushed lull heard between unexpected claps of thunder, lacking rain. Finally, I spoke up.

"If you are finished, Mister French, I see no reason why you should hold us up any longer."

He said nothing. I continued.

"After all, it was not my idea to apply for a job here. It was Amy's."

He looked over at Amy, smiled. She became more relaxed.

"Just because I'm a woman makes little difference," I assured him. "No one is lifting whale oil casks up onto their shoulders or shoeing a horse. It is not hard labor—moving granite slabs or lifting ship tonnage into dry dock. It is work adapted for the mind. Tools are not physical strength but wit, intellect, and determination. Qualities well suited to women. And if need be to complete a mission, I have no trouble taming a troubled heart. Either mine or yours."

He listened intently and appeared quite inquisitive. I was not finished.

"A woman is capable of working for a newspaper just as much as any man. And the fact that we are more empathetic and show more compassion if need be, displays more forbearing than a man. And make no mistake, sir. I may be a woman, but place a deceased body at my feet, whether maimed by accident, slaughter, or natural causes, and hand me parchment and quill, I will report death to you like you have never read before."

Amy sat quietly looking shocked but entertained. I felt better speaking my peace and shedding a pound of inhibitions, while at the same time employing some unanticipated, if not needed, lack of restraint. Sadly, I was feeling like the cat that ate the canary. Poor Mister French sat there and endured my unmasked wrath, although it was not completely unsolicited. Suddenly, he came alive.

"I like it," he roared with a clutched fist. "The girl's got gumption."

"What did I tell you, Uncle," said Amy, looking pleased. "And she can write too."

Suddenly, I felt like I had come down with a verbal hangover. Not so much regret for what I said but for how flintily it was delivered.

"Yes, yes, I think I can find a job here for you."

"You can?" I gasped, slowly sitting down.

"Sure. I have always wanted to expand the paper's contents. Perhaps you can write a weekly piece on cooking or gardening. Advertising is a new and growing sector. Perhaps you could fit in there. Though there's not much writing."

"How about stories about sewing?" said Amy. "That's Emily's career choice at the moment."

"You work the textile mills, do you Miss White?"

I shook my head at Amy's choice of words. I was uncertain whether she was using the term "career" to mock me or had a change toward respect for what I do.

"I work out of home," I said, "most of my clients are in Westport or Fall River."

"I see. Well, young lady, we will talk further." He flapped his fingers at Amy, calling for her to hand him the letters. He inspected one closely and copied down my home address.

"Number nineteen Point Road," he said.

"Er- yes," I replied, somewhat uncertain if not surprised.

"I'll be in touch." He handed Amy the letters. "Now, girls, I have work to do."

Chapter 3:
The Scholar's Tome

We stepped outside and casually strolled along the waterfront toward the city. The spring rain had stopped and the sky was clearing. Chromatic hues in an otherwise dreary day, kindled and the peeping sun's warming rays, heightened the scent of greenery along the side of the road. However, the organic aroma of nature was smothered by the pungent, briny redolence emitted from the busy harbor, along with a stale odor of ambergris and whale oil. These scents were just a negligible distraction to the senses and were put off by the hustling traffic of carriages and people all around us. The din from galloping horses, creaking transports, and the steady hammering from shipyards added frenzy to what should have been a pleasant walk.

"It's all working for the best, I suppose," I said to myself, reflecting on the earlier affair at the *Daily Whaler*.

"It sure is," Amy replied. She ran off and climbed down a small ravine by the side of the road.

"What are you doing?" I shouted, somewhat alarmed.

She fluttered with outstretched arms, trying to keep on her feet while descending a steep embankment. At the bottom was a stony wall in advance of a six-foot drop right into the unctuous Acushnet River.

"Amy! Don't go down there. You'll fall in."

Stooping, she snatched a stray flower growing amongst an apron of grape hyacinth.

"Look, Emmie. Aren't they beautiful," she hollered, climbing back up the hill. She ran over and fixed the plucked flower under my nose. "Smell."

"Wonderful," I said, somewhat relieved.

She closed her eyes, holding the yellow flower under her nose. "I'm trying to think of what it smells like."

"It smells like you," I said.

"It does, doesn't it?"

She drew in compliments like a hubristic sponge. It was not her fault. After all, she was beautiful. And in the end, she would cache the compliment with all the others I had offered her over time.

"They grow by the empty lot across from my house. I forgot what they're called."

"It's a pinkster lily," I said, as we continued our walk.

She broke the floret's stem and weaved it into her hair just above one ear. "Pinkster lily? No. They have another name."

"Daffodils."

"That's what their called. Spring daffodils."

"And if you want to impress your friends you can call them by their practical name, Narcissus Poeticus."

She looked over at me with a wry grimace, as if I was holding a secret from her. "How could you remember such a name?"

"I wrote a poem about it. Did my research."

"You know, Emmie? That's what I love about you. You're so smart … a walking cyclopedia."

"You mean encyclopedia."

"That's what I said. A walking cyclopedia."

"Oh, Amy, stop. You are embarrassing me."

"No really. For example, it was incredible the way you handled Uncle French."

"Think so?"

"I'm very proud of you."

I was at a loss for words. I considered my behavior at the *Daily Whaler* to be beyond absolution, yet it appeared to fit the moment and resulted in a constructive finale. And if I impressed Amy, I'm glad for it. You see, it is not very often that I receive her unconditional badge of approval. Not to label myself a tattletale you understand. Still, I will tell you that Amy childishly reserves most accolades for herself. Ordinarily, I detest such an inflated demeanor in a person. Though her vain conduct in such matters strikes me as comical, if not absurd, and since we are outstanding friends, easily ignored.

"I didn't know Rudolf French was your Uncle."

"He's not."

"But you called him Uncle?"

"It's what I called him when I was a little girl. Still do. Makes him feel good."

"You think?"

"I don't think, I know. Make a man feel good about himself and he will soon be your fool."

Considering Amy's allure, charm, and unequivocal pulchritude, I can see how she would feel in such a way and be so successful at it.

"A fool?"

"Of course. After all, they're just men."

"Oh, Amy." I shook my head in laughter.

"And here comes one now," she announced.

"A fool or a man?"

"Is there a difference? Hello." She shouted, waving.

Driving toward us in his buckboard was Tim, Amy's beau. Well … close friend to say the least. It's a long story. I have noticed that in the past several months they have been spending more time together—the empress and the gallant gentleman, cut from different fabric—she lace and he leather. But lace with the toughness of a steel railway spike and leather as supple as tanned sheepskin. Make no mistake. Though a kind and sensitive soul, Tim Cadman was a paradigm of brawn and perseverance. Now, Amy's father was not very happy about the courtship Tim conducted with his daughter. Where Amy was cultured and erudite, Tim presented himself as an ordinary workhand—one glowing with kindness and practicality but, nonetheless, lacking formal education. Brought up as a farmer, it took very little away from the man who demonstrated acute intelligence and pragmatic judgment far above his station in life.

"Looking for a ride, ladies?" he cheered.

"Come, Emmie."

She sprinted toward the wagon and we climbed aboard. I sat in the back on a pile of rope as Amy plopped herself by Tim's side.

"Thanks, Tim. You saved us carriage-fare," she said, straightening her dress.

"Glad I ran into you two. Running errands is a boring chore."

"I'm not going to get splinters on this old bench, am I?" Amy floundered while scrutinizing her seat.

"You can always sit with the haul," said Tim. He looked back at me and gave me that Cadman wink. "And Emmie can sit by me."

She whacked him on the arm. "I will do no such thing. Moreover, I'm wearing white. I'm not about to soil my dress in a cargo bed. It doesn't matter to Emmie. She doesn't care." She spun in her seat and offered me doleful puppy eyes. "You don't mind if I sit up front, do you, Emmie?"

"Not at all. These are just old things I'm wearing," I said, though it was my best suit of clothing. "Besides, I'm further from the smelly horses."

She furnished Tim a snide facade. "See."

Abruptly, the harnessed team came to a halt.

"Come on, Emmie, you can squeeze up front with us. There's plenty of room," declared Tim.

I climbed over the back of the bench and sat.

"Not very often I have two gals, one on each arm."

Amy jabbed him with an elbow. He rubbed his arm and pretended to yelp. I looked straight ahead and smiled.

"So, where we going to first?" I asked.

"Drop off this load of line."

"Hope it's not going to take all day," moaned Amy.

"Not long."

Tim turned the buckboard down a muddy lane and toward the fishing docks. The wagon sagged along the sloppy soil from one side of the narrow road to the other, up then down, as it dredged through one idle puddle and into the next. The wagon's springs creaked and groaned and the bench we sat on wobbled and recoiled jarring us into one another.

"I hope we're not going to get stuck," cried Amy, looking over the side.

Tim glanced over at me and grinned. We soon arrived at the shoreline and even terrain. The ground was much drier here as the wheels crackled along the stone, lumpy ground.

"Can't you make the wagon stop jumping?" asked Amy. She held onto her straw hat with one hand and Tim's burly arm with the other. "Timothy Cadman, you are doing this on purpose, aren't you?"

The carriage wheel plunged into a hollow. Gentleman Tim shook his head. "I didn't build the road. I can't help it. There are dips and depressions anywhere I turn."

A disgusted grimace grew on Amy's face. She took a deep breath and let out a fading sigh. "I suppose it's not your fault."

"Thank you."

"It never is," she lamented under her breath.

"What did you say?"

"Oh, nothing."

"I think Timothy is doing his best," I said.

Looking away toward the open sea, she hummed, ignoring us and pretending she hadn't heard what I said.

New Bedford was very different from where I lived, though both seaports were in the business of whaling. New Bedford was a proper city. Here the Acushnet River and its anchorage was a maritime megalopolis when compared to sleepy Point Village in Westport. Instead of a sparse grove of masts, there was a jungle of protuberant spars, jutting booms, and obelisk timbers. The southern horizon was a fisherman's web of gnarling ropes, cascading lines, and shackled cables. Commanding bows heaved and bobbed from spindrift jetties like breached whales—unconquered victors, each tied to their throne, tethered by hawsers of rusted chain and awaiting the next aqueous conquest. New Bedford was known by many epithet—Fisherman's Refuge, Baleen by the Sea, Dorsal of New England, or best yet, Whaling City.

On the other hand, Cherry and Webb Harbor, at Point Village where I make my home, was a drowsy one-horse haven. It had but two modest wharfs. Here there were fifteen or more. Each one three times as long.

Tim turned the wagon toward one of the fingered piers. We drove along a claustrophobic isle of iron-strapped barrels. They were everywhere, rows of oily pews in a fisherman's cathedral, buttressed by a baleful, nimbostratus sky. It was a cooper's oasis flanked by crucifix, ship rigging, swathed in vestments of hemp and canvas. At the head of the pier, new barrels were stacked like miniature pyramids, alters of newly hewed casks, waiting to be loaded in the dingy bowels of ribbed vessels, like the dank bellies of the whales they hunted.

Our ride came to rest by the water's edge where Tim unloaded his shipment. He dropped the cargo of rope near a heap of pitched pine pilings stacked by a small shack. He chatted with a group of men. I looked over at Amy who appeared bored beyond measure.

"There sure is lots of activity here," I said.

Amy sat quietly, stared out to sea, and chewed her nails.

"The sun is breaking through," I declared, looking up at the sky. "Turning out to be a nice day after all, don't you think?"

She ignored me and, instead, nurtured her silence. The poor girl appeared restless and uneasy. For whatever reason was a mystery. It always was with Amy. She was very fickle. Her moods swung wildly at times, which made being friends a challenge—one I was happy and always disposed to assume. There was so much going on around us and she could care less. At such times I felt compelled to channel her temperament or lack of inquisitiveness. Moving over on the bench I sat closer to her.

"Timothy sure looks handsome today," I whispered, pointing at him with my nose.

She glanced over. His forearm flexed and bicep dilated as he muscled a large spool of rope up onto a firm shoulder. He dropped the immense twine bobbin by the waters' edge to await delivery to one of the many ships out at anchor. Rolling up a sleeve, he looked up at the sun and wiped his brow with his brawny forearm. I watched Amy as she studied the boy's sculptured physiology. A gleam came to her eye and a forbidding grin flourished on her face.

Much taller than the average man, with golden-brown, feathery hair and polished, sea-blue eyes, Tim was a delicacy of desire—a craving for any girl to feast her sight on and with wicked fancy. I must confess he can stir such blind ambition in a girl. I know. I am wicked. Still, no one is more wicked than Amy. Oh, don't misunderstand me. I mean wicked in a good manner—audacious and bold, with just a pinch of prancing beguilement. Without a chair or a whip, she tames the male beast with a deflected smile or distant wink of the lips. Only she can stick her tongue out at a man and have him find it alluring instead of insulting. And that is wicked. Ultimately, I propose to you that to be wicked is to be captivating or thought provoking. Always ready with a better or more speculative conclusion, whether of clothing, people, or boys. That was Amy—wicked and good.

"He does look handsome," she confessed, examining the boy from head to toe.

Tim smiled and waved over at us. I eagerly waved back. Amy turned her head away. Her face was mournful and somber. Something was wrong. I dared not ask. If so, she would lapse into misanthropic silence. The more one asked the more distant she became. Probing Amy for an explanation to her problem was like trying to untangle a cluster of yarn. The more I probed and pulled the more knots I would create. Amy was a long-steaming stew. The longer I let her simmer the easier she will become to chew.

For the time being, I studied my surroundings, which were teaming with activity, and left Amy to her ruminations for the moment. There were curious people and trappings everywhere I looked. Leaning against a nearby shack stood what must have been a twelve-foot-high anachronistic, bone structure. It resembled a scissored beak from some sort of primordial bird. The parched mandible contained a string of conoidal, ivory teeth, a row of piked molars the size of a large man's fist, and projecting from the elongated muzzle like pointy pegs on a picket fence. I knew full well what it was and had seen it many times, but never with its alabaster teeth affixed. It was a significant if not sad osteological relic. At least to the beast it once belonged to. What appeared to be the bleached skull from some antediluvian mammal or primitive dinosaur was in fact the head and jaw of a once mighty sperm whale—a desecration of a mammoth fish for which New Bedford had bedded its very foundation if not outright existence. And for what? To fashion buttons, make soap, to lubricate the machinery, and light the streets of growing cities—filling the bellies of men far beyond their needs. I call it a desecration, for I know the truth. I have read it in books and have witnessed the confession of a great whaling captain, one named Seabury Cory, who predicted that I would see the fall of the whaling industry as the sperm whale is wiped away from the face of the earth. Will there be anything to stop it?

Dockworkers were everywhere. Several feet away, barrels of whale oil were being loaded onto a wagon to be made ready for market. Behind the ramshackle shack, a blacksmith forged a new chain gypsy for a ship's winch. His steel mallet played one solitary note that pierced my ears and resonated deep within my wisdom teeth. With ceaseless, rhythmic hammering, he shaped a globule of molten metal to his wishes.

Unexpectedly, a pallet of newly-fashioned barrels rose into the air almost directly above our heads. It swung over to one of the ships where it was diligently dropped onto the deck. One's sensory perception was awakened, rattled by the perpetual din and eternal, feisty smell of the place—a pungent fish odor. Noise aside, the scent alone was overpowering and unmistakably familiar. Most of it appeared to come from leaking barrels where the golden whale oil seeped from seams between the wood and oozed onto the pinguid, clay soil. So powerful was the stench that is settled in the back of my throat, varnished my sinuses, and would linger there long after I had left the shore.

Without saying a word, Amy jumped down and walked along the pier.

"Where you going, Amy?" I yelled.

As I could have predicted, she ignored me. There was a point to investigate and a point to let go. Experience told me to let her go. We all have hidden sensitivities or fossils that we keep cloaked, sharing them with no one but ourselves. Inhumed emotions—memories, which dig themselves up to the surface and at the most ill-chosen time, like fervid moles tunneling themselves to our consciousness and stealing the pleasure or mirth of the moment. I find that these intrusive agitations are most obvious when we are removed from familiar surroundings and placed in uncharted landscapes.

As for me, I find that the seaside brings out such invasive burps of sentimentality, leaving me muddled or altogether skeptical to where I want to go, or, more disconcerting, where life is taking me. Perhaps Amy was having one of those melancholy spasms—a state of commotion that evokes a labyrinth of uncertainty and pessimism—a gnawing of aspiration and yearning, leaving one ambivalent to the world around them. The worst of it is when we don't even know what it is that plagues us. Upheaval that conceals its intentions with turbulence lacking motion, disorder absent of confusion, sorrow devoid of sadness, all bundled in gratuitous misfortune that may lack existence all together.

However, I can only speak for myself. I would not be surprised if you thought I was mad. Also, it would be wrong of me to assign fault to the sea for such indisposition, for the sea is when I am most happy—to walk along it, float upon it, or plunge into its arm, especially on a sultry summer day.

Now I am certain that you think I am mad. Think what you must. Can't say I blame you. As for Amy, I should not postulate as to what she may be thinking or feeling ... if anything at all.

In any event, there is one common peculiarity to the malady I have given so much thought to, and that is that most of us wish to be alone at such times. And, with that conjecture, I will leave Amy to her solitary retreat as she places both time and distance between us.

Along the muddy shore and just beyond the docks, a small ship, about thirty-seven feet in length, was sailed up on shore and left hove down. This allowed for its bottom to be cleaned and fastened. It sat on one shoulder with its keel just beyond the reach of the slapping surf. Its towering mast like a fallen tree rose from a pitching deck looking excruciating but proud and pointing west. Two men were hammering its planked underbelly and scrapping off the pallid crustaceans and growth that bonded to the ship's fungus-glazed keel. The two workers appeared to be of African heritage by the color of their complexion. The thinner man wore badly-stained overalls rolled up at the legs. He was shirtless. His black, fibrous muscles gleamed against the algae and bleached barnacles, which he scraped with a chiseled steel bar. His companion was a big man. He wore baggy sailor's slops that hung just below the knee and a blue striped Breton or Mariner's Jersey, apparel often seen worn by young French naval cadets. The garment was ill-fitting and too small for him. It appeared to be painted onto his large frame, its sleeves short and ragged at the ends, torn by the flexing of his enormous biceps. Even though he had his back to me, he looked familiar. I was certain I knew him. His head was shaven clean—a shimmering eggplant glistening with perspiration from its lustrous crown down to the Shar-Pei folds of skin along the base of his neck. He swung a wooden mallet, knocking the ship's loose fasteners and pitch pine sheathing deep into its oak timbers. The hollow banging echoed between the leaning ship and the granite piers along the shore. What always fascinated me was the bewildering way the hammering sound navigated its way to my ears. The striking action and the thud were fractured and askew. Though happening at the same moment, it was true for the hammerer not the far-off listener. One of the Creator's rather empirical gags, I suppose.

The hammering and scraping done by the men was suddenly eclipsed by furious shouting. Rushing just past the wagon where I sat came a tall, gaunt old man. He dragged one leg in an afflictive limp and, waving an angry fist in the air, rushed toward the two black men. Marching behind him came a determined looking scoundrel, stout and muscular, with chestnut skin and wearing a sailor's stocking hat. He looked primed for quarrel and dispute. I smiled as he glanced over. Though a man of color, he had impaling flushed eyes—green—the hue of the moss-covered stones that were exposed twice a day by the migrating tide to reveal their verdurous undertones. Ignoring my cordiality, he continued his militant strut behind the older gentleman, whose conduct was anything but.

The older gent wore a long, navy blue, double-breasted jacket garnished in walnut size gold buttons that spoke to a life of prosperity. The coat had a fine aureate embroidered insignia finely stitched around the sleeve, which he waved ferociously whilst filing his complaint. His creased face spoke to age, one of weathered determination—his eyebrows miniature woolly visors, bulged over sunken cobalt pellets, steely globules for sight that would turn Medusa herself into granite. Under withered, crinkled lips he had a long, flowing, gray beard, parted at the chin and sprouting from his cheeks like two inverted pyramids. It was a sterling image that commanded one to stand alert and salute. He was an old cantankerous whaling captain and one who mandated by fear and onslaught.

Living in a whaling village, I heard many stories of such stern skippers. The men they directed were just as ornery and unrefined. Some of these vulgar captains ruled their ship on the perpetual verge of mutiny. Every voyage they undertook was immersed with deserters, peppered with renegades, and infected by deplorable scoundrels. And there was always one crew member who pushed the captain to his limits. A two-year voyage may even claim a murder or two for which the ship captain is prosecutor, judge, and jury. The convicted wrongdoer, once found culpable, would be tied in chains and used as ballast in the bowels of the ship until he could be let ashore, or kept in the crow's nest, bound and naked, where the roasting sun singed him like a well-boiled lobster. These Captain-masters knew no other way but a cruel penance or the barrel of a gun. At least that is the way it was revealed to me by one of the greatest sea captains that ever lived—Seabury Cory, Samuel's father, who, like every other whaling captain, enriched a tale or two every time he told them.

With lathered temperament, he hobbled along toward the marooned ship, headstrong and willful, carrying his cane under one arm in defiance of his obvious impairment. The wonted din and prevailing drone of the New Bedford waterfront was about to be interrupted by the whirlwind temper ushered in by a most obstreperous individual.

For the moment, it was all a quandary as I watched the two men franticly make their way toward the beached ship. The old captain yelled arbitrary inquiries. "What are you doing? Who said you can be here? Who do you think you are?" His creaky voice became a sputtering siren in the wind.

The man in overalls stopped working and approached the yelping whaling master. By his side he held the iron bar used to rake the ship's bottom. He advanced as the captain backed away. Feeling threatened, the old captain complained to the man in the stocking hat while his shouting continued. They were too far off and I could make out very little of what was being said. The hoary captain appeared outrageously frightened and I could see panic set in even from a distance.

His colleague immediately rushed past him and tore the bar from the black man's hand. The action appeared uncalled for, since I could see no discernible threat. The black man in overalls backed away. Smelling fear, the ill-natured fellow approached him with menacing probability, gripping the bar high above his head. At that very moment, the towering figure with the shaved head placed himself between the bar-brandishing man and his companion. The stocking man lowered the implement. He was promptly taken by surprises when his opponent tore the steel strut from his hand. When he tried reclaiming it, the burly worker tossed it aside and clutched the fellow by the throat, riveting his rival against the bottom of the ship. With one arm and little effort, he lifted his advisory off the ground. The man squirmed as he hung precariously, feet off the ground. He was pinned there, wincing while his shoulders raked sharp barnacles from the keel's glaucous, copper-clad planking.

The old captain scurried off, quaking, toward the center of town, waving a bamboo cane, and crying out for help. I jumped from the wagon and ran toward the ruckus. Tim sprinted ahead. I arrived at the shore and stopped several feet from the quarreling men. Tim immediately rushed over to the big man and clutched him by the wrist. At the end of that wrist was a set of cast iron fingers riveting his suffocating victim firmly against the ship's planking. His desperate plea was asphyxiated with the gurgling foam that dribbled down his chin. Bulging eyes bloated from their sockets. His stocking hat fell from a squirming head while groundless feet dangled in midair. Desperately and miserably, Tim fought to extract the limb that bound the man firmly in place. I covered my mouth with my hand in astonishment and took a deep breath when I finally realized who the big man was. Tim pleaded with him.

"Razor … Let him go, Razor. You'll damage him."

He hopelessly struggled to pry the big man's fingers, which encircled his rival's stubby neck. He clutched Razor by the chin, turned his head, and looked him in the eyes.

"Razor, it's me Tim, Tim Cadman. Razor … let him free!"

The big man couldn't or didn't hear him. I ran over.

"Admon." I hollered.

When I cried out his name, he suddenly awakened from the heated stupor. His fiery temper thawed and, with an addled smirk, he slackened a clenched jaw and eased taut shoulders.

"Please, don't hurt him, Admon," I cried.

A remorseful expression emerged on his face. Abruptly, he released his grip. His hapless prey plummeted to the sodden riverbank. The injured man rolled onto his side, whining, coughing, and clutching his throat. Razor backed away. A gentle smile bloomed on his face as if nothing had happened.

The black man in overalls gently lifted the wounded man by the elbow and helped him to his feet. Once standing, he rebuffed his helper's assistance, yanking his arm away. He staggered off from the shore while clasping his throat.

"Miss Emily," uttered Razor, embarrassingly. He bowed his head in humble greeting.

"What's going on here, Admon," I asked.

Though I called him by his proper name, most knew him as Razor for his glossy head that he kept cleanly shaved.

"I don't know, Miss," said the big man. "It happened so quickly."

Using the term big to describe Razor would be to apply a misleading adjunct. Razor was a giant. When he walked by you, his immense frame severed the air creating its own breeze.

I was acquainted with him from the time when he crewed on Samuel's ship. He was a gentle fellow, loyal, and good-natured, a former slave who journeyed north under the command of Samuel Cory. It wasn't a planned strategy on Samuel's part to help the man but a shared accord. The Confederate South had confiscated Samuel's ship and his desire was to liberate the vessel and sail it north. He recruited a group of free African slaves as crew. Razor was one of those prior captives—men who were unable to find work in the south and on the verge of starving. Taking to gamble, he jeopardized his liberty and signed onto Samuel Cory's ship, the *Sphinx*. They made their escape, but not without difficulty, finally sailing up to Westport Point and his new home.

"My apology, Mister Cadman," said the gentleman in the overalls, extending his hand.

Tim shook it. "What went on here, Frederick?" he asked.

"Who was that elderly gentleman?" I asked. "If I can call him a gentleman?"

"The old man with the cane?" said Tim. "That's old captain Charles Tobias Morse. They call him Tobias. We younger folk call him Charlie. He hates it."

"What was he on about?"

"Trouble, that's what he's always on about. The older he gets the angrier he becomes. Retired whaling captain who resents all the progress and growth along the shore. They say he used to earn some respect. Sadly, now he demands it. And the worst thing you can do is demand anything from a whaling man."

"I must concede, it was my fault," confessed Frederick. "I should have put down my scraping tool before approaching those gentlemen. They must have felt threatened when I approached them with it. Hope we haven't upset the young lady."

"Frederick, this is Emily White," said Tim.

"Frederick Johnson," announced the man, bowing graciously.

"Nice to make your acquaintance, Mister Johnson."

"The pleasure is my fortune, Miss White. Please forgive the actions of Mister Assagai. He is very protective and vigilant of my safety. I venture to declare that the entire incident was a misunderstanding."

"Miss Emily is a steady and plucky young Miss," remarked Razor with a pasty smile. "She's used to a little hoopla. Is that not right, Miss Emily?"

"I've witnessed a brawl or two in my day. After all, I live in a fishing village. Fishermen make sport of fisticuffs. Though I have a question. Who is Mister Assagai?"

"Why, Razor," replied Frederick."I mean, Admon."

He glanced over at me with a broad glimmering and somewhat bashful smile.

"Admon. You have a surname now? How wonderful."

"Yas it is."

"The last time we met, you said you didn't know your last name."

"I had no proper name, Miss Emily. Assagai was given to me by Captain Cory."

"You mean Samuel's father, Seabury."

"The same, Miss." My conversation with Razor was a pleasant one. He was generally a fellow of few words. If not with a friendly smile or the gleam of an eye, he usually got his point across with brawn and might. Once a slave in the south, he never knew his real parents since they were separated when he was only a child. He went by only one name—Admon. As a young man, he was given another calling, one belonging to his slave master. Whether it was Washington, Jefferson, Jackson, or some other presidential sounding moniker is unknown. He never disclosed it to me and maintained not having one. All the time he spent on the schooner *Sphinx* he was only known as Razor. I preferred calling him by his Christian name. Admon— and now Admon Assagai.

"Admon, we have known one another for over a year. Please call me Emily."

"Yes, Miss—Miss Emily. And ya may call me Razor."

I could only smile and appreciate that familiarity with women for him was a colloquial dilemma and one I humorously embraced.

"Assagai … Admon Assagai. I like it. I like it very much, Admon. How did Captain Cory discover your real name?"

"No, Miss. I never knew my real name or if I ever had one. I remember my uncle telling me my father was a great hunter. He carried a long spear that he used to kill game. It was called assagai. The captain said that I should take that name of the spear for myself. It is a proud name."

"Yes. I agree. A proud name indeed."

"You'll always be Razor to me," chimed Tim, patting the big man on the back.

"What did those men want?"

"Charlie had the wharf you see here built for his ships and thinks he owns the entire harbor. Probably objected to having the vessel up on shore and near it. He deals in cotton transports from the south and sells to brokers for use in the mills. Very secretive about his little venture and thinks Frederick and Razor were spying."

"And the other fellow?"

"I have no idea who he is," said Tim, "never seen him before.

"You mean you never saw him."

"Yeah, that's what I said."

I grinned and shook my head. I should have known better than to correct Tim's verb usage. I was accustomed to simple Westport country English and often entangled in it myself, whether knowingly or not.

Razor picked up his mallet from the ground and continued to work.

"Frederick, I have a basket in the wagon for you," said Tim. "I'll fetch it."

Tim trotted away. While he waited, Frederick took a rag from his pocket and wiped clean the iron chisel.

"Are you a shipwright, Mister Johnson," I asked.

"Know something about it," he chuckled. "Work I'm doing puts a cent or two in my pocket."

Frederick Johnson was a tall lean African man with long loopy hair just covering his ears. His nose was wide, cheeks lofty, and lips thinly determined and made placid by gentle, amiable eyes. He was well spoken and with a lexicon much more sophisticated than the average boatyard laborer. He walked over to the granite pier wall and retrieved a straw hat. Under it was a canvas shoulder bag. In the bag were some tools and a book. Where there are books, you can usually unearth my nose.

"I see you read," I said. "May I be forward and ask what your book is about?"

He reached over and pulled the volume from the bag. A facetious smile flourished on his lips. "A very serious topic. Given to me by a colleague, you may say." A forlorn expression dawned as he thumbed through the volume. "May I be audacious and inquire about your sentiments on the topic of slavery, Miss White," he asked.

I was taken aback by his question since not many spoke on the topic openly. "Well ..."

"I know it is a personal matter. I see you raise an eyebrow. That is a good sign in that it is not a disparaging one. More than once I am pitched an angry scowl. So please do not feel that you need answer. One does not make friends when discussing religion, politics, or slavery, at least not among polite company, and certainly not with a gentle lady. But I am obliged to ask if only to answer your inquiry about the book. You have my apology if my pointed question offends you."

"One person's pointed question is another's blunt awl, Mister Johnson."

His demeanor and face contorted, from prying curiosity to a musing smile. It was as if I had opened a door. Though I did not invite him inside, he felt free to enter.

"Please. Call me Frederick."

"Alright ... Frederick. I must warn you. My opinion on the matter may contain convictions for which I make no concessions. And if a scowl exists, you may never witness it for it would be in my heart and not my face. And unless asked, I am careful how I express to strangers how I really feel. It saves me grief and them embarrassment. Then again, judging by the reverence and color of your skin, my thought on the subject of slavery should not provoke you. I have concealed my politics on the matter in the past to maintain approbation, especially around friends. And being a woman, some may find me tenacious in my stance when it comes to delicate issues. Still, I must confess that there comes a time when one must place civic decorum out with the cat, and despite ridicule or mockery, stand tall on principle and educate the ignorant on the constitution behind ethics and civil rights, as it pertains to all men and women."

My little speech seemed to intrigue him. Why else would he be so kind to endure my rant?

"So, it is safe for me to presume that you find slavery an injustice?"

"Is that not what I just explained?"

"I suppose it is."

"To put it plainly, yes, slavery is a perfect example of man's inhumanity to his fellow man. A travesty, to put it lightly."

"And man's inhumanity toward women."

"True. Very kind of you to concede to the plight of women in our society."

"It's not a concession at all, Miss White, but justice, as you mentioned. It was very presumptuous of me to interrogate and snare you in such a way. A gentleman would not have done such a thing. Something in you lured me to ask. Please accept my apology. We need not speak on the subject any longer if it makes you feel uncomfortable."

"You may call me Emily, please. If we are to speak of such delicate matters, one must air on the side of informality. Otherwise, it becomes a debate. And the search for truth becomes more onerous. And I must inform you that the trigger on your snare failed to engage. My dignity, if not my self-esteem, is not impaired and the subject is one that is dear to me."

"I see."

I found my conversation with Frederick Johnson intriguing—that a man without formal education could be so intelligible and eloquent in his elocution. It is the sort of banter that I cherish, a provocative discussion on the thesis of race and culture. Am I being patronizing in my assessment of the man? Has growing up in a tiny fishing village dulled my appraisal of immigrants or outsiders or those that do not necessarily look like me? I pray not. Even after all the reading I have done, I do realize that I have grown up in a white world and have always endeavored to not make the white mistake of judging another by their complexion or language. Grandmamma has taught me well. As she often said, "To exercise judgment on the color of someone's skin is to place our marbles in a yellow jar. All the blue ones will look green and you'll be wrong every time."

"Now my sentiments on slavery are very critical," I assured him. "You see, Frederick, my Grandmamma was a woman of color."

"How interesting. Was she of African descent? Perhaps we are related?" he quipped.

"She was African and Wampanoag Indian. I verily believe I am Caucasian. But Grandmamma's father was a black slave. His owners were the White family. I was an orphan. Grandmamma White took me in as her own."

"There are more orphans in this country than you can imagine, Emily ... most of them in the south. And who is more orphan than a husband and wife who are separated and sold separately."

I knew just what Frederick Johnson meant.

"Grandmamma being a person of color, one may conclude, constituted my upbringing. And they may be right. After all, she raised me. She was the only mother I ever knew. She gave me her name and taught me all her theories about life. I inherited her ethos on humanity and her value of wrong and right. When she held me in her arms and I rested my head on her shoulders, it was the only time I was actually aware of the difference in the color of our skin. To me it was just skin. Every one of us a different tone, even amongst white. Skin color, if not its constitution, is in one's heart."

"I can tell you have a healthy and godly outlook, and your grandmother a teacher of truth. You are uncommon in that you walked in those shoes; you see. Your grandmother was always a free woman?"

"Always. Free in body and mind."

"She was fortunate. Your declaration, though circumstantial, is very powerful."

"She taught me that most people wear their coloration as an emblem or placard. In some cases, it is not a banner we are born with but the one nailed to our soul. And the writing on that banner is often habitually misread or confounded by those who are anthropologically illiterate or fearful. And it's not only skin color but custom, the characteristic of bone structure, the tint of our hair, the place where our forebear's derived—all of it open to critical and unjust assessment and condemnation."

He listened quietly as I continued my rant.

"Now you ask me what I think of slavery and then declare that you find my assessment circumstantial. Allow me to set it straight. I find slavery barbaric and sinful in the eyes of God or man, having no place in civil society. That being said, I am a Christian woman, conscientiously aware that none of us live up to our Maker's intentions. Thus, I forgive those that I know are intolerant and leave it to the Almighty to sort them out."

Frederick stood there, arms crossed, listening and smiling. Finally, I finished. Having surprised myself, I found that my verbal sprint left me subjectively exhausted. He looked pleasantly amused by my rhetorical speech.

"Have you ever thought of giving lectures?" he asked.

"Lectures? Why Mister Johnson, you're joshing now. I thought what I said was commentary on a serious matter."

"Emily, my suggestion is completely earnest and without ridicule. I meant at church or a social gathering. You would be good at it."

"Come now."

"I am serious. I give lectures myself. On the very subject we are talking about."

"He 'as been lecturin' me all mornin'," cried Razor, from under the ship's hull where he was working.

I laughed. Frederick picked up a handful of barnacles and playfully flung them at the big man.

"We are talking about slavery and the crime of immortal, gross indecency, Admon. A subject of great importance to you and me. If you could scrape away human bondage the way you do barnacles, we would all have a saintly world."

The more I listened the more intrigued I became. Frederick Johnson had a charisma that unfolded before my very eyes. He was a man of substance and consequence, with a gentleness and rational authenticity that reminded me of Grandmamma. When he spoke, he ushered into the conversation a level of persuasive wisdom, revealing a foresight that was not only heard but also felt.

"You never told me what your book was about," I reminded him.

He held the book up to the sunlight and stoked the worn volume with his hand. "Oh, it's a memoir written by a friend. He gave it to me during my travels thorough Saratoga, in New York."

"A successful businessman or military man, no doubt."

"Neither."

"Perhaps a whaling captain," I further guessed.

"Slavery he acknowledged. The story of a man named Solomon Northup, a black freeman who was kidnapped and sent south as a slave."

"Kidnapped. I never heard of such a story in print. What is it titled?"

He handed me the rickety volume. At that moment, Tim appeared carrying a large basket and jug of water. Protruding from the basket's lid was what looked like a bottle with milk.

"Give me a hand here, will you?" said Tim. "I'll get the dory ready."

Frederick took the basket and walked toward the shore by the pier where the dory was tethered.

"Coming, Razor?" asked Tim.

All three men walked toward the small rowing vessel. Admon turned and waved.

"Good day, Miss Emily," he cried in his deep gruff voice.

"Nice seeing you again … ah, Mister Admon Razor Assagai." I shouted. I was certain to pronounce every syllable of his name robustly.

He gave out a hardy laugh. He was so proud of his new surname.

The two black men climbed into the dory. Razor took the oars as Tim handed Frederick the basket of unknown goods. Rolling up the cuffs of his pants, he pushed the small vessel out into the harbor. Razor wedged an oar into the pier's stone foundation and pushed the small vessel away. Tim waved as the big man fidgeted with the paddles, struggling to find his rowing cadence. In no time, the dory pulled away and out toward Fish

Island. When I walked away from shore, I realized that I held Frederick's book in hand.

"Frederick. You forgot your book." I shouted as the dory glided away.

"Read it," he yelled, cupped hands to his mouth. "We will meet again."

"Where?"

"Where justice and truth tarry," he bellowed.

"I'll take good care of it!"

I inspected the book. It appeared well-read. The sewing that tied the signatures together was fraying and pages torn and battered. Many of them were dog-eared. The cover was supple cloth, stained and soiled. I opened to the first free endpaper. The hinge was cracked, exposing the gauzy cloth material that held the volume together. The condition of the book reminded me of Grandmamma's tiny library that sat on the self at home.

I turned the first page. It was blank and yellowed. The next page had some writing inked in. It said: "To Frederick Augustus Bailey Johnson. A fellow captive whom, through the grace of God, took back his freedom in 1838 while on his journey to Canaan." It was signed Solomon Northup.

Finally, I came to the title page. The top portion was water stained, as was the entire fore-edge. The title leaf announced: *Twelve Years a Slave, Narrative of Solomon Northup a citizen of New York Kidnapped in Washington City in 1841 and Rescued in 1853.* On the verso was a frontispiece—an illustration of a pensive looking Northup sitting by a barrel and broom. He was dressed in white canvas slave livery. The caption description was thus: "Solomon in his plantation suit."

It stirred memories of tales that Grandmamma would tell about her father's time in captivity. I wondered if he dressed in the same featureless uniform. I thumbed through the pages. Suddenly, a voice from behind called out to me.

"What have you got there, Emmie?

"Amy, where have you been? I lost sight of you."

She pointed. "I was inside that shed at the end of the pier with a man."

"Alone with a man!" I said, shockingly.

"No silly. Two men."

"Amy!"

"I was watching them engraving these long ivory tusks. You know, scrimshanking."

"I think you mean scrimshawing. Carving illustrations—scrimshaw." I pricked her with a slight aspersion. "Scrimshanking is behavior you indulge in on occasions."

"That's what I said, scrimshanking."

"If you insist."

"They were sculpting an arctic scene with polar bears, seals, and ships marooned in ice. It was fascinating. Look, they made this for me."

Around her neck was a rawhide cord. Dangling from it was a white wafer of scrimshaw with an etched image of a whale ship in full sail. She brushed back her long blonde locks with the back of her fingers so I could examine it.

"Is it not something," she boasted. "Cost only a dime."

I appraised the osseous medallion, flicking it between my fingers. I worried about Amy. To encompass such beauty and manage those who may be enraptured by it can be a delicate matter. Unwanted admirers who nibble at you and venture to ensnare your graces. Though allure and elegance in a person may be an advantageous hallmark, I would readily trade it for wit and cleverness. Yes, beauty can be an inimical impediment. Having men constantly at one's feet can get tedious or even downright hazardous—but not for Amy Chaloner. She had an uncanny adroitness for sweeping such conduct out of the way and, when needed, employ it to her favor.

I glanced over her shoulder to the shed at the end of the pier. Two men loafed by an open door spying on us. One had a patch over his eye. The other man, much younger, donned arms stamped in ink. Tattoos, the sailors called them. Body scrimshaw, you may say. I discovered that not only sailors had them but soldiers. Samuel's father, Seabury, had one on his forearm. A mermaid. He had acquired it as a young whaler at a group of islands in the Pacific he called the Marquesas. It's a rare art form and only practiced abroad. It was proof that one has seen the world. One of the men noticed that I was watching him. I pretended not to look. He did a jig while the other pushed him and laughed. I could hear them prattle about Amy and engaging in disparaging hilarity. God only knows what they were saying about me.

"It's beautiful, don't you think," she said. "I'm going to have a silver chain made for it."

"You must take heed with whom you socialize, Amy. Strolling along the New Bedford fishing docks by oneself … speaking to strange men … not sound practice?"

"Oh, you're just jealous."

"I am not."

"It's made of ivory you know."

"I'm just concerned for you, dear … taking gifts from strange men."

"It wasn't a gift. I paid a dime for it."

"Just the same."

"It's better than what you have in your hand," she barked.

She flicked her hair back with a twitch of her head and turned her back to me. “Humph, a book? You can’t slip a book around your neck for everyone to see, I’ll let you know.”

“And you can’t travel halfway around the world at night while cuddling under warm bed sheets with a curio of collagen hanging around your neck. You need a book to do that.”

She suddenly turned and wrapped her arms around me. “Let’s not quarrel. I’m grateful that you worry about me. Even if you do mother me at times.”

“Thank you.” I felt exonerated.

“I’m not as naive as you make me out to be, you know.”

“Never said you were. I must admit to being a little meddlesome.”

“And I do love books. You know that.”

“I know you do.”

“Where did you get it?”

“Belongs to a former slave.”

“To a what?”

Tim yelled over to us. “Come girls. Time to get going.”

Amy took me by the hand, and we walked to the wagon.

The horse reared his head and sniveled as Tim steered him in the direction of town. Amy sat contently, admiring the gift that hung just above her breast.

“What have you got there?” inquired Tim.

“Isn’t it beautiful. It’s ivory scrimshaw.”

Tim steered the wagon with one arm and reached out for the scrimshaw with the other. He took the bibelot in his fingers and closely examined it. First, a puzzled frown then a puffed smirk emerged on his face. “That’s not ivory. It’s bone. Whale bone.”

“It is not,” disputed Amy. “It’s ivory. My father was a whaler. Don’t you think I know what ivory looks like? Besides, the man with one eye who carved it said it was.”

“Well, one eye … that explains it.”

“Timothy Cadman. You’re just jealous.”

“I must admit to being jealous on occasions, but not this time. That trinket is made of bone not ivory.”

“It’s not a trinket. It cost me ten cents.”

“Robbery.”

Outraged, Amy turned her back to him. Whilst they argued, I pretended not to listen. Instead, I looked out for the two black men that had rowed out toward the open harbor and Fish Island. The island sat only a couple hundred feet from the finger piers along the bay front. The two men were tying the skiff along the schooner *Advocator*, which was moored there. Frederick climbed on board and Razor handed him the basket of goods. The companionway, which led to the interior of the ship, swung open and a black man appeared from below. He was dressed in ragged clothing. A woman promptly followed. To my bewilderment, a child suddenly appeared. They seemed to be a family. The small girl, possibly three or four years of age, sprinted along the deck. Her mother gave chase, taking the barefoot child by the arm. She swatted her on the behind and chased her back below. In less than a minute, all three had vanished as quickly as they had emerged. I could only wonder about who they were. And though Tim was not the sort to conceal secrets, he offered no hint as to what was in the basket or an explanation to what business he had with Frederick Johnson.

Amy's curiosity never sparked when the unexpected was glaring. My guess is she had not a clue what was unfolding on the *Advocator* and, if she did, it was not important enough to talk about. You see, Amy views people in a conventional way—observing the obvious and disregarding the unexpected. The unexpected was my specialty.

Our life together is a social reception. I bring the commonsensical, Amy, the eccentricity. Our friendship is a collective of checks and balances that nourish a healthy relationship and help us make our path through life. Yes, Amy is an uncommon girl. At least that is my sentiment on the issue. She would probably see it all the other way around or wonder why I contemplate such irrelevant theories. Right now, her entire focus is channeled to the obvious—the trinket around her neck. As for the unexpected, such as those folks on the *Advocator*, if she saw them, she would have mentioned it. Looks like I will need to go elsewhere to inquire about who they are. As if it were my business. A cattish preoccupation I found difficult to avoid.

Chapter 4: There's No Place Like Home

New Bedford was certainly a busy town and riding through its center a hectic affair. At every street junction there was a throng of horses, freight transports, and a bustling public. They all competed in their rush across intersecting streets. We approached one intersection and Tim stopped abruptly. We jounced and bounced. The scissor springs beneath the bench toiled to support our weight while jarring our bodies together. Every time it happened, Amy would whack him on the arm, as if the uneven ground or unexpected stop was his fault. Her droll demeanor made me laugh. Tim took it in stride and, with every wallop, broke into turbulent laughter.

We rode north up Union Street past the New Bedford jail and the old Cordage Works. The cavalcade of people and buildings lessened. Once we were past the old Tannery Mill, the town of Dartmouth rolled under the wheels of the buckboard. Conversation between Tim and Amy was airy and genial. They were getting along and the issue of scrimshaw had been long forgotten. Before I knew it, we were riding down Old County Road toward the head of the Drift River. As I neared home, a tranquil awareness came over me. A fleecy comfort eased my bones. It was the sort of feeling you get ten minutes after having a glass of wine or, as Seabury Cory put it, "a stiff one in a hard glass" —the same giddy warmth but without the hazy stupor. It had me thinking twice about taking work in the big city. Braided stonewalls and grassy fields became more widespread the closer I got to home. All the complications of the morning visit to the city soon dwindled away. Grandmamma said it best when she declared, "In the city you must think tall and smart but once you enter Westport you don't have to think at all … the countryside will do that for you." Oh, Grandmamma, I miss you so much. How will I manage without you?

The trip home was a long one. I have calculated that if I take the job at the newspaper company it will be an arduous and prolonged journey every morning. I planned on making the trip comfortable. I would walk to the village at the Head of Westport and hitch a ride with Randy Gifford's father, who worked at the Customs House along the New Bedford waterfront.

Tim negotiated the turn at Old County Bridge, through the center of the village, and headed us south on Drift Road. The narrow Drift River flowed to our left. Its waters, black and still, were flanked by a raft of mallards. They meandered while quacking grievances about nothing in particular. Still others sunned themselves along the pitched sodded shore like sculpted, woody decoys, napping.

Overlooking the tributary, and just across a well cultured lawn, was the old stone house of Mister Howland. It was a strange abode with an asymmetrical barrier, a fence made of granite slabs sitting upright out of the ground— a neat string of giant molars. Old Humphrey Howland sat on his white-columned porch rocking in a wicker chair, a spotted dog by his side. I waved—he waved. Yes, it felt splendid to be back in Westport. There's no place like home. Every time I return, old Henry Bishop's song plays in my head. It was one of the first melodies I learned to play on the piano. Grandmamma would sing it while baking bread. She would sing the first stanza and I would finish with the second.

An exile from home splendor dazzles in vain
Oh, give me my lowly thatched cottage again
The birds singing gaily that came at my call
And gave me the peace of mind dearer than all
Home, home, sweet, sweet home
There's no place like home.

I was humming the tune when a squabble erupted between Amy and Tim.

"Why can't we stop?" complained Amy.

"Because we can't," was Tim's vacant reply.

I tried humming louder.

"Timothy Cadman, you stop this beast right now."

"Why do you want to stop?" I asked.

"I wanted him to stop at Macomber Grocers so I could get some apples to feed the ducks."

"You don't feed birds apples," Tim grumbled.

"Actually, I found that ducks will eat almost anything you throw at them," I said. "Most times, they swallow it before they realize what it is."

Tim brought the wagon to a halt in front of the old Bell School. We had passed the grocer and left it some three hundred feet behind.

"I need to hurry," said Amy. "Children will be coming out of school soon. They will scare away the ducks."

Tim and I sat patiently waiting for Amy to get down and go run her errand.

"Well?" she complained.

"What did I do this time?" grumble Tim.

"Are you really going to have me walk all the way back to the bridge?"

"Well, I can't very well turn the wagon around in the middle of this tight road, now can I?"

"And why not?"

"Be realistic, Amy. There's just no room."

"Just pull down someone's drive."

"No."

"Ugh!" She jumped to the ground. Losing her footing, she flopped onto her backside. The sleeping mallards along the grassy strand dove into the river and the squadron swam away.

I tried my best not to laugh.

"Now look what you made me do."

Tim quickly flung himself to the ground and took her by the arm.

"Don't you dare," she warned, hotly swatting his hand away.

"Look at you," lamented Tim. "You've soiled your pretty dress."

He looked back at me with a smiley wince. Amy struggled to her feet and brushed herself off.

"It's all back here," he said, dusting her dress from behind.

She abruptly jumped back clutching her fanny with both hands. "Timothy Cadman. What are you doing?"

"Trying to help."

I could contain it no longer. I turned my face and had a hardy laugh.

"Arg! You're not helping any, Miss White."

"I'm sorry," I mumbled, breathlessly, "but … but …" Laughter doused my words while I entertained tickling thoughts.

Complaining to herself, Amy tromped off in a huff on her way to Macomber's.

"I was only trying to help," he tried to explain. He climbed back up onto the wagon. "A fella just can't do anything right, I grant you."

I gave him an understanding pat on the wrist. "You just keep trying."

We watched as an irked Amy marched up Drift Road. Just then, the bell in the school tower clanged. A juvenile armada burst out its doors carrying books and gripping pencils. One little girl held up her writing slate for us to see as she skipped by. On it was written, "Spring is a cumin, and tulips are a sunin." I smiled. She tossed us a friendly wave and continued her frolic toward Old County Bridge. Another little girl skipped along on one leg then the other. I remember doing the same when I was a child—cavorting down Point Road on the way home from school.

On a dare from his dark-haired chum, a blonde-headed boy climbed up on the wheel of the buckboard and hopped into the wagon's cargo bed. The chum called out to us and complained as he betrayed his comrade-in-mischief.

"Hey you little beetle. Get off there," yelled Tim.

The child dove off and ran. Comrades in fun, they laughed and hooted, with thumbs in their ears and wagging fingers, dauntlessly taunting us to chase them.

"I don't remember being that cheeky when I was their age," said Tim.

"The light-haired one looked just like you when you were in school, Timothy."

He gazed in Amy's direction, unmindfully enlisting no rebuttal. "For the life of me, I cannot figure why she gets in those moods," he said. He stood up and hollered up the road. "The ducks are all gone, Amy. Come back."

She ignored him and continued her trek to Macomber Grocers.

"Oh, let her be. She'll be a different woman when she returns. If there's anyone that can read Amy, it's yours truly."

We watched her strutting her way. Flaunting her anger, she sashayed like a goose on a rampage with velocity in her feet, an ostentatious nose waving to the heavens. Nothing would stop her from her appointed desires.

"Look at her," declared Tim. "The most hardheaded woman who ever lived."

I could swear that the path she levied nearly singed the ground. It was not a time to be walking alongside her.

"You shouldn't fret about it," I declared. "Just let her run her course."

"I suppose your right."

"I'm sure of it."

The last few students vacated the schoolhouse. The schoolmistress, who did not appear much older than her pupils, swept the classroom of mud then latched the doors shut. Up ahead, one of the rambunctious little boys snatched the slate writing tablet from the little girl and ran off with it. She gave chase, caterwauling like someone just cut off a finger.

Tim sat silently and somewhat oblivious to the callow ruckus made by the youngsters around us. It was all of little concern to me. Children can only be children. And I could only be myself … inquisitive. After all, it is in my nature to air on the side of inquiry. However, unlike the proverbial cat that was too curious, I had to approach more carefully and with analytical scrutiny when the peering impulse came over me. There is a difference, you know. Though, when meddling in a friend's affairs, the feline approach is favored.

"What was in the basket you delivered today," I boldly asked.

"What basket?" he replied, mind absent and astray.

"The one you gave Frederick and Razor."

"Oh that."

"I don't mean to pry …"

"No, you're not prying … it, it was just grub for a couple of deck hands on the *Advocator*."

"Oh, I see."

I was unsettled as to why he was being so deceptive. Perhaps I was making too much of it. Could it be that they were really crew? We sat quietly. He appeared distant while I felt somewhat cynical. Tim had never misinformed me before. Perhaps he had good reason and I was just meddling? He sat, elbows resting on his knees, hands folded, looking down at his feet.

"Something bothering you, Timothy?" Looking over at him I lowered my head and tried to make eye contact. "I can tell there is. And it's not about feeding ducks," I told him.

"I suppose it's not."

"Would you like to talk about it?"

He glanced over. Our sight enmeshed. Insecure, blue eyes sparkled. I smiled. Suddenly his face was obstructed by sandy bangs that tumbled onto his nose. With a bulky hand he whisked the silken hair back onto his head.

"Time to get this mop cut," he said with a grin.

I sat admiring him. A limber lip curled at one corner when he smiled, prompting an appealing divot to bloom on his cheek. His nose was fine and dignified, and, if I should be so wicked to say, his face begged a girl to sit closer. One could not help but be charmed by him. He had very fair complexion that left him unable to sport a manly beard. Instead, there was fleecy stubble on his chin and sandy-colored sideburns dripping down his face and fading into a peachy bristle. If you think the absence of facial hair ranks him as less than capable amongst his peers, you would be glumly mistaken. Any man walking by and stumbling into Tim Cadman would be quick to offer an apology. If Razor exhibited the muscle of a bull, Tim revealed his with the grace of a thoroughbred.

The tips of his wispy bangs fluttered to a placid river breeze. He looked out toward the Howland estate.

"Must be grand to have lots of money," he claimed.

"Yes, it must. It doesn't mean one cannot be happy without it."

"If someone granted you a thousand dollars, Emmie, would you not be happier?"

"Well … yes. For a short time. It's not lasting. Having lots of money is like having one too many ales. Sometimes the less you have the better you feel."

"It's not how it can make me feel." He stumbled to think. "It's how it … well, makes a man altogether."

"I don't understand. You never cared about having lots of money before. Samuel pays you well as captain of the *Sphinx* and then there's your employment at the millworks. I can't believe that the lack of spare change is an issue for you."

"I'm not talking about wages. I'm talking about wealth … real money. Money can make a man."

"Yes, it can, in some respects. But what can one do? You can't hang your happiness off a rusty dream. You must be happy with what you have or worked for or you will just pale in misery all your life."

"I can't see how I will be happy without."

"Timothy. You don't believe that do you?"

"Happy without her."

"I'm not understanding you."

"Without Amy in my life."

"Oh, I see. Well, you have no trouble there. Having little money doesn't matter to Amy. She likes you as you are."

"You are not listening, Emily."

I had to stop and think. Amy had her own money. Her family was prosperous. The weekly allowance her father granted her was almost as much as a living salary. Since I have known her, I've discovered that she appraised others by how interesting and adventurous they were, not by monetary self-worth. In that respect she was exceptional.

"Your wages have never been an issue for Amy."

"It's not Amy I need to satisfy."

"Oh?"

"And it's a lot more complicated than that. If I discovered pirate treasure tomorrow it still would not be enough."

"You are right. I don't understand."

"I spoke to Amy's father."

"What about?"

"I asked him what he thought if Amy and I were to wed."

"No! You did not?" His declaration took my breath away. It was great news. Or at least I thought.

"The old man shook his head. Claimed that Amy and I were not right for each other. That she would only cause me grief and we would never be happy. It goes beyond money, don't you see, Emily. It speaks to who I am. A Westport farmer's boy, lacking education—position."

I could render some recognition to Mister Chaloner's appraisal of Tim and Amy's relationship. To Cornelius, no man was right for his daughter. I jumped from the wagon and reached out for his hand. I was determined to purge him of unhappy thoughts and channel them elsewhere.

"Come, Timothy. I want you to show me the giant bass in the river. I remember you said they actually suckle on your finger?"

"Sure. When you feed them."

"Come. Show me."

He leapt off the wagon and I led him by the hand down to the tranquil riverbank. It was a delightful spring afternoon. The piquant scent of freshly cut grass wafted out from the Howland Estate. The nativity of spring was barely weeks old and already yellow trout lilies proliferated the field on the far side of the narrow tributary. Tim's frustration diminished as we approached the Drift River's grassy shore. An aroused tingling left his hand and pulsated up my arm, churning my tummy—like when Mrs. Mosher's little dog tucked his nose in my face. The titillating sensation confounded me. It was the same sensual responsiveness I felt around Samuel—shared only between Samuel and I. It was wicked. Though Tim and I had held hands in the past and kissed once or twice—on the cheek, as a random greeting, you understand—it never kindled such a fiery impulse in me until today. Was it a womanly yearning for affection, to be held and loved, or was I just wicked? My body was betraying my heart while my mind congealed. Instantly, I released his hand before I could melt.

"Right about here." He stooped down onto one knee and rustled his fingers over the water, creating little wavelets on an otherwise glazed surface. "Near this submerged rock. They sun themselves by it."

I stood there discombobulated with a residue of distorted fervor I did not understand. Kneeling by my feet, I envisioned that he was proposing marriage to me. A lascivious shiver flickered up my spine. I became faint and detached.

"They nibble on the kelp and moss along the stones just below the surface," he said. "I usually droop a chum of bread just above the surface and the fish take it right out of my hand." He carefully surveyed the water. "I don't see any at the moment."

As he crouched there, the ducks returned. They kept a wary distance, paddling one way then the other, eager to investigate.

"Do you see any, Emmie?"

"Any what," I stammered, feeling awkwardly withdrawn.

"Fish."

"What fish?"

"Are you alright?"

I was preoccupied, still interrogating my sudden inclination and unanticipated compulsions. Why had I felt the way I did? It was Tim, Amy's beau, Samuel's best friend. Guilt gripped me tightly. He rose to his feet and rested a hand on my forehead.

"Your face looks a little flushed," he declared, running the back of his hand along my cheek. "You don't feel to have a fever."

I warily clutched and removed his limb. "I'm, I'm, fine," I stuttered, aroused from my languorous bewilderment.

"You're behaving strangely."

"I just ..." As I attempted to explain, we were unexpectedly summoned—to my advantage.

"Yoo-hoo! I'm back," she heralded.

"Amy's here." I quickly sprinted up to the road. "Am I happy to see you," I cried.

"Oh? I was only gone for fifteen minutes. What are you two doing?"

I felt a bit contrite as I watched Tim approach. "Oh, nothing, nothing at all."

"The ducks are back," declared Tim. "Where are the apples?"

"Apples?" She clutched a brown wrapper full of sweets. "Oh, the apples, well I forgot. Want some lemon drops?" She held the paper pouch out.

Tim reached in and took a hand full.

"Timothy Cadman, you put some back," she cried.

Tim laughed and handed me a couple. I was careful not to let our hands touch. I felt childish.

"Here, Emmie. I bought you some peppermint sugar sticks. I know you love them." She handed me the neatly tied wrapper of sweets.

"Thank you." I embraced her with a kiss. Holding her tightly, I didn't want to let go. It was contrition for the way I had felt about Tim.

"I must say, that was worth it," she declared.

"How can you forget the apples?" I said, taking a confectionary stick from the wrapper and placing it in my mouth.

"Yeah, what about the apples? A few minutes ago, you were tormenting me about feeding ducks," said Tim.

"I did no such thing." She climbed up onto the wagon. "Besides, I'm tired. I want to get going."

The remainder of the drive took all of twenty minutes. Amy was dropped off on Point Road at her family's summer cottage by the cemetery. Across the road, Mrs. Tripp tended the garden at the old, white Methodist church. She watched as we drove away, wiping her brow with the back of her wrist. Three minutes later, my travels came to an end at my front door.

"Are you sure you're feeling alright, Emmie? You've been quiet on the way home."

"I'm fine, Timothy." I jumped from the wagon.

I know I was being silly. However, I was anxious about making eye contact with him and sparking some sort of amorous acknowledgment between us. I was certain they were feelings which held no validity. I lowered my head and quickly started for the house.

"Emmie."

"Yes?" I tightened.

"You forgot your wrapper of candy sticks."

He extended his arm, handing me the packet. I looked up feeling foolish. Tim was a good friend. I was eager to keep him in that respect.

"Thanks, Timothy."

"You take care," he said. "I'll be in the carpentry shop if you need me."

"Oh, I won't."

He watched me as I fidgeted to unlock the entrance to my cottage. I peered back and waved. He waited until after I was inside before riding away. Slamming shut the door, I slumped up against it. I flung my head back and took a belated breath, exhaling all befuddlements. With the disconcertion of the day swept aside, it felt good to finally be home.

It was nearly dinnertime. I entered the kitchen and pondered what there could be to eat. I scrounged through the cupboard to the left of the sink and the breadbox to the right. There wasn't much. I opened the ice chest. I discovered a fusty scent of stinging mildew and sour milk. I had forgotten that I hadn't had ice for over a week. This was also a good time to reflect on what I wanted to do about earning money. Since Grandmamma passed away, it has made the difference between slurping pea soup and munching on beef stew. Oh, Grandmamma, I miss you dearly—your wisdom, your tenderness. Though there were ways I could make more money if need be, there was little I could do to soothe the broken heart Charlotte White left behind.

I'm certain one could make a claim that affairs could be much more dismal, and I should count my eggs and not my chickens. After all, Grandmamma Charlotte left me a home. Yes, I understand the crux of this argument and it is valid. Take Old Man Hooper, living in a barn up the road, when he's not sleeping under an old dory by the docks. Or consider Alice Soule who owned that neatly-kept cottage up on Cornell Road. You know, the one with the bright yellow shutters. She stumbled on bad times, lost her home, and had to move in with her sister in the city. I hear that her sibling has since passed away and poor Alice is now lodging at the Almshouse in Fall River.

Grandmamma often alluded to the doctrine that, "The good Lord grants us a roof over our heads but it's our burden to supply ourselves with plumage for our bedding." Since she made her perceptive apothegm, the cost of goose feathers has almost doubled, the roof has begun to leak, and cracked windows are in dire need of new glazing. Ultimately, I may need to take the position with the newspaper company in New Bedford.

After finishing my evening meal, I took a casual stroll down by the water. The young whaler *Kate Cory* was making ready to put out to sea on its fourth voyage after being away for almost a year. Her crew toiled, loading a heap of barrels, stockpiled at the end of the jetty, onto its deck. Three burly men hung on a rope, jerking it down, raising a pallet of six iron-hooped casks high into the air and over the ship's gunwales. The vessel's baggy main sails drooped from their yard arms and bull-whipped loosely to a clement breeze. The tenting fabric was left to air and dry by the feeble late-day sunlight after being soaked in a morning of rain. An apricot sun hid behind the oil-stained canvas, winking at me occasionally as the tarnished cloth bloated with air, then lazily fainted and flapped like laundered bed sheets. An orange glow illuminated the western horizon as the thawed, inept ball slithered behind a scalloped, chiffon sky.

At the bow, someone hoisted a flogging jib. Once inflated, the sail violently spanked about in a shredded din until its sheet was made fast. Once tethered, the cleated sail inflated and, like a slivered bladder, heaved and tugged causing the ship to veer. The dock lines clacked and groaned whilst battling to hold the vessel to the wharf. The ballooned jib cloth hid the tepid rays of dimming sunlight, leaving me in its chilled shadow.

A man climbed up the ratlines like a clumsy spider with only two legs, while in the crow's nest above, an associate tightened stays and fastened rope blocks. Along the planked deck rigging, deadeyes were made taut and bolts on chain straps inspected for corrosion, while the first mate shouted orders. High above this nautical theatre, a shrieking seagull circled the harbor, squawking his repetitive chantey, accompanied by the baritone ensemble of laboring men on the whaling brig.

On the other side of Cherry and Webb Harbor, the blowing sand from undulating dunes gave motion to an otherwise static, seaside landscape. The ever-changing sandy knolls were shifted by a perpetual lashing wind and the olive-colored marram grass, which shivered wildly. A saline redolence saturated the cool moist air and engulfed one's desires and faculties, melting all quandary and despair. Cherry and Webb Harbor at Point Village is like no other place I have known.

Now, take the city. Any city. There one discovers the boisterousness, marching band of humanity, barging in one ear, trumpeting the brain, and marching out the other. Once away from such an urban environment, you enter an antithetical world of farm country—another extreme. Here the silence can be obstreperous, a soundless arena of placidity, but for the occasional rustling of breeze-swept leaves or a hidden peeping bird.

However, along the sea, there is that equal measure of sound and movement; like the wind off the water that drifts and sings, caressing every fold and crevice of one's ear—an aged briny breeze that purifies the mind from a day's soiled worriment and dusty concern. Here the ataractic surf, with its slumberous roar, tumbles and surrenders at one's feet, assuaging the soul and rendering one's spirit to tranquility. And the scent—ah, the scent—an incense of freshness, laundering one's sinuses and unburdening the mind of all blunt contemplation. I'll say it again. Point Village is like no other place I have known.

I turned from the whaler *Kate Cory* and walked over to Lee's Wharf, less than a hundred feet away. There the schooner *Sphinx*, Samuel Cory's vessel, sits between the hulking whaler *Janet* and brig *Mermaid*. Lightly built, the double-masted yacht is a gentleman's vessel. Its pure white hull was outfitted for pleasure and rigged for racing. Samuel was captivated with fast sailing vessels. I never witnessed him racing *Sphinx* since most events took place in distant harbors and in such places as Newport in Rhode Island and Boston, where those sorts of activities take place. It requires lots of money to support a novelty vessel such as *Sphinx*. In tiny Westport, where money was as uncommon as a white whale, the sleek schooner had an alliance with no other vessel in the harbor.

Samuel had purchased her with help from his father Seabury Cory. I had sailed on her on many occasions. Seabury lived in the cottage next to mine. He was a venerable whaling skipper who had cached his earnings into a tidy sum. Unlike the wealthy whalers of Nantucket and New Bedford who built gracious mansions and stately homes, old Seabury kept a rather small five-room Cape-style cottage, where Samuel was born, and where he vied on the side of modest simplicity.

Samuel loves his ship. He has taken us sailing on *Sphinx* many times just to spend a day on the waters. Routinely, we ventured so far out that land appeared as a hazy ribbon along the horizon. I confess it takes some time before one feels safe or self-assured. Sailing far from shore is an extrinsic circumstance for most folks and few have done so. The average person has only a slight impression of what it is like to sail afar and lose all sight of solid terrain. Most of us who live by the sea are no different than those who do not, in that few of us have little reason to venture out on the water unless it's to make a living by fishing or trade. After all, not many of us keep a dory in our hip pocket. Of course, there are the affluent city folk who commonly venture out into Long Island Sound on one of the Fall River paddle ships to such places as Providence and New York. The simple ordinary folk, who live on Westport's country lanes, have little reason or money to venture to such places. If they did, the safety of a horse-drawn carriage or train would be more agreeable. After all, how many people have perished in a squall while traveling by coach?

I know I'm being a bit fatuous in making topical conversation. Grandmamma often shouted at me, "Get to the point child, the blunt end is wearisome." Thus, allow me to conclude and declare that I, too, love Samuel's ship. She has taken me to many distant ports—the ship that is. Samuel often refers to sailing vessels as 'she', as do others. Many of the whaling vessels are named after family members—a wife, a daughter.

I will speak to one voyage I was on which took us into the Canadian maritime, to Halifax and beyond—a mission of exploration and rescue. An adventure like no other. On it, we encountered waves as tall and spikey as church steeples—accompanied by pods of gamboling whales, while battered by fearsome tempests. And to make matters worse than spilled molasses, on the voyage home we were pursued by a Confederate gunship, firing canon. I tease you not. It was a chase for our lives, one in which, I must declare, we were fortunate to escape from. It was an exploit that one only reads in books. Such narratives can be very intriguing and, at the same time, frightful. Literary pursuits, while sitting in the comfort of one's study, are very pleasurable. On the other hand, once out at sea, one cannot just shut the cover and shelf the book. In the end, Samuel was able to temper the storms, out run the warship, and *Sphinx* carried us safely home whilst escorted by orcas and humpbacks.

Here in the harbor, the schooner looked restless as it waited for its next adventure, tugging at her lines and enduring a northeast breeze. Its nearly twenty-foot-long bowsprit spiraled wildly, coming in close contact with the whaler *Janet*'s stern. If Samuel had been here instead of away at war, he would have moved her to the west side of the wharf where it would be buffered by the pier. Though I was concerned, I was still reluctant to inform Tim of the circumstance at hand for reasons I need not go into. Instead, I stopped at the Cory store owned by Samuel's cousin.

The Cory store sat at the end of the Road in Point Village, just feet from the water. It was the center of commerce where one could purchase a broom, cloth to make a dress, some peppermint, or have a whaling ship built. It was also the village's post office.

As it was past business hours, I was surprised to find the door still open. I entered just as Mary Ann Cory was emptying a crate of pickle jars that she placed on the store's shelf. The tiny bell above the door jangled as I closed it, announcing my arrival.

"Emily, so nice to see you."

"Good evening, Mary."

"You're in luck, young lady. I was just going to close shop when I realized I needed to put these jars away." She took the lid slats from the top of the empty shipment crate and tossed them aside. "Oh, I have a post here for Seabury." She reached under the counter and retrieved a letter. "Can you drop it off on your way home, dear," she begged, handing me the sealed post. "There's no return address but it appears to have come from afar."

"Oh. Do you think it's from Samuel?"

"I wouldn't know, dear. You will have to ask, Seabury."

"Yes, of course."

"I'm sorry, Emily. I know you haven't received a letter from Samuel for some time. None of us have."

I studied the quivered writing on the wrinkled envelope hoping to recognize Samuel's handwriting.

"It's awful, just awful," she said. "Word has it that hundreds are dying in the war and news is very slow in coming."

"Oh, Mary, I am so worried," I confided, holding the letter close to my breast.

"Well, there's not much we can do but pray."

"Yes, prayer."

I fought back tears. Mary Ann sighed.

"How can I help you today?"

"I was hoping that Alex was here," I said, placing the letter safely in my pocket.

"He should be around the back in the yard working. Is there something I can do?"

"Not really. I wanted him to …"

Alexander Cory, Mary's husband, walked in before I could finish.

"I'm glad you are here, Dear. Emily was asking for you."

"Well, young lady. What do you need?"

Alexander Cory was a thin lanky man. His sleeves were always rolled up just below his bony elbows and a carpenter's pencil sprouted from behind one ear. His posture was of a friendly nature. When happy to see you, he would just stand, stout fists and arms akimbo and resting on narrow hips, with a cordial smirk on gaunt lips. I spilled my anxiety.

"I am concerned about the *Sphinx*."

"Is she sinking," he asked, jocularly.

"Why, no."

"Then there is no concern worth your worry?"

"Yes but … I know docking is tight. Still, I'm afraid that a collision is about to happen."

Mary Ann kissed her husband on the cheek.

"Well, I'm done here," she declared. "Can you lock the door, dear, when Emily leaves?" Removing her apron, she disappeared into the back room.

"The *Sphinx* seems very close to the *Janet*. I was afraid that the schooner's bow would collide into the stern of the whaler."

"I'm aware of it," declared Alexander. "Not to worry. Looks a lot closer than you think. I'll place a couple of extra spring lines on her if that should make you feel better."

"Yes, it would. I promised Samuel that I would watch out for her."

"Aye, we all have."

"Thanks, Mister Cory."

He walked me to the door.

"Have you heard from Samuel," he asked.

My heart skipped a beat as I gripped the doorknob. "No, I haven't. Not for a while."

"Not to worry," he stressed, as he helped open the door. "Samuel's a wise duck."

"Yes," I agreed, glumly. "Thanks."

He held the door as I stepped out onto the road.

"Worry not, young lady. I'll take a look at Samuel's vessel."

I smiled and nodded.

While walking up Point Road on the way home, I took the post and held it up to the light. I felt a tinge of guilt spying on another's mail, but I was desperate for some news about Samuel. The letter appeared to be folded three or four times. All I could make out was a fuzzy amalgamation of merging words. Feeling abashed, I placed it back in my pocket.

I stopped at Captain Cory's cottage and knocked. No one answered.

I knocked again. I held the letter in hand and scrutinized the writing as I waited. Wistfully, I concluded it was not Samuel's handwriting. Disheartened, I took the correspondence and slipped it under the door.

Chapter 5: De Profundis!

After a long walk to Old Country Road, I met Randy Gifford's father in front of Macomber's store, in the old village at the Head of town. From there we rode to work and New Bedford together.

Arriving at the waterfront, I found myself standing and facing a familiar brick building with its weathered oak door. Above me, the same tattered sign hung from its rusty, wrought iron brace with the same gold lettering still advertising the *Daily Whaler*. Gentle gusts nudged the placard. It swung serenely like an infant's cradle while its J-Hook hinges grated and tweeted the melody of a creaky cricket.

It was my first day at a real job. In hand, I brought with me a wrapper containing a sandwich and Solomon Northup's book on slavery, which I hoped to read a little during lunch. This time I was alone. The sun was bright and warming, unlike the rainy morning when I was here last. Even the damaged soffit and gutter along the roofline appeared to have been mended. I'm sure it couldn't be avoided since water from the roof was furrowed to the break in the gutter and dispatched to anyone standing at the door below. More importantly, I was here by my own accord and ready to make a go of things.

I hesitated to enter. Butterflies fluttered in my tummy. I gulped a gallon of moist harbor air and exhaled two. How I wish I had the balletic poise and decisive boldness that Amy exhibited. In Amy's case, she was born that way. Assertiveness was part of her anatomy. Though she could not be here to instill in me courage or self-assurance, I could certainly learn by example.

Confidence is an enigma in many respects—at least for me—constitution of character that is not easy to conquer. It takes practice, training, and, most importantly, moxie. But that is not all. One must know his or her limitations. And once it is discovered, understand them and accept the perfections or sagacity that maturing may have failed to achieve.

The endowment of confidence in one's self can be found between the cover of books. As I get older, I find I am still striving to master that academic doctrine. And if I have mastered confidence to any extent, it is realized by the fact that I have read more books than the average person.

I was about to enter the building when Grandmamma spoke to me. "Paint on your shield of confidence, child, and dispense of fear. For mad dogs can smell trepidation in a troubled soul."

"I will, Grandmamma," I assured myself. "I will."

Similar to the last time I was here, I turned the doorknob and pushed. I pushed again. The door appeared to be locked. The resonant creaking by the sign above my head appeared to mock my attempt. I backed away and looked up to the editor's windows on the upper floor. I did not see anyone. I was unsure of myself as I struggled not to let courage and fortitude thaw.

I turned and peered out to the busy harbor and forest of roped spars and masts. A large square-rigger with a patchwork of fluttering canvas rolled up sail. It navigated its way into the busy harbor preparing to moor. The running ground tackle holding the anchor echoed like distant thunder whilst its rusted iron links tumbled over the ship's gunwale to the seabed below. I restlessly contemplated what I would do next. Perhaps the secured door was an augural harbinger, not to enter, and that I should just start for home. Or, like Amy, I should just push at the door harder. I took a deep breath as anxiety nibbled at my better judgment. But hesitant reflection was soon commandeered by a drone inquiry—just as I started to walk away, the door flung open.

"Having twouble with the dooa, Miss White?"

I whirled on my heels and looked back. "Oh, Mister Hick." I choked on my words. "I'm here," I announced, but for a moment not certain that I really was.

"So, you wa my deea, so you wa. Come in. Mistwa Fwench is waiting."

"Thank you," I muttered as I walked by him. I kept reciting to myself, "Paint on the shield, paint on the shield. I hope I'm not late Mister Hick?"

"Not foe'wa me to say."

"Oh, I see."

I looked down at a pendant watch I kept in my pocket. If anything, I was fifteen minutes early. Or did I mistake the time I was expected to arrive?

"Go wight on up."

I hesitated as I studied the room. I looked up the stairs just behind the clerk's desk. Without Amy to lead me, the staircase appeared much taller.

"Go on, go on," he spurred. "Mustn't keep Mistwa Fwench waiting."

I scurried up the steps. Looking back, I noticed Ezra Hick sitting at his desk and leering at me over his shoulder. I stopped halfway up. I found the moment a perfect occasion to assert some predominate inquiry.

"Something wrong, Mister Hick?"

Ezra Hick ignored me. My austere tone was strongly fashioned to be a rhetorical interrogation than an unfeigned question. To my astonishment, it worked. Ezra Hick pretended not to hear and, instead, hummed while he worked the drawers to his desk. I tried suppressing a priggish smirk as I continued on my way. Amy would have been proud of me.

The short walk down the hall placed me at the door of the editor. Not waiting for ambivalence to simmer, I knocked quickly and loudly.

"Enter," came the muted, authoritative invite.

I lifted my head and threw back my shoulders. My approach of Ezra Hick went quite well I thought. I was determined to continue my newfound tenacity.

"Miss White! Come in and take a seat," said Rudolf, standing to supply me with a chair. "I'm delighted that you are finally here."

"I hope I'm not late?"

I scrutinized the room. I discovered we were not alone. Just over from editor's desk, and by the full light of a window, an older woman stood with her back to us, working by an artist's easel. In front of her sat a girl of nine or younger. How strange I thought. I tried not to stare.

"You are right on time," announced Rudolf French, placing the chair before me. "Sit, right here … please."

I sat quietly. Unexpectedly, everyone else in the room appeared to do the same. Rudolf French sat at his desk and watched silently as the lady by the easel smote the canvas with a brush. The young girl looked displeased and weary.

"Father, can we stop now?"

"Just a little longer, sweetheart." He went over to the canvas and inspected the artwork over the woman's shoulder.

"I'm just about done for today," said the woman. "Molly looks weary and I have a previous engagement for ten."

"I'm tired," said the nine-year-old.

Rudolf bunched his fingers together and threw a kiss. "*Marvaleux*," he cheered.

The woman smiled and shook her head in humor.

"One more sitting, Rudolf, and the painting will be finished."

"Come over, Miss White, come and see how beautiful," he pleaded.

The painting was a watercolor. Far from dry, the damp, blotchy pigment was bright and cheery. It was a portrayal of Molly sitting by the window. In the distance and past the glass pane was a shamrock-colored sea with leaning boats under chalky white sails. Above them, a bright lemon sun hovered, beaming from a robin-egg-blue sky, while along the top fringe of the canvas boomeranged seagulls pimpled the palette. The image of the girl was unmistakable. In the painting, she sat contentedly, savoring the seascape out the window. A serene expression was drawn on her face. It was a contrary depiction of the brooding little girl who actually posed for the watercolor. The entire painting was done in what I would describe as a folksy motif, though not as angular or stoic as most. It had more of a realistic likeness. It was soft and vibrant with scrutiny to detail, right down to the sailing vessels that conveyed movement and a sultry hot sun. One could almost feel its warmth.

"Oh, how beautiful," I declared.

"How rude of me," said Rudolf. "Miss White allow me to introduce Rachelle Devol. Rachelle has been painting for us for many years now."

"Nice to make your acquaintance," said the artist.

"Yes, very nice," I confirmed, recognizing her.

"We know each other, do we not?" she said.

"That's right. Both of you ladies are from Westport," chimed Rudolf.

"Yes. The Devol farm by the Tiverton pond," I said. "I have seen you about town many times, Miss Devol."

"You live by the water on Point Road."

"That's right. I do."

"Small world," said Rudolf.

She washed her brushes in a dish of water and collected them into a small box. "I'll leave everything else here. I will see Molly tomorrow."

"Tomorrow," verified Rudolf as he walked her to the door. "I'll make certain she is here."

"Nice meeting you, Miss White."

"It was a pleasure. See you about town."

"Say goodbye to Miss Devol, Dorothea," directed Rudolf.

"Must you call me that, Father?"

"Molly?"

"Goodbye, Miss Devol," sang Molly, tritely.

The woman smiled and shook her head.

Rudolf stood, studying the painting.

"Come and see, Molly. It's you."

He sounded proud.

The young girl sauntered over and leaned her head against her father, a stray arm round his waist.

"Do you like it?" He adoringly ruffled her hair.

"I suppose," she uttered. "The boats are too small. And there shouldn't be a sun in the sky. You can't see the sun from the window."

"It's called artistic entitlement, sweetheart," explained her father.

"You look beautiful on canvas, Molly," I chimed.

"This is Emily White. She's a new writer for the paper."

"It's a pleasure to know you, Molly." I extended my hand.

"Women can't be writers, Papa," she grumbled.

I put down my hand and smiled. "Sure they can. Who put such a foolish notion in your head?"

"Papa."

"Oh?" I looked up at Papa with a retiring grimace.

Rudolf cleared his throat. "Well … not all women," he assured her. "Things will be different now that Miss White is here."

"If you say so, Papa."

Molly walked back to the window, sat, and opened a book.

"She likes to read," whispered Rudolf. "It's all she ever does."

I drifted over to her. "What are you reading, Molly?"

"A book."

"I can see that."

"Then why did you ask?"

I looked over at Rudolf. He puckered his nose and shrugged his shoulders. Molly was direct if not precocious. Attributes I wish I had at her age.

"Why don't you go back to the house and have Hannah make you some lemonade," he suggested.

"Oh, alright, Papa," she whimpered. Placing the book down, she started for the door. "*Collecting Seashells and Stones*," she uttered as she walked by me.

"Seashells and stones?" I said.

"Yes. You asked me what I was reading."

"You are right, I did."

"Watch out for road traffic," warned Rudolf.

"Goodbye, Miss White."

"Nice meeting you, Moll …" Before I could finish, she was out the door.

"Well … yes, you are here," said Rudolf, rubbing his hands together.

"I see you have a daughter, Mister French?"

"And a son."

"Oh?"

"About your age. However, Dorothea is my precious jewel."

"Does your son work for the paper?"

A despondent expression invaded his face. "Tyler lives with his mother … in Charleston."

"Near Boston?"

"No, not Charlestown. Charleston, in the Carolinas." He sat at his desk and stared up at the ceiling with daunted reflection.

"Dorothea's mother and I are estranged."

I was stunned then humbled by the answer he gave—that he should confide such intimate particulars of his life. I felt somewhat abashed as to what to say next.

"I'm sorry, sir. I did not mean to pry. It was rude of me to …"

"Listen …"

"I am just trying to say …"

"Hush," he thundered.

I was jarred back in my chair.

He threw his arms onto the desk, leaned over, and looked me sharply in the eyes. "Never apologize for a legitimate inquiry. The first rule of a good correspondent is never to leave a report without proper inspection and questioning. And a proper investigation takes bold examination followed by tenacious interrogation. You must wear your bully-badge … be inquisitive … that is, if you are to be successful in this business. Understand?"

"Yes, sir."

"Now, go on with your questioning."

"What?"

"You were asking me about Tyler, my son. Was that not your original question?"

"Ah, yes."

"Continue the interview, then."

I could see the little game that Rudolf was conducting. His approach seemed unconventional, to say the least. Did I have the job or was he testing me first—an extraordinary exchange? I could only hope that it went well.

"Is Tyler at university?"

"Yes."

"Er- and where does he go to school?"

"Very good, very good." He paused. "VMC."

I hesitated as I pondered the acronym.

"Continue."

"Sorry … how old is Tyler?"

"Wait. Do you know what school?"

"You, you said. … VM … C," I think."

"Don't think … know."

"Yes, sir."

"Do you know what VMC designates?"

"I'm not very good at this … am I, Mister French?"

"Virginia Medical College. The story is in the detail. Error in a newspaper narrative is the kiss of death to its reputation. You must not only make certain that the individuals you are interviewing are telling you the truth but also recognize doublespeak, slang, and the idiom and how it is used.

"Yes, sir."

"Of course, in an actual interview you would have your paper and pencil always at hand. Assigning such facts to memory is slippery or dubious at best. More importantly, inquiry is paramount."

"I understand. You mean questions and details such as, how old is Tyler, why he chose medical school, and how his father feels about it, et cetera, et cetera."

"Yes, details, Miss White, details." He placed a booklet and pencil in front of me. "You must get yourself one of these. They are called notebooks … blank pages for taking notes. Write everything down. Any information that may speak to the crux of the investigation or story. In doing so, you may just discover the devil between the crevasses of critical questioning."

He rose from his desk and migrated over to a window overlooking the harbor. He peered out toward the *Advocator*, his sailing vessel moored at Fish Island. From where I sat, I could only see the top of the ship's masts out the window. It spawned questions about the family I had seen there earlier.

"There are things hidden in the depths of humanity destined to destroy all that is good," he declared, burping a sinister scowl. "The Carolinas, the war, and all those black faces."

"Black faces, sir?"

"*De profundis!* And what am I to do about it."

He spoke in philosophical riddles and became more engrossed in what appeared to be painful contemplation. Was it a subliminal experiment, one for me to sort out? Or was his discourse just recollection of much deeper and personal significance. Uncertain, I sat quietly and listened.

"That damnable war … father fighting son, a brother's hostility toward brother. You must forgive my indecent language, Miss White. When talking about war, it can't be helped."

He ran his fingers through his silvery white, wavy hair. Clutching the back of his neck, he moved his head from side to side as if he was grappling with some physical injury or struggling with profound misfortune.

"*De profundis!*" he echoed again.

He paced the floor. Below the soles of his shoes, I could make out the fretful pattern he had worn into the floorboards over time. The threadbare oak that led between the office window and his desk was finely polished, the harbinger of a man preoccupied with worrisome collaboration with himself and the world around him.

"It is a big country, Miss White."

"Yes, it is," I agreed, not certain where this ambiguous conversation was leading.

"No matter how hard one tries to build up there is always someone there to build down … dismantle any productive creation integrity may have constructed. Good annuls evil and evil scrubs out good … the left and the right, human complexity of chasing one another through a meadow and off a cliff and never noticing the beauty the field and pasture they are running through. Left and Right. It's a political term you see. One of never-ending skirmish. They wrestle one another into insignificance and never realize the catastrophe of it all. Meanwhile, the ensuing forces around them; life itself, grinds them into the ground. They never come to understanding or grasp the essence of creation. Humanity should know better. It does not. They never see it coming. And we are here to write about it."

His words had obscure meaning. Rudolf French presented himself as a troubled man. Why he chose this moment to speculate on such personal or metaphysical interpretations of the world around us was a conundrum. Nevertheless, I found myself feeling quite fortunate that a man of position such as his would share intimate if not mystifying sentiments with me. And as Grandmamma's often said, "Allow maturity to speak. Observe and listen. It is a cherry tree ripe for picking." And lo and behold, that cherry tree continued offering fruit.

"Who is to say what is right or wrong, when goodness is sullied by the errant desires of others. Can you tell me?"

"Er-, no, sir," I muttered.

"Take the newspaper business."

"Yes, sir."

"Those in our profession can only write what we see, recount what we hear, report on what others say. What we think about such matters is of no concern or should it be. And while we are toiling to fulfill duty, our very nature works against us. It cries out to address what we see as right or wrong. What is left or what is right … such are the politics of the world."

"Mister French, forgive me for interrupting. The things you speak of appear to be of a personal matter. Should my ears be privy to …?"

"Nonsense, my girl. Minor details," he said, sitting back down at his desk. "That is what I have given you." He searched through his desk draws. "Yes, here it is. This is what is called a photograph. An older daguerreotype image."

He handed it to me. The picture evoked a smile. It was an image of a woman sitting by a lake. Behind her, stood a boy, perhaps ten years of age with a bamboo fishing rod in his hand. He had whitish hair and wore short pants.

"She is beautiful, Mister French. Is this your wife?"

"Yes, Victoria. And that image is the only tangible memory I have of my son Tyler. Last time I saw him he was ten years of age."

"How sorrowful it must be," I declared.

"The difficulty is lack of news … detrimental state of affairs for a newspaperman. The war has interrupted communication between North and South. Making matters worse, correspondence between Victoria and I have never been on the best of terms. She has remarried, you see. Since then, I have learned that Tyler was going to school. I am afraid that he may be recruited by the Southern Confederation into military service."

"That would be terrible news."

Rudolf's concern certainly had valid reason for worry. A doctor would be desperately needed in the war effort. Selfishly, a tinge of trepidation pecked at my heart as concern for Samuel gushed to the surface. It appeared that Rudolf French and Emily White had a collective interest. He worried for his son and I Samuel. Directly, I had a sweeping bevy of questions. What I did with them would shade the complexion of the relationship between myself and the editor. Unfortunately, before I could ask any there was a knock at the door.

"Enter," shouted Rudolf.

Ezra Hick appeared. He looked troubled. "Mistwa Fwench, we have a stowy," he cried, "A boy just delive'wid it."

Rudolf unfolded the note and read it aloud. "Wamsutta Mills. A death has occurred." He sprang from his desk and snatched his coat. "Come, Emily White. Your first story awaits."

I scurried behind.

"Notebook and pencil, Miss White," he shouted. "Must not forget the tools of the trade."

I snatched them from the desk.

After a short trot on foot, we arrived at the red brick Wamsutta Mill, a five-story building with row upon row of large, sashed windows.

"Hurry, Miss White! There," he pointed. "You see? A gathering."

I fell further behind as his long legs covered twice the ground. When I arrived at the scene, I noticed a group of people loitering by a loading door. I pushed past the small gathering. A few of the men looked displeased with me as I shouldered my way into the building. Once inside, I was faced with a ghastly scene. Across the room, between rows of steam-powered looms,

Rudolf knelt over a man who was lying lifeless on the oily, pitch-pine floor. The man's face was unrecognizable and blanketed in blood. A burly-armed man muscled his way over and pushed the gathering of workers and onlookers out onto the yard. I struggled to get back inside but was swept away with the crowd.

"Mister French!" I yelled, waving arms.

"Let the girl in," ordered Rudolf. "She's with me."

Everyone glared at me as I was given free passage. I slithered past gawkers. Once inside, the burly man pushed a few stragglers back and barricaded the doors shut.

I took a breath and slowly walked toward the dreadful sight. Standing by Rudolf were two other men—one I could identify as a constable. The other was a smartly dressed gentleman with tortoise-rimmed spectacles. He inspected the machinery along the floor.

"*De profundis*," cried Rudolf, crouching. His eyes never left the injured man.

I noticed the man was not moving.

"His name is Asha Potter," said Rudolf. "We were very good friends."

"I'm afraid he's dead," reported the constable.

"Asha, Asha … what happened to you?" lamented Rudolf.

"I'll need to summon the coroner," said the policeman. "Can someone let me out?"

"Remove that barricade and let the constable out, will you, Paul?" instructed the other man.

"This is my assistant, Emily White."

"Thomas Bennett," he declared, tipping his hat.

I offered him a frowned smile and nodded.

"Tragic," said Bennett, "just tragic."

"What happened to him?" I asked.

"From the looks of it I'd say he got his hair caught and drawn into the machinery. Once that happened, he was carried by the main drive belt and up to the pulley assembly along the ceiling where his skull was crushed. Terrible way to die. One of my best employees and first-rate loom mechanic."

"Are there any witnesses to the accident we can question?" asked Rudolf.

"I don't know," replied Bennett. "Asha was here very early this morning. He was assembling the new looms. We got them all working just yesterday. Paul here was the first to find him on the floor."

"How are you, Mister Bourque?"

"I'm good, Mister French."

"Your assistant looks a little peaked," said Bennett.

Rudolf placed a limp hand on my shoulder. "Are you alright?"

"Yes, yes, of course," I said, trying to sound able.

"Can you take notes?"

I nodded, pencil in hand, and hovered over the notebook.

"Can we get a sheet or something to cover him with?" begged Rudolf.

Paul Bourque covered the dead man's face and upper torso with some oily rags.

"Paul here is our steam apprentice," declared Bennett.

"Yeah. I was in the engine-house when it happened," said Bourque. "Asha was here with the Negro."

"Negro?" I asked.

"His helper. A Negro from down south. He would come in every once-in-a-while and help Asha."

"This helper has a name?"

"Asha called him Gideon."

"Where's Gideon now?"

"Don't know. When I got here, he was gone. Probably got scared and ran off."

"Oh?"

"You can't trust those kind."

"I see. And what kind are we talking about?"

Rudolf cleared his throat and shook his head, interrupting my line of questioning. I was sounding more like a constable than a reporter in an effort to demonstrate to my employer that I could be as demanding as any male reporter. But chiefly I was more than curious about the man's biased remark, which spoke to what sort of person I was questioning. I was uncertain whether I should invest myself any further. I looked over at Rudolf. He gave me a nod.

Paul Bourque spoke with a slight European accent. The words tumbled over and under his tongue as he regurgitated his Rs and trundled his vowels.

"How did you come to find Mister Potter?"

"Steam pressure dropped. Asha was helping me find the leak. We found one at the collar where the pipe leaves the steam house. I made repairs and Asha went to the loom room before I threw the lever."

"The lever?" I said. "What lever is that?"

Paul Bourque looked over at Bennett, uncertain why this girl was asking so many questions. His expression spoke to annoyance. He was probably asking himself why this girl was even in the building.

"Go on, answer her, Paul," ordered Bennett. "Miss White works for the newspaper."

"If you say so, Mister Bennett."

Paul Bourque would not look at me. Instead, he answered my questions to Bennett as if he were asking them.

"The lever engages the engine … feeds the steam. Asha said he would check the machinery and that I should give him ten minutes before throwing the lever. Said he would be back. Never did."

I scribbled down his retort. Rudolf stood quietly with arms folded, listening. His pose was unmistakable—alert concentration while applauding my examination.

"How long did you wait, Mister Bourque," I asked, as politely as I could.

"I don't know … twenty minutes, maybe longer."

"And what were you doing for all that time?"

"Do I really have to answer this girl, Mister Bennett?"

"Get on with it, Paul," spat Bennett.

Bourque tossed his hands into his pockets and shook his head. "Tightening fittings on the engine and looking for more possible leaks."

"What happened next?"

"When Asha did not return, I went looking for him."

"Were you the first to find him?"

"How do I know? No one else was here. Looms are not ready. Maybe the Negro killed him."

"Why would you think Asha Potter was killed?"

"He's dead, isn't he?"

"And you found him this way."

"Yes, yes!" He wiped his brow with a wrinkled soiled handkerchief, nervously.

"You say Mister Potter was going to check the machinery. What did you mean by that?"

"Check the machinery—the looms. Make sure the main shaft was free and turning."

He pointed to the ceiling. Above our heads was a long iron shaft with a series of cogs. Each cog had a broad, leather strap leading down to a row of looms along the length of the factory floor.

"Where is the engine-house?" I asked

"Behind the building," replied Bennett.

"Can we see it from here?"

"Sure. A stone's throw." We walked to a window. "Just there."

I looked out at a small two-story building toward the back of the property. "I see the mill windows are all opened. Were they opened all morning Mister Bourque?"

"When I got to work, they were."

"So, you could hear the looms working from the engine-house if they were operating?"

"Sure."

"How long were they operating."

Bourque complained to his employer.

I thought about what Rudolf had said to me earlier: "One must be tactful, and do so with assertiveness, and at times, bluntness, get under people's skin." It appeared that Mister Paul Bourque's skin was easily penetrable.

"I protest, Mister Bennett. I don't want to be questioned by this girl any longer."

"That's enough, Miss White," said Rudolf.

"Thank you, Mister Bourque. I have no more questions."

"Good."

"For now."

He glared at me as if my remark was a threat. "Do you need me for anything else, Mister Bennett? I'd like to go to work."

"Lock up the engine-house and go home, Paul. We shall not conduct business today."

I took Rudolf French aside. "I feel like I know that man, Mister French. It was difficult to understand his speech. His accent was so thick."

"You must have seen him around the newspaper office. He's in charge of the paperboys and bundle delivery. Mysterious fellow. French-Canadian accent is what you heard."

"I remember seeing him with Mister Hick, now that you mention it."

"I must thank you, Emily. I couldn't have done a better job questioning him. However, you were just a tinge too aggressive."

"I couldn't help myself, sir. After all I am a woman."

He smiled and shook his head. Bennett walked over.

"You'll have to excuse Mister Bourque, Miss White. These foreigners are very mistrusting of everything and everyone."

"There was nothing to excuse, Mister Bennett."

"Can't blame them, really. But once you do secure their trust, they will move mountains for you."

Rudolf and Bennett discussed arrangements for the body as I walked over to the dead man. The blood oozing from his face blossomed through the gauzy material that covered it. I dropped to one knee and carefully lifted the crimson, sodden cloth. The gruesome image was one that would remain with me my entire life. Since witnessing Grandmamma's passing, death had become an evident companion and an unpalatable one.

I will concede that Grandmamma lived a long and rewarding life.

Though her rewards were tenuous and modest at best, she was a happy soul. I was there to hold her hand when she left us. Though death has come knocking, I refused to allow it to torment me. With time, I had a better understanding of its arrival—that I must keep one step ahead. To do so, I would expunge fear and face it with boldness and resolve. Never to embrace it but, instead, spit in its face. For here it lay before me once again in the image of Asha Potter. This time death had made an outlandish mockery of life—going from unexpected escort to flagrant kidnapper.

I carefully examined the man's bloody scalp and chopped hair. I got up and walked over to the hefty loom. On the leather drive belt were patches of the man's hair and pasty blood. I wandered around the intricate contraption and carefully inspected it, not certain what I was looking for. The loom was a mechanical wonder. A compilation of wheels, levers, and shafts, whose job was to pull, thrust, and spin. I examined it closely. I noticed that at one end of the machinery was a long iron bar or lever. I appraised as to its function.

"What does this do?" I shouted, griping it tightly.

"It's the loom brake," said Bennett from across the room.

"Will I disturb anything if I engage it?" I asked.

"The system is static, Miss White. Do as you please. You can't hurt it."

I moved the hefty lever back and forth. It went back easily but its travel forward was more restrictive. I pulled a little harder. The belt above my head, which operated the loom, disengaged and became slack. Suddenly, the iron handle detached from its crib at the base of the loom. It crashed to the floor echoing throughout the mill.

"Careful, Miss White," shouted Bennett. "Assembly is not completed on that machine."

"Sorry."

"I picked up the three-foot long iron spar. Something urged me to examine it. It was heavy, perhaps eight or ten pounds and painted black. The shaft was wide at the base and tapered toward a knurled grip at the handle. At the base was a greased slot where it slid into a bolt in its crib. The nut was missing. I noticed what looked like blood that had dripped. It was masked against the lever's black paint. The base glistened in sunlight that filtered through a window. I ran a finger over it and held it to the light. It was sanguine and tacky. Blood had mingled with the umber-colored lubricant around the elongated aperture, making it hard to detect. I secured the heavy bar back in its saddle and wiped my hand on a rag draped over the machinery.

I looked out toward the engine house. I watched as the enigmatic Paul Bourque closed up shop and bolted doors. On further inspection of the room, I noticed that the wall to one side of the window was besmirched with blood. Poor Asha must have been thrown against it. I surveyed it from top to bottom. The smear appeared splotched along the brick from eye level down to the floor. The crimson stain was hard to detect against the red brick, but I could clearly make it out.

Along the hard pine flooring below it appeared a heel print in blood. Within the outline of the print were faint but distinct markings, rectangular in shape, like those of rivets or nails. They were arranged in a horseshoe pattern along the periphery of the heel. There were eight of them—tacks, nailed into a shoe to save wear and tear on the heel. But who's footprint was it? Any number of people had walked in, including Bourque and the constable. Perhaps the footprint belonged to the proprietor, Thomas Bennett. Could it have been Rudolf's? I was reluctant about asking to see their feet. My duties were wandering. I had to assert myself as reporter not investigator. But I could not help feeding the insatiable need to know, to uncover, and to expose.

I stooped and looked. Asha had no rivets on the bottom of his shoes. I noticed that the wall smeared with blood seemed a long way from the loom for a body to have been thrown such a distance. Surroundings did not exhibit as they should have. I tried dismissing such notions. For whom was I to theorize such a naive conclusion?

Nonetheless, I jogged my eyes around the room looking for more clues. However, clues to what? Curiosity in such matters is often a messy pursuit and never neatly swathes with a ribbon and bow. "Curiosity is the den mother of discovery," Grandmamma often said. I felt that I must search for pointers or indicators to something other than what appears to be is supported by Grandmamma's aphorism and my compulsion for truth.

I found the way Asha had come to rest exceedingly peculiar. His legs were close together and extended along the floor, straight, like those of a soldier standing at attention, arms were outstretched left and right, just above his shoulders, as if he was nailed to a cross. I fell to my knees and peered down at him once again. I bowed my head and said a prayer. My silent litany was unexpectedly adjourned when I noticed what looked like an envelope beneath him. It was wedged under his body. I picked it up. I was about to examine it when Rudolf French called out to me.

"Come along, Emily. We have to get back so we can get this out the noon edition."

"Coming, sir."

I jumped to my feet and placed the blood-stained letter in my pocket. Making my way, I stumbled over the poor man's outstretched arm. A glittering shape fell from his twisted hand. I froze—my eyes stitched to the object. Making certain no one was watching, I picked it up and gave it a quick look over. It appeared to be some sort of decorative gold button. The red knitting thread which once held it to the garment was still looped around the eyelet. I found the strand odd. As a seamstress, I never saw anyone use knitting thread to sew a button.

"Emily. Hurry."

"Coming."

I turned and looked back at the dead man one last time. "May God comfort you, Asha Potter. No one here can."

The copywriter sat by what was now my desk in the editor's office—a small writing table by the window overlooking the harbor. He finished jotting down what I had written. He read it all back to me.

"Now, is that all of it?" he inquired.

"Yes. Sorry about my abbreviated script."

"It was fine. Now, how about you, Rudy?" Rudolf French stood by the window and stared out toward the harbor. "The presses await us, Chief."

"Yes. I heard you, Edgar, I heard you—the presses."

"I have a little more than an hour to get it typeset for the next edition. What else do you want the story to say?"

"Start writing," directed Rudolf.

"Mister Asha Francis Potter of Forge Road, North Westport, was killed today in an unfortunate accident at the Wamsutta Mills here in New Bedford. Mister Potter was forty-two years of age. He had no next of kin living nearby and no children. Death was caused by blunt trauma to the head while operating a Lancashire loom. Arrangements for interment will be conducted by this paper and announced in tomorrow's publication."

His notebook shook and pulsated in his hand as Ryan pressed his pencil along the page, hectically scrawling down every word.

"Got it."

"That will be all, Edgar. Take Miss White's account, arrange it, and add my commentary to it."

"Right away, Chief. And I'm sorry about Asha. I know you were both very close."

"Yes, we were," added Rudolf, shedding his grief as he looked out the window.

Ryan scurried out. I sat quietly and uncomfortably. Rudolf French was not saying much. I had not expected him to. He had just lost a good friend. Some inner conflicts are best dealt with in silence and unescorted. This is true of those with a strong sense of integrity and position—whether the editor of a newspaper or mother of a large brood. An arbitrator is not really needed when one is trying to tame the conflict between the head and the heart. A wound such as the one Rudolf French was experiencing can only heal after being dressed by the bandages of time. It is a curative process that can take up to a lifetime in some cases, leaving inner scars that fade slowly, if at all. If there is anything fortunate to say about such matters it is that one learns to enjoy the fat times and bear the lean.

"*De profundis*!"

His vociferous declaration startled me.

"Have you ever placed a friend head and shoulders above all others, Emily?"

"Yes, sir. But she died."

"You are too young to have lost such a friend."

"Not really," I lamented. "Grandmamma raised me since I was a babe in a cradle. She was the best friend a girl could ever have."

"When did she pass?"

"Almost a year now."

"I'm sorry to hear it." He sat back down at his desk but never took his eyes away from the harbor beyond.

"Mister French."

He gazed out the window, silently.

"Mister French?"

"Yes, back to work," he said, arranging some paperwork in front of him. "You were going to say?"

"There's a comment you often make … an observation of sorts. De … De profundis. What do you mean by it?"

"Well … it is an incomplete thought, both question and reply … a plea for understanding when one is in desperation … a declaration of the evils that confronts us day in and day out … simply put, a declaration of bewilderment. A plea to God. It's what you want it to mean."

"Is it English?"

"Latin my dear … language of the spiritual and the learned. *De profundis*. Taken from the 113th Psalm. To me it is where one will find one's destiny. It translates into something beyond the state of affliction and anguish, deep down inside us all, inside human frailty, inside the unknown."

"*De profundis*," I said. "I remember reading it."

"From out of the depths."

"A very intriguing word."

"You are a very inquisitive young lady. You surprised me back there at the mill. You exhibited great potential."

"Thank you, sir. I'm afraid I have gone beyond my duty."

"Oh?"

"Yes. I took this." I handed him the letter I found by Asha.

"What is it? Why, it has dried blood on it."

He turned the splattered letter over and examined it. It was addressed to Asha Potter, number 5 Forge Road, Westport, Massachusetts. There was no return address, but the postage had been canceled somewhere in the Carolinas.

"I haven't opened it. I found it lying by Mister Potter. I thought you should have it."

He wedged his finger beneath the flap and slashed the envelope opened. Taking the letter to the window he read it carefully. Folding his arms, he stared out the window toward the water as he often did.

"I do something wrong, Mister French … taking the letter?"

He offered no reply. I knew as an employee of the paper that the letter was not mine to take. And my plan was not to keep it. I never would have opened it. Though, a little curiosity bug climbed into my ear persuading me not to leave it behind. To tell the truth, I was not comfortable with how we discovered poor Asha Potter. I felt that the letter might furnish some evidence. Although to what? Perhaps to why he had to die. Silly presumption, I know. Ultimately, it was an inclination stirred by an intuition that at times I could not ignore. But I was a reporter, not an investigator or policeman. I had intruded and mingled in something that I had no business in doing as a journalist—making myself, along with the *Daily Whaler*, part of the story.

"Mister French?"

He stood silently staring out the window. I waited, unsure whether I still had a job. Worry and indecisiveness churned in my tummy. He was disappointed in me. I was sure of it. And there was more. Arriving at a conclusion, I retrieved the button from my pocket and placed it on his desk. I started for the door.

"Going somewhere?"

"I'm sorry about the letter, sir. I'll let myself out."

"Let yourself out? What in the world are you on about, young lady?"

"Stealing. Taking what was not mine to take and injecting myself into the story."

"What?"

"I went beyond a reporter's duty."

"Nonsense," he said returning to his desk. He picked up the button and looked it over. "What is this?"

"That's another thing I sto—"

I couldn't bring myself to say the word. After all, I felt strongly I did not take the letter or button for my benefit. Still, it was not mine to take. And then again, it was no longer Asha's either. It was all so problematic.

"Confederate coat button. Where did it come from?"

"I stole it."

Rudolf French flung himself into his chair as he often did and gave out a resounding belly laugh.

"You have this angelic obsession with sainthood."

He roared with laughter as tears rolled down his face. Whether they were tears for his friend or for what humor he assigned to my actions, I was uncertain. Perhaps it was a little of both; I was confounded more than ever.

"I made myself part of the story, Mister French, and violated a journalist's creed, and taking what was not mine. Furthermore, it is not a laughing matter, I'll let you know."

"No, it is not, young lady. But you are sure making it so. I commend you for it."

He came around the desk, took me by the arm, and led me back to my writing table.

"Now, sit and wipe the load of culpability from your mind. What you did was a good thing. Asha had few friends, and I was the closest thing he had to family. If anyone had a right to his letters, you are looking at him. Now tell me, why did you leave this button on my desk?"

"Mister Potter had it in his hand."

"Asha? Are you certain?"

"I witnessed it roll from his fingers when I accidentally tripped over him."

He fondled the fastener between his fingers. "It's a Carolina military button. See that image?" He handed me the button. "It's a palmetto tree. If you look closely, you will see an S on one side of the image and C on the other. It's used as the South Carolina state seal."

He took the fastener from my hand, pulled his spectacles from his shirt pocket, and threaded them behind his ears. Holding the button up to the light he read the inscription. "Let's see. *Animis Opibusque Parati*," He recited, stammering over the words. "Prepared mind and resources. Now why would Asha have this in his hand?"

Turning the button over, we discovered some tiny lettering—TDP. We could only guess what it meant. Could have been the maker or fellow who forged it. He sat back down.

"You are certain it was in his hand."

"Yes. I'm sure. I saw it roll out from between his fingers."

He picked up the letter from the desk and looked it over once again.

"It is none of my business, but is the letter relevant to how Asha Potter died?"

He gave me a queer grimace. "Why would you say that?"

"Begging your forgiveness, sir, but do you not sense something wrong?"

He held a dead stare, dazed stupor, looking down at the floor. Deep thought had him by the throat. "Wrong? How so? His question appeared more of a cautious probe than an upright inquiry.

"I think someone was present when he was … er …" My tongue snagged the words before they reached my lips, where they dissolved into hesitant ambivalence. The more I thought about it the more skeptical I became about the circumstances behind the morning's events. I had to ask myself, was I mad or an innocent who had read one too many books, mirroring my adolescent exposure to accidental literature or fanciful fiction and misleading or casting blind aspersion on what should be better judgment? Had I truly discovered a mystery—my Marie Roget? Or have I been reading too much Edgar Allen Poe? C. Auguste Dupin, where are you when I need you? To that silly question I must reply: between the pages of a pretend crime, contrived in the inspired mind of a novelist, is this what I am guilty of? Confusing reality and fable. Or was there clarity where a girl's acumen and prudent wisdom recognized what others had missed. Ultimately, I spilled out a retort to his question.

"Asha Potter was murdered. I'm sure of it. We must consider the whereabouts of the black helper, Gideon? He could have had something to do with it."

Rudolf stared at me, and did so for the longest of time, but said nothing. Probing eyes fell onto the wrinkled letter in his hand and then over at me.

"He was a runaway from the South. We know nothing about him."

"Precisely."

"Asha was Gideon's mentor. Asha helped and clothed the boy, fed him, and found him a place to live … gave him work when he couldn't find any. Does a man slaughter the golden goose?"

"No. That would not make sense … would it?"

He folded the letter and deposited it in his desk drawer. "No, it does not. But stranger things have happened."

"What next?"

"You are dismissed, young lady. Go home."

"Dismissed, sir?" I concluded the worst.

"Yes. Dismissed—done." He circled the desk and opened the door.

I have always been certain that my yearning for adventure and appetite for mystery would be my undoing. Perhaps I should have kept my mouth shut. I would still have the job. Still, would I be able to live with myself when I was certain that an impropriety of the worst genre exposed itself before my very eyes. No, I could not. But why did it have to happen on my very first day on the job?

"Very well, Mister French."

"See you tomorrow morning—seven sharp."

"What?"

He took me by the arm and escorted me to the door. "Don't be late, Miss White. A new story awaits us every day. Whether it's a newborn babe at eight pounds or the death of an unwary victim by villainous hands."

"Villainous hands, sir?"

"Let's leave it all for another day, Miss White, shall we?"

With a straight face and furrowed brow, I made my way out.

"Seven sharp," he said.

The door slammed behind me.

Chapter 6:
A Secret Worth Telling

I was pleasantly surprised, if not happy, by the editor's invitation to return. The workday was only half over, and I still had the remainder of it to occupy my time. I decided to take a leisurely stroll along the waterfront. I was aimlessly wandering without strategy or plan. Well, not all was lost. I had my sandwich and a book to read. It would be almost five hours before Randy Gifford's father would arrive to take me home. I suppose I could visit a nearby stable and arrange for a ride.

I decided that I would explore the city of New Bedford since I have never done so before. The average Westporter does not journey very far from home. If he or she travels twenty miles or more at any point in their lives, they are very fortunate. I, for one, am hoping to amend that established deportment.

I started exploring as a young girl by running my fingers betwixt the pages of books. I have toured Egypt, France, and our American west, circumnavigated the great pyramids along the Nile, scaled Bishop Maurice de Sully's monumental creation, the cathedral of Notre dame de Paris, and inched past the rocky precipices of the great canyons along the Utah and New Mexico Territories.

Today it is not my fingers but my legs that carried me through the streets of one such interesting place. It has been said that New Bedford is the capitol of whaling, known everywhere as the city that lights the world. Would you not say it is a destination of great importance for a curious traveler? I would.

Seabury Cory has often mentioned that New Bedford is the richest city along the east coast. Sailing in from the Atlantic you could smell it before you could see it. The flensing of blubber and trying out of whale oil occupies a good portion of the city's coastal real estate, with oil factories and candle works by the busy waterfront. There exists here a stale fishy odor that I am accustomed to. Today, the wind blows from the north and the rancid redolence of whale is blown out to sea. Though it may not contain the romance or intrigue one may find on European horizons or other worldly destinations, New Bedford has made its mark in the sphere of places to visit. And I get to work here.

I found a small patch of clumped grass underneath the shade of a large maple that overlooked the harbor. Under it, someone had propped a wooden plank between two boulders. It was the perfect bench to sit and have my lunch.

I peeled back the wrapper to my tomato and cucumber sandwich and took a bite. A glob of sour cream oozed from the toasted bread and dripped on to my hand. I looked around and made certain no one was watching and licked the milky wad from my fingers.

"Not very ladylike," I heard someone say. There she stood, arms crossed, and shoulders hunched, delivering her callow reprimand complete with an admonishing scowl. Beaming eyes illuminated from a youthful and amusing face. I tried not to laugh.

"Why, hello, Molly."

"Do you know it's not cultured for a genteel lady to eat out in public," she grumbled.

"Oh?"

"That's what Papa tells me every time we are about town and I ask him to buy me some sweets."

She plopped herself on the end of the plank.

"Oh, I see. Would you like a bite?

I extended my sandwich-filled hand her way. She glared at me, endorsing the declaration she made earlier.

"Sorry," I said, lowering my arm. "Forgot. A genteel lady should never eat in public."

She sat quietly looking out toward the harbor as I wrapped my sandwich and put it away. Out in the sunlight, she didn't look much like the little girl that posed for the painting earlier in the day. Her hair was coiled bronze. Like her father, her eyes were a silver-blue, which gave her a haunting gaze. Her long, suave nose swooped down her face and pointed to heaven in a righteous and dignified manner, where it proudly poised itself between royal, blushed cheeks. She looked tan, though spring had barely matured. She probably inherited her dark complexion from her mother, no doubt. Tall for her age, she wore a graceful ankle-length white dress with a blue fleur-de-lis pattern. Her narrow waist was cinched with a black velvet belt and a large, rectangular, silver buckle. The dress had velveteen-covered buttons in the same tint as the strapped girdle. They ran from her midriff up to the neckline where they were crowned by an elegant ivory cameo.

"Come sit closer," I suggested.

She looked over at me, then down at the seat beside me, retaining her station. She rolled her eyes with raised eyebrows at my request. I was persistent if not compelled to befriend her. Moving over, I sat near her. I fondled a stray strand of her hair and placed it behind her ear.

"You have beautiful hair."

A remote smirk and appreciative glow smoldered on her face.

"I spent an hour ironing it, I'll let you know."

"Why would you do that?"

"To make it straight," she said bluntly as if my question was a careless display of ignorance.

I was in awe of her stunning beauty—far from that of a child but not quite ripened to adulthood. She was at that exceptional age when a girl's most treasured prize is her glowing chastity and exceptional virtues. It is an asset that is often not realized or appreciated by someone her age—an unsophisticated ingénue on the rutted stage of life. And perhaps, looking back, it is that innocence that makes her time precious to a girl my age.

I challenged her unfriendly deportment while studying her face. My gaze was not so much an appeal but a friendly provocation to persuade and engage her in constructive conversation, if not a congenial chat. It did not take long before it worked.

"Are you really going to work for the paper?"

"Yes, I am. Do you think that it's unsuitable work for a genteel lady?"

"Do you want my honest opinion?"

"Honesty is always the best approach."

"Papa says I can be abrasive with my opinions and those who don't know me."

"Oh, I don't think so."

"That's because you don't know me."

"Well, I hope we can get to know one another."

"I suppose it's a good thing."

"That we get to know one another? Yes, it is."

"No, silly. That a genteel lady should work for a newspaper."

"Oh … Well, I'm happy we agree there."

"Besides. Papa has always said that if women ran the world men could retire to idleness and there would be less wars."

"Your father is a very wise man."

She stood up from the bench. "Well, I'm going home. The fish smells are giving me a headache."

"Must you?" I said standing.

"Want to come. I'll show you my room."

I was uncertain if I should satisfy her request since it was the home of my employer and he had yet to invite me himself.

"Hannah will pour us a cup of milk and you can finish your sandwich the proper way. At a table."

"Who's Hannah?"

"My governess."

"Are you sure it's all right with Hannah?"

"Oh, she always complains that her time is filled with drudgery and never company."

"Alright." I said. "I'd love to see your room."

As we left the waterfront, I noticed some activity on the schooner *Advocator* out by Fish Island. Three men climbed down into a skiff while another waited for them to do so. I noticed that they were cloaked in long-caped Macintosh coats and hooded oilskin slickers, though the day was not inclement. One man wore a floppy Sou'wester rain cap the wrong way, hiding most of his face. The man in the skiff waved an arm, frantically urging the men to hurry. The entire scene was peculiar if not suspicious. And although what I was witnessing was probably far from my understanding, more importantly, it was undoubtedly none of my concern.

On the way home, Molly had mellowed. Conversation was spry and plentiful. As a matter of fact, she was quite loquacious, leaving me to scramble for words if I wished to be heard. Just as we embarked, one topic quickly stirred to yet another. It was a pleasant transformation from the silent, somewhat standoffish young girl I first encountered at the waterfront.

On our little walk, I discovered that Molly's name was a sobriquet for Mary, her middle name. Her Christian name was Dorothea, which she didn't care much for, insisting that I call her Molly. My time with her was a delightful change, a diversion from the unpleasant events that unfolded earlier in the day. Meeting Molly was a refreshing surprise at every turn. And the uninhibited manner by which she viewed the world was engaging and vivacious, as it should be for someone her age. She reminded me of Amy, when she was in her youth. Life had tumbled into Dorothea Mary French's lap and she was prepared with solutions, conclusions, and dreams.

The French residence was a two-story brick colonial. It stood between the Brown Candle Works and a dry goods store. Overlooking the river and harbor, Rudolf French had an ideal view of his newspaper company and Fish Island where he moored his schooner.

As we walked in the front door, Molly placed a finger across puckered lips.

"*Shh*. She's in the kitchen."

"Who?" I asked, quietly.

"Hannah, silly. You will like her," she whispered. "She's an Indian you know. She's great."

She tiptoed into the kitchen. I followed. The Indian woman was sitting at the kitchen table. She hurried from behind and wrapped her hands over Hannah's eyes.

"Guess who? Someone you know and not someone new."

"Is it someone near or someone far?"

"It's someone who loves you just as you are."

Hannah gushed with laughter. She leapt to her feet and gave Molly a warm embrace. "My little *qunnequawese*," she gushed, calling the girl her little doe in Wampanaog.

"I didn't see you this morning."

"Had to go into town before you got out of bed, dear."

"I have a new friend."

"You do?" Hannah glanced over the girl's shoulder.

"Hello," I peeped.

"This is Miss White," announced Molly.

The governess walked over and took me by the hand. "Good day, Miss White. I'm Hannah."

"Pleased to meet you … I'm Emily. And you may call me Emily, too, Molly."

"Alright … Emily." She rummaged through the icebox. "We need some milk to go with a sandwich."

"Sandwich?" uttered Hannah, slapping Molly's hand and elbowing her away.

Unperturbed, Molly pulled a chair from under the table and sat.

"What kind of sandwich are you two having?"

"Oh, I'm not having any," replied Molly.

"My lunch," I said, placing it on the table. I unwrapped the smacking amalgamation of cucumber, tomatoes, and sour cream. A stray cucumber slice oozed out from between the slabs of bread. I awkwardly pushed it back in and licked my finger.

"Doesn't look very appetizing," declared Hannah.

"Tomato and cumber. I'm afraid I added too much sour cream."

"My, my. That's not a dinner for a growing girl. Sit and I will fix you a plate."

"Told you she was great," exclaimed Molly.

For the next couple of minutes all I heard was the slamming of the oven door, clashing of lids, and the jangle of dinnerware. With marathon efficiency, Hannah had fixed me a workman's cuisine. She plopped the platter full of food on the table.

"Here you are, young lady," she said, wiping her hands on her apron. "Now sit—eat before it gets cold."

The plate before me was fit for a king. Fried chicken, steamed carrots, yellow squash, and chopped cobs of sweet corn. Hesitantly, I pulled a chair and sat myself down. Placing my book on the table I pushed my sandwich aside.

"Thank you, Miss Hannah?"

"Just plain Hannah, dear, just plain Hannah." She fixed a smaller plate of the same for Molly.

"I'm not hungry."

"Nonsense," yapped Hannah. "Eat."

I took a nibble from a drumstick. Suddenly, a large black dog was circling the table and startled me. He sat gazing with a wistful, begging mien.

"That's Yankee," declared Molly. "He's a Labrador."

She took my sandwich from its wrapper. "Want some, Yankee?"

The hound quickly pranced over to the other side of the table and sat obediently by its young master. A slobbering, ruby tongue dangled over spiked canines as he panted breathlessly and occasionally licked his shiny nose.

"Watch my fingers," commanded Molly, swaying the delicacy in the air.

A wafer of cucumber fell at his feet. Yankee was quick to mob it up.

"Ew! That's disgusting," she chuckled, as the dog licked the floor. "Here. Take it."

Yankee swiftly snatched the soggy delight from her fingers and nearly swallowed it whole. A tomato slice shot across the room. The Labrador gave chase and scarfed it up while polishing the floor with his tongue.

Molly clapped and broke into laughter. "Hurray. Good boy, Yankee." She laughed and laughed.

"Gee, he was hungry," I affirmed.

"That dog is always hungry," grumbled Hannah.

"Want some chicken, Yankee." Molly pulled the crispy, charred skin off her chicken breast and held it in the air.

"No," shouted Hannah. "Out, out," she cried, shooing the dog from of the kitchen. "Your father's going to let you have it when he gets home young lady for bringing that mutt into the house."

Hannah was a tall woman, unlike Grandmamma who was petite. Indian features were prominently striking, though her skin could be identified as a tanned Caucasian. Dark-reddish hair was tied neatly behind her head in a clenched bun. She had elegant, thin lips and her chin was broad and dimpled when she smiled. Apart from an Amerindian bump to the bridge of her nose and slight tawny cheeks, she did not look much different from the average church-going housewife living in New Bedford.

"Rudolf tells me that you may be working for the paper," she said.

"Yes. I'm very excited about it."

"Rudolf's is a fair man. He will treat you right."

"I'm sure he will."

"You from here, in New Bedford?"

"Westport. Point Village to be exact."

"Oh? You must know some of the fisherman who live there."

"I know all of them. Except for a migrant or two, fresh off a whaler. There's always a new foreigner settling into the village every time a whaling ship completes a voyage."

"You must know Lukie, Luke Tripp. He fished out of Westport for many years."

"Old Lukie. Everyone knows Lukie."

"Old Lukie's my uncle." Hannah removed her apron and sat down to eat. "On my Mother's side."

"Lukie was a full blood Wampanoag?" I said, not so surprisingly.

"I'm Wampanoag," she nobly declared.

"Oh? You don't look native," I said, praying not to sound condescending.

"Father was from the British Isles," she said, as if he was an afterthought. "A whaler from Aberdeen."

"That's in Scotland," declared Molly.

The young girl appeared to take great interest in Hannah and her indigenous heritage. The woman had taught her about the native people of the area, how they have all but vanished, and instilled in the child a faultless respect that would only grow. I had gained the same respect through Grandmamma who told tales about the chiefs and guardians of all the land for miles around us.

"Sadly, I don't remember much about my father," said Hannah. "He was lost at sea. I was raised by my mother and the Wampanoag people."

"Sorry to hear about your father."

"Nothing to be sorry about. I was but a child. We lived in Aquinnah at the time."

"The Indian village on Martha's Vineyard," I added.

"Yes."

"See, I told you Hannah was a real Indian," chimed Molly, proudly.

"Grandmamma was born on the Vineyard," I said, elated by Hannah's native history.

"Oh? Your people were from Martha's Vineyard, then?"

"No, not really."

"Oh, that's too bad."

"I never knew my family. Grandmamma was the person who raised me. It was her roots that originated in Martha's Vineyard."

Unexpectedly, shame and embarrassment overcame me. Though I could not discern any reason for it, still I was fraught to admit that I was an orphan, abandoned by a mother and discarded. Quickly, I quelled all contemptible notions of my dubious nativity. As Grandmamma often said, "Child, you were not forsaken, you were gifted. And there was no better gift I could receive."

"From what I was told, I was born in Fall River and left on someone's doorstep."

"No. You're lying," said Molly in disbelief. "When you were just a baby?"

"Yes, an infant. But the recipients had their own children and couldn't care for me, so they brought me to a kindly and good-hearted woman in Westport. She was known for taking in children. Called her Grandmamma since she was much too old to be my mother. She had many happy stories about growing up on the Vineyard. I think she called the place Nunpo. I couldn't find it on the map."

"You must mean Nunnepog," said Hannah.

"That's it."

"Edgartown. Nunnepog was the Algonquin name for the place before European settlers renamed it."

"I must remember it. Nunnepog," I repeated.

"You girls finish your meal. Place the dishes in the wash pan once you are done."

"Where are you going?" chimed Molly.

"I need to go and run an errand." The governess scurried out the room.

"Nice to meet you," I cried as she went. The only reply I heard was the slamming of the front door as she left the house. I glanced over at Molly, tight lipped and bewildered.

"Did I say something wrong?"

"She's funny like that," she exclaimed. "Indians don't like to say goodbye."

I pushed my dish aside and walked over to the window. I could see Hannah scampering toward the newspaper office. Yankee crept back in and took his place by the table. He sat quietly, tail sweeping the floor, waiting for Molly to drop some morsel down to him.

"What are you reading?" she asked, plucking my attention. She thumbed through the book I had left on the table.

"A story about slavery." I sat back down.

"You're interested in slaves?"

"Yes I am."

"Silly question, huh? Why else would you be reading about it?" She turned pages, pausing every once-in-a-while to read a passage.

"What do you know about slavery, Molly?"

"That all slaves are not from Africa," she declared.

"They're not?" I replied, baiting her curiosity.

"Hannah says there are Indians slaves too."

"Yes, that's right. Especially during colonial times."

"Solomon Northup," she said, reading from the title page. "It says here that he was kidnapped. I suppose all slaves were kidnapped, taken away from where they lived in Africa."

I was surprised by the interest she took in the topic. Although, I sensed that she was luring me into something bigger.

"Solomon was a free man who lived in the New York State," I explained. "He was down in Washington D.C. where two men had offered him a job with the circus. Sometime later, he was kidnapped and sold into slavery. Spent twelve years as one."

"He must have gotten free."

"I suppose he did. After all, he did write a book."

She chuckled. "I guess you're right."

She closed the volume and handed it to me. "I like you, Emily."

"Good. Because I feel the same about you."

"You want to share a secret?" she whispered, looking around as if someone in the empty house was listening.

"What sort of secret?"

"Come with me."

I followed her out the back door and into the yard. There was a high board fence that surrounded the entire back portion of the property, making it difficult for those in the street to see over it. Off to one corner was the barn with two large doors that faced the street—a window and another smaller door off to one side. The solitary window was covered with a burlap bag from the inside. The door was well secured with a padlock. Molly placed her finger to her lips warning me not to say a word. We trudged through some brush to the back of the large outbuilding.

"You mustn't tell anybody. Not a soul in the whole world." She crossed her heart with a finger and pounded her chest with her fist. "You must do the same."

"I promise," I said, mimicking her symbolic ritual. My curiosity peaked. "Where are we going?"

She stopped and pointed at the barn wall. "They're in there," she whispered.

"Who," I asked, softly.

She picked at the barn board and removed a knot in the wood. Placing her face up to the hollow she peered inside. "*Shh* … look but don't make a sound."

I placed an eye up to the egg-shape aperture in the weathered barn siding. I could see an old buggy. Just behind it and leaning against the wall was a broom and some shovels. A shelf on the wall held a harness and oily bottles of ointment.

"I don't see anything. What should I see?"

She hastily placed a hand over my mouth. "*Shh*, not so loud. They will hear you."

"Who?" I whispered.

"Didn't you see them? They're lying in the horse stall on the hay."

I looked again, giving time for my eye to become accustomed to the shadowy light. A missing tile and split in the roof's planking allowed a narrow shaft of sunlight to shed just enough brilliance to expose the surprising scene.

"Who are they?"

"Parcels," she whispered, placing the wood knot back over the hole.

"What?"

"Papa calls them parcels."

"You mean like a bundle of goods or a package?"

"Yes. It's a code name. Papa's part of the Underground Railroad and the parcels are his responsibility to deliver."

"Deliver where?"

"To the next post station."

"Hmm, I see. And these … parcels are hiding out in your barn."

"Uh-huh. Malachi and Ruth."

"Their names?"

"Of course, silly. We all have names. I don't know the little girl's name … not that she doesn't have one. Want to look again?"

She removed the bung from the board, and I placed my face up against the weathered wood siding. Through the small orifice, I could smell stale hay and stagnant, musty air that belched from inside the confined space. I took a more careful look. There they were—a young African family. The man lay on his side and appeared to be sleeping. The woman sat perched on a small keg. She wore a colorful headscarf striped in bright yellows and greens and rocked a sleeping child in her arms. Her lustrous, obsidian face faded into the darkness as she stood up and paced the floor. Ultimately, I realized what I was witnessing—the people I saw on the *Advocator* earlier.

Molly gingerly inserted the knot back into the hole and walked away. With pensive reflection I ran the palm of my hand down the coarse, gray barn board and over the clandestine node she had inserted back in place. I considered the hardships that the family must have endured. Revered fugitives hidden from sunlight—whose only desire was to live life with dignity and liberty.

"*Psst*, Emily." She waved for me to follow and we started for the house

"Do you think it was a good idea to expose them? I mean … your father would not be happy if he knew."

"That's why I said. It would be our secret. I just had to tell someone."

"Do you think that was wise?"

"Why … yes. I trust you. You are one of us."

"I am?"

"Sure. Why else would you be reading that book?"

I looked at her—so innocent and confiding. I felt fortunate that she had confidence that I would safeguard the secret we shared. I was still worried that Rudolf French would find me out and consider that I was meddling or, worse, spying.

"You will keep our secret, won't you?" she begged.

"I will tell no one." I ran my finger and held my fist over my heart.

She smiled and did the same. "And hope to die?"

"Hope to die."

After having spent a couple of hours at the French residence, I bid Molly goodbye and left for the waterfront. I was happy that we were finally able to become allies in friendship, but I shouldered the secret we shared with entangled woe and a heavy sadness. I thought about the slave family and what they must have endured.

Rudolf continued to evolve into a very impressive and intriguing person. The man of all seasons was now an abolitionist. And what can I say about his daughter—an unbound catalyst for adventure with a blossoming intellectual spirit. I am willing to wager that she harbored a ceaseless motivation for danger and jeopardy, just like Amy, Molly was a girl after my own heart.

I sat under the large maple by the grassy bluff where I had rested earlier and waited for a ride home. I read my book and enjoyed activities along the harbor. However, I could not help but worry about the slave family back in the darkened barn. Reading Solomon Northup's book about trials as a slave did not help matters.

I observed the busy wharfs that jutted out onto the harbor and the Acushnet River. I noticed a few old vessels deserted and cached off a derelict wharf just north where the river narrowed. The floating hulks looked tired and ignored. All of their canvas and cylindrical spars had been removed. Bronze hardware, try pots, and whaleboats had been stripped. It looked doubtful that they would ever sail again. Many others sat idle, their captains and owners frightened to sail due to Confederate hunters sinking whaling vessels along the eastern seaboard. Since the war started, almost ten whaling ships from New England ports have been scuttled out at sea.

The extraction of a lamp oil from coal, which they call kerosene, has been very popular for lighting and is replacing the use of whale oil. And now the discovery of the fuel called petroleum from deep in the ground in the state of Pennsylvania has further exasperated the whale oil trade. I have read that they have discovered a method of getting this petroleum out of the earth by boring holes and pumping out gallons by the thousands. Where is it all coming from? I could only speculate. Seabury Cory was right. Days of whaling are waning. And that is a good thing, though I am one of the very few souls that think so.

It is a notion that I would not often repeat, especially around impolite company along the seashore, not to suppose that all whale-men are impolite, you understand, which many are. If I could give the command, I would mandate and order to leave the whales be. Although all things must die, they should not have to do so before their time, though I must shamefully confess to having no solution to all the animals mankind slaughters and eats. But whales are different. I must admit at having a bias when it comes to the killing of whales. And I'll tell you why.

I once had an intimate encounter with a one—a right whale to be exact. Really! I will not chaff truth or pitch folly but relay the actual occurrence. It happened when Samuel and I were sailing on the glorious schooner *Sphinx*, just south of Nantucket when, suddenly, we were accompanied by a playful pod of right whales. One particular cetacean and her calf swam alongside the ship. The calloused creatures came dangerously close, almost bumping up against the vessel's hull. When it did, I leaned over the gunwale in an attempt to touch it, but the giant mammal was too low in the water. I moved along the deck to get a better look. I believed that the curious beast was watching me—its beady black eye appraising the image it scoured. I could almost feel the cognitive juices within its large brain stirring as it considered how to introduce itself. I extended one hand out while holding onto the ship's deadeye with the other. All it would take would be a minor rogue wave to toss me overboard. It was then that the whale intentionally and freely lifted its massive torso out of the sea and allowed me to communicate greetings. When it did, I was able to run my fingers over its shimmering, cucumber frame just before it plunged into a breaking comber and receded into the deep. Her calf hesitated. I could almost detect a smile in its pebbled eye, as if it found delight in my presence. When it realized its mother had submerged, it quickly rolled over, dove, and vanished below the foamy, folding swell.

I pulled my watch from my purse and realized it was later than I suspected. In the near distance I could plainly see the red brick facade of the *Daily Whaler*. Waiting by the front door and sitting patiently in his buggy was Randy Gifford's father—my ride home. I gathered my few things and quickly made my way. Mister Gifford is a kind and generous man, however a gentleman of few words—at least not the spoken variety. You see, Mister Gifford loves to sing. My ride home will not be a silent one. I am certain that he will serenade me all the way to the Head of the Drift River in Westport.

As we drove the busy center of New Bedford, I tried reflecting on the relevant events of the day and take in the scenery but could do neither. The distracting Mister Gifford sang and sang. I mean distracting in a charming if not amusing display. His bellowing voice served as a loud warning call to the mundane traffic around us and those who were sure to get out of our way. "Oh! Susanna" would be the melody that was sure to regurgitate in my head over and over long after I arrived home.

The bustling waterfront retreated and street traffic thickened while we rode up Union Street. I glanced over my shoulder as the building which held the *Daily Whaler* receded into the distance. Let's do this again tomorrow, I pleasingly told myself.

Chapter 7: No News is Good News

When I arrived home, I encountered a string of tulips just under the windows along the front of the house—a jubilant splatter of reds, yellows, and whites. What wonderful creations, with their colorful, puckered pedals—velveteen grails sipping the late day sunlight and snagging the eye of wayfarers and village people alike. Strangely enough, such beauty was not there when I set off for work this morning. Where could they have come from? I noticed the side of the Cory house next door. The tulips that were once there were now paraded along my front yard.

"Seabury Cory, what have you been up to?"

Seabury Cory and his son Samuel live in a two-story house just south of my cottage—roughly a whale length away. At least that is how Seabury measures things. A whaler's length to Seabury would be about a hundred feet, the breadth of the average whaling ship. Mister Cory was a whaling man for over forty years, with twenty-five of them as master of his own vessel. He often translated life with a mariner's barometer, paraphrasing everyday descriptions through nautical eyes. It was a language all his own. As an example, when he did not agree with the preacher's doctrine, which he often did not, he would say it was because the minister's binnacle was askew. He often referred to a wife as a necessary craft, and to someone who had too much hard drink as broaching. He was a very independent and captivating personage, as were most sea captains. In fact, he was as close to a father to me as anybody I can think of.

I placed my book and floppy spring hat on the kitchen table. I washed the day's soil and tension from my hands at the sink tub and peered out the window toward the shores of the Westport River. Not far from its bank, the limp pair of willow trees swayed to the breeze. Their drooping branches flowed in the wind like viridescent streamers, softly whipping to the occasional gusts. Grandmamma loved those trees. She shared a kinship with them, describing them as living organisms with the God-given right to subsist and survive according to nature's means. She would often sit by them in solemn supplication or grateful worship. And although she was a devout Christian, she often prayed to the river for its sustenance, to the sun for its warmth, to the very rocks beneath her feet for their foundation, along with the soil for its produce, as if they all were gods. I once found her coming out of Cory's store with ribbons in hand, which were purchased with her last pennies, to tie in the willow tree's branches as a gift of gratefulness and gratitude to mother earth. I asked her once why she would do such a thing since someone soon came along and stole them. Grandmamma never thought of them as being stolen but gifts that were simply passed on. And though she lived life by her King James Bible, ancient and engendered Wampanoag practices were deeply instilled.

In the distance by the muddy riverbank, a squat figure raked the mucky ground digging clams. I could tell it was Mrs. Mosher's brother, since he always wore a smart white suit and straw hat. Who engages in such a burden, dressed in a white suit? Clive Mosher did. He always wore a white suit. It was his uniform. How he kept the clothing spotless and brilliant is a mystery. Every weekend, one could observe him in his pearly wardrobe sailing or rowing upriver. His tiny vessel was also white and as unblemished as his attire. The Moshers lived across the street from my small Cape cottage. Clive Mosher came to live with his sister after the loss of her husband in a farming accident. He was in the habit of cutting through my yard and along the back of the property on his way to the river's edge. But he was not your average trespasser. Later in the day, I was sure to find a pail of mucky mollusks by my back doorstep.

I rapped on Seabury Cory's door. A voice cried out from the other side.

"Ahoy."

"It's me," I replied, nudging the barrier open.

"Welcome aboard," he summoned, meeting me at the entrance. "Come in, my dear."

"Mister Cory, why did you dig up those beautiful tulips?"

"Dug them up and planted them."

"I know, and in my yard, no less. I thought you loved flowers?"

"I do. Still, I couldn't view them looking out the window. They were hidden. Now I can. Besides, I know you have been busy with your new job and I just wanted to give you something to come home to."

"I love you, Mister Cory." I gave him a warm embrace and kissed him on his beard. "You take such good care of me."

After pulling away, he touched his face sheepishly, cleared his throat, and quickly changed the subject. "Yes, of course … well, ah … in any event, how is the new job, dear?" He filled his pipe from a pouch of tobacco he retrieved from a desk.

"I can't really say. I have only started. I am certain that it will be a challenge."

"Well, my girl, I am sure you will navigate the lee shores of employment with little difficulty." He lit the tobacco and exhaled. Billowing smoke concealed his face. "Have you eaten?"

"I just got home."

"Sit. I've got water on in the galley. I'll make us some tea," he said, leaving the room.

"Tea sounds splendid."

"We'll have dinner together," he shouted, from somewhere inside the house.

I sat in a large wing chair by a window in the reception room. The chamber was quite large. Seabury Cory called it the sitting room. I would describe it as a parlor, while my friend Amy referred to it as the drawing room. Nonetheless, it was an attractive and comfortable space.

Across from where I sat was a camel-back sofa and another snug lounge chair. The chair was velvet red, with embroidered, Portuguese antimacassars on its arms—one of many curious items acquired during Seabury's many voyages to such places as the Azores, Sandwich Islands, or Aleutians, to name a few. Along a wall by the fireplace sat a fluted-legged English writing desk, brought back from Liverpool; on another wall a cherry American block-front chest, made especially for Seabury by a prominent Providence cabinetmaker. On the wall above it hung an oval-framed portrait of Seabury's departed wife. It was one of those portraits with eyes that followed you everywhere you moved. The space was formal, delicate, and graceful, and certainly decorated by Mrs. Corey.

By the front door, an impressive-looking tall clock sounded six times. The sixth gong reverberated endlessly; giving rise to the realization that it had been a long day.

I heard chatting just outside the window. I turned and looked. Two fishermen were walking up Point Road. One carried a gaffed spade and a pail full of fish, while the other bore some fish netting over one shoulder. They spoke loudly and laughed. Muffled joviality echoed up the road. At that very moment, Clive Mosher appeared from the side yard carrying a muddy rake and a freshly dug bucket of clams. His jacket was draped over one shoulder, shirt sleeves rolled to his elbows, and the cuffs of his white pants folded to his knees. They were soiled and wet. He stopped and talked with the two fishermen. One unfolded a handkerchief while Mosher filled it with the soft-shelled creatures. The men spoke to one another a while then went their separate ways. Their dampened conversation continued unheard from where I sat, but their laughter rang out quite audibly as they made their way up Point Road.

Seabury Cory entered the room with a silver tray. On it was a sterling teapot and a plate of sandwiches.

"I know you love tomato and cucumber with sour cream. I made you a sandwich."

"You didn't need to bother. Thank you. Love tomato and … cucumber," I croaked, trying to sound delighted if not hungry. After the chicken meal I had at the French residence early in the day, the sandwich before me stunted any hunger that I may have regained. He placed the tray on a short-legged table by the sofa.

"If you wait, I have baked fish in the oven along with clam chowder instead. You will stay and have some?"

"Yes, I will." I said, suddenly regaining my appetite.

"I'll wrap the sandwich and you may take it home."

We had dinner in the dining room. After eating, I followed Seabury Cory into the kitchen where I insisted on helping him with the dishes. The Cory kitchen was a bright and cheerful place. It also had the luxury of being a large space with ample storage and two washbasins, one for washing and one for rinsing. After they were filled, Seabury scrubbed and I dried. The entire time we spent in the kitchen, I found Seabury silent and reserved. I recounted the events of my day to which he displayed little interest.

"And this poor man was actually killed at one of the mills in New Bedford by a steam powered loom."

"You don't say."

"They think his hair became caught in the machinery."

"Sounds terrible," he muttered, staring out the window and washing the same dish over and over. "I hope he was not hurt too badly?"

"Well … as I said earlier, he was killed."

Seabury said nothing, his hands swimming in the sink basin.

"Is there something wrong, Mister Cory? You appear to be somewhere else."

He dropped the dish into the basin, took the towel from my hand, and flung it aside.

"Come, Emily. We need to talk."

Somewhat troubled, I followed him into the parlor.

"Sit."

"What is it?"

He filled his pipe with fresh tobacco and lit it. Opening a drawer in the desk, he retrieved a letter and sat himself down on the sofa. It was the letter I had delivered. Whiffs of smoke pulsated from the corner of his lips and he bit down hard on the tip of the pipe. Removing it from his mouth, he summoned me over while he tapped the mouthpiece on the sofa beside him.

"Come. Sit here and drop your anchor beside me. I have some news."

"Is it Samuel?" I was fearful. I nervously sat on the lounge beside him, staring at the letter in his hand.

"Not exactly," he said, calmly. "It's correspondence from a fellow named Jonathan Gardner. Jonathan's from the town of Swansea and serves under Samuel's command."

"Do you know him?"

He hesitated. "Not exactly. Though this is the second dispatch I've received from private Gardner."

"Why would he write you? Something happen to Samuel?"

He pulled the letter from the envelope and looked it over. "I don't have my spectacles," he said, though I knew he never needed any. "You read it."

He stood and walked over to a window, as if to distance himself from what I was about to read. Standing by the glass he stared into the street puffing his pipe. Holding the letter in hand I began reading.

Captain Seabury Cory:

It is with regret that I write to inform you that we have had no news about the whereabouts of Captain Samuel Cory and Private Edwin Poole. As in my earlier correspondence when I first informed you that Captain Cory was missing, any communication with the two missing men still remains a mystery.

I last saw Captain Cory shortly after we abandoned Fort Moultrie for Fort Sumter in December. After enduring relentless bombardment for two days from Confederate troops, we have surrendered Fort Sumter and marched north. Though no enlisted were lost in the skirmish, two men died through unfortunate circumstances. I assure you that neither your son nor private Poole were one of them.

I personally took it upon myself to approach Major Anderson, our field commander, and ask him about the two missing men. I was reprimanded and ordered not to speak of it to anyone since it was of no concern to me. I sense that he was trying to not worry me, and that he knew what became of them. I cannot really say. The only information he would offer was assurance that your son did not abandon his post nor did he desert.

I would be grateful if you could give news to my mother at the address I sent you previously and tell her that I am well. I will leave it to you to acquaint the Poole family of their son's disappearance, since I do not have Edwin's home address. If I unveil any news of Captain Cory's whereabouts, I will write you as soon as it is possible. I pray that you receive my letter and the photograph which I discovered under a pillow in Captain Cory's bunk. I feel that you should have it before it too goes missing.

God bless us all,
Jonathan Gardner

I clutched the sheet of paper between my fingers and sat stunned and dismayed. So much was revealed yet nothing was certain. Ambivalence and despair washed over me. At this very moment, endorsing truth is a much more difficult reality than wallowing in conjecture. Yet, I must admit at being more fearful than troubled. After all, the letter did not hold any tragic revelation, but neither did it ease my heart that there was nothing to fret about—only Jonathan Gardner's words.

I choose to place my trust in what Major Anderson had said in the letter—that it was of no concern. This disclosure alone gave me hope—hope that there was much more to Samuel's disappearance than anyone had a right to know. Perhaps he was sent on a military errand or transferred due to his naval knowledge or practices. At least that is the reasoning I will subscribe to. Any other would surely be more painful, if not plain dreadful. Nonetheless, I felt unsettled and alarmed. What of Seabury Cory? How insensitive of me to think only of myself.

He stood quietly staring out the window as if I were not even in the room. Holding his pipe in one hand, he rubbed the bitten end along his cheek in embroiled contemplation. Smoldering tobacco drifted like a curling ribbon and mushroomed into a hazy veil along the ceiling above his head. We were the two people who loved Samuel the most.

"This is terrible, Mister Cory. What could have happened? Why doesn't anyone know?"

"I have written to his commander, but I don't expect a reply."

"Where could Samuel be?"

"It doesn't sound like he became lost during any battle. To my knowledge the siege on Fort Sumter is an official start of a war. Even so, no one was killed in the battle. We can take comfort and drop sail in that." He paced the floor, head down, pipe dangling from the corner of his mouth. "Samuel's a resourceful lad. I must exercise a father's optimism that there is nothing to worry about. And you should too."

"Mister Cory, the letter said something about a photograph?"

He walked over to the desk and retrieved a paperboard image. A fatherly smile graced his face as he handed it to me. It was one of those new picture photographs. Some called it a tintype picture.

I held the stiff paper image in hand. I couldn't believe it. There he was. Samuel. Standing along a cannon with his friend, Edwin Poole. He looked proud and noble, resting with one hand on the large gun, the other tucked partially in his knee-length military jacket in a Napoleonic posture. Euphoric elation erupted in my tummy while tranquil warmth tingled all over. Edwin Poole stood close by. A long pole with a swathe of soiled cloth at one end, used to ram or load cannons, was flung over his shoulder. I studied the photograph silently. Samuel looked much older than the last time I saw him months previously. I ran my fingers down the image. How I yearned to caress his face, kiss him softly, let him know that I missed him dearly, and brood over his comfort and happiness every day. I turned the photograph over. On the back was some writing:

Captain Samuel Cory and Private Edwin Poole, Westport comrades.
Mathew Brady photographer.

"Poor Edwin," I lamented. "His wife Nancy will be shattered."

"I have notified Rebecca Gifford, Nancy's mother," said Seabury. "I'm certain that she must have been told by now."

"And Nancy has a three-year-old daughter," I said.

Retaining Samuel's image to memory, I handed the photograph back. He moved to the light and held the picture at arm's length.

"Did you notice the Captain bars on his shoulder?" he asked, proudly.

"I noticed everything about Samuel."

He smiled broadly; eyes firmly fixed on the tintype. "Hope you have the wind at your back, son. You have done well."

He studied the photograph for some time. I sat quietly, allowing him the time with his son's portrait. He propped the photograph on the desk by a candle and peered out the window.

"I must say, those tulips look handsome up against your white cottage," he said.

I walked over to the window. "They do, don't they."

"Did you enjoy your meal?"

"I am stuffed. Chicken for lunch, now baked fish and chowder for dinner, I may explode."

"If you must it will be a joyous explosion."

We both laughed. He put the letter that was sitting on the sofa back in the envelope and placed it on the desk.

"I had a long day. I think I will be getting home."

He walked me to the door. Opening it, I stepped onto the stoop.

"We must batten down the hatches and hove-to dear. It is looking like it will be a terrible war. There is little we can do and to worry would be doing too much."

A tear lingered in the corner of my eye.

"Yes. I suppose you are right, sir."

"The letter did not relay good news but neither did it relate any bad."

"It reminds me of something Shakespeare said in his play *Hamlet*."

Knowing my fondness for reading, he nodded and smiled.

"And what is that dear?"

"*There is nothing either good or bad but thinking makes it so.*"

"Old Bard is right. We shall not forget but nor shall we think about it. We shall tow all ill thoughts into dry dock and speak of the matter no longer; that is, unless we receive any news. Agreed?"

"Agreed."

Chapter 8:
Death Out a Window

There was a drizzly fog. The morning was chilly and raw when I arrived for work. As I approached the *Daily Whaler*, the door swung open and Rudolf French and that Bourque fellow walked out. They were quarreling. I stepped around the side of the building, if nothing more than to hide myself from Paul Bourque. His unfriendly nature made me uneasy.

"And furthermore, I insist you stop abusing the paperboys," I heard Rudolf say.

"What? Pitching pennies?" shouted Bourque.

"You are taking their hard earnings."

"Can I help it if they lose."

"They are children, Mister Bourque, not chums. And if you persist in your little swindle, I will terminate your services. Understood?"

"You're the boss, Mister French."

To my relief, Paul Bourque walked away in the opposite direction. I rushed for the editor's attention before he closed the door.

"Oh, Mister French."

"Ah, good morning, young lady."

"Hope I'm not late."

"Your concern is frivolous. However, follow me. There's a story on the horizon."

Slamming the door, he marched toward his carriage.

"Where are we going?" I asked, chasing after him.

"Just received a note. There's been an accident."

I barely had time to compose myself when I found us dashing down the street in a buggy on our way to a news story. I held onto my hat with one hand and the seat with the other as we stampeded up Union Street on the way to North Second Street. The horse whimpered and squealed in deaf complaint while it galloped along recklessly. Pedestrians leaped aside and the smatterings of mud flung past our heads as the mare's galloping hoofs scooped up the clumpy, wet soil.

Finally, we came upon our destination. The horse fell to a trot before its driver brought her to a standstill in front of an old, shabby three-decker. Clutching my chest, I took a deep breath. For a while back there, I thought that we would be savagely tossed to the street and becoming part of our own story.

In front of the house, a crowd loitered by a gray picket fence. A policeman stood guard, preventing onlookers and gawkers from entering the property. Rudolf scampered ahead. Once again, I hurried to keep pace.

When we approached the gate, we were stopped. But after a few words with the police, we were quickly allowed to enter. I promptly prepared the tools of the trade—flicked open my notebook and drew my pencil. Below a window, by the side of the house, I noticed something was covered with a white sheet. I could see what looked like a woman's leg protruding from beneath the drop cloth. She would be our story.

I went over to inspect. The bottom of the bare foot was soiled and the heel chaffed and callused. Without doubt, this was the limb of a hard-working female. Her ankle was exceptionally delicate and toes neatly manicured—a hint that she was not very old and took good care of herself.

Two men stood by the body. Rudolf French questioned them.

"That's right," said one of the men. "I heard a scream. When I came out, I found the woman lying on the ground."

"You are the landlord," said Rudolf.

"Yeah, that's right. I live on the first floor with my son."

Unfriendly and suspicious, the man was feeble in character and diminutive in stature. He had sharp features, led by a barbed nose, sunken eyes, and a Quaker beard encircling his face.

"Your name is?"

"Dexter."

"Is that your first or last name?"

"Only name."

"What is your Christian name?"

"Just Dexter," he insisted, smugly.

"Can you tell me the girl's name?"

"Allen."

"Miss or Mrs.?"

"Mrs. Allen," he snapped.

"Are you writing this down, Emily?" said Rudolf, glancing back at me with a curvature to his eyebrow.

"Yes, sir."

"What has happened here Mister ah … Dexter?"

"She was beating a rug up on the third floor," chimed the younger man. He pointed up to a window. The boy was tall and gangly and over a foot taller than his father. He stood humped, long arms dangling in front of him, as if they were too heavy for his torso. "She must have fallen out."

I noticed that the window on the third floor was open wide and a dingy floor mat hung from the sill.

"You say the girl's name is Allen. What is her first name?"

"Don't know," retorted the older man. He pulled up the collar of his shirt to ward off the damp air and perhaps our questioning.

The boy quickly gave up the girl's name. "Alice."

His father turned and glared at him.

"Now, Mister Dexter, do you know if anyone witnessed the fall?"

"No. My son and I were inside having our breakfast. Isn't that right, boy? We saw nothing."

"Yeah, Dad's right. He was having breakfast."

"Breakfast you say. How about you, young man? Did you witness anything?" inquired Rudolf, "or were you having breakfast also?"

"No, not really. But I heard lots of hollering and …"

"Keep your trap shut," raged Dexter. "It is no business of ours what others do behind closed doors."

Rudolf shook his head and moved away, annoyed by the man's demeanor. I thought it a good time to try my hand at some gentle interrogation. I raised my notebook and wet the tip of my pencil.

"Did you hear any fighting?" I asked the landlord.

He backed away and scrutinized me from head to foot. "Who the hell are you?"

"This is Miss White," replied Rudolf.

"How did you get past the guard?" he queried.

"She works for the newspaper. She's a journalist. It's alright to answer her questions."

I tried asking once more. "Was there any fighting?"

"No," grumbled the man. "We don't involve ourselves in other people's affairs. Besides, I'm not concerned about that. They have not paid rent for three months."

"He drinks a lot," said the younger man.

His father gave him an inconspicuous hard elbow to the ribs. The boy grunted. Lowering his head, he rubbed his side.

Rudolf had had enough and walked away. "Thank you, gentlemen."

It was left to me to continue questioning the two men. My turn to shine, you could say. "Is the girl's husband at home, Mister Dexter?"

"Upstairs with the police," barked the landlord.

"Who first found Mrs. Allen on the ground, you or your son?"

The man ignored my inquiry and instead snatched his son by the arm. "Come, boy. Our breakfast is getting cold," he huffed as they scurried away.

"Wait, I'm not finished," I implored, holding up my pencil.

"Oh yes you are, girly." cried the little man. "Take it up with the authorities."

I walked the property looking for anything that may be pertinent to the story. The yard was scattered with heaps of lumber and other discarded debris. Along the back of the property sat a string of rickety pigeon coops. Startled, the birds scattered, flew off, and came to rest along the gutter of a nearby house.

I continued my probe. Unexpectedly, I came upon a site that sickened me. Near one of the bird coops was a pile of dead birds sitting on a blood-smeared bench. Here city fowl were butchered and prepared for the evening meal. The ground below the bench was littered with innards and severed pigeon heads. A rusty hatchet stood buried in the bench by the carnage. I quickly moved to the other side of the building.

There I came upon an open shed and some barrels that were overflowing with waste and rubbish. The stench was nauseating. And though the house next door had all its window shutters tightly fastened, it was probably to no avail.

A yellow tomcat suddenly appeared from behind the shed, clutching a mouse. The tiny rodent squirmed in the cat's jaws as the mangy animal darted behind a fence when he saw me. I had come full circle and found nothing of interest—at least in the way of a tip or clue. Once again, I discovered that I was investigating when I should be reporting. The grass was wet and my journey through the yard left my feet cold and sopping. Rudolf walked over as I edited my notes.

"How are you holding up?" he asked.

"Fine, I suppose. Not the most scenic working environment."

He chuckled. "Did you get any more out of those two?"

"They just walked away as I was questioning them. I didn't even get their full names."

"I'll go ask them again. We can question the police later." He disappeared up the front stoop and into the entrance hallway.

I walked over to poor Mrs. Allen lying there on the moist soil like a discarded jumble of flesh. It is said that when our loved ones pass away, they can look down upon us from the beyond. I wondered if Alice Allen was looking down on herself.

I slowly circled the body. A morbid inquisitiveness smoldered inside me. Death whispered its arrival and tapped me on the shoulder with its bony finger of demise. I was compelled to turn and look the Angel of Death in the eye. Stooping down, I carefully lifted the white sheet with the tip of my pencil and exposed the deceased girl's face.

She was beautiful—perhaps twenty-two years of age, with fair hair and skin. Her head was grotesquely twisted to one side and fresh blood trickled from her mouth. She had blueberry eyes that were hauntingly fixed open and glaring. A once supple lower lip protruded pendulously below a gaping red mouth. A runnel of blood streamed from her pearly teeth and seeped down a pale and fragile chin where it dried brown and mottled. I studied her carefully. She was still wearing a gauzy nightshirt.

My attention was drawn to her hands. They were elegant and limber, fingers long and dexterous. Several irregularities and abrasions snagged my eye—especially along her long satin neck and once graceful, contorted fingers. Before I could fully investigate any further, I realized the window on the first floor of the house slide open. The landlord's son had pulled up a chair and sat there, resting his chin on his wrists, arms crossed, with elbows hung in the open air. He surveyed the yard as I sauntered over and tried my luck questioning him once more.

"I didn't get your name," I said.

"Chester," he replied, eagerly.

"Hello, Chester. My name is Emily."

"Father doesn't want me talking about Alice."

His speech, though lucid, was naive. Nevertheless, the boy had to be at least sixteen years of age but sounded like he was six. Earlier I had recognized that there was a simple or hampered nature to his communicative capabilities if not general appearance. And though I didn't choose to take advantage of his affliction, someone had to speak up for the dead.

"Alright. Let's not talk about Alice. Can you tell me your last name?" I poised my pencil over the ledger. "So, I can put it in the newspaper."

"The newspaper! You joshing me?"

"No, really. Tonight's edition."

"I don't know about that. Father might not like it."

"We are not talking about Alice, are we? We are talking about you."

An unassuming smile bloomed onto his face.

"Yeah. You're right. We're not talking about Alice at all?"

"Your last name."

"Allen, Chester Allen. Will it really be in the paper?"

"That's Alice's name."

"Yeah. She's my brother's wife. They fight terrible you know."

"Oh, why is that?"

"Father says it's because Jason drinks too much and gets angry."

"I see," I said, jotting down the man's name. "You say Jason gets angry?"

While I was writing, the window unexpectedly slammed shut. I looked up and captured a glimpse of Dexter Allen drawing curtains.

I walked back over to the body where Rudolf and a police officer stood.

"So, you don't think she fell. It was a suicide, then," said Rudolf.

"That's what the husband said at first," explained the policeman. "But it appears she fell out the window while beating a rug. We found the rug wire beater on the floor by the window. A most unfortunate accident."

"If I may interrupt," I added.

"This is Emily White, my assistant. Emily, this is Officer O'Hara."

The man tipped his cap. O'Hara looked more like a preacher than a policeman. A very handsome man he had a strong angular chin and smiling eyes.

"You say it was an accident?" I inquired.

"Yes. We inspected the window. It is very low to the floor. She must have tripped and fell out."

"With all due respect, Officer, I must dispute your findings."

"Now, now, young lady," said Rudolf. "The officer knows his job. After all, we are not here to challenge authority, but to record the facts."

"No, no, allow the girl to speak, by all means. I have a daughter about her age. Young people today need to be heard."

Rudolf French shrugged his shoulders. "Proceed, Miss White."

"Thank you, sir. Now Officer, as Mister French alluded to, we are here to record the facts. Under no circumstance am I underestimating your ability or overruling your findings, you understand. They are the facts as I see them. I only ask that you consider them."

"Very well, Miss White. What do you think happened?"

"It is my intuition that Alice Allen did not fall or jump."

"Didn't she?"

"No. She was murdered."

The imperturbable Rudolf French crossed his arms tightly, kicked at the soil, and shook his head. He looked somewhat vexed. I was uncertain whether the two men received my notion with critical reflection or dismissed it as a foolish girl's humorous folly. To my delight, the inquisitiveness of Officer O'Hara got the best of him. He smirked, removed his cap, and scratched his head.

"Murder? By murder I surmise you mean pushed. Why would you say that Miss White?"

I reluctantly lifted the sheet over Alice and pointed with my pencil.

"Inspect the deep band of red around her neck. This poor girl was choked with a snare or some sort of ligature."

O'Hara ran his fingers along Alice's neck.

"Hmm, looks freshly made. Didn't notice it before."

"And the nails on her fingers. How many are broken, folded back, even … four, five? And I beg you to consider. Who beats a rug at the birth of light, before sunrise, and undertakes such a dusty chore while donned in night attire?"

"She could have broken her nails in the fall," explained O'Hara, though he knew better.

"Unlikely, Officer. I say it happened before she went out the window. My suspicion is that her husband tried to strangle her and ultimately pushed her out the window. She must of broken her fingernails clawing at him. There should be an abundance of scratches on the man. If you do not find any, you will certainly find some on the window casing from when he tried to oust her."

"Hmm, I see," murmured the policeman.

"Just conjecture, you understand, but worth investigating, don't you think?"

"You've been reading too many Penny Dreadfuls," declared Rudolf. "How did you surmise such a scenario?"

"Well, I discovered that the two of them fight quite a bit and the husband is often drunk. I just put two and two together. And if Penny Dreadfuls helped a little, all the better."

"Who's this Penny Dreadful," asked O'Hara.

Rudolf threw up his arms and walked away.

"Would you like me to question the man on the third floor for you, Officer," I asked, candidly prodding him.

O'Hara just looked at me, as if he remembered some fundamental task he had forgotten to fulfill. His eyes teetered and his mouth took on a permanent yawn. I could almost hear the analytical cogs whirl in his head.

"I never thought he may be drunk," he said. "It was early sunrise when I questioned him. He looked groggy from a night of sleep. Now that I think of it, he kept changing his story—first saying she jumped, then that she fell while beating a rug. Maybe he is drunk."

O'Hara suddenly and without warning ran back into the house. I stood over Rudolf as he knelt on the muddy ground holding up the damp sheet covering the dead girl.

"*De profundis!*" he declaimed, "the evil folks do to one another. You may be right, Emily. There's more to this tale than meets the eye."

"Were you able to talk to the landlord, sir?"

"No," he grunted, struggling with his large frame as he rose to his feet. "Odd fellow … slammed the door in my face when I tried questioning him." He brushed the gritty mud from his trouser leg. "That's the vexed complexion to a reporter's occupation. You get all kinds. What stirred your curiosity?"

"I became suspicious when the younger man told me that the girl's husband drank heavily and that they often fight."

"I'm not surprised." He wiggled a stubby digit toward my note booklet. "Write that down."

"I have."

"Good girl. What else did you uncover?"

"I talked to the boy and got their full names. Did you know that the landlord is the girl's father-in-law?"

"You don't say?" He removed his hat and scratched his head.

"Surprising, is it not?"

"Odd family indeed," he declared, brushing back his tousled hair.

The white strands stood up in the damp air like bristly quills on a soggy porcupine. I was certain that mine did not fare any better. He pitched his hat back onto his head.

"Come, my girl. Let us continue our inquiry."

While officer O'Hara went back into the house to further investigate, we questioned pedestrians and neighbors out on the street. No one had seen Alice plunge to the ground. Those who knew the couple described her as kind and gentle and her husband as distant and aloof.

As we toiled at our profession, Rudolf insisted that I engage in astute circumspection when questioning the public and employ methodical discretion to what was communicated by the average man or woman on the street. With bystanders, every person's story differed somewhat, even though they observed the same event. Some had a tale all their own. It was up to the newspaper reporter to sieve through what was related and endeavor to determine the truth.

We were pretty much done with our inquiries when suddenly O'Hara and another burly officer burst out from the house escorting a man by the arms. The fellow's shirt was sloppily unfastened, and one could plainly see fresh scratches on a hirsute chest. The police marched him reluctantly out through the gate and past the swarm of astonished onlookers. The man instantly lunged and kicked at the crowd as he was scurried along. Gasps and shrieks sounded as the swarm leaped back. He broke into delirious laughter, growling threateningly at the assembly while protuberant eyes nearly left their sockets. The landlord and his son stealthily observed the spectacle out a window camouflaged by curtains as the two policemen hurried their kin on the way to the city jail. The prisoner squirmed and twisted, stumbling as he went, crying out for his wife, though she was dead.

"I love you, Alice," he roared, slurring. "I didn't mean it, Alice," he continued, just before falling into hysterics. "You wouldn't listen, Alice, you wouldn't listen." His pleading and antics grew faint the further away they got. Not long after, they vanished into the vapory murkiness of a foggy day.

Just then, an affable and much older policeman with a rubicund face and protuberant belly came hobbling from the building. Rudolf knew the large man as police captain Frank Ward.

"Morning, Frankie."

"Ah, Frenchie, my lad. How are ya?" said the man in a profound Irish brogue.

"Figured you'd be retired by now."

"Soon, soon. Getting too old for this sort of ting."

"Where are they taking him, Frankie?"

"Aye, to da clink. The bloke confessed to pushin' his woman out da winda. I expect he's gone mad."

I flipped open my reporter's notebook and commenced jotting.

"He confessed, then," echoed Rudolf.

"Aye. Kept changin' his alibi at first. We found pieces of da poor lass' fingernails wedged in the winda casin. And he used this strap to choke her with." Ward held up a rawhide bootlace. "You can tank Officer Patrick O'Hara for a keen eye. Good investigator."

Rudolf French glanced over at me and winked.

"Yes, she is," he agreed.

"The wife must of fought like da devil," declared Ward.

"Takes all kinds," said Rudolf.

"Aye. There's a cozy cot for that kind waitin back at da station. Well, I'll be seein' ya, Frenchie. I'm off to keep da peace." Officer Frank Ward hobbled up the street and soon vanished into the mist.

"Good to see old Frankie again," declared Rudolf.

"Seems like a nice fellow."

"Went to school with my older brother when they were kids. Yes. He is a nice fellow." Rudolf stared at me, fists resting on his hips. "And as for you, young lady."

"What? Did I do something wrong, sir?"

He reached out and tapped me gently on the forearm. "You did a fine job. I'm proud of you. I have discovered a first-rate newspaper girl."

I was elated by the compliment.

"I am very impressed by your natural proficiency for detail. Your presentation and advice to the police was skillful and saved the day."

"Thank you, sir."

I tried to hide the pretentious smile that gushed onto my face. At that moment, I was very pleased with myself. I tried suppressing a supercilious grin. Unexpectedly, Grandmamma came to mind and I could hear her say, "Store your pride under a bushel and wear dignity on your face, for the proud are boastful but modesty respectful and virtuous."

"It was nothing, sir, really," I affirmed, humbling myself. "Just elementary observation."

"Elementary … my left foot," chided Rudolf, chuckling.

"I just added two and two together and came up with four."

"The police added two and two and came up with three. Emily White, you've got what it takes. You will be an asset to the *Daily Whaler*. An asset indeed. Now, let's get back to the office. We should have this story out on the street by noon. By the way, I'm arranging a meeting with some colleagues. I want you to be there."

"Oh?"

"After what I witnessed this morning, and from what I discovered about you yesterday, you may be a precious asset to the gathering."

"Anything you say, Mister French."

The journey back to the office was much more pleasant, even though the weather did not participate. While the horse jogged at a leisurely pace, Rudolf went over my notations, making certain there was nothing we had overlooked. The pages to the journal were damp and moist and the writing smudged, making the jottings a little difficult to read. Still, I had compiled events and details to memory; thus, the blotched script would not be a problem.

The realization of the morning's events and poor Alice Allen finally tugged at empathy. I quickly stored away any commiseration I felt for later in the day when I was alone. I can tell you this—it was no easy task. Suppressing emotions and trying not to let them escape was like holding your breath under water while unable to surface. For now, I had to prove myself to the editor of the *Daily Whaler* that I was tough and capable of performing the job.

To ward off a stray reflection, I focused on the trip back to the office, which was all that more daunting considering the scenery beyond the horse's nose was shrouded in fog.

Unlike a country horse, the animal seemed happier trotting instead of running. Her black coat shimmered, glowing indigo against the muted glow of dreary light. The rhythm of hoofs was mesmerizing. Glory—that's what Rudolf French named the mare, had a talent for seducing one into slumber with just the interminable flicking of a tail.

Although misty rain had stopped, fog lingered. As we approached the waterfront, the hoary brume obscured the ships in harbor. Almost a mile away, I could hear folding waves fizzing out on Buzzard's Bay while thundering upon the open shore. There was also the eerie sound of a barking dog, howling from the shadowed landscape. The incessant yapping had an otherworldly essence to it.

I heard the grinding of wheels along the craggy ground from a carriage behind us, but nothing could be seen. From out of the mist, someone whistled a sea chantey. The pelagic melody moved as we moved. I could swear that the seafaring whistler was sitting right beside me—how far off and from which direction was a mystery. Sounds in fog and their proximity are always more pronounced and surreal. They glide on the silent mist like swarming spirits over an open grave. An image of the girl beneath the sheet was brooding in my mind as the building that housed the *Daily Whaler* materialized from out of the fog.

Rudolf stopped the buggy by the entrance and scurried inside. Visibility suddenly improved as a ray of sunlight broke through a portal in the fog, splashing onto the brick facade of the newspaper company. Thinking of Alice Allen lying on the damp cold ground generated emotions that I could contain no longer. Death was taunting me as it had done with Grandmamma, letting me know that in life it was always present and waiting. Sweet Grandmamma. How alone I felt when looking death in the eye once again, as I did today.

I got down from the buggy. I fondled the horse's silky mane and stroked her cheeks. Rudolf yelled for me to hurry. A tear trickled freely down my face. I lingered, mopping my nose on the gentle mare's cold muzzle. Glory tenderly lowered her head in a whimpered neigh. I wish to believe that she wept along with me.

I sat at my desk and went over my notes with copywriter Edgar Ryan. I handed him a formal report, which I had taken from my dank and wrinkled notebook.

"Is that all of it?"

Edgar Ryan was not much older than I. A short, thin fellow, clean-shaven, hair parted down the middle, with chipmunk cheeks every time he smiled.

"Yes, it is, Mister Ryan."

"It's Edgar, Miss White. Most call me Ed."

"Alright then, Ed it is. But you must call me Emily."

"Ah yes, diligent and industrious."

"I beg your pardon."

"Your name—Emily. It translates into someone who is hard working, untiring."

"I never knew that."

"Ancient Roman, you know."

"Oh?"

"Depending on how far back you trace it. Emily—originally Amelia. Taken from the German."

"German? I always thought it was English. I was named after Emily Bronte, or at least I would like to think so."

"The English took the moniker Amelia from the Germans and adapted it, making it their own, you see. You know those English. A never-ending appetite for colonizing one thing or another."

"Ryan. Is that not English?"

Irish … well not really. I was born in Barrington. That's in Rhode Island, you know. The people on my mother's side are Egyptian."

"Oh?"

"Yes, but that's another story. I know, I know, you would never know it by looking at me." He turned and brandished the profile of his face, lifting his chin with the back of his hand. He held his head up proudly to the light from a window across the room. "See. I have my mother's cheeks."

But it was not his exalted cheeks that I observed but a lingering nose and one which appeared to be an adjunct to a broad forehead. Face to face one would never distinguish it, but from the right angle his facial profile exposed buoyant Amerindian features. Ultimately, it was his rippled, salmon-flushed hair and jovial Irish smile that manifested, revealing his Caucasian attribute. I discovered that I really liked Edgar Ryan. He was full of energy and inquisitive about the world around him. He spoke with discursive vigor, jumping from one topic to another. Once he got started, he just talked and talked. In any event, I found him a refreshing change to the older and ever-earnest Rudolf French, who sat listening—or the austere demeanor of agent, Ezra Hick and his indelible frown. The only nettlesome pickle when chatting with Edgar Ryan was trying to contribute a word.

"I have an uncle named Emil," he continued, in prolix style. "Though Emil is similar to Emily there is no coalition to the two names since Emil is of Swedish extraction. Uncle on my father's side, I must inform you. Of course, Emil not being a feminine derivative of Emily but a …"

"Mister Ryan!" shouted Rudolf.

Edgar Ryan jumped and comically stood at attention. "Yes, Chief," he blurted, saluting and striking his heels.

"We will never get the paper out discussing your enthusiasm with seismology. Let's get the press rolling, shall we?"

"Right away, Chief. And your report on the Allen incident?"

"I have no report. This is Miss White's story. Use her journal and make certain you spell her name right."

"Names are my specialty, Chief. You know that."

"Wish I didn't."

"Miss Emily White. Pup reporter," announced Ryan as he wrote my name down.

"Get to it man."

"Rudolf … German for tyrant," he whispered.

"I heard that."

Edgar Ryan left quickly. Rudolf shook his head.

"Now, we must get down to business. Pull your chair up, Emily. I'd like to have a private word."

I placed my chair by the side of his desk and made myself comfortable.

"I need to tell you that your performance today was exemplary. I don't know what would have transpired if you did not solve that crime for the police. I'm impressed."

"Why, thank you, sir."

"You have earned your stripes, young lady. Now, I wanted to discuss another matter, one we never finished. And now that you have proved yourself, I may have underestimated you. I believe you are on to something."

"Oh?"

"The riddle of Asha Potter and the way he died."

"I see."

"You mentioned that it was murder. I now believe it to be suspicious at the very least."

"I strongly believe that it was murder, sir."

He rolled up his sleeves, crossed his arms, and sat back in his chair. "You see, Emily, I have been a journalist most my life. I report what I witness, or what is observed, or recounted by others. This investigative approach you have taken to journalistic prudence is fascinating, I must say."

"I must confess, it tugs at me."

"I can see why. If it were not for you, Alice Allen's death would have been recorded as an accident. Her husband would remarry and push another girl out the window. How could we have known?"

"Observation, sir. You see, I have witnessed untimely death in the past. You may have reported on one of them. Take Annie Slocum. She was found hanged with a rope around her neck on Cuttyhunk Island."

"Yes, yes, I remember. It was about a year ago. We did not run the story, but it was covered by the Fall River papers."

"That's right. After discovering Annie, Samuel Cory and I brought the body to Fall River on his schooner."

"If I remember correctly it was reported as a suicide."

"Yes, that's correct, but, in fact, it was not a suicide. Annie was strangled after she was afflicted in an unmentionable assault."

"My lord. And the murderer?"

"It's a long story, but they have atoned for their crimes. There were others, but that was my first experience with untimely death. A short while later, it was Grandmamma's time—but of natural causes. She had lived a long life. I was by her bedside when she passed and held her hand as Death departed with her. From that day forward, it has tormented me. The Dark Angel has become an occasional huntress and when it exposes its dreadful facade, I am intrigued, if not compelled, to why it has harvested life. Such as it did today. In this case, death had an expedient accomplice—Jason Allen, Alice's husband."

"It's sad about your grandmother, my dear."

"Grandmamma is always with me. As I had mentioned, it was her time. Nonetheless, death is always burdensome."

"As it was for me with Asha Potter. He was an old friend … a partner in many affairs, both his and mine … closer than you know. Lately, I have felt the heat of skepticism burn my sense of misgiving and concluded that I cannot shroud it any longer."

"I can appreciate your consternation, sir. It is as it should be."

"So, tell me. Why do you feel Asha was murdered?"

"Well, I observed several inconsistencies when I was at the Wamsutta Mill that day."

"Such as."

"Mister Potter's hair. It is believed that it became entangled in the machinery, lifting him off the floor and up to the ceiling where he sustained his mortal wounds."

"That's the way we reported it."

"If that in fact happened, his hair would have been frayed and torn, possibly taking a portion of his scalp with it. I discovered that the hair appeared cut or chopped as if someone employed scissors or a knife."

"Hmm?"

"And the way the body was draped along the floor, sir. As you well remember, Mister Potter was working with Paul Bourque, the steam engineer, who was down at the engine house and out of sight when Asha met his cruel twist of fate. It was very early in the day and just before any of the working staff had arrived. Thus, the incursion had to be expeditious. A fact that was somewhat calculative but rushed."

"Yes, I found poor Asha position on the floor rather incidental but couldn't place a finger on why."

"Well, the body was found close to the loom machinery, if you remember. His legs were placed parallel to one another while his arms were outstretched above his head … if you forgive me, the resemblance—it was as if he lay there nailed to a cross. Think on it carefully. You would surmise that if a man was lifted off the floor by the loom drive belt, and launched to the beams above, he would have been discharged and crumbled to the floor right under the machinery. He was not. In fact, the location of the body was not where he came to rest when he received his injuries but where it was moved."

"Hmm, and your hypothesis?"

"I think he was murdered a good distance from the loom and dragged by the machinery to orchestrate an accident. Still not close enough, though. The way his arms were outstretched would be the outcome of a body dragged by the legs."

"Can we be certain?"

"Unfortunately, in such a case, we can be certain about nothing. There was blood smear, which I discovered on the wall about twenty feet away by the door that led outside. I do not pretend to be an expert on such matters, but I must exercise insight and ask why Asha Potter was discovered away from the machinery that supposedly had killed him."

"Yes, of course."

"The smudge on the wall ran from eye level down to the floor. A good portion of the wall surface was smeared with blood. It was difficult to see since the brick is the same color as the blood. I ran a finger along a dark shadow on the wall and it was sticky and wet … indeed blood—lots of it, with substantial pooling at the base of the wall. Surprisingly, no one seemed to notice or pay it any scrutiny."

"You're right. Everyone just assumed the entire event was an unfortunate accident. Therefore, the police never investigated."

"I ask you this. After he was thrown to the wall, why was the body found by the machinery?"

"Well, one could plainly see the blood smear on the floor. I suppose he crawled over to the loom where he languished and died."

"I can see how you arrive at such a conclusion. However, think how that smearing appeared on the floor."

"It was just blood … smeared on the planking. Didn't give it much thought. Your assessment on the matter, Miss White?"

"It caught my eye right off. The way the blood was uniformly smudged on the flooring … one continuous, unbroken brush stroke, as if applied with a mop, continuous and uninterrupted."

"You are right, it was."

"If indeed Asa crawled back toward the machinery unassisted, the smear would be fragmented, irregular, and uneven as he struggled and twisted along the floor. Instead, what was there was one long, sweeping streak of blood … as if something was dragged along the floor … a body."

Rudolf listened somewhat dubiously but attentively. His face contorted into a frown as his brain wrestled with what he heard.

"What are you trying to say?"

"It is my conviction that Asha was attacked shortly after letting someone into the loom area. I theorize that he was held fast against the wall by his accomplice and beaten with the loom's brake handle."

"Brake handle?"

"Yes. I noticed blood smeared and a patch of hair on the handle's base, where it fits into a cradle."

"How can you be sure?"

"It's an observation upon which I am certain."

"Go on."

"Other than a besmirched patch on the leather drive belt itself, I could find no blood anywhere else on the loom. The blood on the loom's drive belt had hair pasted to it with some sort of slag grease, the same hair as the brake handle did, more than likely placed on the belt intentionally and cunningly."

"Grease! There's no lubrication on those leather belts. If there were, the belt would just slip and not do its job."

"Precisely. Also, there was no hair anywhere else … including the drive pulley where it attaches to the beams by the ceiling, where most of the hair should have been. I questioned how blood could have covered the brake handle base when it was tightly fitted into a cradle that would shield it from soil or blood spatter."

"Blood spatter! The term is revealing. Fortuitous if not noteworthy evidence, I would say." He stroked his chin. "I see how everything fits."

"I also found some peculiar footprints in the blood on the floor."

"Well, that could have been left by anyone. People were in and out of there."

"But these were uncommon. They were distinguishing marks in a horseshoe pattern around the perimeter of the heel—as if the wearer nailed rivets or something to the heel."

"Not as uncommon as you think. Safeguards, placed there to protect the shoe from wear. And your assessment is what, Miss White?"

"If we can find who was wearing those shoe's we should be able …"

"It could be anyone. Though your discovery is preceptive, I'm afraid it deserves little speculation to who may have left them."

"I suppose ..."

"Any other keen observations, young lady?"

"Finally, there was the coat button."

"Yes, yes. I have been asking myself. Why would Asha have a South Carolina military button on his person?"

"Because it was not his. It was torn off in the struggle. Torn from the jacket of the man that killed him."

Rudolf gave no reaction to my attestation. Instead, he slowly got up from his creaky chair and ambled to the window overlooking the hustling harbor. The anchorage appeared to be a meditative refuge for his thoughts—a calming sanctuary for entangled contemplation. He stood by the glass bobbing on his heels, hands clutched behind his back. His gaze soared over the sail-staff jungle of ships and harbor pilings, a sea of spars and cables that overlooked the bucolic Fairhaven coastline just the other side of the tranquil Acushnet River. Fairhaven—a peaceful sanctum where verdurous, grassy fields, ethereal church steeples, and pretty cottages stood sheltered and noble by lofty, patulous awnings of oak and elm.

With slothful stride, Rudolf shook his head. Slapping a commiserative tongue on the roof of his mouth, he recited the now familiar and esteemed declaration.

"*De profundis*!"

Chapter 9: A Most Revealing Account

I awoke to a noise—what sounded like singing or humming, followed by the hollow clang of a bread pan or dish. The burnished light permeated through the flimsy curtain that hung from a solitary window in the small loft room where I slept. I languidly opened one weepy eye, immediately followed by the other. I strained to focus as the newborn brightness made clear the dazzled truth of day. What I heard must have been fishermen out in the street, walking by the house, I surmised.

Feeling drowsy, I lay there, trying to recall the night's dream. Lately, I have been having a reoccurring dream—though not disturbing, still somewhat pestering—eerie, really. But then again, so is the anatomy of most dreams. Some are quickly forgotten while others linger enigmatically—still others hold hidden significance that is usually lost to the fiction of slumber.

Grandmamma had countless, tangled interpretations of her dreams. So decisive were her renderings that she sometimes rearranged her day's intentions around them. Like the time she dreamed that she was walking along Point Road late at night when a full moon fell out of the sky and rolled through the open countryside. She ran for home, fearing the worst. Suddenly, the cicatricose orb rolled right over her. Finding herself sprawled in the road, she picked herself up, only to discover her face and body riddled with fissures and moony craters. When she awakened from her 'mare, she rushed to a mirror. Sure enough—age was upon her. Crow's feet radiated from her eyes. Creases around her mouth and nose were longer and deeper than she remembered. The worry lines along her forehead had doubled in number and crescent pouches grew below her eyes, protruding like billowing chins. But is that not the fate that awaits us all? To Grandmamma, her dream was a warning that she was aging. Thus, a lesson unfolded that she must live a more pious and empathetic life—at least to Grandmamma.

On days when I need not be anywhere in particular, I find that it has become alarming, if not a common occurrence, that the sun ascends the treed horizon outside my bed chamber before I awakened, and my morning poached egg has made its spooned journey from skillet to plate. I have always been accustomed in fulfilling my rendezvous at sunrise and meeting mister daylight dressed and alert by the kitchen stove. It is confirmation of an orderly and salubrious life. But in the past month, I can almost count on all the fingers of one hand the times I have overslept. I have ascertained that this unusual and curious happenstance is a disorder brought on by my recent employment. Who knew having a formal job earning wages would disrupt such a ubiquitous practice as awakening in a timely manner? I must admit to being weary and drained as of late. The trip between New Bedford and Point Village can be very tiring. Even so, on the long drive home, I try to keep up with my sewing, fulfilling my commitment to a number of prosperous patrons that I have groomed over the years. Sewing on a bucking carriage is no easy task, I'll let you know, and I have wee punctures in my fingers to prove it.

As you well know, I operate a small business stitching and sewing. It was how I made a living … until now. Being a newspaperwoman must take precedence. After all, I earn three times what I make as a seamstress working for the *Daily Whaler*—to mention nothing about position and status. Not that I would ever allow such haughty banners to fly over my tent openly or with superior complacency. Such self-seeking attributes are silent distinctions and must never be flaunted … at least not brazenly. After all, Grandmamma would not have approved. Besides, it is not the hallmark of a lady or how she should conduct herself. Still, make no mistake. I have full intentions of making employment work—to be successful at it and be the best the craft can produce. Whoops? Was I swaggering in egotism? Well, a little is not harmful and, dare I declare, almost acceptable around friends. Wouldn't you say?

I rolled over in bed and turned my back to the impinging light and closed my eyes. A few more winks couldn't hurt. Though Grandmamma would be cross if she knew I was dispensing of Sunday service for a foolhardy addendum to a full night's slumber.

Suddenly, I heard someone humming—a woman. It was a popular tune; one I heard many times before. A melody made popular just recently. And if the tune was not familiar the words surely were, for it was a poem called "Annabel Lee." I listened carefully.

It was many and many a year ago,
In a kingdom by the sea,
That a maiden there lived whom you may know,

By the name of Annabel Lee,
And this maiden she lived with no other thought,
Than to love and be loved by me ...,

Hmm, hmm, the voice cheerfully hummed. It sounded like the singing was coming from downstairs and inside the house. I threw the sheets away and sprung out of bed. I got dressed, throwing a nightgown over my head. I listened warily from the top of the stairs. *Hmm, hmm, hmm, Annabel Lee, Annabel lee,* the purring voice continued. I walked one or two steps down the stairs and listened some more. The step crackled. The singing stopped.

"I can hear you stirring up there," the caroling voice yelled "Time to get up. Day is fleeting."

I scurried down the stairs and into the kitchen. There she stood, scooping some fried eggs onto a plate.

"I hope you don't mind," she said, "but I let myself in and started breakfast."

"Amy. How did you ...?"

She continued her babble. "I placed the key back under the mat ... silly place for it. Well anyhow, now I'm here and you are finally up. It's a wonder you got up at all. I knocked and knocked, but no Emmie. Perhaps she's dead, I said to myself. Well, no reason to miss out on breakfast, I thought."

I flung myself into a chair and rubbed the sleepies behind my eyes. Her spikey voice jammed every word into morning's virgin ears.

"You should really find somewhere else to place that key," she chided, plopping a plate before me. "Why with all those feral whalers and scruffy fishermen just down the street. You never know who may invite themselves in. Once inside, I'm certain they would not just start making breakfast for you. God knows what they would do."

"Oh, Amy, they won't bother anyone. I know most of them. Half of them live in the village."

"I wouldn't know," she declared, curtly. "I'm a city girl."

"What do you mean? You grew up here, just up the road."

She ignored my declaration. Amy's family did well in the whaling trade and became wealthy. Soon after, the Chaloner clan moved out of Point Village and to Fall River, where they purchased a large house. Mister Chaloner retained the old homestead on the Point and used it during summer months. Though she loved to boast that she was a city girl, Amy was no stranger to Point Village and its customs.

"Why were you still in bed?"

"I have been tired lately. The job at the newspaper has left me with little time for myself."

"Well, today is Sunday, and you can get some rest." She dropped an overcooked, seared egg onto my plate, "Now how do you like your toast?"

"Ah ...?"

"Singed, blackened, or burnt?"

I grimaced, looking over at a plate of smoldering, charred bread. I shook my head. "Well, yes, ah, just how I like it ... on fire."

"Well, on fire it will be."

She smeared a charred slice with butter. I took the teapot from the stove as the brew overflowed and spilled tea sizzled all over. She sat down.

"I couldn't find the cups and saucers," she said, though they were hanging on the wall in plain sight.

"I didn't know you fixed your own breakfast." I said, lifting a portion of the parched and withered egg with the tip of my fork.

"Never have." She bit into a slice of untoasted bread. "That's what mothers are for," she declared, a mouth full of food.

"I could confirm as much." I whispered. I cut into the tawny yoke with my fork and ate.

Amy flung her bread onto the plate and over her untouched egg and pushed it away.

"What's the matter?"

"Oh, nothing."

"You're not eating."

"Not hungry after all."

"You have three eggs on your plate."

"My eyes were hungrier than my stomach." She wiped the corners of her mouth with a towel.

After chewing some overcooked, oily yoke, I reluctantly swallowed and put down the fork.

"I'm not very hungry myself."

"It's just not the same when you cook for yourself."

I looked down at all the burnt food. It was no wonder. "I know what you mean."

She reached over the table, picked up the book I left there the night before, and thumbed through it.

"This is what you've been reading lately, huh?"

"Oh, Amy, it is so fascinating. I was up until two in the morning. I finally finished it."

"Explains why you overslept."

"I suppose."

"I didn't realize you were interested in the debauched practice of servitude, as Uncle French would put it."

"A first-hand account from the pen of a captive, no less. I would not believe what occurred unless I read it myself. Amy, it was terrible, just terrible, the wretched existence of those poor souls."

"Your employer has more than a casual interest in this sort of business."

"Oh?"

"You know, being a newspaperman and all."

"Oh, I see."

"*Twelve Years a Slave*," she recited, reading from the title page.

"It's the story of Solomon Northrup, a freeman from New York State, who was kidnapped, sold, and implanted into bondage. It's both brilliant and devastating."

"Does it have a happy ending?" she asked, turning over a few leaves in the book.

"Well, if you look at it as story-telling, or in the vein of a fictional narrative, I suppose it does have a happy ending. At least Northrup made it sound that way, though it is anything but fantasy. It is laden with adversity and consternation beyond ethical understanding. Although, old Solomon does find happiness in the end."

"I see that you have folded down the corners of a few pages."

"It was given to me that way. Must have been done by Mister Johnson, the man who lent it to me. It contains the passages with the more dreadful accounts."

"Oh."

"You should know me better, Amy. Doubling over the corner of a page onto itself? Come now. I would never violate a book in that respect. It would be as if I twisted your arm behind your back."

She laughed. "I suppose. Only you would see a book that way."

She placed her finger on a line along one of the dog-eared pages and commenced reading. "Oh my. This sounds terrible."

I rose from my chair and took a station standing over her shoulder. I followed her probing finger as she swept the delicate digit along the page.

"That paragraph talks about the time when Solomon was taken captive," I explained, pointing at the page. "He was attempting to persuade his detainers that he was a free man and that they had made a dire mistake. Unfortunately, we get the notion that the depraved jailers were well aware of Solomon's freedom but ventured to beat, conceal, and suppress the truth out of him. Here Solomon introduces us to two men—James H. Burch and his cruel hired man named Ebenezer Radburn. Together they assault poor Solomon unmercifully."

Amy read aloud. I took a plate of burnt egg in each hand and ambled over to the washbasin by the window. Looking out, the scene behind the house was one of woolly grass fields and moss-covered stone walls, clustered with budding lavender and cream-colored wisteria—a tangle of virgin bloom overlooking the buff mud banks of the serene Westport River.

Having a book read to me is the next best thing to reading one myself. Though I had read Solomon Northup's account, Amy's telling took on a new perceptible dynamic—as if a play was unfolding in my head. I did not have to study each sentence, each paragraph, each page, but, instead, I was free to look inward and construct an uninterrupted scene in my mind's eye as events unfolded. I listened painfully to every word pitched from her lips as if for the first time. She had a coherent and euphonic voice. It was not one measured or metered in poetic timbre but, instead, awash with an absorbing gist that adapted and gripped the moment, abducting the listener with stunning passionate pace and surprising sympathy. Scrutinizing her flowing flaxen hair, crystalline eyes, and angelic face, one would never have guessed that she was so good an orator. Listening to Amy read was like watching an artist apply color to canvas and best appreciated with eyes closed.

As soon as these formidable whips appeared, I was seized by both of them, and roughly divested of my clothing. My feet, as has been stated, were fastened to the floor. Drawing me over the bench, face downwards, Radburn placed his heavy foot upon the fetters, between my wrists, holding them painfully to the floor. With the paddle, Burch commenced beating me. Blow after blow was inflicted upon my naked body. When his unrelenting arm grew tired, he stopped and asked if I still insisted I was a free man. I did insist upon it, and then the blows were renewed, faster and more energetically, if possible, than before. When again I tired, he would repeat the same question, and receiving the same answer, continue his cruel labor. All this time, the incarnate devil was uttering most fiendish oaths. At length the paddle broke, leaving the useless handle in his hand. Still I would not yield. All his brutal blows could not force from my lips the foul lie that I was a slave. Casting madly on the floor the handle of the broken paddle, he seized the rope. This was far more painful than the other. I struggled with all my power, but it was in vain. I prayed for mercy, but my prayer was only answered with imprecations and with stripes. I thought I must die beneath the lashes of the accursed brute. Even now the flesh crawls upon my bones, as I recall the scene. I was all on fire. My sufferings I can compare to nothing else than the burning agonies of hell!

Amy read as I watched Elisha Cornell out the window lead his small herd of prized Guernseys into the sloping field. Immediately, they lumbered over to the picket fence by my garden where I often fed them golden table treacle from the end of a long-handled ladle. The sky above them was a boundless expanse of sapphire blue, blistered with meandering, billowy clouds along a lazy horizon. In the distance, a pair of gangly egrets prowled along the river's marshy edge. Their protracted white necks coiled and thrust while conoid bills snatching unsuspecting prey from ankle-deep waters. Above, a flock of honking Canadian geese soared, impertinently broadcasting their clamorous arrival from points north and beyond. Still, the pastoral and nautical harmony that I witnessed outside my window was unable to ease the anguish I felt as Amy continued to read.

At last I became silent to his repeated questions. I would make no reply. In fact, I was becoming almost unable to speak. Still he plied the lash without stint upon my poor body, until it seemed that the lacerated flesh was stripped from my bones at every stroke. A man with a particle of mercy in his soul would not have beaten even a dog so cruelly. At length Radburn said that it was useless to whip me anymore—that I would be sore enough. Thereupon, Burch desisted, saying, with an admonitory shake of his fist in my face, and hissing the words through his firm-set teeth, that if ever I dared to utter again that I was entitled to my freedom, that I had been kidnapped, or anything whatever of the kind, the castigation I had just received was nothing in comparison with what would follow. He swore that he would either conquer or kill me.

I walked over and placed a hand on her shoulder.

"Poor man. Why, Emmie? It makes little sense. Can it be possible that someone would do such a thing … that there are people out there as he describes? Who were those men?"

"James H. Burch and his hired hand Radburn. Burch was a slave merchant. It's like robbing a bank. They could get upwards of a thousand dollars for a slave."

"Where did this happen?"

"Down in Washington."

"Washington? The capital?"

"At a place called William's Slave Pen where they held and sold human souls. What you just read is a prelude to what Solomon experienced or witnessed until he gained his freedom."

Amy turned a few leaves, stopped at another earmarked page, and started reading.

I remained in William's Slave Pen about two weeks. The night previous to my departure a woman was brought in, weeping bitterly, and leading by the hand a little child. Emily, the child, was seven or eight years old, of light complexion, and with a face of admirable beauty.

"The little girl had your name, Emmie."

"Yes, she did," I said. "A sad affair indeed. Let me disclose what you are about to read. Emily's mother's name is Eliza. She was the slave of a man named Elisha Berry—a very rich man. As the years went by Berry and his wife had fallen into dissipated habits and quarreled. Soon after, they separated. Berry left the house and built his own home on the property. At the time, he invited Eliza to live with him in his new household and they had a child which they named Emily. Berry had always promised Eliza emancipation. She resided with him for nine years, with servants to attend upon her and provide her with every comfort and luxury life could offer. Then things changed and for some unexplained reason the Berry property was divided. Eliza and her daughter, being considered property, fell under the ownership of Berry's daughter and her husband Jacob Brooks. Brooks had promised to take Eliza and young Emily into town so that he could apply for her freedom papers. Eliza got dressed in her best attire along with her young child, proud that her day of freedom had finally come. Instead, after the papers were filled, Eliza and young Emily were delivered to William's Slave Pen. The papers that were drawn were actually a receipt of sale and Eliza and young Emily became merchandise."

"Oh, Emmie. How fiendish."

She closed the book, placed it down, and pushed it away before pouring herself a cup of black tea. Nervously, she guzzled some down. "I can't read anymore," she stuttered, swallowing. Clutching a slice of burnt bread from the tray she buttered it and took a bite. "It is much too sad," she said tossing the bitten bread back onto the tray and posing a sour face. "I'm afraid to discover what unfolds and what fate awaits the poor woman."

"But you must. We cannot tuck our heads in the sands of ignorance. There is much more to Eliza's story." I picked up the volume and searched page to page.

"And you are going to read it to me, is that right?"

"Correct. Now, Eliza previously had a little boy named Randall, a son taken away from her earlier," I said, finding my place in the book. "They were all reunited at William's Slave Pen—mother, son, and daughter, all held for sale. As you mentioned, it is sad … true, but tragic is more explicit. Now this James Burch had a partner or consignee named Theophilus Freeman."

"Freeman. How diabolically prophetic."

"He was indeed the purveyor the day Eliza was to be sold."

I had found my place and fingered the page.

"Here it is. I'll read it to you."

"If you must."

Amy rested her elbows on the table and held her face in her hands.

"Are you alright?" I asked.

"Yes, yes. Just preparing myself for the worst. Proceed."

"Very well. Here Freeman is ready to sell young Randall, Eliza's son."

"How does such a thing endure?" she uttered in a rhetorical sigh.

I cleared my throat.

Mister Theophilus Freeman bustled about in a very industrious manner, getting his property ready for the sales-room, intending, no doubt, to do that day a rousing business. Eliza was crying aloud, and wringing her hands. She besought the man not to buy him, unless he also bought herself and Emily. She promised, in that case, to be the most faithful slave that ever lived.

The man answered that he could not afford it, and then Eliza burst into a paroxysm of grief, weeping plaintively. Freeman turned round to her, savagely, with his whip in his uplifted hand, ordering her to stop her noise, or he would flog her. He would not have such work—such sniveling; and unless she ceased that minute, he would take her to the yard and give her a hundred lashes. Yes, he would take the nonsense out of her pretty quick—if he didn't, might he be d—d. Eliza shrunk before him, and tried to wipe away her tears, but it was all in vain. She wanted to be with her children, she said, the little time she had to live. All the frowns and threats of Freeman, could not wholly silence the afflicted mother. She kept on begging and beseeching them, most piteously, not to separate the three. Over and over again she told them how she loved her boy. A great many times she repeated her former promises—how very faithful and obedient she would be; how hard she would labor day and night, to the last moment of her life, if he would only buy them all together. But it was of no avail; the man could not afford it. The bargain was agreed upon, and Randall must go alone. Then Eliza ran to him; embraced him passionately; kissed him again and again; told him to remember her—all the while her tears falling in the boy's face like rain.

Freeman dammed her, calling her a blubbering, bawling wretch, and ordered her to go to her place, and behave herself, and be somebody. He swore he wouldn't stand such stuff but a little longer. He would soon give her something to cry about, if she was not mighty careful, and that she might depend upon.

The planter from Baton Rouge, with his new purchase, was ready to depart.

"Don't cry, mama. I will be a good boy. Don't cry," said Randall, looking back, as they passed out of the door.

What has become of the lad, God knows. It was a mournful scene indeed. I would have cried myself if I had dared.

I placed the book down open to the page I just read and poured myself a cup of tea.

My mouth was dry, my throat burned, and my eyes watered. Amy sat quietly, staring down. She moved her cup of tea side to side, gyrating the brew inside.

"I have never heard such cruelty," she murmured. "I wonder what happened to little Emily."

"Don't you want to know?" I said, picking up the book.

"May as well," she said, despondently, lifting her teacup to her lips.

After some further inspection, and conversation touching prices, he finally offered Freeman one thousand dollars for me, nine hundred for Harry, and seven hundred for Eliza.

As soon as Eliza heard it, she was in an agony again. By this time she had become haggard and hollow-eyed with sickness and with sorrow. It would be a relief if I could consistently pass over in silence the scene that now ensued. It recalls memories more mournful and affecting than any language can portray. I have seen mothers kissing for the last time the faces of their dead offspring; I have seen them looking down into the grave, as the earth fell with a dull sound upon their coffins, hiding them from their eyes forever; but never have I seen such an exhibition of intense, unmeasured, and unbounded grief, as when Eliza was parted from her child. She broke from her place in the line of women, and rushing down where Emily was standing, caught her in her arms. The child, sensible of some impending danger, instinctively fastened her hands around her mother's neck, and nestled her little head upon her bosom. Freeman sternly ordered her to be quiet, but she did not heed him. He caught her by the arm and pulled her rudely, but she only clung the closer to the child. Then, with a volley of great oaths, he struck her such a heartless blow, that she staggered backward, and was like to fall. Oh! How piteously then did she beseech and beg and pray that they might not be separated. Why could they not be purchased together? Why not let her have one of her dear children? "Mercy, mercy, master," she cried, falling on her knees. "Please, master, buy Emily. I can never work any if she is taken from me: I will die."

Freeman interfered again, but, disregarding him, she still plead most earnestly, telling how Randall had been taken from her—how she never would see him again, and now it was too bad—oh, God! It was too bad, too cruel, to take her away from Emily—her pride—her only darling, that could not live, it was so young, without its mother.

Finally, after much more of supplication, the purchaser of Eliza stepped forward, evidently effected, and said to Freeman he would buy Emily, and asked him what her price was.

"What is her price? Buy her?" was the responsive interrogatory of Theophilus Freeman.

And instantly answering his own inquiry, he added, "I won't sell her. She's not for sale."

I gingerly closed the book and placed it down on the table. My tea had cooled, and I poured myself a half a cup. She sat quietly. I had very few friends that were as resilient and of burly resolve as Amy. Her emotions were made of armor, her sentiment hardened oak, and her compassion dispatched with caution. Still, it was apparent that she was disturbed by what was written by Solomon Northup. I ambled to the window and looked out, standing there till I finished my tea. Along the open field a striped tabby perched on a fence post and licked his paw. He wiped one of the clawed mittens over his snout, licking and washing. In the distance on the Westport River, by Jug Rock, a small sailing vessel lay grounded on the muddy flats. Its sails drooped on deck as its sailor waited for the tide to return. Amy embraced me from behind and kissed me on the cheek.

"Poor Eliza … to live a life of luxury only to be betrayed and endure such despicable injury and unimaginable loss. Makes one think, doesn't it? Can it be possible that we live in northern bliss?"

"Living in the North has little to do with it."

I turned and gave her a peck on the cheek. "It's all about skin color, dear."

She pulled up the sleeve of her blouse and examined the color of her arm. "Who would think," she said, somewhat bemused.

"Well, I'm going to get dressed."

"By all means, please do. We need to meet Tim on the *Sphinx* by nine."

"Meet Tim?" I said, somewhat puzzled. I placed my cup in the sink basin.

"Yes, silly. Don't you remember? Why do you think I'm here?"

"A friendly visit."

"No?"

"Oh, yes. We were sailing to Fall River today to pick up some parcels."

"Then it's on to New Bedford. We will sleep on the schooner after we anchor and on Monday, if the wind is with us, then we can dispatch you to the *Daily Whaler*."

"Yes, the *Daily Whaler*. My second home from home."

"I'll help with the dishes. You go upstairs and get dressed."

"Won't take long." I started for the stairs.

"Emmie."

"Yes?" I paused at the stairwell.

"What do you suppose happened to little Emily?"

"Northup doesn't tell us."

"If she is still alive, she would be around thirty years old."

"I would think around that."

"I have decided. I must read the book."

I grinned and silently rushed up the stairs.

Chapter 10:
An Excursion for Fall River

Professor Winton Macartney nudged his gold-wired spectacles up the sweaty bridge of his slender nose with his pinkie. His long, platinum hair was matted to his broad forehead, and perspiration trickled down the flushed cheeks of his round, boyish face. Though the bilge of the ship was generally a cool place, since it was well below the vessel's water line, today it was made unbearably hot by spent engine steam. Winton sat contemplating his work. The hot morning sun shined down on him from an open hatch up on deck.

But the heat did not bother him much. He was of diminutive stature and accustomed to working in uncomfortable, confined spaces, such as the keel bay of a ship. At present, he was engaged in the completion of a new steam engine in the sailing schooner *Sphinx*. Winton was in his element. Drudging in such dank places was somewhat gratifying. The odious odors and musty air were but a slight nuisance to the spry ambition of conquering the inner workings of a cranky, marine steam engine.

Of course, Winton had his way of doing things and, when it came to steam-powered craft, few engineers were more knowledgeable. Still, a problem existed with those who worked with him. So engrossed was he in scrutinizing, dissecting, and solving problems that when it came to explaining a practical application, he would digress into theoretical implementations and historical developments of the machinery he worked on, leaving most listeners scratching their head, if not stranded with a faint headache. Of course, Winton was oblivious to the actuality that a captured audience had no idea what he was going on about. The worst anyone could do was express perceived ignorance, if not total lack of understanding. This would only open more rationalization by Winton, and he would pontificate about some obscure concept or comparative supposition that appeared more convoluted than the original explanation.

Yes, it was true. Winton's intellectual prowess and aptitude were equal to none … at least when it came to his occupation. And when he furnished a solution, or expounded on cause and resolution, a wise observer should best pretend that he or she understood every word. When it came to the complexity of a faulty steam engine, asking Winton Macartney too many questions only added to the quandary.

Aaron Kerr, Winton's assistant, extended his burly arm and pulled Winton up and out of the bilge. If Winton was a David, then his helper, Aaron, was Goliath. Aaron Kerr was a giant of a man. Nearly the size of Admon Assagai, he had an egg-white complexion and red, fiery hair—cropped to his head and ablaze like an autumn leaf.

"Get the manual out of my bag, will you Aaron?" requested Winton, wiping his hands with a scrap of cloth.

"Aye, reit awa', sairr," replied Aaron, with a guttural Scottish accent.

"Did you find the problem?" asked Tim, as he entered the ship's saloon from up on deck.

"The top compression plate needs a new membrane, Mister Cadman," replied Winton.

"Compression plate?"

"Precisely. The head plate that confines the piston. Steam is escaping between the plate and cylinder chamber. The membrane that seals the two is fabricated of oakum, impregnated with a dehydrated gum by-product. Not used much these days, I'm afraid. It will need to be replaced."

"It's a new engine," insisted Tim

"New engine … bad assembly," remarked Winton, pushing his slippery glasses back up his nose. "I don't understand it. John Penn and Sons, the builders of that trunk engine, haven't been known to skimp on standards. Surprising, really. Penn's low-pressured steam engines are constructed with the exceptional precision of a fine German timepiece. Made to last forever, you know."

"Where can we get one of these, ah … membranes."

"Hinkley's, in New Bedford. We should also consider mounting the engine a little higher."

"Higher, you say?"

"Yes. We must concern ourselves with water that enters the bilge. If the engine is too deep into it, it could become swamped."

"Here ye ur, sairr," announced Aaron, handing the professor a large black volume.

Winton placed the book on the saloon table and pulled out a diagram illustrating the inner workings of a trunk steam engine. "You see, here on this technical schematic, Mister Cadman. It is a integumental membrane that acts as an impermeable mucilage, bonding the two castings." He pointed out the problem on the drawing with a pencil he always kept tucked above one ear.

Tim exhibited a baffled frown. He knew nothing about steam or the apparatuses that it fed. And the diagram in front of him was of little help, since it had esoteric elements that he just did not understand. Sails and anchors he understood well—even the inner workings of a ship's capstan. Automation and controlled explosions mixed with machinery was another matter.

He looked up at Aaron, overwhelmed by the engineer's intricate explanation. Perhaps the professor's assistant could explain it to him in simpler terms. Standing behind Winton, Aaron covertly signaled with raised eyebrows and a quick nod of the head telling Tim to agree with everything the professor said.

"Yes, yes, of course, an integratival membrane."

"Integumental membrane, Mister Cadman. Integumental," said the professor working his pencil across the drawing. "You see it here in the schematic represented by these parallel lines. A protective impenetrable seal between the head and chamber. It's what all new engines are using these days. Made of several elements that have undergone vulcanization and taking on the properties of packing."

"Vulcanization? You don't say?"

Winton peered annoyingly over the top of glasses perched on the tip of his nose. "Vulcanization, Mister Cadman. Named for Vulcan, the Roman god of fire. Although, I'm sure this is all familiar to you—don't mean to waste your time."

"Not wasting my time, Professor."

"Then you are wasting my time, Mister Cadman."

"Well …"

"You understand everything we just went over, do you not?"

"I find it all, ah … very riveting."

Making certain the professor was not watching, he glanced over at Aaron, shrugged his shoulders, and shook his head. Aaron offered him a dry smile and did the same. Tim finally realized that the less said the better. Endorsement of his ignorance was best kept to himself.

"Yes, it is riveting. The actual process of vulcanization has been around for years now." Winton wiped his glasses clean with his shirt tail. "A discovery by a chap named Charles Goodyear, you see. Died just a short while ago, sad to mention." He plopped the glasses on the bridge of his nose and wrapped the fine wire temples around his ears. "Goodyear's book, *Gum-elastic and its Varieties,* is a intriguing thesis. You should get a copy, Mister Cadman. I think you would find it fascinating, if not indispensable."

"I'll be sure to add one to the ship's library," replied Tim, roguishly.

"A rubber gasket is whit we need, Keptin," interrupted Aaron. "Is at nae right, sairr?"

"In layman's terms, you are correct, Aaron. A rubber gasket indeed."

"Yes, q-quite right," stammered Tim, fearing that Winton would continue to minister to him about the properties of rubber gaskets.

Winton tucked the diagram back into the book and stored the volume away in his bag.

With the professor's back to him, Aaron offered Tim two celebratory thumbs up, signaling that the lesson on the properties of engine gaskets was over.

"We are sailing to Fall River to conduct some private business, and then we hope to sail onto New Bedford," said Tim. "You will sail with us, will you not, Professor?"

"I just happen to be on a sabbatical from my teaching duties at University. You have me for as long as it takes to tame this wonderful steam dragon."

"Great. I will inform you of our little venture once we arrive in Fall River. Should you choose to stay aboard, I will designate you as chief engineer."

"Very well," replied Winton. "In any event, I must travel through Fall River on my way to Providence and home. Should it not work out I can disembark there and take the paddleboat. Otherwise, it is on to New Bedford." He shook his head. "Dreadful place."

"And you, Mister Kerr?"

"At yer service, Keptin."

"Let's see, what should your position be?" pondered Tim.

"Ah am a carpenter by trade, Keptin. But mah lest assignment was as stoker oan th' passenger vessel, *City of Glasgow*, before comin tae the States."

"Intriguing. I know that you and the professor are a team. Should he sign on, we will appoint you as ship's carpenter, then."

"Aye, aye, Keptin." He cried, saluting—standing at attention.

"Very well. Errr … at ease, sailor."

Tim found humor in the Scotsman. He was good natured and their temperaments seemed to mesh. Aaron's large, fearsome size was intimidating and revealed little about the gentle essence of the man. He was a gentleman very much like Admon Assagai.

"I'm certain that you would not object to sharing a cabin with Mister Kerr, Professor," asked Tim.

"It would not please me to have it any other way."

Tim was showing the two men to their cabin when a call came from up on deck.

"We are ready to depart, Captain," bellowed Eli Monroe, the *Sphinx*'s helmsman.

"Very well, Mister Monroe."

"Wind still from the west and on the nose. So, we cannot sail her out. The crew of the *Janet* are braced to pilot us with the whaleboat."

"Do you think they will have any trouble?"

"I would expect not, Captain. Winds are light and a two-knot tide is with us."

"Any sign of the girls?"

"They are boarding as we speak."

"Very good, Mister Monroe. Prepare to cast off."

While the actual captain of the *Sphinx*, Samuel Cory, was away fighting in the war, Tim was delegated as acting captain. Regardless, he felt uncomfortable with formality and protocol, such as addressing his friends by their surnames or serving them orders. Nevertheless, the framework of decorum was pressed on him by Samuel in a written dispatch. Tim pulled it from his pocket and read it.

Discipline must be observed and of main concern—rules of conduct implemented with poise and conviction and, above all, orders obeyed and carried out without exception.

Out at sea you are the law, the leader, and commander. But you must also remember to exercise authority with a level of compassion and measure of tolerance. After all, you are not a tyrant but a guardian—the ship is your wife, and you are Captain Cadman and lover of the sailing vessel Sphinx.

You and the ship are one. You are king and the crew your subjects.

Once beyond the Knubble and out of harbor, make certain the crew addresses you by title and with proper respect, as you do them. Otherwise, you will lose their esteem and, more importantly, their confidence. Adoration on a ship, as anywhere else, is earned, not appropriated.

Do not forget all that I have told you. It is the creed of a successful ship's Captain.

It was an honor and a privilege to be given command of such an amazing vessel. *Sphinx* was one of a kind, built in the spirit of the American racing yacht, *America*, which was sent to Great Britain nearly ten years ago and entered in the Annual Regatta around the Isle of Wight, where it won. Samuel often reminded Tim that *Sphinx* was one of the fastest, if not the fastest, yacht of its size on the east coast. Being built light and fast made sailing her a challenge. However, Samuel had confidence in the young carpenter and, with the exception of Eli Monroe, he could think of no one more capable to sail her. It was a challenge that Tim Cadman recognized and a responsibility he was determined to shoulder.

Tim climbed up on deck just as Amy approached, lugging a floral carpetbag containing an assortment of personal items. She was always over-prepared and the scene that confronted him was a familiar one. With arms about to pull from their sockets, she struggled with the large duffel as it dragged along the deck.

"Here, let me help you with that," declared Tim, snatching the heavy bag.

"Oh, peanuts," she cried sucking on a finger. "I think I broke something."

Tim smiled, shook his head, and handed the carpet duffel to Eli Monroe. "What do you have in that thing, anyway?"

"Some books I want to keep on board along with necessities and other essentials … oh, careful with that, will you, Eli, dear. I have my favorite tea set stored in there."

"You can depend on me, Miss Amy," said Eli, scurrying below.

"Place that bag in the forward starboard cabin, Mister Monroe," ordered Tim.

"Hurry, Emmie," cried Amy, her injured finger in her mouth.

I threw my duffel bag up to Razor. Amy extended her free hand and helped me up.

"What's wrong with your finger?"

"I think I broke it," she said, expressing a desperate frown.

"Here, let me see."

I pulled her hand from her mouth. She immediately snatched it away.

"Come, don't be a child." I tugged it back.

She winced and looked away as I carefully inspected the trembling digit.

"Hmm, a little redness. Not much more. Probably from sucking on it."

I knew all along there was no injury—just Amy's narcissistic approach to seeking sympathy and attention from anyone who was gullible enough to fall into her trap, one I was routinely happy to stumble into. Giving in to such misconduct was part of being a friend. However, on this day, for whatever reason, I was not in the mood.

"Your finger is perfectly fine."

"How would you know? You're not a doctor."

"Well, let us summon the ship's doctor, then. Timothy!" I yelled. "We have some inflicted trauma that needs immediate assistance."

He rushed over. "What happened?"

I held up Amy's hand and waved it in his face. "Look. This finger. I think it's busted."

"You're joshing," he said, inspecting it carefully.

Amy turned and grimaced. "Don't, you'll hurt me," she cried.

"No one's going to hurt you," assured Tim. "Let me look."

With gentle assiduity, he gingerly bent the delicate appendage up and down and side to side. I held tightly onto Amy's hand as she tried to pull it away. With a smug wearisome smirk, I directed my yawning sentiments at Tim.

"Feel anything?"

"Yes, annoyance," sniveled Amy.

Tim glanced over at me and frowned, realizing he was duped.

"Nothing broken that I can see. You are fine. If you want, I'll kiss it better."

I rolled my eyes. Just as he puckered his lips Amy snatched her hand away and whacked him on the arm. Tim and I laughed.

"Oh, you two," she protested, marching off, as we continued laughing.

"Alright, everyone, cast off lines," ordered the captain. He ran up to the bow by the boat's sprit.

"Just about ready, gentleman," he hollered to the eight rowers in the whaleboat. Tossing them a towline, he tied the bitter end to the schooner's capstan and returned to the quarterdeck where he took command of the ship's wheel. Once the vessel was on its way and pointing true, he tied down the helm.

"Just active crew up on deck, ladies. You must get below until we have hoisted sail and cleared The Knubble."

The Knubble was an outcropping of granite ledge at the mouth of the Westport River and entrance to Cherry and Webb Harbor. It was a narrow and precarious inlet. Maneuvering a large vessel past The Knubble was not always a straightforward venture. Seabury Cory called the inlet "The Camel's Needle," comparing the narrow passage to Jesus' revelation about the rich man and his narrow path into heaven. However, today the seas were duteous to a caressing breeze that flowed off the craggy granite ledge, as it wafted over the tapering, disjointed bight along the rocky shore.

Amy flung her nose in the air and, with a sneer, retreated down the companionway ladder, bumping straight into the arms of Winton Macartney.

"Ah, good morning, Miss," said Winton. He quickly pulled his arms away and wiped his hands on his clothing as if he was just groped by a leper.

Habitually, Amy did the same.

"I must get on deck," he maintained, climbing the ladder, somewhat overwrought.

"I must get below," she countered, as she continued her decent.

A conflict of egos tussled along the companionway steps until Amy pushed the engineer out of the way and continued down into the cabin.

Winton quickly dismissed her and started up the ladder. He walked past me without saying a word. I looked below, making certain the way was clear. A second man appeared. He ogled up at me then backed down the ladder. Immediately, he removed his pork pie cap and waited for me. Working the curled brim of his hat between his stout fingers, he lingered as I made my descent.

"Hello. My name's Emily," I chirped, extending a hand.

He reached out to shake it just as he dropped the hat. It rolled on the floor behind him. He backed away to retrieve it, only to step on it, pancaking its pork pie shape.

"Oh, I beg your forgiveness," I declared. "I'm in your way."

"Ah, nae, lassie. I am in yer way."

He moved back and allowed me by. There was a loud thump. He had walloped his head on one of the saloon's ceiling beams.

"Oh, dear. Are you alright?"

"Aye," he sputtered, rubbing his head. He closely inspected the beam. "Nae damage tae th' ship at ah can see."

"Ah, yes? Well … I'm, Emily White."

"Aaron Kerr," he declared, extending his enormous paw. He stood staring, gently gripping my hand.

"Is there something wrong, Mister Kerr?"

"Ye ur a lass." He declared, with mislaid astonishment.

"Yes. Been one all my life."

"Ah pray ye ur friendly body fur a change."

"So, I see you spoke to Amy."

"Aye. Is 'at 'er name? She did nae hae much tae say."

"I wouldn't worry about that. When she does, you will be sorry she did."

"Aye, ah think ah noo wat ye mean."

Just as the conversation was getting started, a shout was heard from the deck.

"Ah must get gonnae. They ur callin fur me."

"So they are," I said, stepping out of his way. "It was nice meeting you, Mister Kerr. I'm sure I'll see you about."

"Aye. Ye can call me Aaron."

He started up the ladder. Halfway up, he dropped his hat yet again. He looked down and winced. I quickly picked it up.

"You dropped this."

Abashed, he delivered me a coy smile, placed the cap on his head, and rushed up on deck.

A few minutes later, Amy emerged from her cabin and meandered down the narrow passageway that led into the main saloon.

"Who are those men?"

"Don't know," I replied. "New crew I suppose."

"The big fellow has fabulous fiery hair. A shame that it is squandered atop a man's head."

"He was a gentleman," I said.

"I wouldn't know." She placed a straw hat on her head and fastened it to the bun in her hair with a pearl crowned hatpin.

"Did you not speak to the poor fellow?"

"You know me better than that, Emmie," she remarked, curling the hat's brim. "I never talk with strangers. Besides, I didn't understand a word the man was saying."

I was thrown back by her declaration that she did not talk with strangers. I knew it was not true. Then again, she was not assuredly telling a falsehood either, I should let you know. On closer assessment, one would quickly discover that Amy, in fact, does not talk with strangers—just at them.

"He's a Scotsman," I declared.

"Well, you would know," she sighed, giving my disclosure no particular interest. She examined her hand, the one with the finger that was supposedly crippled, turning it over and wiggling it around.

I tried to reinvigorate any curiosity that may exist in her. "You know what they say about Scotsmen, don't you?"

"I am dying for a cup of tea," she said, ignoring my dubious query. "This salt air makes me thirsty."

"I will have to ask Timothy about lighting the stove," I said, relinquishing all attempts at arresting any enthusiasm.

"Never mind. I don't feel like waiting. I'm going to my cabin and unpack," she declared, sounding fatigued. "Perhaps I'll take a nap. Making breakfast this morning took a lot out of me. I don't know how Mother does it." She hummed the tune she was singing all day— "Annabel Lee," then sauntered off to her cabin.

You have to love Amy. No, really—you *must*. If you do not, she will tire you out with capricious demands and a fleeting temperament. You may find those distinctions to be undesirable in a person, when in fact we all have our unappealing tendencies. She has always stood by my side in hard times. When it comes to loyalty and trustworthiness, Amy Chaloner has never failed me—one of the many reasons I call her my friend. If you find that surprising, don't. On the other hand, I have no defense for her audacious and vainglorious nature.

I filled the kettle and placed it on the unlit, cast iron stove.

I could hear water splash outside while one of the oarsmen cheered his companions on, yowling, "Put yar back into it, ya mangy dogs, row, row, row."

Climbing halfway up the companionway, I looked out for Tim to ask permission about lighting the cook stove. *Sphinx* was drifting effortlessly behind the whaleboat while Eli steered the vessel and nursed a pencil-thin stogie. A blue braid of smoke spiraled around his head then quickly blew away.

"How are you, my-lady," he asked, pinching the cigar from his mouth. "We have not had a chance to talk since last summer."

"No, we have not. It's nice to see you back behind the wheel of *Sphinx*, Eli. Perhaps we will have a spirited conversation later when I'm allowed on deck."

"By all means, my lady," he replied, in his Bermudian cadence.

"Will you be cooking on this trip?"

"You missed my cooking, have you?" He chuckled.

"Especially your chowder."

"I'll make some Bermudian chowder with baked scrod and yams for supper. Would you like that?"

"That would be splendid."

Eli Monroe was the oldest and the most respected member of the crew. At thirty-four years of age, he was helmsman, cook, and senior adviser. Finding someone to take the wheel while Eli toiled in the galley was never a problem, since Eli would always reward the steerer with a hunk of his sugary apple and cherry pie. Born in Bermuda, Eli was the child of slave parents and a twenty-year veteran of the Royal Navy. Speaking three languages, he was educated in London and a seasoned sailor.

Tim came parading up the deck, shouting orders while the schooner prepared to hoist canvas. "Make ready to af the wheel, Mister Monroe."

"Aye, aye, Captain," he acknowledged, tossing the spent stogie over the gunwale.

Tim looked at me and winked as I peeked out the companionway hatch. "Where's Amy?"

"Taking a nap."

I was about to ask him about lighting a fire in the stove when, to my surprise, he summoned me up on deck.

"I know you like to watch the sails unfurl. But stay on the quarterdeck. Sit behind Eli. And try not to get in the way."

"Yes, sir," I cried, giving him a flat-handed salute.

He saluted back in Cadman fashion—with a wink in his eye.

I was thrilled to be up on deck where the bustle stirred. I peered over the gunwale to the water below. The busy crew of the whaler *Janet* had established their stride and the whaleboat rowed us along at a good fetch. Their success, and the distance we covered, had all to do with a dropping tide, which helped ferry us along quickly toward The Knubble and out into Buzzard's Bay.

How exciting, I thought to myself. I licked my finger, wet my nose, and held my head up. Once I turned it in the right direction, I was able to discern which direction the wind was blowing, as a gentle breeze chilled the tip of my damp nose. It was one of many little tricks taught to me by Samuel's father, Captain Seabury Cory—retired. Wind currents were gusting from the direction of the granite ledge and picking up speed. Once at The Knubble, *Sphinx* would lift sail and make a ninety-degree turn to port toward the harbor entrance. This would place the air on our starboard beam and, eventually, pull us out to sea.

"Hoist main number one," came the cry.

The crew scurried along the decks. Razor and Aaron Kerr pulled the halyard from over their heads, milking the main sail up the mast. The beefy gaff spar swung to port as the wind picked up and canvas shimmied and unfurled beneath the weight of its supporting spar.

"New heading, Helmsman," shouted the captain. "Two-hundred-and-thirty-degrees south, south-west."

"Aye, aye," acknowledged Eli, as he stood ready to steer.

It was all so exciting to be sailing again.

"Casting off, Captain," came a shout off the starboard bow, as the whaleboat released the towline.

With its sails idly flogging in the breeze, *Sphinx* slowly drifted past the smaller whaleboat. Razor pulled the towline back on board and the whale-men waved us off.

"Ya owe us a grog of brew," yelled the skipper of the whaleboat.

"A bucket of beer for each man when I get back," hollered Tim.

They all cheered.

"Head her south, Mister Monroe."

Tim assisted one of the crew setting the jib and staysail as the schooner slowly turned toward The Knubble. Sails were made trim and the swan-colored cloth quickly ensnared the spiraling gusts. We quickly slipped past the estuary's narrow aperture while the ship picked up speed. With a clear view of the open sea, the wind strengthened. Once we were beyond Half Mile Rock, most of the schooner's canvas was up and fixed, and *Sphinx* was nearly making hull speed, which is as fast as a ship her size could go.

Suddenly, the bow lifted effortlessly into the air and dropped violently into a curling swell. The conditions and surface of the water between Cherry and Webb Harbor and the open ocean crests of Buzzard's Bay were noteworthy—how quickly things could change! On the Westport River, there was nearly a wave. Here, the coiling seas were nearly three feet high, with winds that could only be described as remarkably robust. Seabury Cory would describe it as a fresh breeze or a force five blow on the Beaufort wind scale. I would describe it as invigorating.

Sphinx's nineteen-foot-long bow sprit pierced the breaking swells, burying itself at the base of each wave and stitching them together one after another with every knot made. The gleaming white schooner leaned ever so slightly to starboard as the foamy crests exploded into a fine spray and streaming rainbows, glistened along the ship's gunwales. From the many voyages I had undertaken with Samuel, I would venture to say, but not bold enough to mention, that we were carrying too much canvas for the existing wind conditions. The ride could be greatly improved and made more pleasant by shortening sail and lowering the center of effort being prescribed by a strong breeze.

Sure enough, it was like Tim was reading my mind—or perhaps I, his.

"Mister Assagai. Place a reef in that main," he commanded. "You, Sailor, take down that staysail and lash it to the deck." He stood by the wheel at Eli's right shoulder while the Bermudian steered, keeping a keen eye on sea conditions, crew, and ship.

I got up and stood by them. "Isn't this exciting, Timothy," I declared.

Eli cracked a friendly smile and nodded. Of course, this was just routine for a Royal Navy man. Nevertheless, his smile was cursory acknowledgment that he found humor, if not comfort, in my simple declaration.

"What a great sail. I never tire of it," I said. "This is wicked fun."

Tim did not appear in a chatting mood. I could see unexpected anxiety in his face. He was grinding his teeth. His jaw staggered from side to side as he looked up toward the masthead and watched Razor and Aaron lower the gaff and reef the sail. I remember the same presence in Samuel, which was often exhibited at the beginning of every one of his voyages. But Samuel had a better way of hiding it—the only hint that he felt uneasy was the rapid clenching of his fists and a slight squint of one eye. Once we were well on our way, I was certain that Tim would feel more relaxed—or as relaxed as a ship's captain can be.

He quickly stepped forward. "No, Mister Assagai, the other cleat." He roared. "Tie that halyard off at the other cleat … the one above."

He observed carefully as Razor fastened the line in place. "Make certain you tie it off with two bights, Mister Assagai." He shook his head. "You would think he knew the routine by now," he muttered under his breath.

Once we were well beyond Two Mile Rock, the schooner turned west toward Sakonnet Point, where we once again changed our heading north, this time up the calm waters of the Sakonnet River toward Fall River. The wind had altered and now was blowing out of the south. *Sphinx* sat upright and comfortably as we were pushed from behind. It was a serene, if not hypnotic, ride; one you would never experience over a gravel road.

The huge rectangular main sail extended well out over the water on our port beam. We sailed quietly, with the only sound coming from beneath the bow as it cut the waters, emitting its effervescent song. Occasionally, the boom rubbed against one of the roped deadeyes and made a clattering noise. A paunch wrapped around the polished spar protected both deadeye and boom from chaff. Abrasion and corrosion were two irritants that constantly plagued a sailing vessel. There was so much that could go wrong on a ship, or its crew, and a captain had to stay vigilant. It was no wonder that gentleman Tim Cadman was anxious and demanding.

We continued our sail up the Sakonnet, with Aquidneck Island to port and the villages of Little Compton and Tiverton to starboard. The large spar supporting the main lifted gently, and the gaff above it swung lazily with random gusts of wind. Occasionally, the sail hardened to an isolated squall and the schooner would surge forward at great speed. The staysail had been unlashed from the deck and hoisted once again. Number one jib hung potbelly and proud over the end of the protruding sprit, now dried by the late morning sun.

With nearly fifteen miles under its keel and another ten before arriving at Fall River, the crew of the *Sphinx* had plenty of time to rest. Everyone appeared at ease and cheerful. Even Tim was witnessed laughing as he exchanged banter with Eli and playfully wrestled with sixteen-year-old seamen, Robert Cuffee.

I walked over to Razor and Aaron who sat along the deck with their backs to the cabin house. Aaron carved an apple and handed Razor a sheared wafer of fruit.

"How are you, gentleman," I inquired.

Aaron immediately shot to his feet and removed his hat.

"Ah, lass, will ye nae sit with us?"

"Only if you sit first."

He threw himself down, making room for me between them. I must have looked like a rag doll plopped between these two titans. But two gentler giants would be hard to come by together, considering one was as white as the other was black.

Aaron looked past me and over at Razor. "A lassie oan our ship. Is that nae stoatin, Razur?" he declared.

Admon Assagai leaned over and whispered in my ear. "Nice fella. Wish he talked English."

"Will ye nae have a slice of mah Macintosh, lassie?" He cut me a chunk of apple and handed it to me off the tip of his slip joint knife.

"Thank you."

"Mah pleasure."

"So how are you fellows liking the sail?"

"Braw," bellowed Aaron, taking a bite of his apple and practically swallowing it whole. "Reminds me of haem."

"See what a'mean," muttered Razor. "Can't understand a darn thing the man says."

"He said the trip is grand," I whispered. "And that it reminds him of home."

"Oh? I see. Wish I had someplace as nice to compare it to," replied Razor.

"By the way, where are you living now, Admon?"

"New Bedford."

"You like it there?"

"Beats livin' in Baltimore," he chuckled. He lumbered to his feet. "Well, back to work. The captain has been after me to grease the capstan. If it jams when we drop anchor, he'll have my hide."

"Oh dear. We wouldn't want that."

"Talk some more later, Emily."

"Yes. I'd like that."

Razor got up and walked away. It was with sober humor that I envisioned the captain having his hide, as he put it. After all, he was five or six inches taller than the captain. Built like an ox, he had arms practically bigger than my legs—to which I must add, when it comes to the size of my limbs, it is probably more than you need to know.

"Whaur are ye gonnae, Razur?" hollered the good-natured Scotsman. "Ah still hae two apples fur us tae eat, mon."

Admon Assagai shook his head and continued walking.

"Braw fellaw," said Aaron. "Jist wish he did more talkin'."

"Admon never has much to say," I told him.

"Aye, Admon. Is 'at is nam?" he said, a mouth full of fruit.

"That's his name."

He nodded and chomped while he studied the apple, deciding where to take the next bite.

"So you're from Scotland?"

"Aye."

"How long have you lived in the States?"

"Two years noo."

"Like it?"

"Aye. Lots tae do and lots tae see."

"Still, you must miss home. I know I love where I live. I would not want to live anywhere else."

"Aye, lassie. Ah miss mah family, but don't miss th' weather."

I laughed.

Just as we were getting to know one another, Winton Macartney came walking up the deck, wiping his hands with a dirty cloth.

"I've been waiting for you, Aaron." He sounded a bit miffed. "We need to lift that engine out of its cradle. It's quite heavy."

"Aye, sairr." Aaron jumped to his feet. "Will ye nae say hello tae Emily?" he asked boldly, folding the blade of his knife and slipping it into his hip pocket.

"Of course. Should have introduced myself earlier." Winton continued wiping his hands as he spoke. "Professor Winton Macartney, steam engineer. You must be Emily White."

"Why, yes."

"The captain has mentioned you. You're a correspondent for a New Bedford paper. Are you along for a story?" He crossed his arms and surveyed me as if diagnosing a faulty steam valve.

"Why no. This is my … well, the *Sphinx* belongs to my fiance. I'm just along for the ride."

"I see."

He took the apple core from Aaron's hand and flung is over the side.

"You must excuse us, Miss White, we have work to do. Come along, Aaron." Winton Macartney scurried back toward the rear of the ship.

"It's a wee ship, Emily," declared Aaron, polishing a fresh, uneaten apple on his sleeve. "See ye again suin." He handed me the fruit. "We will hae an apple together, heh?"

"An apple a day. It's good for you," I said.

"Aye, keeps the physician away," he added.

"That's what Mister Franklin claims."

"Come along, Aaron," shouted Winton.

"Got tae go." He scampered away.

"Don't lose your hat," I shouted.

What a delightful fellow, I thought to myself, as the two men disappeared below deck.

I sat on the cabin house, nibbling on my apple while a marvelous, salubrious breeze tamed the noonday sun. I weaved some strands of loose hair, that danced across my nose, around my finger and tucked them under my sunbonnet. I made certain that the black India silk scarf that held the raffia straw hat to my head was tied firmly below my chin and holding the loose hair in place. After I finished eating my apple, I got up and moved, tucking myself by the ship's main mast and a trunk used for storing ropes. I made myself comfortable. It was the perfect niche, since the main sail had cast its shadow on me, tempering the sultry, mid-day sun. I felt so fortunate that the first sail of the season was a pleasant one. A girl could not ask for better weather or a more relaxing ride on the sea.

The schooner handily glided over the sheltered waters of the Sakonnet River as the waves playfully spanked the ship's bow. Conditions here were a far cry better than what we experienced earlier out on the tidal waters of Buzzards Bay.

As we sailed along the shores of the town of Tiverton, its georgic landscape displayed itself in a patchwork of greens and browns, depending whether a field was freshly plowed or covered in weed and grass. I could see an unending row of stone walls that hemmed the sloping hills one to another. It was the planting season, and one could make out farmers busy in their fields. Here and there, a small hamlet would appear clustered around tall, acicular church spires. Buildings of worship were central to many a village along the New England countryside. The scenery reminded me of home. And although Westport was only a few miles away, as far as the crow flies, here on the water it may as well have been a world away. Still, there was no other place I wanted to be at this very moment.

Open water, salted air, and gentle breezes had a tranquilizing influence. I soon found myself dozing off. I felt as if I had just consumed a full bottle of one of Grandmamma's medicinal elixirs, laced in spirits. It was not long before the sound of *Sphinx* cutting through the water and the river wavelets fizzing by the ship's bow had serenaded me into a deep slumber.

An undetermined amount of time had passed when I was suddenly awoken by a loud, crashing roar. It sounded like a mountain was about to come down on me. I quickly sat up straight and looked around. I had forgotten I was on a ship. Out on the bow, where the rolling rumble originated, Razor and young Robert Cuffee were letting out the anchor. The chain thundered and clinked as it left the locker. The booming sound reverberated throughout the deck as the rusty iron loops progressed through the capstan's cog and out through the ship's hawser. The descending anchor hit the sea floor. Suddenly there was silence.

"Everything alright, sleepyhead?" I heard someone say.

"Oh, Timothy, I must have fallen asleep. I have been so tired lately."

"Well, you're a working girl now."

"Don't remind me." I straightened the bonnet, which was cocked on my head.

"I'm happy you got some rest. Here, give me your hand. I'll help you up."

"Are we here already?"

He lifted me to my feet.

"Don't know how you slept through it all. As soon as we approached the city, I was certain you would have awoken. This is not a peaceful harbor. Anyway, you just went on sleeping. Amy was doing the same below. Don't you girls sleep nights?"

I sheepishly ignored his inquiry.

Indeed, it was not peaceful here. Whilst I stood there, one of Fall River's paddle ships startled me by blowing her whistle. Tim laughed.

"Wake up, kiddo." He patted me on the elbow and went about his command.

The paddle ship, better known as the Fall River Boat, maneuvered precariously close to our stern. A couple of men on a small, overloaded coal barge cried out with clutched fists as the boat created a nasty wake. The schooner rose gently to the slipstream of mounting water; leisurely its stern rose, then its bow, but rendering no urgent consternation.

I looked around. Sounds of city life resonated from every direction. It was not so much the noise or traffic that I found troublesome, but the smells—city smells. Where New Bedford Harbor reeked of dead fish and whale oil, Fall River dispensed a stench of toxic chemical dyes and stifling, textile chimney exhaust.

The treed bluff that was once the hamlet of Fall River was now a tangled and unending construction site. Everywhere one looked, buildings arose. Matchbox apartment flats piled one upon another pinpled the countryside. Mills burdgeoned from the foothills—featureless castles with clock-less towers—gruesome, granite dominoes entombed in the earth and creeping up the high ground to the city's town hall at its sloping summit. Grandmamma often spoke of the beauty here when she was a child, and the bucolic waterfalls cutting through the town and flowing down to the river like a cleansing distillate. Now all the trees had been removed and the rapids covered by granite mills and bricked factories as commerce swallowed the beauty the city once had—as textile barons transformed the countryside into greenbacks and coin. As Grandmamma often told me, "A forest is beauty until it is profit, and though they are both green, one gives while the other takes."

"I need to have a little talk with Professor Macartney and his associate about the purpose of this trip," said Tim.

"Oh?"

"Yes. Give me a moment. I need to go below. Then we'll all meet up on deck."

I waited while Tim gave instructions to Razor and his companion about deploying the ship's dory and making it ready for us to go ashore. I watched them from a distance as Tim spoke and Razor nodded. Patting the big man on the shoulder, he returned and we both walked back toward the quarterdeck.

"I've been wanting to ask you what this trip is all about," I told him.

"You have, have you?"

"Yes. Can you give me a hint?"

"Sure. It's about slaves."

"Slaves?" I echoed.

"Slaves."

Chapter 11: A Narrow Escape

Aaron Kerr sat on the capstan at the bow of the ship while his boss, Winton Macartney, stood by looking restless. Winton found it imperative to remain occupied. It was irritating and a stagnation of spirit and mind to stand idle waiting for the unknown. For Aaron, the free time was always a welcome moment to enjoy his surroundings and contemplate the simplicity of life on the water. As a trainee of steam powered marine machinery, and under the watchful eye of Winton, Aaron was no stranger to drudgery and labor, thus he cherished the brief hiatus. As for Winton, he paced the deck as a delinquent brain eroded his patience. With almost spiritual devotion to his profession, he accepted nothing short of progress without delay. Aaron, on the other hand, was quite content with his apostolic duties and at being an uncomplicated acolyte. Though a pair of more extreme antipodes would be difficult to find, the two men worked well together.

Tim called on the steam engineer. I was ushered behind.

"Mister Cadman, I understand you wish to speak with me," grumbled Winton.

"It's Keptin Cadman," insisted Aaron, whispering the hint over Winton's shoulder. Having served on other vessels, he was respectful of a captain's title. "It is proticol, ye noo."

Winton pitched him a provoking glare over the top of his wire-rimmed glasses.

'How is the engine installation coming along, Professor?" inquired the captain.

"Aaron is building the new cradle from some oak timber we discovered stored in the forecastle. The engine will sit almost a foot higher once completed. We should have plenty of room for the boiler and for a man to work it, though it will be blazes down there. With its slack bilges, this vessel was never meant to accommodate a motor."

"Will you be able to get it in there and working?"

"Oh, yes. We should be finished by the end of the day if you don't further detain us. Inaugurating the boiler in place will take longer."

"Sounds like things are coming together, Professor. You're a genius."

Winton Macartney relaxed some and came alive. Discussing the specifics of his vocation was almost as satisfying as engaging in them. Nonetheless, whether he thought of himself brilliant or not, Winton felt compelled to explain the intricate workings to his client.

"That I'm a genius is, of course, a flattering compliment, Captain. However, I do have ample years at university, and I am a very accomplished mechanical engineer. But let us dispense with all my obvious credentials and speak to the issue at hand, shall we?"

"That's why you are here, and the ship's owner is paying you."

"There's one little problem. Allow me to explain." Winton pulled a notepad from his shirt pocket with an outlined drawing of the work needed to be done. Retrieving a pencil from behind his ear, he dampened the lead on his tongue and began to sketch. "The new location of the engine will change the dynamics between propeller and keel, as you can see, but will make little difference in the overall propulsion. Though we do not have to raise the boiler to accommodate the surging steam to the piston chamber. Steam rises, as you know."

"I understand," replied Tim. He gnawed at his lip.

"Now, the shaft orifice will remain parallel to the schooner's keelson; with a slight twenty-degree angle to the rudder and off to starboard. Of course, we will have to cut a slight bight out of the rudder under the vessel to accommodate the drive unit."

"Drive unit?"

"The propeller, Captain. That work will be accomplished once the vessel is placed in dry dock."

Winton Macartney worked his pencil across the notepad as he doodled a rough drawing of his modifications. "As you can see here, tolerances may be a little tight between the relief valve flange and this cabin floor member just above it. However, I am certain everything should clear once the impulse damper is installed."

Once again, Tim was overwhelmed and stultified by the technical facets of the project. His teeth grated and he grimaced. Indeed, listening to the professor was very unpleasant. He wore his bewilderment on his face like mud on swine. I didn't blame him. It was Greek to me also, or Latin, if you prefer. In fairness though, steam engines were a new and specialized technology and few men, let alone woman, were familiar with how they worked or how they were integrated into a sailing vessel. Weary by Tim's dubious awareness, the professor abandoned any further practical explanation.

"Your apathetic enthusiasm is overwhelming but appreciated, Captain," groaned Winton, stuffing the notepad into his shirt pocket. "Now, what is it you want to talk to me about?"

"I wanted to explain the mission of this trip, since it will take some time to install the boiler and complete the project, and you may not approve."

"Oh? Proceed."

"I'll come to the point, Professor. How do you perceive slavery?"

"Slavery!" shouted Winton. "Why, you insult me."

"I didn't know you felt so strongly. If you can't …"

"Yes, I work Aaron hard, but he is not my slave. I take exception to the fact that you insinuate that I am treating the man as one."

"Aye, Professor. But ah dorn't min' th' hard wark," Aaron capitulated.

"Quite," snapped Winton.

"Professor, that's not what I mean."

"Then exactly what do you mean, Captain?"

"Let me put it this way. I have a crew that is made up of former slaves or sons of slaves. I noticed that it doesn't seem to concern you."

"Why should it?"

"Well then, let me explain it to you this way."

"Captain Cadman, I have work to do. Will you get to the point?"

"All right. We are picking up some runaways from Fall River and transporting them to New Bedford, where they are to board a ship for Nova Scotia."

"Aye. Ah loove Nova Scotia, ye noo."

"Quiet, Aaron," howled Winton.

"Jist tryin' tae be helpful."

"Yes, yes. Go on, Captain. You are picking up some runaways and your point is?"

Conversation with the professor did not appear to be getting any easier for Tim, even though they were not discussing steam engines. At this point he preferred that they were.

"No point at all Professor—no point at all."

"Then stop wasting time, Mister Cadman. I have work to do." Winton Macartney stomped away.

"Ye hae tae forgive th' Porfessur, Keptin. He's bin workin' aw day an' aw he had was a cup ay tea early thes morn. He's lock a baby without his bottle when he's hungry. He is nae a bad chap once ye get tae know heem."

"And how about you, Mister Kerr? How do you feel about this black slavery business? Any objections to this mission?"

"Nae ah don't, Keptin. After all, look at mah skin." He held out his pale rosy arms. "A coople ay more days in th' sun an' ye will not be able tae teel Razur an' ah apart."

Tim smiled.

I climbed down a rope ladder to the dory. Tim wrapped his hands around my waist and helped as I stepped into the small boat.

"I hate that rope ladder," cried Amy, from up on deck. "My feet get tangled in the rungs."

"Ah can help," said Aaron, reaching over for her hand.

"No," she yelled, pulling it away. "You'll drop me."

"Ah hae drapped many things, lassie, but ne'er someone as bonnie as ye."

"Oh, let him help you, Amy," I said. "He looks very capable to me."

"Haur, place yer hans in mine, lassie," he instructed, holding his large paws out.

"My name is Amy," she said, looking up at him, defiantly.

Amy had a way of beating down a man and training him to her measure—if not by blunt assertiveness, then by blinding him with her exceptional beauty. But Aaron was different. He didn't appear to be impressed by her adroitness or charm. Perhaps it was his large frame or the flaming crop of hair on his head that derailed Amy's stratagem. If you were to ask me, in the short time I have known Aaron Kerr, I would say it was his gentle manner and disarming demeanor that appeared impervious to insult or disparagement.

"Dae ye nae troost me, Amy," beseeched the Scotsman, still offering her his hands.

With eyes like a pup begging as his master eats his dinner, Amy could no longer resist the benevolent giant. She placed her hands in his. Like Jonah being swallowed by the whale, Amy's hands were lost in his, as he gently folded his fingers around them. Raising his prodigious limb high in the air, he lifted her off the deck as if picking up a child's doll.

She yelped.

Leaning over the side rail, he lowered her carefully down into the boat. Amy let out a lingering shriek expressing fear and delight as she hovered in the air. Promptly her feet slowly came to rest on the bottom of the rocking boat where Tim was there to steady her.

He anchored his brawny arms around her. Amy looked up at him. He let fall his lips upon hers. For a short moment, Amy had forgotten herself and surrendered to the passion poised to accept her hidden yearnings. They kissed vehemently. Their heads vacillated and wavered as Tim's enamored finger meandered and caressed her arched back. She capitulated to his affection and tempered him with indulging wet lips. Sitting at the rear of the dory, I turned my head in polite embarrassment. I waved to a nearby lumber barge that tolled its bell in cursory approval. Awakened from an ardent stupor, Tim and his ingenue conceded to compose.

"Ye see, Amy, ah hae delivered ye intae th' arms of yer angel," declared Aaron.

She lowered the brim of the floppy hat over her face, concealing a sheepishness rarely witnessed in Amy Chaloner. Tim held her by the arm and steadied her as she sat. She clutched my arm as the dory rocked from side to side to a passing wake.

"Welcome back," I said.

She lifted her nose with smug disregard and turned her head. "I have no idea what you are on about," she sneered.

The sangfroid that ruled her fortitude exposed a hairline crack for just a short moment. That she was no different than the rest of the world was a fault Amy would never admit to.

"We may need you, Mister Kerr," said Tim, looking up at the big man as he hung over the rail.

"Aye, Keptin. At yer service." He straddled the gunwale nearly six feet above our heads.

"Razor is our customary rower. We can't take him on this errand. It's unsafe for a runaway to come along considering where we are going. Would you like to come instead?"

"Ah would. Shood ah lit th' Professur knoo?"

"I would not worry about it, Mister Kerr. Hop in."

Arron climbed down into the small boat. "Would ye loch me tae row then, Keptin? Ah am very good at it."

"Row, Mister Kerr," said Tim, shuffling to the bow.

"Ah won th' Isle of Skye Charles Edward Stuart rowing contest in the year of fifty-five." He sat and gripped the oars.

"Who was Charles Edward Stuart," I asked.

"Aye, Emily. My hero. Bonnie Prince Charlie."

With the first stroke of the oars, the boat thrust forward, jostling us back. I clasped onto the side of the sixteen-foot-long boat. Amy hung unto my arm with one hand and her hat with the other. When not rowing, Tim sat at the bow. Meanwhile, Aaron was doing what he did best. Using his muscle and driving us quickly to shore.

Small boat rides are always satisfying—being down close to the water and weaving between larger vessels—riding over their silent, trundling wakes as the rolling humps of water pitch toward dry land. It is always wicked fun. However, with Aaron Kerr rowing, the short journey to shore took on a more breathtaking jaunt. Boat traffic was everywhere. Though the ride was an enjoyable one, I would much rather be loafing in a dory on the Westport River near home, where the loudest sound one hears is honking geese, and the only wake thrown by rafts of grousing ducks or the occasional dilatory, fishing vessel. Westport is a place where the scenery is a blanket of verdurous fields and enchanting bungalows—where one becomes replenished by the reinvigorating fragrance of the salty ocean nearby or the blooming honeysuckle dangling over stonewalls surrounding pasture and meadow.

The dory plowed onto the stony beach and came to an abrupt halt. Tim vaulted over the bow and tried pulling us on shore so we could disembark without getting wet. But the boat would not budge, not with Amy and I, and the two-hundred-and-thirty-pound Kerr, still sitting in it.

Aaron Kerr promptly jumped out and helped pull the small vessel up the riverbank, while Tim tied the bowline off to a nearby tree. Aaron gallantly offered Amy his arm. In chivalrous poise, he removed his cap and swept it from left to right—a cavalier bow, clearing the air in her path. He was quick to learn what made her happy. She pompously gripped his burly arm, held high her head, and gave him an autocratic simper, as she stepped out of the tethered pram. I was next. Unlike my best friend, Aaron offered me outstretched arms. I threw mine around his neck as he swept me up and shuttled me high onto the sandy embankment. Amy watched as the surf lapped by her feet and looking swindled.

She walked by me on her way to the main road above the bluff. "You should not be throwing your arms around the neck of strange men," she cautioned.

Tim gathered a hand-drawn map from his pocket and unfurled it. "Now, listen carefully everyone, and I'll explain the mission at hand. We are at the base of Ferry Street. A block up is Broadway Avenue and the train station. Across from the station is our destination, here."

"Columbia Street," I said, looking down at the map.

"Colombia Street is all up hill, I'll let you know," complained Amy.

The Columbia Street was an incline leading from the train station near the waterfront to Main Street. Living in the city, Amy was familiar with many of its byways.

Upon hearing her grievance, Aaron eagerly, if not kindly, offered his services. "Ah would be happy tae carry ye, if ye loch, Amy."

"Never you mind," she blustered. "It's not that steep."

"Number 28, Columbia Street, to be exact," announced Tim. Folding the map, he turned it over and read some writing on the back.

"It says here that the house is built of large granite block, with a flat roof, capped with an enclosed widow's walk, that overlooks a church across the street."

Snooping over Tim's shoulder, I read the rest of what was written. "Once you have found the house, you are to meet with a gentleman named Andrew Robeson, at which time you shall escort one Isaac Sinclair safely to New Bedford, where he will board a ship for Nova Scotia."

"Nova Scotia. I have so many memories of our trip there on the *Sphinx* with Samuel. Remember, Timothy?"

"How can I forget? I learned a lot on that trip about sailing the schooner."

"What a great adventure it was," chimed Amy.

"Nova Scotia. Ah would loove tae see th' place again," added Aaron.

"I'm sure you will," declared Tim, patting the big man on the back. "Now, let's be on our way, shall we?"

The leisurely walk up Ferry and Columbia Streets was a short one, with very little protest from Amy and her piffling concern about clambering up hills. Soon we arrived at our destination. As I looked up, my mouth gaped at the sight of the place. The home at number 28 was impressive in both Brobdingnagian breadth and raw, unorthodox design. The pluton structure, with its finely cut stone, looked like it had grown from deep in the earth. The structure had the appearance of a public building more than someone's home. It was exclusively constructed of stacked granite blocks and secured by towering pilasters at its corners, with traditional bracketed cornices. It was an exceptional example of architecture and a home that the Greek goddess Hestia would be proud to live in.

The abode was surrounded by a stately wrought iron fence and supported by granite pillars and dividing curbstone. Chiseled granite stonework was everywhere. The yard itself was a shaded croft—a marquee of mature oaks and ancient elms, which took up almost the entire block. The building's front door and portico were paired with smoothly carved Greek columns and adorned by immense windows, one on each side of the impressive, quarried veranda. The walkway from the street led to an enormous, picture-framed oak door and was paved in hewed cobblestones, bordered by red brick.

Tim and I looked at one another. We were probably asking ourselves the same thing. Was this a sanctuary for runaway slaves? We climbed onto the granite stoop leading to the front door when, suddenly, it opened.

"Good day, good people. I'm Station Master, Andrew Robeson. Come in quickly, please."

We entered as the man anxiously ushered us in by the elbow one at a time. Before closing the door, he peered up and down the street. "The house is being watched," he informed us. He slammed the door and fastened the bolts.

Unexpectedly, we were greeted by another gentleman. He was short, stocky, and somewhat jolly. He introduced himself as an agent and abolitionist and expressed his delight at our arrival.

"So happy to see such courageous faces," he beamed. "Which of you is Captain Cadman?"

"That would be me, sir," said Tim, extending a hand.

"Nathaniel Briggs Borden," announced the man. "But you can call me Briggs."

Robeson came over after fastening the entrance door. "I see you have all met Mayor Borden."

"That's very kind of you, Andrew, but to be bestowed with such an accolade as mayor, after being retired for years, is a bit much."

"Nonsense, Briggs, once one holds such an office he is christen with the epithet for life."

"This man here is the captain," said Borden, taking Tim by the arm.

"Captain Cadman," said Robeson, "we awaited your arrival, eagerly."

"Yes, sir."

"Happy to meet a fellow agent and his conductors. Welcome to my home. Please, come and take a load off your feet. My lovely wife just put out refreshments."

We followed Robeson and Borden through what must have been a common hallway but could only be accurately described a majestic gallery. Our footsteps echoed off the glazed tile floor beneath our feet and up to the gold-leaf adorned vaulted ceiling above. To my left was a stairway with a landing illuminated by a basilican stained-glass window in an exhibit of radiant color and encompassing a baroque floral medallion at its center. To the right was a wall of portraits and landscapes, overlooked by statuette busts of Robeson ancestors clinging to marble pedestals.

Andrew Robeson led us to a palatial room just off the gallery.

"What does he mean, conductors," I whispered tugging at Amy's elbow.

Amy cupped her hand to her mouth as we paraded into her room. "It's code talk. This slavery business has its own secret language."

"We are the conductors, then?

"Yes. Conductors are those who help slaves along on their travels."

"I see. And being the captain, Tim is the head conductor or agent. How exciting. How did you know all this and never shared it with me?"

"*Shh.*" She hushed me as if we were walking in late for a prayer service at church. "We'll talk later," she said, as we entered another room.

"This is the study," announced Robeson. "Please sit and make yourselves comfortable."

The chamber where we were received was full of books and many comfortable places to sit, read, and enjoy. Shelves were everywhere. I have never witnessed so many volumes in a private home. In the center of the room on a round mahogany table sat a steaming, silver teapot and a platter of biscuits resting on a silk tablecloth. Tea, cookies, and books, I marveled. I felt as if we had stumbled into a heavenly asylum.

Tim sat nervously twiddling his thumbs as if waiting to see a physician. Amy draped her arms out over the chair with legs crossed, looking queenly and quite at home, while Aaron sat quietly, staring at the biscuits on the tray. Not one of them looked impressed, let alone aware, by the athenaeum and awaiting volumes.

It was an opulent space. Chairs and settee were upholstered in fine silks and fleecy satins and in dazzling colors that seduced the eye. The lavish drapery on the windows was as thick as a winter quilt and made of fine tulle fabric, which puddled onto the floor in an overflowing fishtail train or ruffled bouquet of posh material. The plush rug radiated a fancy splash of rich color, a floral palette of carnations and roses, intertwined in a spiral composition that leaped from its rich vermilion background. I was truly in the lap of luxury.

All this opulence was overwhelming. At times I had to close my eyes and wipe the images clean from my mind. If you can forgive me, I find such a lifestyle an iniquitous contortion to the natural order of things—the way ordinary working people lived. Grandmamma often described such diplay as a mutant anomaly of civility and an obscenity to common graces.

On the other hand, what these two gentlemen were undertaking could only be described as admirable and compassionate. After all, they had the capital and channels to do so. And I am certain, though Grandmamma was critical of those with too much money, she would gladly confess that there was a special place in heaven reserved for such guardians as Andrew Robeson and Nathaniel Briggs Borden.

"And you must be Amy Chaloner," declared Robeson, bowing as he took her hand.

"Yes, I am," she replied, as if it were about time she was noticed.

"You fit the description your father gave me of you, entirely—attractive and beautiful."

She looked over at me and gloated.

"He informs me that you are interested in our war against human bondage."

"Well, Rudolf French is my mentor in the matter. He persuaded me to participate."

"Then you must know that Rudolf is a station master and a major associate of ours in New Bedford. This little venture you are about to engage in today is collaboration between our two stations. We are delighted that you have accepted this noble calling."

"How could I refuse? Uncle French can be very convincing."

"Rudolf French. A general of the Underground. Praiseworthy solider in our campaign," proclaimed Borden, as he poured tea into cups and passed them around.

I was bewildered by how much was being revealed to me and how little I knew. More importantly, I was astonished that Tim was so involved in what has come to be known as the Underground Railroad and kept it secret all this time. I had read about the Underground Railroad in the papers but never suspected that I would one day ride its rails.

"And you, young lady," said Robeson, extending his hand.

"Miss Emily White."

"It's a pleasure, Miss White. How long have you been a conductor?"

"I suppose I was baptized just today."

"Bravo," cheered Nathaniel Borden, handing me a cup of tea and saucer.

"And you, sir," addressed Robeson, looking over at Aaron.

The young carpenter appeared to be intimidated by his hosts and surroundings. He was quieter than I had expected and sat huddled in his chair as if something would break if he moved.

"Your name, my good man?"

"Aaron Kerr, sairr."

"And how long have you been interested in our cause?"

"Ah hae nae cause. Ah am jist a seaman lendin' a hand if need be," admitted Aaron.

"Fine, then," concluded Robeson. "Judging by your size, sir, I would say you are worth ten of them."

Robeson, sensing Aaron Kerr's awkwardness, walked over and shook his hand. "I am honored to welcome a fellow Scotsman into my home. I have a deep admiration for those who are willing to sacrifice time and integrity to pitch in, my good man. And although there are those that may tell you different, your integrity will grow by leaps and bounds once you have fulfilled your brief commission. Coming from a long linage of proud Scotsman, I can say that I am certain you will become a superlative conductor, even if just for a day. Our challenge is a great one, Mister Kerr, and our army minuscule, but we must not fail. For failure is not the hallmark of a Scotsman. We shall prove ourselves."

"Yes, sairr."

"At the very least, in the eyes of God. I do not confess as much with any hyperbolism, you understand. So, it is with great appreciation that I must thank you, sir, for … how did you phrase it? Ah yes, lend a hand. Yes. And a fine hand indeed."

"Ah appreciate th' ken' words, Mister Robeson."

"Have a biscuit," said Briggs holding out the platter of cookies.

I could tell that Aaron had been patiently waiting for the sweets to come his way. He studied the tray like a child at the candy counter at Macomber's store. Ultimately, he snatched one. And just before the tray was pulled away, he reached over and plucked two more.

"By all means, Mister Kerr, fill your pockets," insisted Borden, chuckling. "There's plenty more from where those came from."

Looking guilt-ridden but unable to help himself, he sheepishly clutched another cookie.

"Mister Cadman, we here in the city are under siege," proclaimed Robeson.

"Scoundrels, I say, every one of them," conceded Briggs, placing the treats back on the table.

"Under siege?" repeated Tim. "I'm afraid I don't understand."

"We are under surveillance, Mister Cadman," replied Robeson. "We have been very successful in our little operation of delivering our parcels north, thus we have attracted considerable scrutiny, I'm afraid."

"They have come up from down south," chimed Borden. "A group of hunters, migrated here to track runaways and return them to their—and I hate to use the term, rightful owners."

"We heard that they had recently arrived and are scouring New Bedford for runaways. Nonetheless, it appears that they have pursued their prey here to Fall River," said Robeson.

"Come, come, Andrew. Prey is such a harsh word," maintained Briggs. "Victims would be more appropriate, or, if you like, parcels."

"Quite right, Briggs."

"Parcels?" I said.

"Forgive me, Miss White. I forget you are new to abolitionist terminology. We have a language of our own, you understand. Parcels, or baggage if you like, are the souls we are assisting: the runaway slaves."

"Grandmamma often mentioned the Underground Railroad. I always wondered how it got its name."

"Legend has it that it was coined by a slave catcher and his master," explained Briggs. "You see, there was this slave named Tice Davids down in the state of Kentucky who was running away from his overseer and owner. He had swum across the Ohio River toward the town of Ripley, Ohio. Once on dry soil, he sprinted for his life along some train tracks. His hunter was almost upon him. Just as the overseer was about to apprehend him, old Tice vanished and evaded capture. When the owner caught up to the overseer, he asked him what had happened to the runaway. The overseer told him that the slave was running along the tracks when suddenly they swallowed him whole. Thus, the term Underground Railroad."

"Is that true, Mister Robeson?" inquired Amy.

"No one can really say. Though it sounds like folklore, it only goes to prove that there must be some truth in the fable."

"I find it an enchanting tale," I said. "Even if it's not true."

"Originally, Mister Sinclair was expected to travel the inland route to the next station in Providence. However, Mister French suggested that a straight run from New Bedford to Nova Scotia on his ship would be quicker and safer. I'm afraid that now we have little choice."

"What happened to Tice Davids must now happen to Isaac Sinclair," said Briggs. "He must vanish … today."

"He is right," confirmed Robeson. "It is no longer safe for him to remain at number 28 Columbia Street. The hunters know he is here."

"Are they in the area?" I asked.

"As we speak," declared Robeson.

"They may even be just outside the house, waiting," said Briggs. "I encountered them at my place this morning, and I'm afraid they may have followed me here."

I placed my teacup on the table and walked to a window overlooking the street.

"I assure you, Miss White, they are somewhere out there," he warned.

"They may suspect something is astir," declared Robeson. "Whether it's a southern party or a local hero. They have multiplied their troops by placing a bounty on every head that is captured. With the war and all, these are rough times. There are many supposedly local kind-hearted citizens eager to earn quick money."

"To say little about those who are sympathetic with the South," said Briggs.

"Good point, Nathaniel."

"There's a carriage by the church with two men in it," I said. "They are just sitting there, smoking cigarettes."

Robeson walked over to a window and inched back the curtain slightly. "Very suspicious, are they not, Miss White?"

"We must engage with caution," warned Briggs, as he looked over his comrade's shoulder and out toward the street.

"What should we do?" inquired Tim.

"One must be prepared and willing to undertake the mission. There could be conflict."

"Did ah nae teel ye that conflict is mah middle nam … on mah mother's side," said Aaron. "We Scots dinnae fear it or rin from it."

"Well said, Mister Kerr," said Robeson. "Fear not. We are not without a plan."

"Yes, yes, they are crafty, but we are artful," sneered Briggs, rubbing his hands and looking blissfully sinister.

"Are you with us, Mister Cadman?" inquired Robeson.

"Of coorse he is. 'hat nae reit, Keptin?"

"Yes. Aaron is right. We did not come all this way to fail."

"I remember reading about the Fugitive Slave Act," I reminded them. "Cannot we all be fined and arrested for harboring slaves?"

"The Slave Act has been suspended and ignored since the war has started. And though some communities are abiding by it, my colleague Nathaniel here has many friends in the state house and senate," explained Robeson. "We have ways around it if need be."

"Congress is trying to make changes," explained Briggs. "But it will take time, my dear. The fear is for the slave, not the conductor. They may try and fine us but no one pays and no one enforces the regulation. And with the war, the law is in disarray. Let's call for Isaac, shall we?"

Andrew Robeson walked across the room to a cabinet full of books. Clutching the case with both hands, he moved it aside, as if opening a door on hinges, exposing a staircase leading to the cellar beneath the house.

"Come on up, Isaac," he summoned. "And bring your things."

Isaac Sinclair was not much taller than Amy or me. Looking to be around sixteen, he had spiraling cropped hair and chestnut complexion. There was almost no stubble on his face, a gentle broad nose and cautious coal-black eyes. He was given a new suit of clothing along with a wool jacket and Concord slip-on shoes, sporting buckles. He carried his old things in a pouched bag wrapped around the tip of a walking stick.

"Come, Isaac," said Robeson. "My wife will prepare you for your trip."

While Robeson went with Isaac, Briggs explained to us where to find our next safe house and two new parcels.

"Here is the next station," said Briggs, handing Tim written instructions. "It's the William Canedy Homestead near Steep Brook Village. You can approach the place north up the river and avoid any overland travel."

"How will I find it?"

"The Canedy property has a flagpole by the waterfront. Old Glory will be flying at half-mast. That is a signal that the parcel is ready for delivery. Once there, you will be assisted by a gentleman named Philander Canedy. He will release to you two parcels. One named Old Jim and the other

Levi Taft. Once they are safely aboard your vessel, your mission here will be accomplished."

"We are prepared to leave," announced Robeson, entering the room, followed by a woman in a long, flowered summer dress and shrouded bonnet concealing the wearer's face.

"A-ha, well, what do you think," said the once mayor, feeling clever.

We were all puzzled by who it may be.

"Are we ferrying two people, then?" inquired Tim.

"Where's Isaac," I asked.

"Here," exclaimed Andrew Robeson, removing the ruffled bonnet off the face. To our astonishment, it was not a woman at all but a smiling Isaac Sinclair.

"What do you think of our little disguise?" uttered Briggs, somewhat satisfied.

"Ye hud me fooled," declared Aaron.

"Might just work," tittered Tim, trying not to break into laughter.

"Of course, it will," maintained Briggs.

"One of the girls will have to stay behind," said Robeson. "Four arrived—two men and two women—the same must be seen leaving."

"You are right," said Tim.

"I'll stay behind," offered Amy. "I can walk home."

"Splendid," affirmed Robeson. "Mister Cadman, take my coach. That way there is no delay, and it will make it more difficult if you should be followed. Just tie the transport off to one of the bollards along the waterfront. I'll send a boy down for it later."

We marched through a long, carpeted lobby leading toward the back of the house. I stopped and looked up. The ceiling was nearly twelve feet high. It was painted a pale sky blue and adorned with cherubs wrapping a coil of white silk stoles along the plastered border. The moldings at the cornice were gold leaf, crowning a dental motif and encompassing the entire perimeter of the narrow chamber. Once again, I found I had to shut my eyes and wipe my mind's slate clean of the sizzling, opulent images that singed my psyche.

"Hurry, Emmie," hailed Amy, running back and towing me by the arm.

We all bid the two men farewell and climbed into the well-appointed black coach. Tim sat up front at the reins with Aaron while I took my place on a rear bench with young Isaac. Nathaniel Borden tied the bonnet strap tightly beneath the black man's chin to bunch the material around his face for cover. After a short goodbye, we were on our way. Evidently grateful, a twinkle sparked in the boy's eye as he looked back at the two gents that were so kind to him. Instead of turning down Columbia Street toward the river, Tim steered the coach uphill toward Main Street and in the opposite direction of the church, which stood across from the house. We drove away from number twenty-eight.

"Where are we going?" I asked.

"I need to know whether we are being followed by the two men by the church."

I looked back at the carriage with the two smoking men. As we made distance, they did not move or attempt to follow. I felt we were safe.

"They are not following."

Isaac Sinclair sat with his head down. His arms shook with fear.

"We should be safe now, Isaac," I told him. I tucked the bonnet down over his face. "But we must maintain vigilance."

Tim took the main road toward Globe Village, but away from the waterfront.

"Should we not be getting back to the ship, Timothy, before someone else sees us?"

"Someone has."

"Where, where?" I looked over my shoulder.

"Ah see two men, Keptin. Ridin' horseback weel behin' us."

"Let us turn here," said Tim. "See if they follow. It may be nothing."

Tim navigated the coach off Main Street down a dirt lane and behind a small chapel on Middle Street. We waited.

"Do you think they were following?" I asked.

"We will soon find out."

Tim circled the rear of the churchyard and advanced toward the main road. The two men on horseback lingered as if admiring the park across the way. One could tell they were endeavoring not to look over. We continued south, driving down Main Street and away from the direction of the waterfront and safety of the *Sphinx*.

"They are following," I cried.

"Hold on tight!" warned Tim.

Unfurling the whip, he wheeled the cracker, splitting the air between the horse's ears. Suddenly we were sprinting down Main Street, weaving amid startled traffic and scurrying pedestrians.

"They ur givin' chase, Keptin!"

Two men on horseback could gallop much faster than a gentleman's coach carrying us. Approaching the wide intersection at Globe Village, Tim robustly spun the veering coach and poor bolting mares down Globe Street toward the river. I hung on for dear life. The two horsemen bolted at a rapid trot, outpacing us. The coach's wheels clattered and skittered against the craggy shale road, jarring us in our seats. Aaron Kerr sat on the edge of his bench reveling every minute and cheering Tim on.

By the time we had reached Bay Road, running along the waterfront, the two riders were abreast of us. I clutched onto a frightened Isaac. The bonnet on his head fell off his head and down his back while the slave inside shuttered with dread. Without the bonnet, the disguise was made black and naked. To the chasing horseman there was no mistaking the basis for our insistent retreat.

One of the men came alongside and reached out and attempted to seize the mare's throatlatch to bring the horse and coach to a halt. Aaron stood up and dangled his broad torso perilously over the coach's spiraling wheel. Holding onto the rail supporting the sun awning, he swung a hammered fist, pummeling one of the riders from the saddle to the ground. Upon doing so, he raised a clenched fist and wailed an affirmation of victory. While Aaron Kerr delighted in the skirmish, Isaac quivered with fear. The poor fellow must have thought that all these white people were raving mad.

The remaining rider receded a bit but continued his unrelenting pursuit as his companion lay in the road well behind us. The chaser's horse once again came closer, its snout trumpeted and snorted. I could practically feel the stallion's breath at my neck. The man brandished a pistol from his jacket and fired a shot directly over our heads. Indignant, Aaron dove over the front bench and into the back of the coach where the boy and I sat.

"Ur ye awl reit, lassie."

"Yes."

"Hoow abit ye, lad?"

Startled by the gunfire, the boy's roving fingers searched for injury. Finding none, he nodded that he was fine.

"Whit ever happens, Keptin," declared Aaron. "Keep on gonnae."

And with that advise, he stood up on the bench behind me and dove into the air off the back of the speeding coach.

"Aaron!" yelled Tim, looking back.

With his hands firmly around the man's throat, Kerr landed on the horse and chaser, using the culprit's body as a cushion as they hit the ground.

"Oh, Timothy. What do we do? We need to go back for him."

Tim kept racing onward. I watched as both men wrestled on the hard pan road and faded further and further away. The coach neared a bend. I lost sight of the brave Aaron Kerr.

"What shall we do, Timothy?"

"Crazy Scotsman. We shall get Isaac to the ship. That is all I can think of doing right now."

Finally, we were at Ferry Street, where Tim tied the horse to a hitching post at the end of the road. Isaac Sinclair took off the dress and tossed it into the coach.

"Tank ya, sur," said the boy.

"It was just good fun," said Tim. "Now you stay with Emily. Emmie, can you take the dory and get Isaac back to the ship."

"Of course. You know I can."

"I'll be back. Don't follow me."

"Where are you going?"

"To look for that crazy Scotsman."

"But that man had a gun, Timothy."

"Tell me something I don't already know."

"How about the fact that he may shoot you."

He gave me an absurd look and that persuasive Cadman wink. "I'll be alright."

Tim and the boy pushed the boat into the lapping surf. I tore off my shoes and tossed them into the pram. Wading into the chilly water, I climbed in.

"Get inside, hurry," Tim told Isaac, as he shoved the boat into deeper water.

I pinned the oars along the boat's gunwales and proceeded to row. We floated slowly toward the anchored schooner. I watched as Tim disappeared over the bluff, sprinting up Ferry Street. Isaac Sinclair looked back toward shore, unsure for his safety. An apprehensive stroke of fear still smeared his face.

"You are safe now, Isaac," I assured him. "A couple more minutes and we will be on the ship with friends."

"Tank ya, Miss Emily," he said, folding his hands to the heavens and reverently bowing his head in prayer. "Tank ya, oh Lord," he recited over and over.

Razor, Eli, and Winton Macartney met us at the ship's rail as the dory slammed up against the hull. I threw the bow and stern line up to Razor. He tied us off.

"Where is the Captain?" asked Eli, hurling down the rope ladder.

"We ran into some trouble. Timothy went back to look for Aaron." I helped the boy up the ladder.

"Aaron should have never left without my permission," said Winton. "Is he alright?"

"I don't know, Professor. We got separated. But I'm going back to shore and wait." I sat back down and prepared to row. "Untie me, Razor."

"You better go with her," suggested Eli.

Razor pelted down the rat-ladder and into the dory.

"I'll row now, Miss Emily," he said, in a gruff but obliging tone.

I hopped over a bench and sat myself down at the bow. Razor took the oars and steered us back to shore.

We waited by the riverbank, as I was very mindful of Tim's instructions not to follow. There was so much to see and so much going on in the harbor. But I could enjoy none of it. Until I could discover Tim and Aaron safe, anguish and concern was the only course on my agenda. Meanwhile Admon Assagai trudged the rocky shore, passing his time while skipping stones athwart the surf. I sat and waited along the sandy bluff where I could plainly see the road above and any possible sight of my two missing crew members. Suddenly, in the direction of the pier along the shore where the Fall River Boat made its home, a man came trekking toward us looking worn and exhausted. Razor jogged over to him. The two men talked. I stood up to get a better look. To my relief, I noticed it was Tim.

"Where is Aaron?" I desperately inquired as I ran over.

"I don't know." He struggled for breath. "I ran back where he left us but there was no sign of Aaron or the assailant. They both vanished. I have been combing the waterfront looking for them with no success. I did encounter the first fellow we evaded."

"Did you speak with him?"

"Yes. He didn't recognize me. He was limping badly and leading his horse, which was doing the same, poor animal."

"What did he say?"

"I asked him if he was hurt or needed help?"

"And?"

"He appeared upset. Told me to mind my own business."

"What should we do, Timothy?"

"There's nothing we can do—at least not for now. We will get back to the ship and wait. If Aaron does not return, I'll have little choice but to report the incident to the authorities. Perhaps by then he will materialize, or someone will have some news."

"I'm so worried. He took such a tumble."

"I know you are. But don't underestimate the man. He may yet surprise us. Let's get back to the ship, shall we?"

The trip to New Bedford was now delayed. In the morning I would need to go into town and have a telegraph sent to the *Daily Whaler* explaining my dilemma. Tim assured me that it would not be a problem since I was doing Rudolf French's bidding and saving someone from a life of slavery.

Tim and I observed the waterfront all evening with the spyglass, hoping that Aaron Kerr would appear. The sun hung low in the west and would soon be below the horizon. I was on my way below deck when, unexpectedly, Eli Monroe called Tim over.

"Yes, what is it Mister Monroe?"

"Where you landed the dory—about a hundred yards north. I think I see our crewman sitting on some ledge." Eli handed Tim the spyglass.

Hearing the news, I ran over. Soon, the entire crew stood watching.

"I see him," I cheered.

"You must have hawk-eyes," noted Eli. "I could just about make him out with the spyglass."

"Come now, Eli. Look how big he is. And who else wears a pork pie hat?"

"No one that I have ever known," chuckled the helmsman. "And how you can make out the man's hat, I'll never know."

"That's our boy," said Tim, collapsing the spyglass. "Let's try and signal him so he knows we will be out to get him."

"He keeps a Scottish flag in his duffel below," declared Winton. "It's how I have signaled him in the past."

"Good idea, Professor. Fly the Scottish banner up the port halyard."

Eli helped Winton raise the white and blue Saint Andrews flag high up with the staysail halyard while Razor and one other crewman departed for shore in the ship's dory.

"He sees it," I cried.

Handing me the spyglass, Tim disappeared below. I held it to my eye and got a better look. The good news was that Aaron looked in one piece. I threw up both my hands and waved. He confirmed and did the same.

Once back on board everyone rushed over to shake Aaron Kerr's hand or pat him on the back. Winton Macartney even gave him a hug, followed by a slap in the back of the head, knocking the pork pie hat over his eyes.

"Next time, let me know where you are going, you big lunkhead."

"Follow me, Mister Kerr," said Tim, sounding like a ship's captain once again.

Both men went below where Tim quizzed the Scotsman on his exploit. I followed. Once below, I pulled the copper teakettle off the hot stove.

"You must be dying for a cup of tea, Aaron." I grabbed a cup and poured.

"Aye, lassie, loove a cup jist about noo."

"What happened back there, Aaron, after we rode away?"

"We werstled a bit, then, th' scondrol got awa, Keptin."

"Did he say anything to you?" I asked.

"Nae. He got back oan th' horse an' rode aff. Ah think he may hurt or broke his arm."

"Where have you been all this time? I went looking for you, but you were nowhere to be found."

"Got lost, Keptin."

"Lost? You could see the river from where we left you. How could you get lost?"

"Weel, you see, Keptain. Ah foond this wee place th' serve th' best haggis an' Scotch whiskey ah ave tasted in a long while."

"Haggis and whiskey."

"They waur out of haggis, but their scotch was marvaloosly aged."

Tim leaned in and sniffed.

"Are you drunk, Mister Kerr?"

"Blooter'd but able, Keptin," shouted Aaron, jumping to his feet and saluting.

Tim shook his head and tried not to laugh. Though Aaron's shirt was torn and he wore a lump on his head, he was not any worse for wear for a man who dove off the back of a barreling coach and tangled with a gunman.

"That bump looks nasty," said Tim, inspecting the injury on the Scotsman's forehead. "You must have hit the ground pretty hard, huh?"

"At is nae when 'at happened, Keptin."

"It's not?"

"Ye see, Keptin, thaur was this lad at th' other tavern. Th' one out of haggis."

"You mean you visited more than one tavern?"

"Haggis is hard tae fin, Keptin."

"I'm sure it is."

"As ah was sayin, Keptin, this Irish mon asked me wa ah was drinkin that Scottish dreg sewer watar. Of coorse, ah burst th' Paddy reit in the beak."

Tim and I looked at one another, flabbergasted.

"Of course, you did," blurted Tim.

"Alas, we becam friends, efter ah booght heem a whiskey."

"You don't say."

"Fur a wee fellaw, he had a fist loch a hammer." He rubbed his head.

"I've heard enough, Mister Kerr." Tim patted the big man on the shoulder. "You have earned your bruises and drink today."

"Ah did retrieve a gift fur ye, Keptin."

He lifted his shirt and revealed a pistol.

"A revolver?" I blurted.

"Th' scoondrel dropped it when he rode aff."

He handed Tim the weapon.

"It's loaded. Do you know anything about them, Mister Kerr.

"Nae, Keptin. A shotgin is mah choice of weapon."

"Ah, here's the professor," I said, as he descended the companionway. "Perhaps he knows. …"

"Nae, nae don't ask …" warned Aaron.

"Do you know anything about pistols, Professor," I inquired.

"Mah Lord, haur comes th' lesson fur th' day." Whimpering, he shook his head. His boss was about to kidnap an audience and he was once again caught in the middle. Making matters worse, Tim handed Winton the pistol.

"Be careful, Professor, it's loaded."

"I am not a fool, Captain," said Winton, looking into the gun's barrel.

"I'm not very familiar with pistols, Professor. How can we unload it?"

He turned the weapon over and carefully studied the unconventional instrument. The professor was a methodical man when talking about what he knew. And the curriculum he was formulating in his brain was carefully amassed before the scholarly lecture on all things pistol was delivered.

"Ah, yes a LeMat revolver. They are relatively rare."

"So, you are familiar with guns," I said.

"I am familiar with all mechanical machinery encompassing compression chambers, my good lady."

He turned the pistol over, looking for any markings.

"These guns are exclusively used by the Confederate military. Invented by a gentleman named Alexandre LeMat in Orleans." He swung out the reloading leaver and moved it up and down. "The shot ram device is coming apart. Inferior design, I'm afraid. You can see the revolver has two barrels. Fires lead balls and buckshot. I suspect the manufacturer has been experimenting with various calibers of ammunition. I believe this one is the new thirty-five caliber. Older models utilized a larger forty-caliber slug. You can tell the model by the larger smooth bore shotgun barrel with bone shattering twenty-eight-gauge buckshot. I have handled early models and they appear to have a smaller shotgun cylinder."

As Aaron Kerr tried to warn me, Winton Macartney proceeded to tell us everything he knew about the weapon.

"They started making them in Philadelphia, but they were never accepted by the military as a standard Union firearm, you see. Since the war began, LeMat stopped production in the states and they are being assembled and smuggled in from France. Very unique mechanism, really. It discharges nine black powder rounds and single buckshot from an independent barrel. Devastating at close range." He lined up the sights with one closed eye while looking down the gun's barrel. "Of course, a substandard piece of equipment when compared to a Navy Colt."

"Yes, but how can we safely unload it, Professor," asked Tim.

"You need to remove the assembly pin below the barrels. But if you just want it quickly unarmed for safety reasons, it is probably more expeditious to just fire the loaded chambers."

He held the firearm by his ear and listened, as if the device was ticking and about to go off.

"Shall we, Captain?" He started up the companionway ladder.

Once on deck, Winton Macartney walked over to the rail. Pointing the loaded weapon down at the water a few feet from the ship, he pulled the trigger. Cocking back the hammer eight times, seven shots were discharged.

Unaware of the reason for all the noise, a fearful crew came running over. Isaac Sinclair cowered by the rope locker. Terror dripped from his face. I ran over to assure him that there was no danger.

The sound emitted from the firearm reflected off the hilly streets of the city and targeted the entire harbor with explosive clamor. After the gun was purged of its projectiles, Winton flicked the specially-made firing pin on the pistol's narrow hammer, discharging the round of solitary buckshot. The gun leapt in his hand as it was fired and emitted a roar of cracking thunder that echoed off the city's mills. Promptly, he spun the gun around and handed the weapon to Tim, grip first.

"Empty, Captain," he concluded, smugly. "It appears this weapon was fired once. It contained an empty chamber. Careful. Don't burn yourself. The barrels are still quite hot. Come, Aaron, we have work to do."

Tim handed the empty revolver to Eli. "Mister Monroe. Store this thing in the captain's desk drawer and make certain the drawer is locked, will you?"

Eli Monroe carried the revolver below. Tim and I stood at the rail looking out toward the cityscape. Behind us a salmon sun was setting and mirroring its light off the windows of homes and factories that spotted the hillside of the city like countless flaming lanterns.

Aaron Kerr rested his hand on Tim's shoulder as he walked by, smiled, and followed Winton along the deck.

"I like him," said Tim.

"Never met anyone like him," I admitted.

"Too late to go over to the Canedy residence."

"We can go first thing in the morning."

"What an incredible day," he marveled.

"Yes, incredible indeed."

Chapter 12:
The Freedom Train's a Ridin'

The next morning, I was awakened by Winton and Aaron laboring on the steam engine, deep in the ship's bilge. Tim was at the captain's desk making an entry into the ship's log. I placed my hand over the teapot on the stove. It was hot.

"Good morning, Emmie."

"Morning," I uttered, still nursing some grogginess. "What time is it?" I poured myself some tea.

"About six," he replied, looking at his pocket watch and entering the time in the ship's log.

"I slept like a nesting hen."

"Well, best get above," he advised. "Enjoy the calm morning before harbor traffic gets hustling."

"Where's young Isaac?"

"Wandering the decks," he chuckled. "I don't think he likes being confined below. He cannot believe that he is free to move around and banter with the crew. Slept under the stars last night."

"Poor fellow."

"Had not enjoyed a peaceful sleep since he left the Carolinas, he told me."

"I can believe it." I looked out the companionway hatch. "What a beautiful morning."

I carried my copper mug of tea and stepped out on deck. The river was a black mirror imaging the industrial architecture along the glutted shore. The crinkling reflection from the water was one of soaring smokestacks and heaps of coal, staring down on awakening brigantines and barques moored motionless around us.

In the not-too-far distance, the Slade's Ferry crossed over from the city to the town of Somerset like it had been doing for nearly two hundred years. I watched its undulating wake lazily slithering toward our vessel like a subaqueous serpent. Ambushing the hull, it bounced off the bow with a playful *whoosh*, wrinkling the emulating images of the reflected world around me.

I crossed from the port to the starboard side of the ship, which faced the divergent shores and the tranquil outskirts of the town of Somerset. The bucolic lowland, with its sleepy dairy fields and provincial homes, was surrounded by agrarian grassland and walled off by hedgerow and wild shrub. The contrast between the two shores could not be more different. Down the deck, young Isaac was sitting by the mast eating an apple, probably given him by Aaron who appeared to keep a sack of them on his bunk. Razor and most of the crew were still in their bunks below. Up on the bow, Eli Monroe was scrubbing the deck with a bearded mop. Our eyes met and he dropped what he was doing and walked over.

"Good morning, my good lady." He pulled a pouch of tobacco from his hip pocket. "Sleep well?"

"Yes, and you?"

"When I am out on the water, I always sleep well."

"I know what you mean. The salt air has a splendid influence on the soul."

"You are right there," he said, rolling a stogie with proficient skill. "On land one just lives, eats … sleeps. On the water one knows he's alive, that food is delicious, and rest rejuvenating. When you wake up in the morning out at sea every morning, rain or shine, you feel born again and every day sparkling new."

"That's what I love about you, Eli. You remind me of Grandmamma. She was full of life."

"Your Grandmamma must have been a loving soul." He lit his cigar. "If I may ask, what happened to your mum?"

"I never knew her. I was an orphan."

"My Lord, Sorry to hear it," he said, with his Provencal Island inflection.

"Nothing to apologize about. Grandmamma raised me and I could not ask for a better mother."

I took a sip of tepid tea and reflected. Eli nursed his freshly rolled cigar. He had moved down wind so as not to allow the spent smoke to blow in my face. Eli was a gentleman.

I did not like talking about my abandonment when an infant. I remember Grandmamma and I often spoke about it freely. And though her advice was like a spoon of castor oil, and not always swallowed with any ease, somehow, later I always felt better. "To heal you must purge, to purge, confess, and only then can you mend," she often advised me.

"I was dropped off on someone's doorstep somewhere on that hill behind us. Perhaps that is why I have never been fond of Fall River."

"Oh, did they take good care of you?"

"I don't think they kept me very long. Probably had too many mouths to feed. I was delivered to the home of Charlotte White of Point Village in Westport. She was known for taking children in until a home could be found for them. I was an infant when I came to her. She never let me go and I never had a reason to leave. But she did."

"Leave?"

"Yes … last year when she died. She was in her eighties. A long life."

"I am sorry, young lady, if you allow me to be."

I looked at him. "Yes, you have no reason. But it's appreciated."

Eli looked at me with a comforting twinkle in his dark eyes. I never realized how much he reminded me of Grandmamma. Not only by the things he said, but by how he looked. Though he was much younger, the sea and sun had prematurely aged his face. He had the same crow's feet radiating from his eyes and a sympathetic smile above a dimpled, clean-shaven chin. Like Grandmamma, perhaps it was his dark skin that I trusted.

"You know, your first foot fall in life was but a mere inadequacy, my dear girl," he explained. "What you endured as an infant is of no memory. Your hurt was not felt then and you should not reconstruct it now. Your mother could have had good reason."

"Think so?"

"Yes. You may ask what in God's name could be a good reason … to abandon a child? And I must confess that I don't know … just that good reasons do exist. But look at you now. It is a new day. Think only of joyful things."

"Yes," I agreed, "joyful things. Grandmamma often said that an ounce of joy would wipe clean a pound of sadness. And I have had enough joy in my life to cleanse tons."

"What are you two talking about," asked Tim, strolling over.

"I was telling Emily that the sunrise over Fall River is no match for the ones on Saint George's Island in my hometown in Bermuda."

"That's not fair," said Tim, pointing toward the city. "All those buildings are in the way."

We laughed.

"We are going to pick up the other two runaways. You coming, Emmie?"

"Oh, yes, I wouldn't miss it for the entire world."

"Deploy the dory, will you, Mister Monroe."

"Aye, aye, sir."

Razor had been rowing for almost thirty minutes as we glided along on our journey toward the northern part of the city. It was serene here with almost no boat traffic. Down river where the *Sphinx* was anchored was considered the aquatic commerce center of the city. Here it was much like the Westport River with its thalassic environs and occasional sailing vessel. Tim sat in his usual berth at the bow and I at the stern.

Razor hummed as he rowed, at times closing his eyes and venting a smile, his nose sniffing the freedom of air around us. I tried to reserve the tune to memory and hum with him.

"You are kindly, Miss Emily. Ya sing just fine."

"It a haunting hymn," I told him. "Is it not?"

"Ya know the notes now. Ya hum it and I will sing the words."

"There are lyrics?"

"Oh ya. A song with no words is like a bird with no wings."

"Alright, then," I said, eager to oblige.

I began humming the harmony. A few seconds later he began to sing.

On my shoulder I shall carry
n' my brother I shall bear
we shall pray for one another
n' the Lord will get us there.

We shall not endure the cane
in our travels true and far
n' forsaken all the pain
on that freedom railway car.

I continued to croon the woeful tune, though my harmony was askew. But he didn't care, nor did I. His voice boomed from deep inside. From there the lyrics filtered through his heart before drifting off his lips and down the river valley. It was a soulful, resolute voice—a rejoicing affirmation—like the crack of distant thunder made close. Though his eyes were closed, Razor rowed true and on course. My meager humming was nearly censored by his loud baritone resonance.

N' the freedom train's a ridin'
n' to Canaan we shall roam
for the Lord we are abidin'
up to heaven by His throne.

N' my soul it is willin'
as my spirit starts to glow
when that train comes a singin'
it's to freedom I shall go.

Tim appeared oblivious to our melodious vocalization. He sat gazing ahead. Contemplation and scrutiny were integrated to his face. He looked worried. After all, our last attempt as conductors and picking up a parcel was an adventure we both did not care to repeat.

I was done humming. Razor continued, softly. The thrum of his voice was a purring murmur now, barely audible. His eyes opened as he looked at me and smiled.

"Miss Emily we is a team, we are," he said, gleefully.

"Another pair of impassioned vocalists would be hard to find," I bragged, laughing.

"There it is," shouted Tim, pointing. "Behind those trees about three hundred yards ahead."

"I see it," I replied.

"Steady as she goes, Mister Assagai."

"Yeas, sir."

The flagpole was visible just beyond a grove of trees. Old Glory was flying at half-mast. At its base were two chairs and in the chairs two people. Tim waved. A man in the chair waved back and walked over to the water's edge. Tim looked back at me and winked.

Up a slight incline and near the road stood William Barnabas Canedy's homestead. It was a modest-looking two-story early American, though some would maintain that the structure had a late colonial motif. I didn't much care what its architectural era was. It looked welcoming and humble, a far comparison from number 28 Columbia Street. Oh please, don't get me wrong. There is almost nothing I could say that was disparaging about the Robeson estate. Just that the Canedy house looked more inviting to the constraints and heart of a country girl. And I would bet that the inside of the home was just as unassuming.

Razor turned around and took a bearing. Pointing the dory toward shore, he rowed us toward the ubiquitous Underground Railroad station.

Once we were all on dry land, and after a brief introduction with Philander Canedy and his sister Annie, Canedy left for the house to accompany the two black gentleman. Unlike the exuberant and friendly Andrew Robeson and Nathaniel Briggs Borden, Philander Canedy was quiet and, not unlike his residence, reserved and unassuming. Annie, on the other hand, was gregarious and sociable.

"You must forgive my brother," implored Annie. "He is not always so austere."

"Oh, please, don't take on such a concern. We found your brother quite pleasant. Didn't we, Timothy?"

"A gentleman."

"No, you don't understand. He is the life of conversation and a whip of whimsy. But he's not himself. You see, we just received news that his son William Barnabas Canedy, has died in the war."

"My God, Miss Canedy. What sad and tragic news."

"By all means, our condolences," lamented Tim.

There are very few people I know as courageous and fearless as the gallant Timothy Cadman. However, the mere talk of dying unhinged him. Having had an intimate encounter with it, death was a foe that desperately haunted him. Though we had experienced the expulsion of human life together, unlike Tim, I had found it an adversary who needed to be acknowledged and confronted, despite any dread or horror I may feel. To Tim, the mere talk of loss of life, let alone the sight of it, unhinged him.

Still, it surprised me, since he was with me when Grandmamma passed away. The fellowship we shared at the moment she left us had been enough to subdue what fear we both felt at that moment. In such hardships, there is truly solace in numbers. However, Grandmamma's death was unlike that of his close friend who had been very ill and died alone as Tim held his hand—or the demise of Annie Slocum, who we discovered hanged by the neck in a barn at Cuttyhunk Island. Both deaths had plagued him. But with Grandmamma's passing, I was sure that he had turned a corner, that death had become a lesson in disguise—that he would see it for what it is, an unavoidable and challenging encounter. At the time of Grandmamma's passing, I found Tim surprisingly dauntless and uplifting in helping me through a jarring time, with a display of courage and support. I thought that he had tamed the existential fear that death held over him. It was apparent that he had regressed.

Grandmamma often said, "Fear is an illusion that has no analytical understanding beyond life itself. And if it cannot be accepted and dismissed, the only other defense is defiance, if one can bear it." I have chosen the latter. Don't misunderstand my view on the matter. I do not take an insentient approach to death. However, living life to its fullest, making a sword from a plowshare, and fighting the good fight while I am able, is a prescription that alleviates, if not domesticates, any practical fears I may harbor. Yes, Grandmamma, "Fear can be but a splinter that stings or the scythe that removes the legs of stability from under you."

"If you can excuse me, ladies I must help Razor with the rowboat," claimed Tim.

I knew Razor needed no help with the small craft. I chose to believe him.

The news Annie Canedy relayed to us brought fresh memories of Samuel and his whereabouts. That old splinter of fear buried itself deep into my resolve. But as Seabury Cory said of his son, no news is good news. Yet, it was a systematic torment. The best way to deal with it was to not think about it. To do so would be to worry if the sun would rise tomorrow or the moon tumble out of the sky. Worrying about something that I had no control over was infertile and senseless—not doing so, easier said than done.

"Is this not the William Barnabas Canedy homestead," I asked.

"Yes. He was my father. William, Philander's son, was his grandson. They both shared a name. My father had thirteen children. And all those that haven't died have moved up town. Only Phil remains."

"Do you not live here?"

"No. I live in the center of town, where I teach at the High Street Grammar School."

"A teacher. Such an admirable occupation."

"Yes, if not an indelible one. Everyone remembers his or her teacher. Once you are gone, you go on living in the memories and impressions of fledgling mature minds. Most of my sisters are teachers. And yes, you are right. It is an admirable occupation. And what do you do, Miss White?"

"Seamstress …" I said, pausing. "Actually, I am a writer for a daily in New Bedford."

"A correspondent?"

"I suppose I am," I said, unsure what my title was.

"Must be fascinating. Whereby I mold the minds of children, you do the same with adults."

I thought very hard about what she said. "I suppose there's some truth to it. In any event, I just started working in the newspaper business. I have a lot to learn. And I'm certain that my editor, who is an honorable man, reports the news and life as it is."

Philander Canedy came down from the house, escorting the two runaways. The men toted burlap sacks containing their personal belongings, while Philander carried their lunch pails.

"This is their food for the day," he explained, handing me the two containers. The hot meals radiated through the steel lids and up to my hands. "They may keep the tins. They were donated by our church, you see."

Taking the small sacks from the men, containing gifts, such as a comb, straight-razor, soap, and other mementos, Tim carried them down to the dory. I helped store them, along with the hot meals, beneath the bench at the stern. Excited, Razor ran up to greet his two new comrades.

"*When the train come'a singin it's to freedom we shall go*," he chimed, proudly. Joyful, he shook the free slaves' hands, nearly jouncing their limbs from their sockets.

"Come, Mister Assagai," called Tim. "Help me push the boat out."

I climbed into the dory as Tim and the big man shoved the craft into deep water. A few yards away, the two black men and the Canedys stood silently, heads bowed, arms around one another, reciting prayer. After long good-byes, we were finally out in the middle of the river and on our way back to the ship.

I looked toward the old, cedar clapboard homestead and Annie, who tarried along the shore waving. Her brother had taken down the flag and, with a lumbering stride, trudged up toward the house, carrying the Stars and Stripes under his arm.

Philander Canedy was a sad man—a spool of pain trying to keep the thread of social propriety and normalcy wound tight while silently mourning the loss of a beloved son. His abolitionist calling could only strengthen his resolve to help the runaway slaves, if only to grant his son's sacrifice just cause. My heart could not envision what a father must feel. With Samuel's whereabouts uncertain and classified as missing, I could only pretend to know how Seabury Cory was enduring. As with Philander Canedy, I prayed that I would never need to know.

With all the weight in the small sixteen-foot dory, Tim hoisted a small sail. Since the wind was out of the northwest, the uplifted canvas helped push us along, making Razor's job at rowing easier.

I sat in the bow while Tim trimmed sail. Old Jim, as he liked to be called, sat on the floor. His companion, Levi Taft, sat abreast of him. They played a game of dominoes. The painted wood tablets were a gift by Annie Canedy, which were cut and fashioned by her brother. Delighted with the leisurely sail, the two men played quietly. While he rowed, Razor was distracted by the game, wishing he could play. Enthusiastically, he would distract one player or the other and offer his advice on which domino to plop down.

With the canvas trimmed and tied in place, Tim climbed up to the bow and sat by me. He looked around, making sure there were no horsemen in boats following.

"Sorry about not being very friendly back there," he said.

"I understand. Hearing about someone dying is not pleasant news."

"To tell you the truth, it wasn't that."

"No?"

"It's all that has happened since Sam left us. Philander Canedy's misfortune just brought it to the forefront."

"Oh."

"I am not the real captain of the *Sphinx*. It is not my ship. I'm just caretaker. And that's fine. But my best friend is away at war … well, I know you feel the same … more so. I wish Sam were here. I miss his companionship. Philander's son reminded me of the perils he must be facing, and I needed to occupy my mind with labor as to not get muddled. You know how I can get around tragedy. I'm sorry for my weakness."

"It is not weakness," I insisted. "You are a sensitive and compassionate gentleman, Timothy. Those are rare qualities and exceptional virtues in a man, proof of strength and consideration for others. Look at yourself. You are tough and able, a man's man. Few men are as fearless and valiant as you. I have witnessed it on exploits we have taken with Samuel on the *Sphinx*, and you know it. Everyone knows it. The feelings you have for Samuel are praiseworthy. But try not to think about the worst. It is only cruel to do so. Make it easy on yourself. I do … I must."

"You handle these things better than I do, Emily. How can one make things easier … change the way you feel?"

"Listen. Seabury Cory's advice is what we must follow. There is no proof that misfortune has befallen Samuel. If his own father is not worried, why should we. I have chosen to take his advice and not worry about things I have no control over, nor know for certain. Yes, it is easier said than done, but adopting such a neutral posture will make you stronger. It has me."

"I suppose," he said looking away.

In a ploy to advance his spirit, I kindheartedly gripped him by the arm.

"That is what Samuel would want from us … to be strong and resolute, not think of him every minute of the day. Do not mourn or grieve the unknown, Timothy?"

"I will try," he reflected, relinquishing a placid smile.

"Besides, you are the conscript mistress to Samuel's metaphoric mistress, the *Sphinx*. That schooner is precious to Samuel. The confidence he has placed in you can only be thought as commendable. And to be near the *Sphinx* and take care of her is like being with Samuel."

"Sometimes I think you should have been born a man and I a woman," he chortled. "I hate it when I get so sentimental and emotional. You are one of the few people that has witnessed it. You handle such matters so much better."

"You cut yourself short, Timothy."

"What can one say about that day on Cuttyhunk when we discovered that poor girl hanging from the rafters of that fish shed. Confronted with it,

I ran from that scene as quick as I could. You, on the other hand, remained."

"I had no choice but to confront it, Timothy. Annie was a friend. Even though she was dead, she needed me, just like your best friend needed you when he died. Did you not tell me that you held his hand as he departed?"

"Yes. You are so sensible."

"So are you. You just don't give yourself any credit."

"You may not know this, Emily, but I have learned about life and death by watching you. I'll never forget when Charlotte died. I like to think that you and I helped her find her way into the afterlife."

He placed his hand over mine and held it tightly. "Why are you so wise, Emily White?"

"You should read more books," I said, feeling somewhat uneasy. The touch of his hand was warm and pleasing. It stirred something inside me, something I was afraid of expecting. I was at a loss for words. Such a fine specimen of a man, tall, muscular, handsome, yet his most valued male trait was sensitivity. But to Tim, it was a signpost to weakness, as it is to most men.

He squeezed my hand. I finally remembered. His touch made me shiver. Not with trepidation, you understand, but with unanticipated delight. Wicked, wicked, delight. I was suddenly bombarded with sensual awareness. I tore my hand away and pretended to fix the hat upon my head.

"My, it's getting windy all of a sudden," I affirmed, though the breeze was but a whisper.

"You're a good friend," I heard him say as my thoughts went elsewhere. "Sam is so lucky to have you."

"He is," I said, uncertain about what I just said.

"Thank you, Emily," he squalled.

And with those words, Captain Timothy Cadman leaned over and kissed me.

Now, I must explain, for I am flustered. I believe Tim meant to innocently kiss me on the cheek as friends often do. Be that as it may, a small wake jostled the boat and, unintentionally, my face swung to meet his, and warm lips settled upon one another. Impetuously, I laced a hand around the back of his head, to steady myself on the rocky boat, you understand, and entwined my fingers firmly between his silky, brownish hair. Wickedly, I held his subtle, irreproachable lips onto mine. It was short, seductive, and wrong. However, I could not help it—I did not help it. Flushed with unanticipated craving, I prayed for forgiveness while holding him captive in a fury of merciless kisses, bathing his lips with my raping tongue while relishing in corporeal passion and egregious, if not manic, desire. If I had been standing, I would have plummeted into the dory's bilge and onto my back and satisfied this rousing fury of passionate arousal I was feeling—taking him down with me. These were unexpected sensations, a delirium I never realized I would be stricken with, let alone espouse to. This occasion was more forceful, if not more shameful, than the last time I engaged in such concupiscent feeding. When I realized my behavior, I immediately pulled away, pretending the event never happened.

"You are a good friend, Emily White," I heard him say as he stood up and casually moved toward the stern of the boat. Not heeding, or perhaps unaware, Tim went about the business of trimming sail as if nothing out of the ordinary had occurred between us. He was much braver than I could give him credit for.

I was left alone with my fiery thoughts and simmering heart, attempting to decipher what had just taken place. I had to keep reminding myself with restrained regard. Tim and I were simply friends, as he declared. Samuel Cory my only true love. Memorandum about how I had promised Samuel that I would wait for him kept stinging my brain. Disloyalty washed over me. Bizarre thoughts filtered through my mind. What if this were not a dory with five people on it? What if Tim and I were in a dark room alone instead—a mattress factory—with feathered cushions paving the floors? I had to make light of it—induce comical excuses, you see. For, if allowed to happen, such unfaithfulness could spawn so many casualties—Samuel, Amy, all my friends, to mention nothing about betraying myself. To indulge in such elicit behavior would be to brand myself with the letter 'A' by Hawthornean measures and excommunicate me from the world I love. It would strike deep in the heart of my village where I live. Good God! I would have to move to a place where I could hide, like New York City or Boston, or wrap myself in sacks and move to Istanbul where no one would ever find me.

I placed my hand over the side of the boat and dipped it into the cool river water. I ran my fingers up and down my face. It did little for the guilt I was feeling and raging desire that still lingered. Was it carnal lust or just a girl wanting to be held and loved? Was my need for Tim, for Samuel, or was it for any man that could hold and love me? I knew I was getting older. Although I felt I was still just a girl, my body was telling me I was a woman. I immersed my hand in the river water once again and tried convincing myself that I was the rogue. If anyone needed to be rescued it was Tim, not me. How could I have mistaken friendship for anything more? Grandmamma, where are you? Your advice is needed now more than ever.

Once we were on the schooner, Tim raised sail immediately to take advantage of favorable winds. *Sphinx* weaved between anchored ships as the mill town of Fall River receded. With the three runaway slaves aboard it made for a joyous celebration. They sang and danced as we raised sails, tugged halyards, and winched sheets. I leaned on my elbows along the port rail watching the Fall River Steamboat maneuver away from its assigned pier. Aaron Kerr came over with an apple.

"We finally hae some time tae hae an apple together," he said, handing me one.

"How's the bump on you head?"

"It's nothin,' Emily. It helps hold mah hat on mah heed."

I laughed. "You're a hero, you know?" I took a bite of my apple.

"At' is foolish tock, lassie."

"Not to Isaac Sinclair," I said, munching on the fruit.

The Fall River Boat rang its bell and hooted its whistle as it nigh our stern. With Eli at the wheel, Tim ran to the quarterdeck and admonished the captain of the backing paddleboat as it nearly collided with the dory that was being towed behind the schooner.

"Crazy buggers," grumbled Aaron.

"Such a busy harbor," I declared. "Look how fast the city is growing." I pointed. The gnawed fruit hanging from my hand. "All those houses. People piled onto one another. I could never live that way."

"Aye. It's a wee Glasgow. Look at aw those new mills."

"Did you know that they use steam engines to run the looms?"

"Aye, we hae done work in a mill ur two." He named a few. "The Metacomet Mill, the Oliver Chase Thread Mill. An' jist before comin' ontae th' *Sphinx,* we worked at th' Wamsutta."

"The Wamsutta Mill in New Bedford?" He promped my curiosity.

"Aye, waur that fellaw was foond dead not long ago."

"Was the professor there with you?"

"Ye mean, was ah thaur wi' th' Professor. Aye."

"How long ago was that?"

"Oh, main hae ben a foorth nicht, now. Th' engine ne'er worked correctly. We arr still haven' trooble with it."

The revelation that Winton and Aaron were at the Wamsutta Mill around the same time Asha Potter was discovered dead was serendipitous to say the least.

"Ye see 'at rubble granite mill just thaur, wi' th' big red chimney … 'at is th' Metacomet Mill, a dark an' gloomy plaece tae wark."

He pointed to still another building, a smaller one, on a slight incline and near the shore. It was difficult to see with all the construction along the waterfront.

"Noo, ye see 'at other mill thaur, lassie, th' wee one... 'at is th' Chase Thread Mill. But ah could find nae mice working thaur."

"Mice?"

"Aye. Workin' mice weavin threid."

"I'm to believe that they employee mice to weave thread," I inquired, sounding silly even asking.

"Aye. In Scootlund. Dornt they use mice in America, too?"

"You mean mice. Instead of people."

"Aye, mice, tae run th' machinery."

One had to lend a sharp ear when Aaron spoke. His bumpy accent was thick and in concurrence with a Scottish idiom, making it difficult to understand him at times. Though I heard him quite clearly, this time he made little sense. However, I made less sense since I was still asking questions.

"You mean a rodent … a rodent spinning thread."

"Aye. Wee rodents. Have ye nae heard about it."

"Can't say I have."

"There's thes fella in Scootlund who has an entire mill of mice weavin threid.

I laughed, though I didn't want to appear disparaging or gullible. I had been acquainted with Aaron but a couple of days and he could very well have been teasing me. However, he sounded sincere, if not sober.

"Mice weaving thread." I pondered, hoping he would stop talking about it.

'Aye, David Hatton frum Dunfermline, Scootlund. Mice eat a wee bit. An' dornt mined workin' oan Sundays."

I was reluctant in asking him anymore about the Mouse Mill. Then I thought … *why not? Silly stories spawn silly questions.*

"Did the mice get a dinner break?" I giggled.

"Aye. A tea break, even. Hatton was a kin' mon an' gave lots of his money awa tae beggars an' pour."

"Money to the poor."

"Aye, lassie, th' pour and penniless."

As it often happened, Winton Macartney came marching over, looking for his apprentice. And though Aaron enjoyed his free time, unlike the mills where he had worked and had countless places to hide, on the *Sphinx* there were none. And up on deck, out in plain view, was as good a place as any.

"Aaron, has the stack been bolted down like I instructed?"

"Almost finished, Professor."

"Then get to it, man. That boiler is not going to install itself."

"Aye, Professor."

"Idle hands and an idle mind, leave intentions in decline."

"Aye, Professor. I'll get it done Sairr, reit away."

Impassive by his employer's reproach, Aaron lingered, drew an apple from his pocket, and handed it to me.

"Remembe' … an apple a daee, Emily."

With Aaron off to work, the professor finally addressed me with a simple greeting. Not that I was looking for one. Winton Macartney was a practical man and one with priorities. And his priorities were imperative and came before casual conversation or superfluous salutations. We have been on the same sailing vessel for two days and we barely exchanged a word.

"Good morning, Miss White, I trust you are well."

"Yes, thank you."

He leaned on the gunwale rail and looked out toward the shore.

"Can I ask you a question, Professor?"

"Questions are fodder for the brain, Miss White. Ask away."

"Have you ever heard of a … a mouse mill?"

"Yes."

"You mean they really exist?"

"If you mean the Hatton Mouse Mill, yes it did, long ago. What of it?"

"Just curious," I marveled, unable to suppress the notion that I was being played.

"They tell me that you are a writer for a local periodical."

"They, Professor?"

"Yes, your man."

"Man? What man would that be," I asked, having no idea who he was talking about.

"The captain, of course," he said, with a slothful smile.

"The captain is not, 'my man', as you put it, Professor, but if you would like to know, I do work for the *Daily Whaler* in New Bedford."

"A writer? So, though intelligentsia does not grace the unassuming decks of this ship, there is one person aboard that may actually understand the difference between coordinating or subordinating conjunctions."

"Or dangling and participle modifiers, if you prefer," I sneered.

I can't say that I liked Winton Macartney. He was either mercilessly professional or unmindfully contemptuous. His only loyalty was to his profession. His personality was an amalgamation of an algebraic mind and mechanized heart. If I could describe the man in one word it would be dismissive. For that was how he treated any topic or individual he did not have a common interest with.

"You know, Miss White, newspaper writers may be proficient at uncovering a story, but most cannot project the written word with any expertise or fundamentally translate it onto parchment with any perceived competence."

"Oh, did I say I was a newspaper writer, Professor?"

"So, you are not a writer?"

"I did not say I was not."

"Miss White, do you or do you not write for a newspaper."

"I do not write for any newspaper, Mister Macartney. I write for myself. The newspaper pays me a wage for my work."

"Is that not the same?"

"No. What I do I accomplish with pride and as you mentioned, competence, I assure you."

In my conversation with Winton Macartney, I discovered that he thrived and found gratification in rivalry. Everything and everybody were an algorithmic equation. Unless you gave him a challenge or able to match wits, he would quickly dismiss you.

"You work for a paper but claim you are not on this vessel for a story and that the captain of this ship is not your man?"

"This ship is on a clandestine and perilous mission, Mister Macartney. Now would it make sense to announce it to the world in a public journal?"

I had quieted him for a minute as he gathered his thoughts. Once they were released, they were blistering.

"A woman on a ship full of men but not married to any of them?"

"Your point, Professor?" I finished my apple and thought twice of flinging it at him. I tossed it over the rail.

"No point at all, Miss White. But do you really think it is appropriate conduct. After all, voyaging offshore is a man's occupation."

"Mister Macartney, for your information, I may not be a wife to anyone on this ship, but in regard to the *Sphinx*, I am her mistress."

He frowned. "You refer to the ship in an effeminate gender yet claim to be her mistress. Quite the sapphic declaration."

"I suppose that disturbs you."

"So, you admit as much? You are proud of it?"

"I am not proud. I am honored. Honored to be a fiance-in-waiting to the proprietor of this vessel and a mistress to his ship."

"Now you confess to androgynous behavior."

"If you wish to think so. In the interim, I shall wait for my man. And as for the ship, if you are vigilant, Professor, and stay up late enough, you may just realize me making mad love to her."

I finally left him speechless. I took advantage of walking away before he could assemble a vile thought. I did not look back and allow him to witness the smirk on my face. What great banter! What fervid deliberation! It was wicked. Of course, I may have sounded agitated. However, if I did, it was for a purpose and to feed the professor's constitution. Having watched

Winton Macartney's curt interactions with officer and crew, I decided that somebody had to put him in his place, if such a place existed. Nonetheless, I found his inquisitiveness peculiar. Was this idle conversation or was he on an exploration expedition? And if so, what was he looking for?

I glanced back to the stern, but he was gone. Soon, I heard metallic hammering from deep in the ship. Winton Macartney was in the bowels of the schooner making love to his steam engine and interacting with what he understood and made him happy—if indeed such a man knew what happiness was.

I gave the matter with Winton further thought. Why was he so inquisitive? I would like to think he discovered an adversary who could match his wit and not treat him as an aberration, even if that adversary was a maiden in waiting and a mistress to a ship.

Chapter 13: The Anti-Slavery Whaling Society

To the captain's pleasure and the weary relief of the three escaping slaves, the sail to New Bedford was pleasant and uneventful. Regardless, it took us forever. The wind direction kept changing and *Sphinx* was made to tack from shore to shore as it tediously snaked its way down the murky Sakonnet River. It meant that our meandering jaunt would make it five times the distance by sea than by land—well worth it, considering we evaded any chance of capture or detainment.

We anchored just before nightfall. Once darkness fell upon the waters, we ferried the three black men from the *Sphinx* to the schooner *Advocator,* moored at Fish Island. The men were ushered below and made comfortable where they hid just beyond the clutches of those who would do them harm.

At low tide the next day, the venerable *Sphinx* was tugged into the dry dock just north of the whaling fleet. The barn doors to the berth closed, shutting out the sea, while an enormous steam pump drained the confined compartment. As the water was belched into the harbor, the schooner was buttressed from underneath and made to sit on its keel. By the end of the day, the berth was made dry, leaving only a few inches of water and exposing the barnacle pimpled bottom to the dry salt air. Here Winton and Aaron would continue their work installing the steam engine's bronze shaft and propeller.

Before the ship was towed into dry dock, Tim had shuttled me ashore. The now familiar facade of the *Daily Whaler* awaited me as I pushed open the door.

"Well, well, the juniow newspapwa giwl, Miss Emily White," trumpeted Ezra Hick. He circled his desk to greet me. "Have you weturned for the benefit of the papwa ow have you'wa good gwaces been exhusted elswhewe?"

I discovered early on that one must push back on Ezra Hick before he gets a running start and wears you down. Ezra had a charming pomposity that one had to approach carefully and with a courteous ferocity that did not sound scornful.

"Absence makes the heart yearn fondly, Mister Hick. Your greeting only exposes your longing for my company."

"I beg mewcy, young madam. I have no idea what you mean."

"Come now, Mister Hick. You miss me, and my arrival pleases you." I removed my coat and hung up my hat.

Miffed, he quickly retreated behind his desk. "Thewe's a meeting in Mistwa Fwench's office. He was hoping you would be able to make it in today."

"What sort of meeting?"

"Miss White, I am the executive clewk, what happens in administwation is beyond my duties."

A bit concerned about my absence, I hurried up the stairs to the office. Ezra Hick vigilantly watched me over the top of his spectacles as he usually did. I stopped my climb and gazed at him. Ruffled, he cleared his throat, turned his back to me, and made himself busy.

I could hear a murmured cacophony of voices coming from inside Rudolf French's office. The tempestuous exchange became louder as one shout interrupted another. Surprisingly it was a woman's cry that mitigated the lively flutter of conversation.

"Well, here I go," I said, turning the tarnished brass knob.

Once inside, the talk ceased and a consortium of heads, like a parliament of owls, turned to face me.

"Miss White, come in, come in," bellowed Rudolf, rushing over and finding me a chair. "For all those who do not know, this is Emily White—correspondent, writer, and now an agent on the freedom train."

The group applauded. I must confess to being very uncomfortable with such acclaim when I had done nothing to deserve it. Sheepishly, I sat down as quick as I could as to curtail the affirmative scrutiny given me.

"Miss White has been on one of our recent excursions to transport three parcels from Fall River. As a matter of fact, those parcels were forwarded just this morning."

"God bless you, Miss White," cried someone in the group.

"Let me introduce you, Emily."

Rudolf walked around the room with formal introduction. "I believe you have met Frederick Johnson."

"I told you we would meet again, did I not?"

"Yes, you did, Mister Johnson."

"And this is Zoeth."

Zoeth had a jocular smirk and gleeful twinkle in his eye when he noticed that I was surprised to see him.

"I know Zoeth well. He lives a few doors up from my cottage. I didn't know you were interested in this sort of thing, Zoeth?"

"Life's full of surprises, heh, Emily?"

"Yes, it is."

"And to your right is the eminent Box Brown," said Rudolf.

The black man bowed his head in greetings.

"Box Brown?"

"You may call me Henry, Miss."

"Of course. I know who you are. Henry Box Brown. Grandmamma spoke of a slave who escaped from a Virginia plantation by mailing himself north in a two by three-foot box."

"One and the same. I'm afraid that Box is how everyone knows me. But you can call me Henry or 'Freight' Brown, instead."

Everyone laughed.

"Mister Brown has been attending our little meetings for some time now. But I'm afraid this will be our last encounter since he is moving overseas," said Rudolf.

"Overseas. How exciting," I said.

"I hope it will be exciting, Miss."

"Box is on the run," Rudolf explained. "With all the rumors that his overseer has been spotted here in New Bedford, it is no longer safe for him to stay."

"On reflection, we will mail him in a much bigger box," piped Zoeth.

Everyone laughed.

"And to your right is Doctor Silas Brownell," said Rudolf.

Silas had a jolly, plump face and modest smile. A brown Quaker beard circled his face. Scant strands of glinting hair were pasted on his head with a popular pomade ointment made from whale blubber and beeswax.

"And, of course, you have met Hannah."

Hannah rushed over and embraced me. "Wompi wauchaunat," she recited proudly.

"It is a pleasure to see you once again," I told her. "I'm afraid I don't understand."

"It means White Guardian," she proclaimed. "And that is what you have become."

She tenderly stoked the side of my face. Since I was now part of the group, a conductor, an operator, helping those escaping bondage, it meant a great deal to her.

"You are now a defender of the black and the brown, supporter, and white sister to the Wampanoag. I welcome you to the Anti-Slavery Whaling Society stockholder's meeting."

There was applause all around. Silas Brownell got up and offered his chair to Hannah so she could sit close to me. I was relieved when he did, since the oleaginous salve he used in his hair had a pungent and nauseating odor.

"You have met everyone, Emily," declared Rudolf, sitting back down. "Back to business. Now as I was saying earlier … the *Advocator* just needs a minor refit, and she could make the voyage easily."

"Rudy. Be realistic. Half the planking on her is rotting or sprung," implored Zoeth. "If you were not using her as a station on the Underground Rail, she would be under water by now. The only thing that is keeping her afloat is slave labor."

Rudolf glared at him. Zoeth cleared his throat.

"Sorry, Rudy … poor choice of words."

"There is some truth to it, Rudolf," reflected Silas. "The runaways have been pumping out her bilge while they live on her. Otherwise, you would need to hire a man every day to pump her out or place her in dry dock for extensive repairs."

"Look, Rudy, I may not know much," claimed Zoeth, "but I come from a long line of coopers and shipwrights—my father, my grandfather. One thing I do know is how to build a watertight vessel. Ships are not that different from barrels. I have been a craftsman for over twenty years, and I must tell you that vessel is less than seaworthy."

"Alright, alright," howled Rudolf, vaulting out of his chair.

"So, you see, Rudolf, we need that money for vital commodities such as food, clothing, and transport," insisted Silas. "Repairing the ship with donations is out of the question."

Rudolf paced the floor. "What if I donate a thousand dollars of my own money?"

"Rudy, almost a third of that would go just for dry dock fees," theorized Zoeth. "And another two thousand just to re-plank the hull, replace hardware and spars—new sails."

Rudolf turned to Edgar Ryan, the *Daily Whaler*'s typesetter. "Edgar, how much does the society have in the kitty?"

Edgar, who was sitting at my desk taking a narrative of the minutes, pulled open a ledger and swept his finger along a page. "Three hundred and … forty-five dollars, chief. And the Methodist Episcopal African Church on Mill Street promised us a donation of fifteen dollars by the end of the week. That leaves us three hundred and sixty."

"If I can have permission to talk?" chimed Frederick Johnson, pushing back his chair and standing.

"By all means, Mister Johnson," said Rudolf. "For those of you who are unaware, Frederick has doubled our contacts since he joined our group and given up valuable stations and routes, most of them run by free blacks and former slaves. We often forget that there is a chain of free men, black and brown men, all along the Underground Rail route. Until recently, our little venture has been limited in both scope and color. We forget that most of the saviors to the slave population are the slaves themselves, is that not right Frederick?"

"I dare say if one traces the Underground Rail from Washington to New England, one will find that most safe houses are run by black brothers and sisters. Black folk are the unsung warriors in assisting runaways."

"Well, you are right, of course. And I'm sure you understand. It is just that we live in this little ivory world of ours here in New England and … well. I have pontificated enough. Go on Mister Johnson. You have the floor."

"Thank you, sir. Since I arrived, I try and stay out of financial matters. My major interest is in sustaining peace and harmony amongst agents and operators—good people such as yourselves. Let us not reject entirely the renovation of the ship outright but, instead, consider it as a future probability. We must pray on it and hope the Lord will hear our plea and supply the needed funds to raise the *Advocator* from its infirmity. Until then, let us map out conventional land passages north."

"Here, here," shouted Silas.

"Unfortunately, the Miller family in Providence has had a fire that destroyed their home," explained Edgar. "We will need to find a new safe house to deliver our parcels, should we choose that specific inland route."

"How about the Wilson place on the east end of Providence, just by the town of Seekonk," inquired Rudolf. "It is very rural there. Should be easy as a hideaway."

"I went over to speak to them," said Zoeth. "The Wilsons have closed their doors. They were raided a couple of weeks back and, though no runaways were discovered, they are now reluctant to use the home for a station. Afraid that now that they have been found out someone will burn down the house like they did the Miller place."

"There's no proof that anyone burned down the Miller place, Zoeth," maintained, Edgar. "The way I heard it the fire started in the kitchen."

"Yes, yes, the fire probably had nothing to do with their Underground Railway Station duties, but we do not want to press the matter," declared Rudolf. "We will have to look elsewhere." He looked over at Frederick Johnson for some answers. "What say you Mister Johnson?"

"I was just about to add. I know a couple of free black families that will certainly aid us. One in Providence and another in Worcester. As I mentioned earlier, most of those I assist in helping our people to freedom are other black folk."

"Yes, yes, we have established this. Where in Providence?" inquired Rudolf.

"In town—Federal Hill area. Reverend Joseph Lawrence. He has helped me in the past."

Rudolf walked over to the window and looked out toward the harbor and his schooner, the *Advocator*. A ribbon of smoke escaped from an open hatch. Inside, the group of runaways were cooking the noon meal.

The *Advocator* had served Rudolf French well over the years. Unwary neglect had crept up on her. From the *Daily Whaler*'s office window, the old girl still looked able and royal. She was a grand lady who had battled ocean pyramids in high latitudes, transverse the equator's distressful doldrums, and circumvented the tumultuous southern capes of South America and the Dark Continent. However, that was many years in the past. And like the decaying gutters on the building just outside his window, or the ligneous whaling vessels that had battled years of sun, wind, and rain, that sat in harbor in disgraceful decay, the *Advocator* had aged … and so had he. He studied his vessel in the distance and wondered where all the years had gone.

"*De profundis*."

"Well, Rudolf. What do you think?" asked Silas.

"Think?"

"Yes."

"About what?"

"Frederick here suggested we try Reverend Lawrence at Federal Hill."

A somber silence fell on the room. Someone coughed. A chair scraped along the floor in a high rasping screech, and the pendulum on the Seth Thomas hammered a thumping resonance.

"Yes, yes, the sooner the better, Silas. We're not getting any younger. And with all the fugitive hunters careening the countryside, we need to rush delivery of our parcels as soon as possible."

I looked over at Hannah. She smiled. For a short few seconds Hannah's mind and mine were as one. I could hear her inner voice endorse what I was thinking—urging me to air any proposals I may have.

"I have an idea," I blurted, holding up a finger.

There was a raucous shuffle of chairs as everyone turned to face me. Rudolf French hurried back to his desk and sat upon it.

"By all means, Miss White, let's hear it."

"I just wanted to mention that …"

He interrupted.

"Now listen everyone. I have confidence when this girl speaks, so let's hear what she has to say, shall we."

"As I was about to say. …"

"I know, she's just a woman," he pontificated. "But most of you have wives and I'm certain you lend them a credible ear. So, let's hear what she has to put forward."

"If you let the young lady speak, Rudolf, then we'll listen," protested Silas.

I sat quietly waiting in the event Rudolf had more to say. I was grateful that he was giving me an opportunity, even if I was, as he coarsely characterized me, just a woman. However, I couldn't hold old Rudolf's principles and moral standards against him—only work to change them. If I made the practice of attacking every man that expressed his common callowness, there would be very few men left to talk to.

"Yes, go on, Emily. We're waiting," he implored, somewhat impatiently.

"Right. As I was going to say—how about *Sphinx*?"

"*Sphinx*?" echoed, Silas. "What's a *Sphinx*?"

"What about her?" inquired Zoeth.

Having lived only a couple hundred feet from the schooner's berth at Point village, Zoeth was wholly familiar with Samuel Cory's thoroughbred schooner.

"What *Sphinx*?' sneered Edgar.

"Samuel Cory's schooner. The ship we just transported the three men from the Robeson and Canedy stations. We can use her to ferry them to Nova Scotia … at least this one time."

Everyone peered at Rudolf. Hannah reached over and threw her arm around me in thankful homage.

"How about it, Rudolf?" inquired Silas. "This *Sphinx* just may be our way out, until we can make other arrangements."

"I know Samuel Cory well," said Zoeth. "It is just the sort of thing he would vow to. After all, is that not what he is fighting for? But Samuel is away battling in the war. Who is in currently in command of the *Sphinx*?"

"Samuel's first mate, Tim Cadman," I confirmed.

"Can you inquire of him," requested Rudolf. "I mean … we would pay for the privilege and time, you see."

"I'm sure he will agree. Doesn't hurt to ask. But only if we could volunteer our services—free of charge." It was very bold of me to make such an offer. And I was uncertain whether I had overstepped my authority.

"When can you speak with him?"

"Timothy should be down at the dry dock where the *Sphinx* is having work done."

I pushed back my chair. Everyone got up with me.

"I'll go speak to him right now."

I walked toward the door. Everyone followed and watched me go. Ezra Hick scrutinized me as I descended the stairwell to the main lobby. At the top of the stairs, the Anti-Slavery Whalers Society congregated and pondered my success as I walked out of the building.

I sat at the table with an empty plate in front of me. Tim, on the other hand, was still eating. Hannah stuck a fork into a pork chop from the kitchen platter and dropped it into Tim's plate. He looked up at her and smiled.

"Thanks, Hannah. These chops are so great."

"Secret Indian recipe." She looked at me and rolled her eyes. "Men," she uttered, with tedious amusement.

Pork, potatoes, corn. Watching Tim eat was a cognitive if not feral exercise in famishment. He exercised the curious habit of eating one food group at a time and finishing it before moving onto another. First came the potato. When it was all devoured, he scooped up the vegetables, quickly and forthwith moving onto the meat. He carefully inspected the charred pork chop from all angles as if the severed chunks from the poor animal were still moving. He cut them into small, uniformed cubes, lining them up on his plate one by one, like a row of Royal Navy cadets, ready for inspection.

"You didn't eat much of your meat, Molly." I told her.

"I only eat the squashy part around the edges," she said.

"She loves the fat," chimed Hannah, cutting some and placing it on the young girl's plate.

"Some more?" she offered, holding the platter by my plate.

"Oh, no, thank you. I have had enough."

"Eat your corn, Molly," ordered Rudolf. "And stop playing with your food."

"Oh, Papa. I don't like corn."

"You don't? Everyone likes corn," I said. "It's an interesting vegetable."

"What can be interesting about corn?"

"Well, did you know that the average ear of corn has eight hundred kernels and sixteen rows, or that an ear of corn is really a flower and the kernels seeds and that Indians used it as money?"

"Money? Oh, you are joshing me."

"No … I'm not."

"Is that true, Hannah?"

"Yes, it is. The Wampanoag use maize in exchange for tools and cloth. They also used furs and dried fish."

"Yeah, well, I still don't like corn," moaned Molly.

She could be charming but, at times, challenging. Molly was a precious jellyroll of maturity and adolescence, further sweetened by a keen sense of mischief. If she should sink your boat, you will find Molly French floating priggishly nearby.

Rudolf threw down his knife and fork, sat back in his chair, and rubbed his belly. "Hannah, that was very tasty."

She took my empty plate away. Before Rudolf could intercede and insist his daughter finish her dinner, she did the same for Molly.

"How old are you Molly?" asked Tim.

"Depends on why you ask."

Tim was taken aback by the young girl's reply.

I was a veteran to Molly's quick wit and somewhat sullen manner. It was a pleasure to watch someone else with their tongue in the trap.

"I ask because I would like to know."

"Not a good enough reason."

"I need a reason?"

"Yep."

"I bet I can guess."

Handing his empty plate to Hannah, he smiled and prepared himself for the game … a game he was sure to lose.

"Good luck, Mister Cadman," said Hannah leaving for the kitchen.

"You can try," baited Molly.

"I'm good at guessing a girl's age."

"I doubt it," she said, crossing her arms.

Tim glanced at Rudolf. The old newspaperman closed his eyes and shook his head. He enjoyed when his daughter exchanged witticism with adults. In doing so, he was uncertain what he enjoyed best, the way Molly chewed them up or how she spit them out.

"Seven," blurted Tim.

"Nope."

He winced, "Six? … no wait, you must be older than that … seven, did I say seven?"

"Not on your best day," she snarled, tossing him a duped smirk.

"Nine, then."

She glared at him and shook her head. "I thought you said you were good at this?"

The only other person I knew who engaged in such standoffish sport was Amy; a practice Amy never outgrew. With Molly, this haughty behavior was in its infancy. Already she was a whiz at it.

"Ten. Eleven. Come now, you have to be one of those."

"I don't have to be anything," she said, smugly. "But if you must know,

I'm nine years, three months, and two weeks old."

"Wait a minute. I said nine."

"You left out the three months and two weeks. That makes me nearly ten."

"She's nine going on forty-two," declared Rudolf. "Now, Molly, be polite with our guest."

"You win," said Tim.

"Papa, when can I go down to Charleston to see Mother?"

"Soon, dear, soon."

"You said when I was of age. I'm nine now, going on ten."

Rudolf shook his head, trapped by a conundrum of his own making. He had promised his daughter that he would take her to South Carolina to visit her mother when she was of age, and he had no intention to do so any time soon. "When you are a little older," he said.

"You say that every year. Don't you think a girl who is nine plus three months and two weeks is old enough to travel on her own, Mister Cadman?"

I stretched my limb under the table and gave Tim a swift kick. Abashed, he looked over. I shook my head.

"That will be all, Dorothea. We will talk about it another time."

"But, Papa, you said when I was old enough you would take me."

"That's enough, I said." He wiped his mouth with a towel and got up. "Now let's help Hannah clear the table."

"Can I go to my room, please?"

"If you like."

The young girl pushed back her chair.

"Must you go Molly?" I asked.

"If you stay, I will guess how tall you are," pledged Tim.

"Do you have a ruler?"

"You mean a yard stick?"

"If that is what you call it."

"Ah, no."

"Then we would never know how tall I am, would we?"

Tim grimaced. Molly got up and walked away.

"Say goodnight, Molly," insisted Rudolf.

"Goodnight," she sighed.

Working a toothpick between his teeth and shaking his head, Rudolf affectionately watched as his offspring ambled away. "Shall we retire to the parlor?" he said, chuckling at his daughter's sulking charm.

We sat discussing the newspaper business, slavery, and a glimpse into Rudolf French's analytical view on how life used to be and should be. The parlor was small and unassuming, typical of a colonial style home. The sofa we sat on faced two double hung windows overlooking busy Front Street, and had intimate proximity to pedestrian traffic. The brick structure was built right up to the sidewalk where, occasionally, a child or two were discovered, noses smooched against the glass and peering inside—as one just did. Rudolf rushed to the front door and chased the youth away.

"This sort of thing happens quite frequently around this time," explained Rudolf, closing the door. "There's a school around the corner … and well, they are probably looking for Molly."

He went over to a corner cabinet and retrieved a bottle of liquor. "You will have a drink with me, will you not, Mister Cadman?"

"Can't say I'll refuse one."

"It is exceptional stock, my boy, and I only bring it out for special occasions."

"I see."

Rudolf poured the liquor into a stout crystal glass. "It's French brandy—cognac, you know. Straight from the fields of Angouleme on the banks of the Charente River in the west of France."

"I have never had Brandy," said Tim, sniffing the glass.

"Or been to France," I said, stating the obvious.

"You're a connoisseur already, my boy. Always sniff your brandy before you drink it. It tutors the palate … enhances the flavor."

"I can smell the grape in it," declared Tim, nose in glass.

"White grape, my good man. This cognac is one of the little treasures given to me by one of the whaling captains, you see. Drink up, my boy, drink up."

Tim took a sip of the amber spirits, shut tight his eyes, and grimaced as the burning elixir seeped down his throat. "Good." he grunted, finally coughing.

I took a sip of flavored milk from my glass, pondering why men drank such harsh refreshment.

"How's your chocolate milk, Emily? Warm enough?"

"Fine, sir."

Rudolf poured himself a brandy and swished it in the glass. Walking to a window, he held it up to the light and studied it a while. "Some men drink this nectar for the flavor—others simply because they can afford it. And then there are those who feel they need to observe life through its glorious, luminous glow." Bringing the glass to his lips, he threw back his head and promptly emptied it. He looked down into the small goblet as if it was never filled. "And there are those that use this distilled ambrosia for medicinal purposes … at least that is what they tell themselves," he continued, somewhat somberly. "Only to realize, in time, that the nagging obstacles of life only return stronger and with a vengeance the next morning. Restraint and forbearance, Mister Cadman. You know what I mean?"

"I do, sir," said Tim, quite aware that he had trouble holding liquor.

"Have another, my boy."

He filled Tim's glass before it was emptied. Tim looked over at me with a cringing glance. Rudolf poured himself a double.

"The secret to mixing business and drink is to pour your adversary two glasses to your one," he advised. "Unless amongst friends."

He moved across the room and settled into a plum-colored wing chair. Done with metaphysical notions and conceptual speculations on the merits of serving hard drink, it was time to get down to business.

"When do you expect the grand lady to be back in the water, Captain?"

"Tomorrow or the day after, at the latest."

"Excellent."

"She is being equipped with a steam engine and having her shaft and propeller installed."

"When can you leave?"

"Immediately. How many people are we transporting, sir?"

"The same three you picked up in Fall River. And stop calling me sir. It's Rudy."

"Very well," said Tim, asserting himself with a manly gulp of brandy. I reached over and placed my hand on his arm.

"Be careful of your condition," I warned him, under no uncertain terms.

"Condition?" blurted Rudolf. "Are you alright, my boy?"

"How about the family in the barn," I said quickly.

"Family … what family?" stuttered Rudolf.

I gave my question rational scrutiny. I knew I had said something I should not have. I had promised Molly that it would be our little secret. The fact that I was aware of the runaways shrouded in the French barn became an element of indiscretion. I felt guilty. Betrayal was not a lesson I had wished to teach young Molly French.

"Molly," uttered Rudolf, as the revelation washed over him.

"I'm sorry, sir … I mean, I did not see any reason … well, the poor darling had a secret and she wanted to share it with somebody. I promised her I would keep her secret."

"That's quite alright, my girl. Have no fear. I will not forsake your trust. I'll just tell Molly that I told you about the Bonneau family. I don' mind that she has shared it with you, after all you are part of the anti-slavery society now, but she must remain careful with who she shares secrets."

"The Bonneau family?" I said.

"Yes, they escaped from two different plantations, a hundred miles apart. Quite extraordinary ... really. We rarely see complete families on the run. It is common practice that they are separated when sold and lose touch."

"Why don't they just come along when we leave for Nova Scotia?" suggested Tim.

"I thought of that," said Rudolf. "But I have been waiting. They are unsure whether they want to continue north. They have been to the black church on Mill Street and have made friends and come to like it here. I promised I would try to find them work. But it's not safe at the moment. Every day, more and more plantation overseers are emerging with edicts of seizure. A couple more weeks and they may not have a choice in the matter."

"What sad news," I said.

"I hear you had some trouble in Fall River smuggling out one of the men."

"With the superlative on trouble," I added.

"Oh, it was nothing," said Tim, trying to put good light on the incident. "Aaron Kerr, one of our crewmen, had a scuffle with one of the men who were chasing us as we made our way back to the ship from the Robeson estate."

"Scuffle? What sort of scuffle?"

"Let us show you," I said. "We thought that you might know something about it. Do you have it, Timothy?"

Tim stood up, reached under his shirt, and pulled out the pistol he had hidden. Rudolf flinched in his chair nearly spilling his drink.

"Where did you get it?" he asked.

"Aaron took it from one of the men that was chasing us as they tussled on the ground."

Tim handed the newspaper editor the weapon. The man swept the gun away with the back of his hand.

"Never point a gun at a man unless you mean to shoot him, my boy. Grip first, always hand it over grip first."

"Oh, it's not loaded."

"Makes no difference. Not polite, not etiquette, and never safe."

"Yes, sir."

"Such a sinister-looking thing," I declared.

"Never handled a pistol before," acknowledged Tim.

"Quite alright, my boy," said Rudolf, turning the gun around in his hand. He made certain it was not loaded. "Not everyone is familiar with the weapon of choice for killing your fellow man."

"My father had a rifle for shot. I used it for hunting, but you don't see pistols that often."

"There are so many of these being developed nowadays. Those with good ideas or money get their patterns manufactured. This little hostile is an uncommon one."

"We had someone on the crew who was familiar with such things look at it," I said. "He was very familiar with the manufacturer. Said it was called a LeMat."

"Yes, see here, stamped on the frame just above the trigger. CS TDP," said Rudolf.

"CS. Does that not stand for Confederate States," asked Tim.

"You are correct, my boy. TDP, TDP," recited Rudolf. "Where have I seen those initials before?"

"You seem to know something about pistols," said Tim.

"Follow me," directed Rudolf, handing him back the gun.

He led us past the front door to a room adjacent to the parlor. The room was Rudolf's study. He took us to a stately desk and removed the things that lay on top, including books, old publications of the *Daily Whaler*, and other newspapers.

"This is my work desk away from work," he said. "Inside is a rare collection of … well you will see."

Inserting a key, he lifted the entire top of the desk exposing a secret compartment. What was exposed was an assortment of weapons—pistols. Half of the guns lay neatly placed for display while the other half were strapped to the compartment lid or desktop.

"Wow, that is impressive," exclaimed Tim. "Look at all that glimmering hardware. What are you doing with all these guns?"

"An abridged compilation of weaponry used by our military and the average gentleman. It's what I collect."

"Collect? For what?"

"For pleasure," I informed him. "I collect books, Amy collects seashells, and Mister French collects … well, guns."

Tim scratched his head. "If you say so."

"Well said, my girl. Your captain friend is not a collector and may never be. Collectors are born. Few are steered toward such a habitual pastime as collecting."

"That one there," directed Tim, pointing. "That's an attractive weapon."

"Good eye, young man. It's a percussion cap Colt Navy. One of the most popular revolvers made today."

Rudolf unstrapped the revolver from its resting place and handed it to him, pistol grip first. With one eye closed, Tim looked down the barrel and spun the bullet cylinder. Though I was almost certain he had no idea what he was looking for.

"This is what naval personnel use?"

"That's a misconception. It's issued to ground forces. See here." Rudolf took the revolver in hand. "That engraving on the cylinder is a naval scene, a battle in Texas and why it has adopted its name."

"That one there is a similar weapon."

"That one is also a Colt. An early model. The 1848 Dragoon. Larger caliber."

I ran my hand along one of the guns in the cabinet. This peaked Rudolf's desire to expound on his prized gem.

"Like it, Emily?'

"Well ... I like the artwork ... how it's made."

"Henry Derringer pocket pistol. Single shot."

"The scrolled engraving and ivory inlay is beautiful," I pointed out.

Looking into the concealed compartment, I would have to admit that the machinery of weapons lying there, with their polished brass, garnished blue steel, hand rubbed wood, and embellished scrolling, made for wonderful displays of art and ornamentation. No wonder Rudolf French would want to collect them. It is bewildering that such alluring grandeur and instruments of death could consolidate the eye and mind into appreciating their value, whether as a piece of art or a merciless firearm.

"Here," said Tim, handing the gun collector the LeMat revolver. "You should have this for your collection."

"Are you sure, my boy?"

"I have no use for it."

Rudolf proudly strapped the revolver in the case between a Stocking Pepperbox pistol and a Remington Navy. At least, that is what he called them. He backed away and admired his new acquisition.

"Looks fine there, don't you think?" He patted Tim on the back.

"Sure does, sir."

Rudolf locked his desk and we all returned to the parlor where Hannah was waiting with a fresh cup of chocolate milk.

"I am taking a cup up for Molly," she declared.

"Good idea," said Rudolf. He finished his drink. "Another one?"

"No thanks. I need to negotiate with the dry dock warden about the fee and the use of the pit. I don't want to be at a disadvantage."

"Good thinking, my boy." Rudolf poured himself another. "One more, just to blind the devil," he claimed.

Rudolf's drinking concerned me a little. A drinker should know his limitations and I could only trust that he knew his.

"Mister French, have you heard any news about Asha's death," I asked.

"I'm afraid not. I'm sure you remember Officer Frank Ward. He looked into it and uncovered nothing."

"Did he not find anything at the site?"

"Afraid not. By the time the police got to the Wamsutta Mill to investigate, the scene was scrubbed clean."

"What about the letter?"

"Letter?"

"Yes, the one I found on Asha."

"What about it?"

"Was it of any consequence?"

"Oh, it's just about two runaways."

He took the letter from a table drawer and handed it to me. I was reluctant to open it.

"I was hoping you could find a clue about Asha's murder."

"No, nothing like that, I'm afraid."

The letter was watermarked with a stamp or seal on the top left-hand corner.

"Mister French, what is this stamp."

"Some sort of letter head, I suppose."

"Have you looked at it?"

"Yes, but it is smeared and hard to read."

I had the strange feeling that he was being somewhat ambiguous, if not evasive. I walked to the window and held the letter to the light. Along the bottom of the seal it read *E pluribus unum*. Along the top was written "Tyrone Dukes Plantations." In the center was the familiar illustration of the palmetto Tree with the letter S to its left and C to its right. I had wondered why the name Tyrone Dukes was familiar, when it finally dawned on me.

"Mister French, have you looked at the name on this seal?"

"Dukes Plantations," he verified. "It's where Victoria lives."

"Is that not odd?"

"What do you mean?"

"Do you have that coat button I retrieve from Asha's hand?"

"Let me get it." Leaving the room, he returned with the fastener.

"If I remember correctly, you said there were some initials stamped on the back side?'

"Yes, ah …?" He studied the back of the button, quietly, "TDP," he blurted.

"The initials on the gun."

"That's right. That is where I had seen it … on the button. *De profundis*!

"TDP, Mister French. Is that right?"

"Yes."

"Tyrone Dukes Plantations."

"My good Lord, Emily—the fastener, the gun, the letter? They are all connected."

He scurried over to the liquor cabinet and poured himself another brandy.

Chapter 14: Escape from New Bedford Harbor

The massive oak gates to the dry dock slowly swept open and *Sphinx* was carefully floated out of the enclosure. Two small whaleboats towed her clear of the docks as Rudolf and I stood watching from the quay. We were waiting for Tim who was off settling dry-docking fees with the dock master, while the newspaperman and I watched Eli Monroe steer the old girl out a safe distance. It was a breezy day. So even without canvas, *Sphinx*'s hull and rigging soon seized the wind, which helped steady her to a safe anchorage where she dropped her kedge. The small anchor would hold the schooner temporarily until we could row out to her.

"All the boys were placed on the schooner late last night," declared Rudolf. "Hidden away like smug chipmunks in a hollow log."

"I am very excited about sailing to Nova Scotia again."

"So I've been told."

"Last year with Samuel. This time with Timothy."

"Speak of the man, here's the captain now," declared Rudolf.

The newspaper editor and Tim shook hands.

"We're taking Frederick along to help settle the newcomers," informed Tim.

"I'm so happy you are coming along," I said.

"Hope I'm not in the way," said Frederick.

"Nonsense. If anyone's in the way, you are looking at her."

"I was not aware that you paid the dock fee, sir," said Tim.

"Tis nothing, my boy. The society is taking care of all expenses on this voyage."

"But the prop work had nothing to do with the voyage. It was essential."

"Are we not all?" declared Rudolf. "This is an engagement in righteousness, a campaign of benevolence, for, after the grapes are pressed, we all drink out of the same decanter. I will hear no more on the subject."

While the two men spoke, I noticed activity on Rudolf's schooner, the *Advocator*.

"Mister French, who are those men?"

A small party climbed down from the schooner and into a skiff—one in uniform. A policemen's uniform. Another man had his jacket sleeve pinned to his shoulder and struggled to get down into the small boat.

"Who in God's world?" snapped Rudolf.

"Who are they?" inquired Tim.

"I have no inkling, but they should not be boarding a vessel without proper authority."

"There's a policeman with them," I said.

"A good captain always carries one of these," said Tim, handing Rudolf a spyglass.

The old newspaperman brought the folding monocle up to his eye. "I see someone I recognize. Bulldog."

"Bulldog." I echoed.

"One of Morse's boys. Edward Bull. He's known around the docks as Bulldog."

"I can see the constable, but I don't know the other men," said Tim.

"May I look?" I held up the optics to the skiff as it rowed away.

"The one you call Bulldog. Is he the fellow with the stocking hat?"

"Yes, the heavily built one," replied Rudolf.

"That's the gentleman that Razor had trouble with down at the docks if you remember," said Tim.

"I doubt he's a gentleman," declared Frederick.

"They're rowing out to that big ship drifting near the light house at the mouth of the harbor," I announced.

"Palmer Island Light," Rudolf stated. "And that's Morse's ship."

"Something is up. We best get going," declared Tim.

"By all means, my boy. Go quickly. I pray you pay heed. I smell trouble in the air. And a newspaperman's nose can sniff danger miles away."

"It was a good thing we moved those men onto the *Sphinx* last night," I added.

"Now remember, you are a reporter for the *Daily Whaler*, my girl. I expect you to report and have a story when you return."

"I will, sir."

I extended my hand. Rudolf swept it aside and wrapped his arms around me.

"Take care, my dear."

Tim sat at the bow of the dory with the spyglass and studied activities on the ship by the lighthouse. It drifted by Palmer Island, waiting for the skiff to return. I looked back toward shore. Rudolf was arguing with a man in a stove-top hat and black wool tailcoat. I recognized him as Charles Tobias Morse. Morse danced with rage conducting a dispute with his contorted cane while throwing his arms in the air and pointing out to us. Rudolf French turned his back on the man and walked away. The cantankerous sea captain remained, complaining to a nearby mooring post or anything that would listen.

"I have a dreadful feeling about this."

"I think your concern is warranted, Emmie," agreed Tim.

"Those men on the ship by the lighthouse are pointing at us," added Frederick.

We arrived at the *Sphinx* about the same time the men in the skiff boarded the brigantine by Palmer light. The ship drifted along tiny Palmer Island, a small spit of land, which sat at the mouth of the harbor. As soon as our feet touched the schooner's deck, we made preparations to depart.

"Do we have everyone on board, Mister Monroe?"

"Everyone, sir."

"Very well. To your posts, men! Raise sail and let's get out of here."

We hurried toward the quarterdeck.

"Ready at the wheel, Mister Monroe."

"Aye, aye, Captain."

"Where are our parcels?"

"In the forecastle, hidden away but comfortable," said Frederick.

"Very good, Mr. Johnson. You are free to move about and lend a hand if you wish."

"My pleasure, sir."

Watching Tim give commands was an inspiring demonstration of a capable student addressing his mentor's instruction and directive to the letter—practically like watching Samuel himself in action.

"Get that anchor on board, Mister Assagai. Mister Cuffee, prepare to raise number one and number two jibs. James, help your brother. Hurry, hurry."

The Cuffee brothers were twin boys of color and not much older than sixteen. Sons of a Wampanoag father, they lived on Drift Road not far from me. When commanding the Cuffee brothers, Tim treated them as a unit. Thus, jobs assigned to them often required two men.

Razor raised the main sail. Aaron helped. With most its canvas airborne, the schooner began making speed rather quickly. Being a racing yacht, *Sphinx*'s advantage was its immediate acceleration and sustaining speed under calm conditions. She was a bit tender under a good blow and known to bury her rail in a seaway. Still, she gave all competitors a run for the bank.

Tim took the wheel from Eli and sent the helmsman forward with Frederick to raise the foresail. Looking up at the twin masts, he appraised wind condition and direction. With a busy harbor, he had a tricky maneuver ahead of him and everything had to be just right. Winton Macartney appeared from below and rested his hand on Tim's shoulder, computing the chances of leaving port safely—if at all.

"I'm certain you are aware, Captain?"

"You have something to add, Professor?" inquired Tim, looking down on the man's hand resting by his face.

"To the southeast … a black sloop just off Fort Phoenix."

"Don't you think I see her, Professor?"

"That vessel is on a converging course with the brig by the lighthouse. There's a conspiracy afoot, Captain. And that's not all. Just beyond, off on the horizon, is the Vineyard ferry steamer coming in fast. It's a narrow channel and bound to complicate things. You can't sail to the west. Palmer Island is in the way, and to the east you have the sloop and the shoal off Phoenix Beach. *Tsk*, *tsk*, what's a captain to do?"

"And your point, Professor?"

"It is obvious they are preparing to block our departure. I think they object to us leaving. We will be lucky to make it betwixt those two intersecting vessels. In the event you do pull it off, you may just collide with that approaching steamer. The laws of physics are against you, I'm afraid."

"Well, Professor, I am not afraid."

"Come now, Captain. You must concede. The portal out of this harbor is nearly blocked. Just return and drop anchor. See what they want. Why create a quandary?"

"I know what they want, Mister Macartney."

Though Winton Macartney had no objection to having runaway slaves on board, it was obvious that he was not concerned for their safety. They did not serve his interests. After all, they were just men. There was nothing mechanical about them.

The schooner continued on its way as Tim ignored any advice that Winton hinted to. With a stiff wind on the nose, the schooner made short tacks on its way to open waters. With the main, foresail, staysail, and jibs all hoisted, we approached hull speed as we soared toward the Acushnet River inlet. At the entrance of the estuary, it was obvious that the brigantine was slowly crawling to block our path. The foolhardy sloop, coming from the opposite direction, was doing the same. Both ships were working in unison with only one possible mission—to derail our floating underground train and apprehend its black passengers.

"All hands … prepare to come about," hollered Tim.

Eli emerged by his side. "Those two vessels look like they are going out of their way to obstruct our departure."

"I'm not turning back if that's what they think, Mister Monroe."

"If you try and sail out, there is bound to be a collision, Captain," the professor reminded him. Winton's advice was more meddlesome than helpful.

"Don't you have work to do on that steam engine, Professor?" barked Tim.

The two sailing vessels at the mouth of the river continued making headway—one from the New Bedford shore and the other from Fairhaven. It was like two sliding barn doors closing, with *Sphinx* the stallion that was trying to get away. Making matters more difficult was the paddle steamer *River Queen*, completing its trip from Martha's Vineyard. She chugged up the channel for her home port of New Bedford. Its impulsive captain had the brash reputation of preserving course and speed, and ignoring sailing craft until the last minute. It was one worry more for us.

"We will be threading a needle, Captain," declared Eli. "Channel's very tight through here."

"Hope you know what you are doing, Captain," blurted the cool-headed professor as he disappeared below.

With Winton gone, I took his place by the captain's side. Tim winked and smiled.

"Prepare to come about," was the order given.

The crew hastened to their stations.

"Ready about," bellowed the captain. "Release sheets."

"Releasing sheets," yelled a crew member.

The wheel was quickly turned to starboard. *Sphinx*'s tilting masts sprung upwards and its swan-white hull spun gracefully on its heels. Abruptly, all the sails whipped violently from one side of the ship to the other with a mad flutter. Jibs flogged uncontrollably, while sheets belted like lashing bullwhips.

"Mister Cuffee belay those jib sheets. Don't let any of those lines overboard," bellowed the captain.

The twin crewmen scurried along the deck, one to starboard the other to port, a mirror image of one another. Suddenly, and without warning, like a felled tree, and with just about the same impetus, the main boom hurled across the cabin top, sweeping the full girth of the ship's deck and slamming against the shrouds and deadeyes along the starboard rail.

"Mister Assagai. Secure that spar before someone gets hurt," ordered the captain.

At the halfway point of its tacking maneuver, *Sphinx* lost momentum. However, once the lines were fixed and made true, the old girl fell onto its new tack and accelerated on a course toward Palmer Island and the cryptic brig.

"What do you think, Eli?" said Tim. "Should we tack down the middle or behind her?"

"If you try down the middle you will surely lose the wind. Maybe safer to take a course around her stern."

"Think that's wise?"

"Shallow waters. The chart shows rocks there. But we should have room."

"Shoal waters are not an option, Mister Monroe. I rather deal with a danger I can see."

"Let's wait."

"Are we not traveling too fast, Timothy? The Island's coming up on us."

"We need speed, Emily, in the event we decide to sail between those two ships up ahead."

"If you stay close to the brig's stern, we can certainly avoid the rocks," suggested Eli. "since she is going in the opposite direction to the danger. There should be plenty of deep water to tack behind her."

"We shall see, Mister Monroe."

"Now remember, we will be carving the wind closely. The slightest change in its direction, and we could lose headway and drift up onto the rocks."

Tim looked worried. "What do you think I should do, Emily?"

"Only your best, Timothy."

"If only the ship was mine this would be an easy maneuver. This is Sam's ship. You know how much he loves her. What if I sink it? What of the crew? What … what should I do?"

He was very unsure of himself and becoming frantic. That was not good. The present circumstance beckoned absolute fortitude and gritty determination—tenacity that not all men were able to summon at a time like this. In any other situation, taking cavalier contingencies may have been considered arrogant but, in the existing circumstance, it was the distinction between the lives of those on board and freedom. Not an easy choice to make. I felt that brash confidence was Tim's best teacher. And he had to dig deep to find it.

"Getting close to the island, Captain," cautioned Eli. "She may ground herself soon if we don't take action."

"What do you think?"

"Not so sure you have room behind her now, she's moving too slowly."

"Choose on the side of freedom, Timothy." I encouraged him. "Samuel would be more disappointed if the ship were seized—especially if the runaways are apprehended. He would not want you to fail for the sake of not trying."

He sunk his teeth into his lip and nodded. "Prepare to come about!"

Spinning the wheel to port, he tacked the graceful schooner away from the ship and Palmer Island.

"This one's for you, Sam," he said to himself.

The mastheads swept a cloudless sky in a ninety-degree arch—the bow swung swiftly from west to east. The crew was vigilant and flogging sails were tamed quickly. From shore, it must have appeared that the *Sphinx* was manned by highly accomplished seamen instead of the unskilled, but keen, bunch that sailed her. Just as we accelerated in one direction, the ship was suddenly spun back onto the other. Practice made perfect, and the crew improved with every new course change. It was a cat-and-mouse game along a narrow channel. With the wind on the nose, and blowing from the direction we needed to go, the only way out was a series of calculated short tacks. Winton appeared on deck to witness what he predicted as certain catastrophe.

"A shame it's not ready. The engine would unquestionably be beneficial at the moment."

Tim ignored the engineer's blunt remark.

"Stay close, Mister Monroe. I may need to hand you the helm."

"What route are we taking, Captain?"

"Behind the stern of that brig. We will try again."

"A very close-haul. That option is closing. If she blankets our wind, we will flounder behind her. The current may push us onto the reef off the island."

"On the other hand, if the puffs are in our favor, it will quickly carry us by her."

"Or send us crashing into her stern."

"Looks like a prayer to the wind gods is in order, wouldn't you say, Captain?" aired Winton.

"Fingers crossed should suffice, Professor."

The *Sphinx* glided toward the brigantine and the possible pitfall that lingered behind its stern. I kept one finger tangled over the other and hidden behind my back.

"By God, we may just about make it," declared Eli.

"She's swinging around, she's swinging around," yelled James and Robert Cuffee.

Unpredictably, the brigantine slowly turned toward the island in an ambush to intercept our course.

"Our window of opportunity is closing, Eli."

"Options are called for, Captain. Abort. Fall off and place her on a beam reach across the inlet toward the Fairhaven shore … buy us some time."

"Then what?"

"Once past the black sloop, you may find room to cut behind her. However, we will need to sail on a reach across the entire inlet and do it quickly."

"Coming about," hollered Tim to a scrambling crew. The schooner tacked yet again.

"You are the proverbial mouse, Captain," declared Winton. "Clawing up one wall and down the other." A chuckle dripping with contempt left his lips. "It will get you nowhere."

"Your observation is falling on deaf ears, Professor."

"Just alluding to the obvious."

Things began happening quickly. The wrong decision one way or the other could fault any attempt for success.

"I must warn you, Captain," said Eli. "There is low water along the Fairhaven shore."

"I'm aware of it."

"That sloop can navigate much faster than that old brig. If she turns and tries to impede our track, the mud flats along Phoenix Point are sure to trap us."

"Then our only choice is to take her down their throats, Mister Monroe. In-between them, before they converge"

"You are the captain," proclaimed Eli.

"It appears so," declared Tim, chucking me a smile.

"We are making good time," Eli pointed out.

"Yes, but we must sustain momentum if we are to spring any element of surprise."

"You are right, of course."

"Do you think we have enough room to sail between those two ships, Timothy?" I inquired.

"If not, we will make room."

"How?"

"Once we are close to the sloop, we will tack hard to starboard to avoid her and try to squeeze by her nose and past the brig."

"She's much larger than we are. Will we have time?"

"Yes, she's bigger but sluggish. Takes her time to maneuver and make headway. I'm done dancing. We will deflect her …"

"Deflect her?" I cried. "How?"

"With backbone … take the fight to them. I shall confront them on my terms and with the likelihood of imminent collision. It's what Sam would do."

Tim was absolutely right. The practice was common in yacht racing, and the quandary handed to us at the moment would be a classic challenge for Samuel—a duel he would gladly assume.

"At the last minute, we shall attempt to cut across her bow and sail toward the opening between her and the other ship."

"Did you say attempt, Captain?" taunted Eli.

"A wholehearted one, Mister Monroe."

Eli gnawed on his cigar and pitched me a droll and playful squint. The urgency and danger of the moment excited him.

"Let's show them what this racing girl can do, shall we?" said Tim. He glanced over and winked. "Everyone, prepare to come about!"

Hands scurried to their posts as we changed course. Lines and sheets whipped and sails flogged. The schooner swung and stood up from its starboard lean. The sweeping bow spun eighty degrees—west to east. Promptly, the crew heaved and yanked, making lines taut, as the ship gracefully pitched to port and accelerated. It was a glorious maneuver. One felt exhilarated when bellied canvas held its breath and stiffened to a clotting breeze. This was sailing, and I never tire of it. We were now well-trimmed and on a track away from the black sloop as it attempted to catch us.

I hurried to the rear of the ship and snugged myself low and out of the way. Half the men stood by the helm vigilant, their legs sprung and loaded, anxiously awaiting the captain's next command. As expected, orders were issued. We tacked yet again. This time right toward the black sloop.

"You are going to get us killed, Captain," cried Winton. "My work … my beautiful engine … it will go down to the bottom with this ship."

"Then we go down in glory, Professor—me with my ship and you with that vaporous contraption you call an engine."

While Tim and Winton engaged in an unfriendly verbal tussle, Eli was immersed with the events unfolding before us.

"Captain, we have the option to cut around the back or the front of her depending what she does."

"We shall make way in front of her. I can't take a chance with shoaling along the flats."

"I don't think we will have open water in front of her if she remains on course."

"Then I will open some."

We approached the black sloop with profound speed. Up until now, we had been evading the two vessels. Now we were sailing right for them. *Sphinx* accelerated, offering the sloop no alternate contingency but to take evasive action or be lanced by the schooner's ominous sprit. Eli Monroe's posture had changed from captivated excitement to cautioned anxiety as the spark in his eyes diffused into a sulking grimace.

"You must choose a course, Captain," implored a worried Eli.

Tim's courage and confidence grew by leaps and bounds. "I have chosen my course, Mister Monroe. We are on it at the moment."

As the schooner bore down on the sloop, its crew stampeded along the deck. Panicked shouts echoed from her quarterdeck as the captain wailed ambiguous commands. The bewildered helmsmen froze with a gaping stare as the twenty-foot-long battering ram barreled down upon him. We all held tight for what appeared an inevitable collision.

"We are going to collide—we are going to collide!" shouted the Cuffee brothers.

Without warning, everything changed. In the impending seconds that we had left, the threatening sloop slackened sails and rounded up, endeavoring to avoid the *Sphinx*'s menacing pike. Tim spun the wheel hard and furious. The obedient schooner spun like a top. In the final moments, its bowsprit delivered its opponent a glancing blow, removing a portion of the cap rail along the ship's beam. The impact jarred our rigging. The shock sent a quaking tremor throughout the entire ship. Spars shuddered and the main mast quivered, while white chips of paint splintered from its surface—raining down on deck like confetti. We continued to turn into the eye of the wind. The black sloop went from a port reach to a close-haul as it slowly moved away from us. Unexpectedly, its massive sails snatched our wind as it ghosted by. *Sphinx* stalled and its canvas slackened right in the middle of an evasive maneuver. Immediately, we lost headway.

The fickle wind circled the point along Fairhaven's southern shore and suddenly took an unexpected approach, pinning us in place and further complicating matters. We found ourselves immobilized—dead in the water. We slowly drifted backwards, carried by the current, unable to fill our sails while they flogged relentlessly. The sloop continued in front of us and headed out into open water toward the oncoming steamer *River Queen*. On our starboard side, the brigantine was closing in on us. The steamer blasted its horn. We lay helpless in the center of the channel. On the brig, its sails throbbed fiercely as sailors attempted to gain control to avoid striking us and the oncoming passenger ferry.

"Why are we not moving?" I cried.

"We are being held in irons by the incoming tide," explained Tim. "The wind blowing on shore is offsetting the current and trapping us."

"In essence, we are hove-to by a strong current," added Eli.

"The brig is coming awfully close," I said. "What can we do?"

"Not much, I'm afraid," said Tim. "Not until the sails catch some wind."

"Try turning the helm to port, Captain," suggested Eli. "The current may push on the rudder and twist us into the wind."

Tim turned the rudder every which way, but nothing worked.

"The black ship is changing course ahead," wailed one of the Cuffee brothers.

The sloop and the *River Queen* were on converging course. With not enough wind to work itself through the eye of a tacking maneuver, our opponent was left with little alternative but to veer off, downwind, away from the single-minded captain of the Vineyard paddleboat and toward us.

"The black sloop. She's sailing straight for us," I uttered.

"She will have to pass on our port side," declared Eli. "Otherwise, they will collide with the brig. We are trapped in the middle."

"Glory be, Captain, ship a'commin," announced Razor.

"She's going to pass really close … trying to get a good look at us," declared Eli.

"Frederick, stay below with the boys. Don't show your faces," commanded Tim.

Frederick huddled in the cabin with the three freed slaves. Up on deck, the sails were still flogging loosely as they spiraled and thrashed, begging for breeze. The lashing sound they produced was deafening.

"Here they come," said the Cuffee brothers, cautioning in unison as the sloop approached.

"Everyone on your toes. Make ready to come about," ordered Tim. "Take the wheel, Mister Monroe, quick."

"Come about? How are we going to come about? We're not moving, Captain."

Eli and I wearily eyed one another. The helmsman shrugged his shoulders and took the wheel.

Tim dashed to the rope locker where he procured a heavy rope and a grappling hook. Tying the line to the grapple, he threw the line's bitter end around the capstan post. Standing precariously along the ship's rail, he patiently waited, twirling the iron hook on the end of the rope as if he was about to lasso a steer. The black sloop approached with its boom jutting out well over the water while its enormous mainsail suckled a following breeze. The curious crew of both ships hung over the rail, assessing one another while watching as the enormous, canvased spar nearly struck the schooner's port rigging. Just as the blunt stern of the sloop passed us, Tim flung the grappling hook over the gunwale and onto the deck of the fleeting vessel. Moving away, he steadied himself by a flogging jib, waiting for his astute plan to unfold.

The rope paid out rapidly. The grappling hook tumbled and rolled along the sloop's deck as a crewman gave chase and the ship sailed past us. Before he could seize the oversized, iron-barb and fling it overboard, the line sprung from the water and snapped taut, digging the fingered snare firmly into the sloop's rail. With her snout tied to the sloop's stern, the schooner lurched to port, listing, as the cable heaved, and the bow deflected. The capstan post on the schooner's bow creaked and the deck heaved and buckled while the rope strained to hold the two ships together. Tim ran back toward the helm praying the line would not part before the sloop could veer us into the wind. A sailor on the tethered ship worked fiercely to cut the manila umbilical tying the two ships together. His captain cursed and brandished his fist. The schooner continued to slowly twist to port as her crew watched with gaping fascination.

Finally, the cable was severed. It catapulted into the air as if shot from a cannon. Swiftly, *Sphinx* fell forty degrees to port while its sails flared. With canvas filled, the schooner inched forward. The crew cheered and danced as they watched the black sloop continue away from us.

Tim cupped his hands to his mouth. "Thanks for the tow, boys!"

We all looked up and marveled at the sails blustering with air. We were so preoccupied with the black sloop that we had forgotten the brigantine, which loomed over our starboard quarter. Its golden-haired, mermaid figurehead glared down on us as it made its perilous approach.

"He's going to hit us—he's going to hit us!" alerted the Cuffee brothers in a forewarning chorus.

The southern wind that had stopped *Sphinx* in her tracks was now pushing the menacing ship toward us. The brig was difficult to maneuver and slow to turn. As we slowly began to move, the brigantine endeavored to change direction to avoid hitting us. Off on the horizon, the captain of the incoming steamer was true to his reputation. His course was straight and unwavering. The *River Queen* was barreling directly for us while sounding its horn with frenzied alarm.

Tim returned to the quarterdeck. He examined the sails as the brig got closer, assessing wind conditions and the certainty of escape.

Looking down on us from the towering ship was the constable and the man named Bulldog. Standing beside him was the fellow with the sleeve of his jacket pinned to his shoulder. The man had appeared to have only one arm, but I could plainly see the other just under his jacket and hung from a sling. Under his cap sprouted fair hair the color of corn silk. His tapered blonde mustache was as thin as his upper lip and perched just below a sweeping narrow nose and ladled chin. He had a patch over one eye. The remainder of facial features were buttressed by scantly coiled sideburns and foreboding cheeks.

Luck was with us, if just for a fleeting moment, as the brigantine perilously wafted several yards off our stern. We were well by her now. Just when it looked like we would get away safely, the dory, which we towed, became wedged beneath the bobstay on the big ship's bow. Immediately, the *Sphinx* came to a halt, tethered to the large ship by the small boat and its painter. We made almost no headway as our ship and dory pulled the ponderous brig into the path of the impending *River Queen*. It was no one's fault, really. We had left shore hastily and failed to bring the dory aboard, deciding to do so once out at sea. Disastrously, the small rowboat was now wedged firmly between the brigantine's hull and its bobstay and tied to our stern. It was a wonder that the cable did not part.

The policeman on the brigantine shouted over to us. "Who is captain of that ship?"

"I am!" hollered Tim, stepping forward.

The incoming ferry sounded its frantic horn.

"Your name, skipper?"

"State your business."

"We have suspicion that your vessel is carrying contraband, Captain. You must return to port immediately and your vessel searched."

The crew of the brigantine hung over the bow wildly assessing what held them in place … A crewman tossed a rope ladder overboard and shimmied down to the dory in an endeavor to free the ship. The *River Queen* continued thundering its horn. Tim glanced in the direction of the echoing sound giving it a slim measure of curiosity.

"Under whose authority?"

"Under the authority of the Slave Act of 1850," declared the constable.

"Captain, we need to move from here," chimed a nervous Eli. "Shall I cut the dory free?"

"Hold off, Mister Monroe."

"But, Captain?"

Ignoring the helmsman's plea, Tim scrutinized the incoming ferry. The act of engaging the men on the brig in conversation appeared reckless on his part. He peered over the side at the dory then back at the ferry. The sailor on the rope ladder abandoned his effort and climbed back up as crew helped him get on deck. The sound made by the blaring horn on the ferry echoed off the planking on our hull. Call me foolish, but I was certain gentleman Tim had a plan.

"The *River Queen*, Captain!" shouted Eli, frantically. "We must cut the line."

Sphinx was on a port reach with the wind on her starboard beam and sails pulling hard. Downwind, the black sloop, which had passed us earlier, was maneuvering to sail back. Both *Sphinx* and the brigantine drifted deeper into the center of the channel. The line tied to the dory strained and creaked. The tiny boat splintered and began to break up amidst the strain.

Aaron Kerr leaned over the side. "Shud we noot cut the line, Keptin?"

"Who brings such charges?" demanded Tim, neglecting the Scotsman's suggestion.

"One Captain Charles Tobias Morse," the lawman yelled.

"Captain!" cried Eli. "You must cut us free … now!"

"Will you not return to port, Captain?" continued the lawman.

"I will do no such thing," replied Tim.

"Captain!" cried Eli.

"Razor, cut the rope to that dory, hurry!"

Admond Assagai took out his straight razor from his pocket and, with a quick swipe and flick of the wrist, instantly parted the line. Suddenly, we were all jarred back as *Sphinx* surged forward, leaving the shattered dory and the helpless brig behind.

The *River Queen* approached quickly while blasting its horn. The crew of the brigantine trimmed sail and turned the lumbering ship down wind. We all rushed to the stern to watch. It was now obvious why Tim hesitated in cutting the dory's painter. He had intentionally towed the brig into the path of the oncoming paddle ship, buying us time to get away. The boisterous ferry's horn was still blaring when it carelessly collided with the bow of the brigantine ship. As it approached, the black sloop made a bearing away from us in an attempt to avoid casualty. Tim swung the helm, turning *Sphinx*'s stern away from the passing ferry. It steamed by just a few yards from our rudder.

The panicking crew of the brigantine floundered as the impulsive *River Queen* removed its bowsprit with a thundering crash. The brightly painted matron effigy, which once hung proudly beneath the ship's bow, now lay in the water, splintered and deposed. The ferry continued to scour and abrade the bow of the large ship as it slithered by unimpeded and without losing headway. *Sphinx* sailed safely away as we all watched, stunned and amazed by the astonishing circumstances that had just unfolded.

"Take the wheel, Mister Monroe, and get us out of here."

"Aye aye, Captain. Heading?"

"Into the open sea. Anywhere but here."

"The open sea it is, sir," said the gleeful helmsman.

The schooner made one last maneuver, falling onto a starboard tack and heading southwest. With a clean and unobstructed path, we sailed past

Fort Rodman toward Cuttyhunk Island and the open Atlantic.

The black sloop was now well behind. There was no way it could catch us. Though the brigantine and paddleboat were in no danger of sinking, the damage to the ships was significant. The brig lost its sprit while the *River Queen* had its port paddle housing swept away. Tim spied the scene through the optics.

"What do you see?" I asked.

"Most of the damage to the ferry is superficial. She appears to continue her sail to port. The brig lost its sprit. Its foremast looks in danger of coming down."

"The ferry had room to maneuver out of the way," I pondered. "Why didn't it change course?"

"I expected it to. A collision between them was not part of my plan."

"Cheeky buggers. They ur th' same in Scootlund," declared Aaron, watching the ferry steam away. "They sail fest an' stop fur noo body."

"Mister Kerr, get up front and inspect for damage to our bowsprit."

"Congratulations, Captain," said Winton Macartney. "I must admit. That tactic you employed with the grappling hook to turn this vessel into the wind was brilliant. It should have proved a foolish undertaking. It's a wonder the rope did not break."

"A wonder indeed, Professor."

"That was a splendid display of seamanship, Captain," said Frederick. "I am confident that the remainder of this trip will be uneventful. And if not, that we have a captain capable of handling almost anything that is thrown at us."

"Powerful game 'a chicken." added Razor. "You is the rooster, Captain."

The entire crew showered Tim with accolades and handshakes. Gentleman Tim took it all in stride, endeavoring to keep his composure and not look too pleased with himself—which if you knew him like I did, he was not.

In the distance, the *River Queen* continued blowing its steam horn while sailing into harbor. Behind her, the brigantine had dropped anchor and began to take down canvas and assess its condition. The black sloop circled the damaged ship. Tim studied them through the spyglass.

"Thaur is nae damage tae th' bowsprit, Keptin. The cranse iron took th' brunt ay it."

"Very well, Aaron," said Tim, breaking from formality and addressing the man by his familiar name. "Go down below and get yourself an apple. You've earned it."

The fiery haired Scotchman lumbered away taking the captain's glib request seriously.

"Do you think anyone was hurt on the ferry," I asked.
"Don't think so. Paddle is still turning. That's a good sign."
"I'm glad."

Chapter 15:
The Bonnie Blue Off Sow and Pigs

The wind was brisk and blowing out of the south as it often did in the summer months. With the New Bedford waterfront well behind us, Eli took soundings twenty miles off Nantucket to make certain we would miss the shoals to the southeast of the island before turning north. Once deep water was established, *Sphinx* swung toward our destination—Canaan.

"Shame we lost the dory," said Eli, lighting a cigar.

"No problem," said Tim. Having been a carpenter at Seth Howland's carpentry shop, he was well aware of what it took to build one. "Mister Kerr, can you build us a small pram, something to get us around in harbor until we can replace the skiff."

"Ah sure can Keptin. Hoo large dae ye want it?"

"Ten foot long should do it. We have all the lumber you will need in the bilge. If you run out, you are welcome to take down the bulkheads around the captain's cabin and use that. It's not structural and we can replace it when we return to Westport."

"Reit awa', Keptin."

"Mister Cuffee, will give you a hand?"

"Which one Keptin, ah cannae teel them apart."

"James. He's the one that's always smiling."

"Smilin' Jimmy, reit awa' Keptin."

It was not long before the sound of a wood saw and hammer rang true up on deck, along with the clang of pots and pans in the galley as Eli prepared the evening meal. We had spent the entire day becalmed and drifting to a bloated ocean swell just north of Georges Bank. Aaron and James Cuffee spent the day building the small skiff, while Winton kept mostly to himself, seasick, and laying in his bunk reading technical compendiums that he kept in his traveling library. Razor humored himself by whittling small toy soldiers and farm animals from blocks of wood that he would give to children along the New Bedford shore. The three runaway slaves played endless games of dominoes, cheering, hooting, and laughing, having a great time while anticipating the challenges that existed in a new world. Tim was below making entries in the ship's log and tending to navigational duties. The sun was nowhere to be found, which complicated things for the new captain and the use of the ship's sextant. I sat under a leaden sky, sunning myself to opaque rays that glistened behind a milky veil. Nonetheless, one could feel the heat that the obscured orb emitted.

By the third day we found ourselves very close to the Nova Scotia coast. Robert Cuffee, or was it James, climbed the ratlines on his way up to the crow's nest.

"Now you be careful up there, Robert."

"I'm James, Miss White."

"Oh … just the same."

I settled into my favorite retreat by the rope locker and watched as the young man climbed to the top of the mast. Frederick Johnson came over and sat on the cabin house beside me.

"Ah, the lovely Miss White," he declared.

"Am I to take your cheer as a compliment to a girl on a ship full of men?"

"There is a difference between a compliment based on flattery and one that rests on truthfulness. My personal toast draws its candor from the latter."

"You are very kind, Frederick."

"We have been out on the sea for over two days and yet no time to speak to one another."

"I spend most of my day on deck—in the fresh salt air and meditating over ocean waves. Like snowflakes, one wave is different from the other and no two breakers are alike. It's a performance that relaxes me. You, on the other hand, have been spending all your time in your bunk and below with the boys."

"You must forgive my unintentional absence, but I have been tending to obligations and duties, preparing the runaways for a free life. When not doing that, working on a narrative I have been writing."

"Oh?"

"The captain and I have been discussing our landing port in Nova Scotia. I have deliberated in length with Rudolf French about the matter and he thought it wise that I was along on the voyage to orchestrate the entire affair once we arrive at our destination. I am familiar with a couple of black churches and communities there. And as we are getting close to Nova Scotia, I must decide which one to choose."

"And have you?"

"Not certain."

"Where are they in Nova Scotia?"

"Halifax for one. A small village called Africville in the northern part of Halifax on the shores of the Bedford Basin. It's a thriving little village with a church, general store, and ample black folk, consequently finding work there can easily be arranged."

"Sounds promising."

"Yes, Halifax has a population of nearly fifty thousand souls. Thus, chances of blending in are more advantageous. Some people in our community favor it."

"Is there another?"

"Yes. The other is very rural. Many runaways who have settled up north prefer rural settings. Perhaps it's the remoteness of open country and the choice to move around, change scenery at will—exercise your freedom. The place I have in mind is a small village called Greenville, just north of Yarmouth. That is where I think we are heading."

"How far do you think we are from Yarmouth?"

"The captain estimates fifty miles or more from where we are at present"

"Are we far from land itself?"

"I would think about thirty miles off the coast of Cape Sable. Greenville is along the west coast while Halifax is on the east. From here, we have to decide which way to turn."

"I'm certain they will be happy no matter which community you choose."

"I'm sure of it."

"Ah, it is peaceful out here, don't you think?"

"It is, Emily. Unfortunately, it takes me back to the tobacco plantation of Maryland when I was in bondage. I remember the stillness in the fields at night, the serenity of the hour, the corrupt hush of enslavement."

"How tragic, Frederick, that such placidness should evoke bad memories."

"On the contrary. The quietness of that moment was an escape by some means to the cries I would hear at night—suffering through my brethren's anguish, torched by remembrances of sons and daughters sold like meat at market never to be seen again."

His words left me barren of thought. What could I say that was supportive or comforting? The pain endured by one in bondage was beyond my understanding. It would have been impertinent of me, a white girl from the north, to pretend to realize it.

"Well, you are away from all that, Frederick."

"Am I?" he said.

His rhetorical question opened up new queries. Did a black man really have freedom up north? Dispirited by any further investigation, I kept quiet, staring out at a vanishing horizon.

"The calm conditions we find ourselves in at the moment are fortuitous," he said, breaking a moment of discomfort. "In that it gives us some time to disengage from the hard terrain under our feet and swarms of people back home. A few days out here and a man will feel like he was born again, once he steps back on hard ground."

I knew just what he meant. Lacking any wind, the only man-made sound one hears amid a placid sea is an occasional creak from a swaying spar or the whisking whoop of flaccid cloth, as rust-stained sails are tossed to-and-fro by benign rolling waters. Out here, there is a cleansing of intentions and grand schemes one may have harbored back on land. When out of sight of land for days, nothing else matters but the open sea. The present moment is all that is relevant and, if not, given enough time, the sea will make it so.

"When will we know which place will be chosen?"

"As soon as the sun returns, and the captain is able to take a sun site to verify our coordinates. Once we know where we are, we will determine where we are going."

"Where do the runaways prefer?"

"They are so joyful to have escaped bondage that anywhere will suit them."

"Well, Greenville sounds pleasant enough," I said.

He smiled. "Anywhere one can be free, Emily, sounds pleasant enough."

I got up and walked to the rail looking down at the tall humpy swells. They lifted *Sphinx*'s hull like a seesaw on the open ocean. In the distance, I could see a playful zephyr coming toward us as it rippled the waters into shivering crinkles. We were hove-to with slack canvas. But the newly stirred breeze reverently caressed the sails. The nimble breeze stirred the cloth, filling them. Soon, the schooner was making progress as its bow scored the undulating swells, leaving a virgin sea to effervesce with a rustling murmur and fizzling crescendo.

Frederick got up and stood by me. "Have you read the book I lent you," he asked.

"Oh, I forgot to return it. I have it with me," I said. I took the volume from my purse that sat on the lid of the rope locker.

"I must thank you for such an enlightening memoir. It has opened my eye to the injurious and destructive and cruel practice of slavery. I could hardly believe what I was reading."

I handed him the book. He held the volume in his hand, caressing the cover like a long-lost friend.

"The printed word is a catalyst for the soul, a stimulus for the senses, and, in some cases, an anthology of adventure and folly. However, the escape from slavery is a salvation that, though one can transcribe to paper or engrave events and tactical memory into a book, is difficult to instill in white perception and understanding of what it is to be a slave. Northerners may hear or read an account of a poor black man suffering under the whip and chain and feel candid compassion but never really understand the extent of anguish and adversity—not only to the body but the mind and heart. For no man may have lien or ownership over another."

"I think I know what you mean, though I may not know how it feels."

"Mister Northup has a special gift of telling a story and placing you there, your back to the whip, your ankles and wrists in shackles, and your empathy through solicitude and trepidation. Unless you have lived a slave, had your family torn from your arms never to be seen again, and for complaining about it, whipped naked and raw, until a lie becomes truth and that vile lie your only reality … you can never truly understand."

"It comes down to walking in one's shoes, does it not, Frederick? Until you do, you will never bear their heart."

"Well said, Emily. In any event, I am happy that Solomon's book has opened your eyes and brought you here to this chariot of manumission."

"You said that you were writing a narrative."

"A novella about bondage and flight."

"Like Solomon Northrup?"

"Actually, about another gentleman's struggle for emancipation."

"Would I be impertinent if I ask you about it?"

"Not at all. I call it *The Heroic Slave*. The story of Madison Washington and a fictional account of what happened to him."

"You have captivated me, Frederick. I love story telling."

"The story is imagination—the man in it is authentic."

"Madison Washington?"

"Yes, Madison was being transported on the slave ship *Creole*, carrying one hundred and thirty-five souls from Virginia to New Orleans. Madison led a mutiny on the ship, took the crew prisoners, and compelled their captives to sail them to Nassau in the British Bahamas, where the slaves aboard the *Creole* were set free by the sanity of British rule."

"I must read it when you are done, Frederick."

"I would be honored if you did." He displayed an unassuming smile. "If you love to read, I recommend you acquire the works by an acquaintance of mine, William Wells Brown—a reformed slave and abolitionist. Though William and I do not see eye to eye on many things, I can take nothing away from his literary prowess."

"What has he written?"

"On many topics."

"Such as?"

"If you like story telling I will mention his novella. Very provocative and imaginative, I must warn you. And perhaps it would be infelicitous of me to mention such unprincipled subject matter as the one written by Mister Brown. However, it is probably the first novella written by a black brother and that makes it of consequence."

"He's your brother?"

Frederick laughed. "All black people are brothers and sisters to one another, Miss White. Once your family has been torn away from you, one comes to realize that we are all one family."

"Sorry. How naive of me."

"Not at all. You are not expected to know how the term is used in a black man's world."

"You mentioned Mister Brown's novella … said it was written on an unprincipled topic. What is it? I think I am mature enough to hear it. And I have an open mind. You should not fret about mentioning the title."

"Very well. It is called *The President's Daughter* … about the infidelity of Thomas Jefferson."

"Oh, my. Is that not libel? It's not true, is it?"

"I will say no more. It is the only story telling narrative I can remember written by Mister Brown. He has also written accounts of his travels in Europe, literary plays, and, more importantly, about his life in bondage. But if you wish to know whether Mister Jefferson is guilty of such breach in fidelity, I am not the one to tell you. You must research it for yourself."

"I will. And I must get myself a copy of *The President's Daughter* … is that right?"

He smiled.

Our chat was suddenly adjourned by James Cuffee's cry from the top of the mast.

"Land ho, at two o'clock!" he yelled.

Before I knew it, Tim was on deck with his spyglass.

"Ah, the captain," said Frederick. "Appears that land is near."

"We need to make a choice about land fall," I told him.

"Come on down, Mister Cuffee," shouted Tim. "Good job."

"I don't see any land," I declared, looking over the horizon.

"It's over twenty miles off," said Tim. "You can only see it from above."

"Land, Captain. That's great news."

"Have you decided, Mister Johnson?"

"Yarmouth would be best."

"Yarmouth it is."

Tim went below and returned with our new heading just as the wind got stronger. Eli steered the schooner on the new course and headed us northwest as we sailed on toward Yarmouth, Nova Scotia.

It was early the next day when we arrived at snug Yarmouth harbor. Rather than bringing *Sphinx* alongside the quay, we chose to anchor in shallow water, off Doctors Island, a couple hundred feet from shore, and retain the privacy of the three runaways. By late in the day, after the tall tide had dropped, the schooner lay on her side, resting on her port shoulder and keel, in five feet of water. Tim had expected as much, since *Sphinx* had a ten-foot draft.

Much smaller than Halifax, Yarmouth still had twice the population as the tiny town of Westport where I lived. Coastal villages are some of the most beautiful places and Yarmouth had all the charm and loveliness of the average New England township.

Apart from a few leaks, the pram built by Aaron Kerr served its purpose. About half the size of the dory that was lost in New Bedford, it had a limited-load accommodation and flexed and creaked when the oars were buried and engaged. Built with a flat bottom, the tiny skiff could only carry four. The ride was slow and clumsy. Aaron tried not to work the tiny boat too hard, hoping she would stay together and not leave us all in the drink. Still, I found it a bit of fun and, with my trusty copper tea mug, I volunteered to be official bailer.

I waited on shore as Aaron returned to the ship for the three runaway slaves. Once on shore, the one called Old Jim dropped to his knees, threw his open arm into the heavens, and thanked his God. By example, his younger companions did the same.

Later in the day, the men were introduced and handed off to Reverend David Dize of Greenville African Church. I felt regretful that I did not have more time to be acquainted with the three freed slaves as they rode away in the Reverend's wagon, joyfully waving. Frederick accompanied them to help with their liberty in Greenville.

While waiting for Frederick's return, Tim and Aaron stumbled upon sanctuary—a quaint two-table tavern overlooking the tranquil waterfront. After waiting several hours, Frederick Johnson had yet to return. Along a dramatic horizon somewhere over the state of Maine, a coral sun was ebbing behind a ribbon of noctilucent clouds. It would be dark soon. With a little diplomacy, I had convinced Tim that we should return to the ship and wait for Frederick there.

For the remainder of the evening, I was the designated chaperon to two inebriated five-year-olds. Following a staggered promenade and some ill-advised acrobatics along a six-foot high brick wall, we finally arrived at the small skiff, floating below the quay. When we rowed over from the ship, we had left the boat sitting on the mud and walked up the spongy shore into town. But the tide had rushed in and now our tiny ferry was floating in ten feet of water with no way of getting down to it. None of us had remembered Yarmouth's fourteen-foot tides. It was a wonder that someone thought to tie the small boat to a piling before we left her along the waterfront. Considering their flushed condition, the boys found our predicament hilarious. They argued about who was at fault. They soon reconciled and concluded that the blunder would be mine. Of course, accusations were not made without some juvenile hilarity. The three of us lingered along the edge of the wharf wondering how we would get to the small boat. A resolution was reached, when without warning, Aaron Kerr dove into the frigid waters, leaving Tim in irrepressible laughter.

Aaron swam the boat to shore and we all climbed in. The two men clung to one another while Aaron taught Tim a Scottish ballad. The cold plunge did nothing to sober the enterprising Scotsman. The two laughed, and sang, and cried. I rowed. For if I did not, we could have very well ended up in Newfoundland.

The next day, the *Sphinx* was moved along the small-town quay and a ton of coal was scuttled into the newly built fuel bunker deep in the ship's bilge. Frederick Johnson had returned from Greenville earlier in the morning, while Eli and I made plans to go into town and purchase provisions for the day's meals. To his chagrin, Tim kept a low profile working at his desk and nursing a headache from a night of hard drink. Up on deck, Aaron Kerr did not appear worse for wear as he spent most of the morning hammering the gaps in the skiff with oakum to help make her watertight. I poured Tim a cup of tea. He winced every time Aaron struck the caulking mallet. I smiled and shook my head since Captain Tim Cadman, of the sainted schooner *Sphinx*, should have known better.

The ship was moved back into the intimate harbor and anchored while we made ready for the long slog south against prevailing southerlies. We had been in Yarmouth three days waiting for a favorable wind. On the last day, Winton Macartney and Aaron spent most of their time stoking the boiler and preparing to engage the steam engine for the departure. Wind direction would no longer be a factor in our leaving.

"We are ready to throw the regulator throttle," announced Winton.

Uncertain as to what he meant, Tim gave Aaron a hollow grimace.

"We ur ready tae leave anytime ye ur, Keptin."

In the belly of the ship, the steam engine chugged and clattered. The noise made was deafening.

The clattering appeared nimbler, accelerated, as Winton threw a lever and pulled a bar. There was a loud hiss and baritone purr. The entire crew gathered around the cabin and companionway watching with curious fascination as bulkheads trembled, deck pulsated, and the entire hull cried out in reverberation. Disinterested, Eli sat at the wheel, prepared to steer us out of harbor. After all, he had been around ships of all sorts most of his life and a steam-powered vessel was nothing new or dear to him.

"Throw the reversing mechanism," ordered Winton.

Aaron pulled on a leaver. A thrust of steam exhaust blasted out and through the stack on the cabin roof with a whooshing blare. The clamor and roar were loud and unpleasant.

"Two hunder an' thirty fife poonds," yelled Aaron, striving to be heard, while he studied the pressure gauge by the engine.

"Good, good. Leave the throttle full open," directed Winton. "We'll control her with the steam cut off."

"Two hunder an' forty," bellowed Aaron.

"Ready to engage, Captain," hollered Winton.

Aaron looked up at Tim and pointed up at the sails and hinting that they were prepared to set sail.

Razor and one of the Cuffees boys set the capstan in motion. The anchor was lifted, while its chain rattled and clattered into the locker deep into the forecastle.

"Hoist the main and number one jib," came the order. "Ready when you are, Professor."

Winton gradually engaged the propeller, and the bronze shaft began to spin.

"Close that valve, Aaron," ordered Winton. "We need more pressure."

Gradually, the ship began to move. Though the mainsail was hoisted, it only waved like a flag, since the wind was on the nose. Magically, *Sphinx* moved forward. There was a resounding cheer from the crew. For the first time, I witnessed Winton smile. His entire face had changed. He looked approachable and happy, sporting a little-boy grin. Aaron was poised proudly, steam cut off, lever in hand, while monitoring the clock-faced pressure gage.

"We are moving," I shouted, astonishingly, watching out a port while the scenery ashore glided astern.

Tim scurried on deck, not believing his eyes. Eli stood, casually steering and cherishing his stogie.

"We are moving, Captain," he uttered, impassively. "Cannot call it sailing."

Once we were out in open water, the schooner was allowed to voyage under full sail on the prolong journey home. The propeller was disengaged, and the engine allowed to vent, or sit idle, while the canvas did all the work. Though the steam engine was usefulness in calm seas, the small engine could not compete with full sail out in the open waters.

I retreated to my comfort ground by the rope locker, sitting with my back against the mast, in the shade of the large standing mainsail. I felt pleased with myself and with the entire crew for the good we had accomplished on this trip. To our benefit, the wind direction had changed, but a northern breeze ushered in a stinging chill. I moved to the port side of the ship where the sun's dazzling glimmer warmed my bones. The bright sunlight glinted off my cheeks, generating a winking glare that tingled my nose. Its intense rays anesthetized my conscientiousness as ambition and spiritedness was hove-to and where I fell into a languorous slumber.

Sphinx was finally in home-waters and making ready to circle Cuttyhunk Island. From there, it was a short hop to New Bedford harbor. We began our approach off the western tip of Cuttyhunk. Getting too close to the Island would place us in perilous waters. Tim made certain he was on deck to help navigate us safely past the island and into Buzzards Bay.

"Make sure to keep us on course, Mister Monroe. We don't want to get close to Sow and Pigs Reef off the west coast of that island."

"Aye, aye, Captain. I cannot forget Sow and Pigs and I will not let it trap us."

"Oh, you are familiar with the reef, are you?"

"No, sir, not really. But when I served in the Royal Navy, I was on Her Majesty's Ship *Valiant*. We got hung up on some rocks just off Hornby light in Sydney harbor in Australia. It was also called Sow and Pigs Reef."

"Then I have the best man at the helm," proclaimed Tim, patting Eli on the back.

"Sow and Pigs. What a peculiar name for a reef. Why is it called Sow and Pigs?" I asked.

"Don't rightly know," replied Tim. "But every year it swallows a ship or two."

"Do you know, Eli?" I asked.

"Not the one off Cuttyhunk Island. But the Sow and Pigs off the South Bend in Sydney Harbor was named because the rocks lined up like a Sow parading with her piglets."

"Then it should be Sow and Piglets," I suggested.

We laughed.

"I've been watching that vessel coming in our direction, Captain," said Eli.

"Looks like we are on a converging course," I pointed out.

"Yes, it does," agreed Tim. "Change course a little, Eli. Ten degrees east."

The schooner's heading was altered. By steering closer to the island, we would pass the oncoming vessel safely. Just as we adjusted our heading, the oncoming ship did the same.

"Captain, she's altering course," declared Eli. "Right at us again."

"Another ten degrees east."

Sphinx slowly pivoted closer to Cuttyhunk to avoid a collision. As we did, deliberately, the approaching ship changed course yet again.

"I think she's on to us for one reason or another," declared Eli. "Why does she keep changing her heading?"

"Well, we can't adjust ours again. At least not in an easterly direction. We may lose our wind and drift onto the reef."

Winton came walking up the deck from the bow where he sat with the crew observing our approach to land.

"Flirting with oncoming traffic again, I see, Captain?" he accused.

Tim ignored him.

"She is still a way off. But we will need to decide what to do soon," explained Eli.

"Keep our heading. If she wishes to fence, we shall brandish our sword. I'm going below."

I looked over at Eli. He shrugged. The run, though pleasant, was invigorating as the schooner's bow plowed through a short, breaking swell and disturbed reef waters. *Sphinx* was being pushed by the stern and traveling as fast as it could. The air blew over our port stern rail and an occasional wave was shattered by the bow into a pellet shower of shivering spray.

Tim soon appeared with an enormous sack. Inside was a sail. While he removed it from the duffel, I noticed it was made of very light cloth, bed sheet cloth, not much thicker than the dress I was wearing. It was unlike all the other sails onboard, which were much heavier and made of thick canvas linen. This sail appeared to be made of cotton. Tim unfolded the fabric. It took up the entire length on the port deck. Curious, Winton worked the material between his fingers and shook his head.

"Bad time to hang out your wash, Captain."

The captain pulled the sail along the deck, getting it ready for deployment, just when Aaron Kerr came scurrying over.

"Some rocks, Keptin, jist under th' water. Off th' starboard bow."

"Everyone to your stations," yelled the captain.

Tim quickly tied a line to the clew on the cotton sail and measured it out.

"Razor, take this line and attach it to the cleat by the helm port rail."

"Aye, Captain."

He then took another line, this one only a couple of feet in length, and tied it to the tack or other end of the sail.

"Take this, Aaron, and walk it out to the very tip of the bowsprit. Tie it off there. Use a double knot. Think you can do that?"

"Did ah' nae teel ye, Keptin, 'at ah worked th' tightrope walker in a circus once?"

"Make like a monkey then, quick, Mister Kerr."

While Aaron shimmied up the bowsprit, dragging the tack of the sail with him, Tim tied the head of the cotton sail to a spare jib halyard. All three corners of the sail were now attached.

"Take your positions, men. Prepare to jibe and place her before the wind to port, Mister Monroe.

"Aye, aye, Captain."

"On my command."

"She's out to get us," shouted Eli. "Still coming."

I watched as the other ship got closer. Running below, I retrieved the spyglass and ran back up on deck.

"Alright!" hollered Tim. "Let's teach that sloop how a schooner does it, shall we? Mister Monroe, eighty degrees west."

"Eighty degrees? But that will send us into her path, Captain."

"Robert, James, quick, give me a hand pulling this sail up."

"But, Captain?" cried Eli.

"I said now, helmsmen."

"Aye, aye, sir."

Eli spun the wheel. The schooner began to turn.

"Watch your head, everyone!" hollered Tim.

In a successful jibe, the unbridled fore and aft booms gracefully swept the ship's girth, while flogging jibs followed obediently. Tim and the boys yanked rapidly on the halyard as the large cotton sail rose into the sky like a mammoth theater curtain.

"Mister Assagai, take down the jibs," ordered Tim.

As the headsails were lowered the new sail promptly bloomed, filling the entire western horizon just above the bow. It was like no other sail I had ever seen. The only time I remember that much cloth sewn together was when the circus came to town, bringing with it an enormous domed tent. The sprightly light cloth hung above the schooner like a thousand bed sheets sewn together and cast to the wind. Though I thought it was unlikely that we could ever go any faster, the schooner immediately picked up speed. The nose of the ship was heaved high above the water while the bow wave sucked the stern squat and low. At any moment I felt like the ship would lift from the sea and fly. Aaron struggled as he made his way back onto the deck. The sundered waves created by the hull gurgled and gathered astern, collapsing behind us as we made our escape with tremendous speed. It did not seem natural that a sailing vessel could sail so fast and continue at such a rate. Tim scurried up the deck while captivated by the deployed sail.

"Stunning. I was uncertain what to expect, but its done the job," he said.

"Breathtaking," I said.

"Fascinating, Captain, just fascinating," commented Winton. "I'm impressed with your competence thus far."

Tim and I looked at one another and smiled. Winton peered over the side.

"I don't understand it," he commented.

I looked over the rail uncertain what he was looking for.

"What is it, Professor?"

"The progressive disturbance through the water propagated by the hull and the water it displaces should dictate our apparent velocity. The crests of the bow waves are moving at tremendous speed and yet we are accelerating much faster than the seas ahead of us. Physics dictates that it is not possible for us to be traveling at such a speed."

Eli struggled with the helm as the vessel twisted and yawed from its intended course. With the stub of the damp stogie hanging from his lower lip, he clung onto the wheel tightly with both hands. A captivating smile graced his face. At that very moment, Eli Monroe was having the ride of his life and loving it.

"Hold on to her, Mister Monroe," advised Tim.

"You bet, Captain. This is the most fun I have ever had at the wheel of a sailing vessel. There's no way that sloop will collide with us now. We will clear her by a mile."

The crew hung on as I did. Everyone was mesmerized by the colossal handkerchief that hung from the sky and how fast it drove us.

"Where did you ever acquire that rag?" Winton asked.

"It's called a spindrift sail. Samuel Cory had it imported from England. They use it on racing yachts over there."

We were now well out of the path of the oncoming ship as it passed behind us.

"Why do you suppose they were trying to collide with us," I asked.

"Don't know," replied Tim. "Give me the spyglass."

I handed him the monocular.

Aaron hinted at my inquiry. "That is th' sloop 'at tried tae run us doown when we left New Bedford."

"He's right," said Tim. "It's the black sloop. I wonder what their objective was to harass us way out here?"

"Misguided pride," said Eli. "We had made fools of them."

"Can I see?"

Tim handed me the glass.

"Aaron's right. It's the black sloop."

I studied the mystery ship through the spyglass. She sailed on a starboard reach just west of Sow and Pigs and heading south. I could make out a couple of men along the deck, but we were too far away to make out their faces. I thought I recognized one of the men. He looked like the fellow with the injured arm. I could not say for sure. Suddenly, a flag ran up the backstay and up to the masthead.

"They hoisted a flag, Timothy."

He took the glass from my eye.

"What is it," asked Eli. "I have never seen that flag before. Is it a state flag?"

"Don't know. It's a blue flag with a large white star in the center," said Tim "They ran it to the top of the stay and now they just brought it down halfway."

"They are dipping their ensign," Captain," declared Eli.

"What does it mean?"

"When one ship approaches another, it lowers his flag to half-mast as they pass," explained Eli. "It's an act of respect, a salute, if you may."

"A salute?"

"They are taking the flag down." I cried.

"They have just insulted you, Captain," noted Winton. "An act of defiance … a slap to the face."

"Is he right, Eli? Are they mocking us?"

"Can't say. Though after they dipped the flag, they should have raised it back up to the masthead once again. It's protocol."

"Don't you see, Captain, it is an action of ridicule," insisted Winton.

"What can you possibly know about it?" snarled Tim.

"It is the Bonnie Blue banner. And I know that much."

"Bonnie Blue? What does it stand for?" inquired Eli.

"I suppose it stands for the right of secession," jeered Winton.

"Secession? From what?" I inquired.

Winton beamed at me with a priggish smirk.

"Why … from the Union, my dear lady."
"The Union?"
"Yes. You see … the Bonnie Blue is the new Confederate flag."

Chapter 16:
Hick's Dreadful News

With *Sphinx* safely anchored in New Bedford Harbor, Tim and I started for the *Daily Whaler* while Frederick Johnson followed. Once I arrived, I discovered the old squeaky sign above the newspaper's door gently waving in a habitual breeze, as usual. It had become a friendly concierge welcoming me to work on most mornings. Once inside, the ovation was less subtle.

"Ah, the duchess of twavel and pleaswa," announced Ezra Hick. "We awe pwivileged with youw pwesence as always."

I turned a deaf ear to his disparaging wit and instead kept walking. "Morning, Mister Hick. Is he in?"

"Mistwa Fwench is always in."

Slyly, he scrutinized us, his glasses to the cusp of his nose, while shuffling papers along his desk. I led Tim and Frederick up to the office and found the door wide open. Inside, Rudolf French was thumbing through several newspapers with journals strewn upon his desk. Zoeth Winslow was standing by the window. The two men were discussing a trip Zoeth had taken to Providence where he was scouting for new underground stations. I knocked.

"Ah, look who's here?" wailed Rudolf. He ushered us in. "Welcome back, my girl."

There was the shaking of hands all around. The editor escorted me to my desk.

"Thank you, sir." I placed my purse and a few of my things down. "A pleasure to see you again, Zoeth."

"We were witnessing your arrival out the window. I pray the trip was a rousing success."

"It was wonderful."

"Went without a hitch," declared Tim.

"You mean with a hitch, my boy," chuckled Rudolf, with a nudge of the elbow. "Sailing vessels are full of them, eh?"

Tim smiled while the jovial editor patted him on the back.

"The only trouble was here in harbor when we left," Frederick, explained.

"Yes, I know. We need to talk about that. Most unfortunate. Come."

We followed him to his favorite window overlooking the harbor.

"There, tucked between that cluster of whaling ships along Leonard's wharf. See her?"

I looked out the window in the direction he pointed. One ship looked very much like the next, especially here where over fifty whaling vessels called New Bedford their home. Still, with its newly built bowsprit and freshly hewed wood, the brigantine stood out, though the imperial, mermaid figurehead once stationed off the bow was missing.

"That's the ship that was hindering our departure," I said.

"It's the brigantine, alright," Tim added.

"It is undergoing repairs," declared Zoeth. "New spars and bow structure."

"I watched from this very window the day you left for Nova Scotia. I must tell you my boy, that was some astonishing maneuvering."

"Captain Cadman bears brilliant sailing abilities, Rudolf," boasted Frederick.

"I am quite aware of that … mastery behind sail. It was a rather spectacular performance."

"I assure you. It was not my intention," complained Tim. "If only I could have avoided them, I would …"

"Oh no. It was not intentional on Timothy's part," I quickly helped explain. "He did the only thing he could do. And handled it brilliantly."

"I realize that. He was left little choice," said Rudolf. "It was a blockade."

"Thank you, sir. Apparently, they knew I had runaways aboard and wanted us to return. I was not prepared to do that," I said.

"They had a policeman aboard. He was ordering us to return," I said.

"It was a fraudulent demand," proclaimed Rudolf. "There was not a thing they could have done to stop you. Besides, I have since discussed the matter with the policeman that was aboard that day. He explained that he was hastily swept off the street by Morse and persuaded to try and stop you. They had no proof of any wrongdoing, nor did the police employ any sort of commissioned warrant."

"But how did they know we were carrying runaways?

"Gossip, chatter, my good woman." Rudolf sat himself down at his desk. "Come, everyone, sit."

We all pulled a chair. I, for one, had questions. "You said you spoke to the policeman."

"I know all of the badges," declared Rudolf. "I was assured that they have more critical duties on their plate than to chase down runaways. Besides, it's a federal matter. Local police shouldn't be sticking their noses into it."

"Who were those men we saw on the brig the day we left?"

"Can't say for certain. But I'm afraid that I may have uncovered a clue." He got up and walked to the window. Consternation suddenly occupied his thoughts. "I roamed the docks and did some snooping. That's how a newspaperman inhabits his time, opening doors, upsetting every stone. When the damaged ship was towed to the wharf, it became very clear to me what their intentions had been. Four gentlemen disembarked."

"Who were they?" asked Tim.

"Did you know them, recognize anything about them?" I asked.

"No, but Bulldog was one of them. That's Morse's strong arm. I tried to get a story. I introduced myself and asked for their names. They turned their backs to me and walked off. But I wasn't done, you see. As they went, I inevitably shouted out, welcome to New Bedford, Mister Dukes."

"You said you did not know any of them."

"That's right. However, the tall one turned and glared at me. And though I did not know him, I had the impression he knew me."

"Must have been very unsettling."

Rudolf French fell into a silent stupor, clasped hands behind his back, jouncing on his heels, and glaring out his meditative porthole to the world. It was an introspective posture, one that had become very familiar. An axiomatic certainty that he was preoccupied with unsettling memories … memories of the past, unexpected obstacles in the present, and challenging burdens for the future. "He knew those Black men were on your ship," he declared.

"Was it this Tyrone Dukes?" inquired Tim.

"Never met the man. I could not tell you if it was or was not."

"What did he look like?" I asked.

He just stared out the window shaking his head.

"Sir, the man. Can you tell us? What were his feathers?"

"Much younger than I. Blondish, mustache, sparse goatee, breaking into a scanty beard, very tall … had a patch over one eye. The other man had his jacket sleeve pinned at the shoulder … arm in a sling. Kept it inside his jacket."

I had a hunch that the men Aaron Kerr had wrestled with and the ones on the brig were the same. I felt strongly that I was right and was compelled to further investigate.

"Do you think those men had anything to do with Asha Potter's death?"

"Why would you say that?"

"Why wouldn't I? We must suspect everyone with ties to a Confederate state."

"I don't know. I just don't know," he bemoaned, his face in his hand.

"Did you notice the jacket the man was wearing? Did you look at the buttons? Were any missing?"

"I'm a newspaperman for heaven's sake, not a police investigator. Besides, he wouldn't have been wearing military gray, not here."

"Calm, Rudy, calm," advised Zoeth.

"Yes, of course. I just have a lot on my mind."

My reporter instinct simmered as the questions belched. "I'm sorry, Mister French. I was only trying to …"

"Not your fault, Emily. You can ask me anything you like if it will help solve the mystery behind Asha's death."

"Did you get to see what sort of buttons were on the jacket he was wearing?"

"I don't know. Silver metal, I think."

"Military?"

"He wouldn't be wearing anything military up here. It would raise suspicion and he could be detained as a spy. They were buttons, plain and simple. That's all I can tell you about it."

My inquiry was angering him. I was desperate to expose any sort of evidence or indication as a conspectus that would help promote my suspicions or bolster any suppositions I may harbor. However, questioning my employer so harshly may not have been the best approach. Still, I would continue to try.

"We should question this Bulldog fellow."

"They are not the only men up from the south searching for runaways. At present there are others … plantation overseers. Nevertheless, some of the whalers have informed me that those men on the brig were from the Carolinas. Considering the reward being offered, there are those that would turn in their dear mothers for a blue penny. We were lucky to get the boys up to Nova Scotia when we did."

Rudolf returned to his desk and shuffled through some periodicals. He handed me one. "Here … see what it says."

I read the paper's title, "*The Fall River News*." Below the paper's title and in larger script it declared, "North Carolina Secedes from the Union." And in a column toward the bottom of the paper, "Slaves make daring escape from Fall River on sailing vessel."

"Slaves … escape? How can they print such a thing without any concrete evidence?"

"News, my girl, news. One can fabricate and circulate any story which is presumed 'fit to print' … when the means to an end is selling of papers. Gossip and certitude is in the mind of the reader, whether veracity or blather. If there is no story you simply construct one … focus on questioning and interviewing those who allege to be in the know … those who appropriate assertions and allegations whether based in truth or not. Once the presses have cooled and the evening edition circulated, patrons are left to sort it all out for themselves and, in the end, left to arrive at their own conclusions. Before the truth can be unveiled and propagated, the rag has been torn and salvaged to carpet the tray of birdcages or appropriated as a doormat. Then it's on to the next sensational story. At least that is how some run a newspaper business. Very profitable, I may add. We do not operate that way. Here, at the *Daily Whaler*, it's about the facts, based on merit, plain and simple."

"I thought slavery was done away with here in the north," I proclaimed.

"In Massachusetts it has, since the 1780s," explained Frederick, "but southern slave lords still have the power to apprehend anyone the law spuriously considers lawful property. Even here in the Bay State."

"If you turn to page three," instructed Rudolf, "you will discover that a substantial reward of fifty dollars is being offered for information leading to the capture of runaway slaves. That's almost two month's pay for the average working man."

"Do we know who tipped them off?" inquired Tim.

"In all likelihood it was Tobias and his henchman. He holds shares in the brig that tried to run you down. He's also a slave sympathizer."

"Do you mean the old whaling captain that walks with a cane?" I said.

"One in the same," said Zoeth. "He's transporting well-needed cotton from the south. All the whalers along the wharves know about it."

"I noticed that not much news gets by them," said Frederick.

"Textile barons have been lobbying Washington for access to southern cotton," declared Rudolf. "There are so many politicians with their hands out that the price of cotton has doubled."

"I thought there was a blockade of southern ports," declared Tim.

"Charles Morse is not going to a southern port. He's been buying cotton in Nassau. If he has trouble getting past the blockade, he transports this haul to the British Isles. Indirectly, this helps the south raise cash to support the war effort."

"Nassau?"

"Of course, the cotton is coming directly from the port at New Orleans and piloted via the islands."

"Along with guns and other supplies," remarked Zoeth. "The danger is not in Morse bringing cotton home, for which many here have turned a blind eye, but that he may be dealing in contraband, weapons even.

Greenbacks are scarce in the Confederacy. They are desperate for supplies of all sorts."

"Ultimately, it is not our affair," declared Rudolf, getting up to pace the floor. "Until we have boldface confirmation, it is not a story fit to print. Our concern at the moment is to safely escort runaways that have been moving through our city and lessen the time they spend here."

"I agree," said Zoeth. "Since this war started, slaves have been arriving off the waters by way of New York at the count of three or four a week. We need to keep them moving before they are found out."

"Is it really practical to use a sailing vessel to transport one or two men?" Tim asked.

"You are right, Captain. I have reassessed," declared Rudolf. "The use of the *Advocator* or even *Sphinx* is out of the question at the moment. There are several whaling captains willing to take runaways and stop along the Canadian coast on their way to the arctic."

"Some slaves have even been hired as crew on whalers, which is of great fortune," Zoeth pointed out.

Zoeth Winslow was very much involved with the abolitionist movement—an actuality I was never aware of. The opposition to slavery was recondite and stealthy. Unless you were part of the Underground Railroad, others had little idea who its members were. Underground Stations were clandestinely scattered all over the countryside and, in many cases, where one would least expect it, for bondage knew no economic eminence nor did those willing to fight it. There was one fundamental factor that was prevalent in the antislavery cause—that was the complexion of someone's faith. I say complexion for not every believer was an abolitionist, but most abolitionists were cohesively bound to their godly beliefs. Point Road had its own little Underground Railway station at the Zoeth Winslow cottage, and no one in the village ever spoke about it or suspected it.

Zoeth lived with his mother a few doors up from me. His father had died long ago. He was old enough to be a big brother. When I started school as a child, Zoeth was the age I am now. Still, we complemented one another. We were about the same height though, for a girl, I can be considered ample and leggy. He is median complected, with brown eyes and brown hair. Zoeth could easily lose himself in a crowd. He lived a life of moderation. Proof of it was revealed in his abstemious physique and healthy appearance. He retained a very practical nature. Like Tim, he was easy going and tolerant of his fellow man. Devout and spiritual, every endeavor began and concluded with prayer. The more hardship he endured the more thankful he was. I must confess that I am but a pagan when uniformly juxtaposed with Zoeth's Christian devotion. Grandmamma and he often talked about their faith—and wrangled over academic precepts for hours.

"I pray to the trees in my field, to the rocks by the river's shore, and to the sun that warms me every day. For they are all God, and God is in all," I often heard Grandmamma sermonize.

To Zoeth, this spoke to nihilistic and primitive practices. "One needs to have salvation," he would preach to her.

"Talk to a tree," she would remark, "and you shall find it," at which point I would have to leave the room or be consumed by Christian doctrine and native tradition.

Though Grandmamma practiced Christianity, her native roots were deep, and she weaved tribal ideology and scriptural creed into one. Zoeth was certain that Grandmamma was wandering down the wrong path to heaven. She was convinced that every path leads there.

"I need to get back to the ship," announced Tim. "Get it ready for the short sail back to Westport."

"I'm sure we will see one another again," declared Rudolf.

"You know who to talk to if you need me," said Tim, meaning me.

"See you back at the ship tonight, Emily."

"Hold up. I'll walk out with you, Captain," cried Frederick.

After Tim and Frederick left, Zoeth sat by Rudolf's desk and the two men discussed the trip Zoeth had taken to Providence and the Underground Station houses he visited. I took to my desk by a window and tidied up. I watched Tim row out to the *Sphinx*, stopping, every once in a while, to bail. It was apparent that the small makeshift boat was still leaking.

I updated the journal I had kept on our trip to Nova Scotia. I have discovered that, since working for the newspaper, I post a narrative every day. Along with my personal account, I was faced with the challenge of writing something for the paper without substantiating the account of escaping slaves that was written in the Fall River paper. I began writing when, unexpectedly, the office door burst open, slamming the wall behind it. It was Ezra Hick. Molly was close behind.

"Mistwa Fwench, Mistwa Fwench, we have a cwisis."

"Oh Papa, Papa," cried Molly running to her father.

She bundled her arms around him as Ezra tried to explain.

"Thewe's been a kidnapping. They tied hewa up."

"Kidnapping?"

"At the house, Mistwa Fwench?"

"Now, let us all calm down."

Rudolf knelt and clasped his daughter by the arms. "Now, Molly, what happened?"

"Some men, they took her."

"Took who?"

"Hannah," sobbed the young girl. "They took her away."

"What do you mean they took her away? Who took who away?"

"Three men. They came to the barn. Hannah and I were bringing a meal to Malachi and Ruth. We were just sitting and talking when I heard some men outside the barn."

"Men?"

"Yes. Ruth and Queenie ran and hid in the hay loft."

"Who is Queenie," I asked.

"Ruth is the runaway. Queenie is her daughter," explained Rudolf.

"They took Malachi and Hannah," cried Molly.

"When did this happen, Molly?" asked Zoeth. A worried Rudolf paced the floor.

"Hours ago."

"Hours ago?" I uttered.

"I was locked in the barn with Ruth. We were afraid they would come back. We hid for a long time."

"I'm going for the police," declared Zoeth. He scooped up his coat and walked out.

"Have them meet us at the house," begged a frantic Rudolf. "Ezra, make certain the evening edition is out on time. I may be gone for the day."

"I will Mistwa Fwench."

"Let's get to the house." Rudolf grabbed his hat. "Come, Emily."

"No, Papa. I'm afraid."

"Come, Molly, take my hand," I encouraged her. "We will go together."

Molly and I got to the house a full minute behind her father. When we arrived at the bungalow, Rudolf was whisking from room to room with frenetic shouts, calling out for the governess. We waited by the front entrance. Molly had her arms around my waist, her head tucked beneath my arm.

She kept reciting under her breath. "They took her, Emily. They took her."

"Don't worry," I said. "We'll find her. I promise."

I am not one for making assurances I ultimately could not fulfill, especially when I had no idea what the unfolding circumstances were at the French residence. It was one of those thoughtless axioms we utter when we are lost for words. For now, it was all I had to offer her.

Rudolf dashed by us and ran across the grassy yard on his way to the barn. The outbuilding was off to the corner of the property and well behind the house. With Molly clutching my arm, we scurried over together.

The side door to the barn was swung open. Nailed by the side of the door was a small plaque that read *Morgan Stables.* A studded padlock hung from the latch and was torn from its rusty hasp. The barn was where Morgan horses were housed during winter months, fattened, and sold. In the summer, the animals were kept in a field across the river in Fairhaven at Rudolf French's breeding farm and country home. Raising cavalry horses was one of his many pastimes. I noticed that all the horse stalls were scrubbed clean and bedded with fresh hay. Able to bunk horses comfortably, the barn appeared huge inside. For stables, it was well kept, with two-inch, pine-planked flooring and walls lined in lacquered oak wainscoting. Up until today, it was home to a slave family—the Bonneaus—Malachi, Ruth, and their daughter.

Molly and I shuffled in cautiously. Rudolf was already there, calling out for Hannah. We made our way to the back of the building beyond the stalls to the tack room. Molly anxiously peeked inside. "This is their room," she said. "Papa removed all the saddles and grain bins and fixed it up. It's almost as nice as my room, don't you think?"

The space was newly painted and made comfortable. There were two cots with clean blankets and, between them, a small table and oil lantern. On a far wall was a small coal stove topped with an enamel teakettle. Though the space had no window and felt a bit stuffy, it was recently whitewashed and made bright and homey. There was even a floral rug on the floor by the bed brought over from the house. But it was the small cot that was along one wall that caught my eye. This was Queenie's bed. Hung on the wall well above it was a Wampanoag cradleboard, adorned with a kaleidoscope of wampum beads, colorful ribbons, and twine made from willow and cattail fibers. It was embellished with fancy stones taken along the beaches and cliffs of Gay Head and woven with buckskin and rawhide. I walked up to the small crib-like bunk and ran my hand along the Indian blanket that covered it.

"That's Queenie's bed," said Molly. "And that's Hannah's cradleboard from when she was a baby. She stored it there to help ward off evil spirits."

"It's beautiful," I said. I was very familiar with the Wampanoag baby hamper. Grandmamma often used one to transport infants when she cared for them.

We wandered around the little room while Rudolf called out for Hannah. Suddenly I heard shuffling on the ceiling above my head. Hay dust came drizzling down from between the ceiling boards.

"It's Ruth," said Molly. "She's hiding." She ran outside the small chamber and hollered up to the rafters. "Ruth, it's me … Molly. Papa is here. You can come down now."

I looked up to the bales of hay stacked up to the roof beams just above the tack room. Abruptly, a ladder appeared and was lowered to the floor. Rudolf helped as Ruth handed him five-year-old Queenie.

"What happened here, Ruth?" inquired Rudolf.

"Some men busted in ayn' done took Miss Hannah ayn' Malachi, Mistuurr French." She sobbed, her daughter clinging to her leg. "They'a gone. They'a gone."

"Did you see any of them?" I asked.

"No, Miss. Molly and me done hid in the hay loft. Ay were afraid ta look down."

"I saw them," trumpeted Molly.

"You saw the men, Daughter?"

"From between two bales. They couldn't see me."

"Would you know what they look like if you saw them again," I asked.

"Uh huh. I sure would. At least one of them. I saw him very clearly. The one that was beating on Malachi had a scrap or mask over his face."

"How about the other two men?" said Rudolf.

"Well … not as much. They were wrestling and punching Malachi on the floor. I was afraid. One of them was a giant. They quickly took Malachi away."

"A giant?" I said.

"Uh huh. When they carried Malachi out the door, the tall man bumped his head."

Rudolf and I looked at one another. Concerned consternation flushed onto his face.

"That door is almost seventy-six inches high," he said.

"They must know Malachi. They kept calling him by his name," said Molly.

"Did you see them take Hannah away?" I inquired.

"They choked her from behind and held a sponge to her face."

"A sponge?" said Rudolf.

Molly began to cry, as the image of Hannah being dragged away was made fresh in her mind. "There was nothing I could do Papa, nothing I could do."

"Where did this happen?" I asked.

"There," she pointed. "Hannah was hiding behind the door. They choked her," she sobbed uncontrollably, "they choked her until she died."

"Now, now," said Rudolf embracing his daughter. "I don't think she's dead."

"You don't?" she sniveled.

"If she was dead, they wouldn't have taken her."

I looked behind the door. There was a large chest with a wooden lid, used to store coal. On the floor near the chest, I discovered a bottle. One similar to the bottles Grandmamma used for her potions. It was empty of its contents. On it was a paper label with large lettering that read: *Chloropormum Purificatum* and, below it in smaller script, *Kirby Druggist, No. 3 Main Street, Charleston, South Carolina.*

"What do you have there?"

"Looks like an empty bottle of anesthesia."

"You mean like ether?" he asked, taking the bottle from my hand. He raised the small flask to his face and wrinkled his nose. "It's a biting scent."

"Yes," I said. "Like syrupy vinegar and a peppery smell. It's chloroform. Works just like ether, though doctors don't use ether any longer. This compound's not as dangerous or flammable."

"Where did you find it?"

"Behind the door … on the floor."

Rudolf was an exemplar of nimbleness under duress. Not much rattled him. This did. Though not panic-stricken, he certainly appeared overwrought. I would not consider him of sound mind if he were not. Though he was composed and unflappable at first, Rudolf French perspired. He paced in short strides, the bottle in his hand, and holding his head as if it was about to explode.

"It must be what they used to incapacitate her," I said. "We had a doctor on the *Sphinx* who carried a bottle in his medical bag. I saw him use it once. He poured it over a sponge and placed it over the face. Used it when stitching lacerations or to assist in childbirth."

"Did you say you saw the man use a sponge, Molly?" asked Rudolf.

"Uh huh. He held it over Hannah's face. I saw it. He suffocated her with it."

"What did this fellow look like," I asked.

"Like any other man."

"That's of little help, Daughter."

"What sort of hair did he have … the color of his eyes. Was he tall, fat?"

"Regular hair. He had a beard. I couldn't see the color of his eyes. They were very narrow. He was a little taller than Hannah. She was struggling as he held her from behind. He made faces."

"What sort of faces?" I asked her.

"Like this." She squished her face and gritted her teeth. "And he had teeth missing. He wore a gray jacket, and it was buttoned with one button."

"One button?"

"Uh huh. The top one … at his neck."

"A gray jacket, sir," I pointed out. "It may be a Confederate jacket."

"Everyone wears a gray or black jacket. I'm afraid it's of little help."

"I would know him if I saw him again," said Molly.

"You would?" I said.

"Oh, yes. I would know him."

"Molly, take Ruth and Queenie to the house and show them to the spare room upstairs," instructed her father.

"Would you like to see my room, Queenie?"

"Use the back door so no one sees you."

"Follow me, Ruth." Molly took Queenie by the hand.

Ruth Bonneau, still sobbing, would not move. She was afraid and uncertain.

Rudolf placed a friendly arm around the young girl. "Come, Ruth. Go with Molly. You will be safer inside the house."

Queenie reached out for her mother's hand and the three of them walked out. A minute later, Zoeth sprinted up the drive with a policeman in tow. Rudolf rushed over to meet them.

As the three men spoke, I inspected the inside of the barn. I picked up the oily chloroform bottle where Rudolf had left it sitting on a bench. I looked around the floor for the missing cork stopper. Swinging the barn door, I searched behind it and around the coal bin. Finally, there it was. As I knelt to pick it up, I was distracted by something that quickly snagged my eye. An icy tingle crept up my spine and a palpitating heart skipped a beat. With listless approach, I got down on one knee and scrutinized what was there.

The floor was coated with a sheer blanket of coal dust. Embedded in the black talc was a distinct impression—an infamous signature. One left by a boot. It was clear and undeniable—an etching of evil. I hovered a trembling hand above what had become an unintentional endorsement of a trespasser's presence—possibly someone diabolical and fiendish. I did not dare disturb the sullied stamping. Though faint, it was there. I counted carefully. Four, five, six, yes … seven, and finally eight. Eight dints made by square nail heads and dimpled into the coal dust in the shape of a horseshoe. I paid particular attention to the spacing between the markings. The first two were very close and almost touching. The remainder of the indentations had nearly a half-inch spacing between them. They were uncommon impression by rivets on the sole of footwear.

Rumination quickly found me back at Wamsutta Mills and the footprint I had discovered in blood. They were the same. Were they really made by a killer's foot? Or was it all just a faultless clue, one made by a pawn, an innocent bystander, erroneous evidence that was prescribed to be what it was not—all by a young foolish girl who thinks she is clever but, in fact, has no business musing such assumptions? Nonetheless, it could not be ignored. Although I had no intention of mentioning it to Rudolf French, I was sure not to forget it.

Chapter 17:
A Bold Proposal

Seven worrisome days had gone by since the disappearance of Hannah and the black slave, Malachi. After having offered a reward of two hundred dollars for their return, and a number of newspaper articles associated with the fiendish kidnapping, Rudolf French called for an emergency meeting of the Anti-Slavery Whaling Society. The usual members were all present. Though not officially a member of the society, I had asked Tim to be there.

Rudolf suspended the evening edition of the paper and excused employees for the remainder of the day. This included a bewildered and less-than-willing Ezra Hick, whose only interest in life was working at the paper. The building's doors were bolted and window shutters secured. Secrecy was of utmost importance.

Rudolf struck the gavel and Edgar Ryan flung open his ledger. The society had come to order. The editor appeared tired and disheveled, with shirt wrinkled and necktie hitched into a rumpled bow. He had not shaven for days and his ashen hair was a spectacle of fleeting tangles.

"Shut it, Edgar," he ordered. "We are not taking notes over what is heard here today. I'd like to start by announcing that Zoeth here has spoken with Edward Soule, the master of the whaler *President*. He has offered to transport Ruth Bonneau and her daughter to Shelburne, Nova Scotia, on their way to Arctic waters."

"Is that not far from Halifax or the settlements at Greenville and Yarmouth," I inquired.

"I can explain," said Frederick Johnson.

"By all means, please do," said Rudolf.

"You see, the master of the whaler *President* is more than happy to supply transport, but not to swing west toward Yarmouth, which would place them into headwinds and ill currents. Shelburne, along the east coast, will be their destination. From there, Ruth and her daughter will be taken to Birchtown, just outside Shelburne. There is a small community there of loyalists of color who can help."

"Great news, Rudy," wailed Silas Brownell.

"Loyalists?" I said.

"Precisely," said Frederick. "Black runaways who populated the small community of Birchtown and Shelburne after the Revolutionary War. I have written to the preacher of the African Baptist church there. He is prepared to take in Ruth and her daughter and render them shelter."

"Wonderful," I declared.

"Rudy, have you heard any news of Hannah?" inquired Silas.

"Nothing." Rudolf rubbed his face in his hands. "Consequently, I cannot sit idle while these turncoats violate those I value. Many of you feel as strongly as I do—together with those in the whaling community and other mariners who have been attacked offshore by Confederate renegades. Most of us here at the newspaper may be beyond military fighting age, but it does not mean we cannot contribute and consolidated some muscle and do something."

"Easier said than done," said the doctor. He reclined in his chair, balancing his weight precariously on the chair's rear legs, and rocked. "As you made plain, Rudy, we are no longer pups."

"No. But we can still deliver a bite. I have consulted a few whaling captains and ship owners … received an enthusiastic response." Rudolf got up and slowly walked to the window. We followed him with our eyes as he sauntered across the room—hands in pocket, head down, and thinking with his feet. "Tell them, Zoeth," he said.

"We have plans to sail a fleet of ships down to one of the major Southern ports, perhaps Savannah or Charleston, and set up a blockade."

"A blockade," sneered Edgar. "With what?"

"Whaling vessels."

"Whaling vessels!" he barked. "Why, they would deploy a gunship in minutes and sink them like crippled ducks."

"Precisely, my good fellow."

"What are you on about?" begged Edgar.

A contemptuous chuckle cackled from across the room.

"Presumptuous youth," roared Rudolf. "They have all the answers but none of the solutions. Conclusions adorn from a naked wardrobe, one lacking critical observation and foresight. These are today's spiraling luminaries, you see." He wagged a finger of adjuration at the boy. "Now, if you are quiet and let the man finish, my young prodigy, we will all discover what it is about."

"In all fairness, Edgar's not a military man," I interrupted in a somewhat feeble endorsement of juvenescence. “I am certain once he hears the entire plan, he will agree that it is brilliant.”

“Ah, the accommodating strategy of diplomacy, my girl,” declared Rudolf. “It’s to your credit, Edgar, to have comfort in one so loyal.”

Edgar Ryan timidly shook his head and bit his tongue.

Of course, I had no inkling as to Zoeth’s proposal. I may have spoken too soon to judge whether the plan was brilliant or even contained an ethos of success. The error in Edgar’s remark was that it was fashioned prematurely and rudely. As Grandmamma often said, “Fasten not your doors and humble yourself with truth. Never disparage the jester. Or he may laugh at you.” Valued advice, if only I was certain what Grandmamma meant by it. Nonetheless, I am sure it would have served Edgar well if they were spoken to him.

“Would these whaling vessels be fitted with weaponry?” I asked.

“No, no, nothing of a sort,” explained Zoeth. “We are not qualified or trained in such militant measures.”

“Allow me to make it plain and simple,” added an exasperated Rudolf, as he returned to his desk. “Our plan is to sail down to a major southern port with old and noncommissioned whaling vessels, many which are rotting at the dock and taking up dockage. I have spoken to their owners and they are prepared to sacrifice them for the Union cause. Now, once we sail them south, our plans are to sink them at the mouth of the harbor and construct a man-made reef of beam and timber. As it stands now, the whaling business is severely in decline. The old ships will go to a righteous cause.”

“How many vessels are we talking about?’ asked Silas.

“We have over twenty commitments as we speak,” declared Zoeth. “There will be more. We are holding our first meeting with captains and owners this week.”

“Captains Wood, Bailey, Tilton, Swift, Childs … nearly twenty of us in all,” explained Rudolf. “We will compile a magnificent flotilla of majestic whaling vessels. Once we enter a southern harbor, we will sink one ship after another. And since they are not sloops of war, the citizenry ashore will have no idea what is happening until it is done.”

“Especially if we arrive at night,” added Zoeth.

“A blockade will have been established.”

“It can take a good amount of time for a large ship to fill with water and sink,” added Tim. “Scuttled vessels do not always stay in one place. A minor storm and tide change could drive them ashore or out to sea.”

“We have thought of that,” explained Zoeth. “Four-inch holes, ten in each ship, will be drilled in the hull—sealed with bungs. Before we leave New Bedford, we shall fill the ships with stones. When the time comes, we knock the bungs out. Once the ships sink, they will surely stay on the bottom."

"Stones?" I said.

"Yes, stone and rock donated by farmers in the surrounding towns. They are all more than happy to assist—ready to donate the stones that cobble the walls around their fields. We shall use them as ballast ... to weigh down the ships."

"Brilliant!" exclaimed Edgar.

Everyone broke out in laughter.

Tim remained stoic. "I don't think they have thought this through," he whispered.

"You don't?"

"Not wise to poke a nest of hornets."

"How do you mean?"

"A move like this will only anger those in the Confederacy. They will retaliate and hunt down every whaler that leaves harbor, from here to Greenland."

"Oh, don't tell me that, Timothy."

Tim's grumbling undertones attracted the editor.

"You have a question, Mister Cadman?"

"Not at the moment."

"I have one." Frederick Johnson rose to his feet. "What does the Anti-Slavery Society have to do with any of this?"

"Nothing," replied Rudolf. "Future meetings will be curtailed, and advocacy decreased while I work on the whaling Stone Fleet, that's all."

"Stone Fleet? How suitable," remarked the good doctor.

"What of our Underground Rail duties as a society," sounded Frederick.

"Of course, we shall not waver in our labor to help runaways," assured Rudolf. "And, if any complications arise, I shall simply call for an urgent meeting. I am certain we can work things out."

"What of the search for Hannah?" I asked.

"We shall speak of it later. Are there any other questions?"

We all sat somewhat mystified by the grand scheme of things. With the exception of Dr. Brownell, who sat quite contently cradling an unlit pipe in hand while chewing on its mouthpiece. It was all beyond our ability and faculty as lowly members of an anti-slavery guild. But the meeting appeared important to the newspaperman and he had the means to carry it out. Hannah's kidnapping had awakened an angry abolitionist in Rudolf French. The war in the South has come home for us.

"I adjourn this meeting of the Anti-slavery Whaling Society," announced Rudolf, slamming the gavel on his desk.

With the meeting over, everyone left, with the exception of Zoeth Winslow. I returned to my desk and began to work on an outstanding story about affluent city dwellers and the time spent at their summer seaside estates. Such places were emerging all over the New England coast as those with the wherewithal escaped the heat of summer to oceanfront properties—cool breezes and quiet surroundings. I had nearly finished editing the first few sentences when I was ordered to stop what I was doing.

"Come over and pull up a seat, my girl," instructed Rudolf. "I have a proposal to put forward. Your services will prove beneficial."

Zoeth took a chair and slipped it beneath me. In my hands were the tools of the trade—a pencil and notepad.

"That will not be necessary. This is a personal matter," said the newspaperman.

"Yes, sir."

"I am certain now. As you have suspected, Tyrone Dukes had something to do with Hannah's disappearance … and dare I say, the possible death of Asha Potter—whether directly or by someone in his party."

"Why would they have taken Hannah?"

"Revenge, perhaps," said Zoeth. "For helping slaves escape."

"You see, Malachi was familiar to Dukes," explained Rudolf. "He was one of his slave hands. Ruth and her daughter, on the other hand, came from another plantation nearby."

"You think Tyrone Dukes would stoop to kidnapping?"

"He doesn't see it as kidnapping," said Zoeth. "To him, it's more like taking back what's his. He sees Hannah as just an Indian, retribution. You take my property, and I will take yours."

"But they are people. People like you and me. Not property."

"Those in the slave trade are intolerant and unforgiving in their creed," added Zoeth.

"A creed the French call *racisme*," said Rudolf. "An attitude that favors a particular color in people, using hostile measures to control and censor them."

"How would they have known that Hannah was Indian? She didn't look or dress like one."

"Molly said she was dressed in Indian attire when they kidnapped her. You see, she was leaving that day for Aquinnah on Martha's Vineyard to attend a powwow, or spiritual celebration."

"Most unfortunate," declared Zoeth, shaking his head.

"I am hoping you would be willing to help, Emily. Investigate Hannah's kidnapping."

"Of course, I would. Anything I can do."

"Well then, here is the plan. As you know Molly has been begging to visit her mother in Charleston."

"Yes, I know."

"I have decided to let her go."

"Oh?"

"Yes. However, this is a time of war."

"Do you think it wise?"

"There is free movement between North and South at the moment. Both sides exhibit a constitutional respect for the average civilian and the freedom to cross borders."

"Unless you are an able-bodied fighting man," cautioned Zoeth. "In which case, one may be suspected of being a deserter, spy, or saboteur."

"When crossing the border, youth has its handicap," declared Rudolf.

"Is it not a long way for Molly to travel alone?"

"She will not be alone … that is, if you will accompany her."

"You mean down …"

"To Charleston and Dukes Plantation. Since the battle of Fort Sumter, Charleston has become a Confederate stronghold. It should be safe there. I don't see that changing in the near future. Most of the fighting is being done south of the Bull Run River … closer to the border."

"Charleston?" I was taken back by the possible prospect of travel.

"Charleston's a city of forty thousand—a southern citadel. Little fear of military conflict there," declared Rudolf. "Both sides are avoiding cities with large populations."

"Civilian casualties are avoided at all costs," said Zoeth.

South Carolina. How titillating. When I think about it, the furthest south I had ever been was Cuttyhunk Island, a few miles across the bay from where I live. For me a trip to the Carolinas would be comparable to a sojourn to Europe.

"Why now?" I asked, knowing Rudolf had been reluctant to let Molly visit her mother.

"Molly can identify the man who kidnapped Hannah."

"And possibly the killer of Asha Potter."

"At the moment, our concern is to find Hannah and bring her home. That is where you come in."

"And what if Molly does identify the man? What can I possibly do?"

"That remains to be seen. In any event, you will need to do your share of snooping while retaining confidentiality. If you find Hannah, you will notify us of her location, and we will dispatch a contingency along with authorities to deliver her."

"Do you think Hannah is on the Dukes Plantation?"

"Don't know," replied Rudolf. "The possibility does exist that she has been sold anywhere between Virginia and Louisiana."

"What if she has, sir? How could we possibly find her?"

With impetuous frustration, Rudolf threw his hands in the air and jumped from his chair. He walked to the window running his fingers frantically through his hair. "Well, we can't very well sit here and do nothing," he roared. He paced the floor.

"Composure, Rudolf. The young lady asked a valid question."

"Unforeseeable circumstances call for unpredictable measures. We will never find her if we lollygag around here just praying for something to happen."

"Still, prayer is a factor we must consider, Rudy."

"Yes, yes, pray, Zoeth, pray! But prayer without works is to no avail. God helps he who … well you know the rest."

"Grandmamma often said, 'If we supply the hook and rod, God will supply the bass and cod.'"

"Dear, dear, Charlotte," said Zoeth, sounding pleased.

"In that regard, Molly will be the line and hook and you, my girl, the rod. To insure you arrive in Charleston safely, Zoeth will be the vessel."

"Vessel, sir?"

"I will chaperon you and Molly," declared Zoeth. "Make certain you arrive at the border safely."

"Will we encounter fighting on the way?" I stuttered, suddenly feeling somewhat fearful, if not untutored.

"Little chance of that."

"It's a long way, Rudy. Anything can happen, Lord forbid."

"We need not go there," declared the editor. "I have already made accommodations … reserved passage for three on the steamer *Vanderbilt*. Destination Washington. From there, Molly and Emily will take a carriage to Richmond and the train to Charleston. You, Zoeth, will return home."

"When do I leave?" I asked.

"End of the week."

"Oh?"

"Problem."

"Not at all, sir."

"You appear disconcerted."

"Just a slight burp of anticipation."

"Quite understood. After all, it is short notice. But fear not. We have the remainder of the day to do some shopping and get ready."

"Shopping?"

"Yes … get you girls steamer trunks and clothing to fill them."

"Oh, that will not be necessary. I have my own …"

He interrupted and quickly raised his hand in resolved opposition. "We shall not entertain dispute. I insist. We shall write it off as business expense. You will bear no cost. You shall be considered on duty, you see. After all, you represent the French household. You must portray it with regard and competence. To do that you must display the requisite of function and license as a governess. That, my girl, starts with how you present yourself. A finely dressed governess speaks mastery to authority. And to do that you must first consider appearance."

"Governess?"

"You will accompany Molly as her guardian, for all intents and purposes. No time to waste, my girl." He sprung from his chair and put on his hat and coat. "Time to go shopping."

Before I could summon any practical assessment, we were all scuttling out the door.

Chapter 18:
The Boat to Washington

Tim gripped the cowhide strap handle with both hands. At the other end a red-headed boy did the same. They shuffled along, lugging a camelback travel trunk out to an awaiting carriage. The chest, overlaid with drab green canvas and bandaged with studded, oak slats, swung precariously from side to side, as the boy floundered out the front door. Coiled fiery hair dangled over his eyes as he fidgeted with the leather strap, barely clutching onto it. Waxen knuckles and protracted fingers labored precariously. He bit an extended tongue while exhibiting a trying frown as if the grimacing mien amplified the strength of twiggy arms.

"Oh, please don't hurt yourself," I begged.

"Come on, Billy. It's not that heavy."

The boy tripped over his untied shoelaces.

"Don't drop it," instructed Tim.

"I, I won't," groaned Billy, teetering over the threshold.

The trunk continued its journey out the door. I followed while looking back and inspecting the cottage's small interior. Dishes were washed and put away, floors swept, and curtains drawn. All that remained was to secure the door and hide the key. I could not believe that I was leaving home for parts unknown, away from slumbering Westport and Point Village, uncertain when I would return. Butterflies fluttered in my fluctuant stomach and a cool breeze snatched my breath. I sighed. Apprehension and unexpected ambivalence hijacked all the enthusiasm and desire I should have felt. Suddenly, I was unsure of things. But this trip spoke to the duties of my employment and that was not an obligation I was about to shun.

At that very moment, I must tell you, I felt troubled by the absence of any news about Samuel away at war. Missing, they described it. Just what does that mean? I was too distressed to give it any worthwhile thought. Nonetheless, I longed for him terribly. I felt abandoned and deserted, disavowed of affection—bound in a plight of loss—selfish sympathy, perhaps. It was a consciousness that I've acquired since Grandmamma passed away and one that I was unable to thwart.

Across the room sat the well-worn thatched rocking chair where Grandmamma spent her evenings reading. The woven straw seat was torn and sunken. A puffy pillow covered the damaged reeds. It was positioned between a south window, facing the wharfs, and the exposed brick fireplace. On one end of the hewed mantle above the hearth sat an oval basket of dried herbs and flowers and on the other an assortment of empty bottles—vacant flasks that had been washed and made ready for the next batch of healing potions that Grandmamma would have brewed and filled. Once ready, she would peddle the homemade elixir, persuading patrons of its medicinal endowments and curative properties, and offering their money back if the remedy did not work. Most of these mixtures were made of simple fruit and vegetable juice blended with sour mash alcohol and tainted with pepper or garlic. But no one ever returned for their money. The more expensive potions had a pinch of laudanum in them, medicine prescribed to her by her doctor for joint pain. At a dollar a bottle, the opiate-fortified potions were a penance—monetary profit in exchange for ache and discomfort—inflammation of the joints, and a cost that Grandmamma suffered as a method of placing food on the table. Sometimes her ailment got the best of her and, when she could endure the pain no longer, she would consume her own elixir.

The green-colored glass sat in a cluster on the oak mantle, like empty vessels of ale or cider left on a dank table at the local tavern. I did not have the heart to remove or toss them out. Perched where she had left them, they had become a cryptic memorial of hollow glass. It was an assortment of doting memories of the woman who raised me.

Cherished remembrance lingered as a pair of arms embraced me from behind. A delicate chin rested on my shoulder and a silky cheek cloaked in wispy hair nestled against my face.

"Oh, Emmie, I'm going to miss you so much."

I reached back, wrapping my arms around hers. "I'll miss you too, Amy," I assured her, cuddling my cheek against hers. "But before you know it, I'll be back home … you'll see."

Walking across the room, she tossed herself into the rocker. She grimaced as she sank deep into the chair's damaged webbing.

"Not the most comfortable place to sit, I'm afraid," I acknowldged.

"This was Charlotte's favorite chair, if I remember." She rubbed her hands along the rocker's burnished arms and rocked away.

"Yes, it was. Needs mending."

"Must be a year now since she died."

I was about to reply when my words dwindled on my tongue and dissolved away. I swallowed my thoughts and abandoned any retort. Instead, I turned and looked out the window. Down by the fishing docks, Lilly Mosher wagged a finger of objection while arguing with one of the fishermen about the price of his catch. Holding the striped bass high in the air and away from her, he shook his head and, with his free hand, rubbed his forefinger and thumb together while they haggled over the cost of fish. Just beyond them, the whaler *Janet* raised its main, a curtain of oily sail, allowing the ashen canvas to air and dry in the crisp morning sun. Soaring along the shore, a clever seagull dropped a clam from up high onto the rocky beach, cracking open his dawn meal. Yes, I will miss Point Village.

Tim stood by the door, arms crossed, waiting. "Trunks all loaded, Emmie. I've paid the boy for the help and sent him on his way."

"Thank you, Timothy, let me pay you." I reached into my small handbag.

"Please don't. It was just pocket change."

"Are you sure?"

"I'm sure. Now, we are going to Fall River, is that right?" he said.

"Yes. They should be waiting for us there. We are taking the *Bay State* steamboat to New York."

"Well, I'm ready to roll anytime you are."

"I should let you go," sighed Amy, springing to her feet.

I slipped on a waistcoat and flung my reticule over my shoulder.

"I love your dress, Emmie," declared Tim.

"Do you really?" I looked down and inspected my outfit.

"Very smart. Don't you think so, Amy?"

"It's that blue-striped blouse," observed Amy. "Believe me. I know fashion. Plays nicely off the flutes on the white tussah ankle dress." She circled me admiring my apparel. "I never knew you worked with silk, Emmie."

"Oh, I didn't sew this. It was store bought."

"Store bought. Well, I never ..." She pinched the material of the dress, caressing the cloth between her fingers.

"I thought you made all your clothing?"

"Mister French insisted I buy an entire new wardrobe for myself. Took me to every dress shop in town."

"You don't say?"

"Paid for it all himself."

"Where did he take you?"

"Well, there was a small shop, ah ... Lady's Attire by Rose. Another called La Mode Elegant and Women's Garment and Apparel, to name a few. Oh, yes. And a couple of shoe stores."

"Shoe stores? I'm jealous."

"I had never even been inside a woman's dress shop before. The money they ask for store-bought clothing these days is disgraceful."

"No worry. Uncle French has a bottomless billfold."

"I still don't feel right about spending that sort of money."

"I would," Amy concluded.

Not accustomed to being dressed in such fine clothing, I tugged at my blouse and straightened the pleats on my dress.

"I feel swaddled in these clothes. That trunk that left here is full of such frills and ruffles. And hats … one for every day of the week. He just insisted on buying and buying. Said I had to look professional for my assignment."

"Lucky girl."

"Even the travel trunk was his idea."

"While you girls chat, I'll be in the wagon," proclaimed Tim, tired of waiting.

"Better get going," said Amy. She picked up the key I kept on a small table by the front door. "I'll lock up for you."

"I'll write as soon as I'm settled."

"You better."

She took the ribbon and straw bonnet I was holding and tied it on my head.

"Oh, Amy. You are so good to me."

"What are friends for? Now, best get going."

She pushed me out the door.

We rolled into the steamboat yard at the bottom of Central Street in Fall River. Rudolf French and his daughter were waiting. Molly rushed over. She jumped up and down with elation while waiting for me to step down from the carriage.

"Hello, Molly."

"Miss White, Miss White, is this not marvelous?"

"Sure is."

With my feet barely on the ground, she threw her arms around me. "We are going to have a grand time, aren't we?"

"I expect so. Why are you suddenly calling me Miss White?"

"Awh, Papa said I should address you with respect. Said you are not my playmate."

"Nonsense. You may continue to call me Emily," I whispered. "As soon as your father is gone."

She grinned and ran off to meet Zoeth who was just arriving.

Rudolf French walked over to greet him. Covertly, Tim took me by the arm and swept me around the side of the baggage shed.

"Listen Emmie. As soon as you get to this Dukes Plantation, I want you to write Amy and let us know exactly where you have settled. One never knows what may happen while you are away."

"God forbid, I'm not expecting anything to happen to you … or Amy."

"I'm not talking about us. I'm talking about you. You are stepping into enemy territory."

"Oh, Timothy. I'm not off to Cameroon or Central Africa. This is America. We are all one country."

"Not since Sumter. I mean it. I don't trust that Rudolf French."

"Timothy Cadman, I can't believe you just said that."

"No, no! He's a nice enough fellow and all that. It's his judgment that lacks reliance. Why, he's a … an eccentric idealist. Talking about sinking whalers in southern harbors and all that. Who would do such a thing?"

"Oh, Timothy. Do you think he would send his daughter into harm's way?

He grasped me by both arms. "Just promise to write … straight away."

"I promise."

I looked up at him. I could discern a disquiet woe in his eyes. Reaching out, I gently stroked his cheek. "We will be alright. Please don't worry."

He took my hand away and tenderly kissed it. The butterflies in my tummy returned, this time in swarms. A kaleidoscope of desire drew me closer. Compulsive craving raised me to my toes and I softly kissed his cheek. Without warning, I somehow knew something was about to happen, as he promptly stooped and kissed me adoringly, if not passionately, on the lips. My chin trembled as we gazed longingly at one another, studying each other's face, meditating on audacious thoughts and desires—throwing crumbs of passion to feed illicit yearnings and forbidden ardor, rituals only shared between wedded couples, in lustful darkness. Auspiciously, and with virtuous conduct, nothing happened, as we knew it never would. My friendship with Amy was worth more—more than heated flesh and a perfervid desire one felt for just a fleeting moment.

"You must miss Samuel," he said, pushing me away.

"We all do," I replied, sheepishly. "I'll write, I promise."

He nodded, turned, and walked away.

Running my fingers ever so lightly along parted lips, I watched as he climbed up onto the wagon. His trousers were tightly fitted around his hips. Rugged legs and the broad muscles just below his lower back flexed firmly, lifting his burly frame up onto the wagon. Wrapping the reigns around his brawny forearms, he whipped the horses forward. Stout shoulders contracted and hardened as he maneuvered the wagon around shipyard traffic and up Central Street. I was watching him pull away, thinking over the moment, when my reflection was unexpectedly averted.

"Well."

"Oh, Molly. I didn't see you standing there."

"Obviously," She clamored, boldly. "Is he your boyfriend?"

"Boyfriend! Timothy? Of course not. He's just a friend."

"Friends are not supposed to kiss one another on the lips, you know."

"They're not?" I uttered, still dazed as Tim trundled up the Fall River hill.

"No, they are not. It's improper."

I swiftly awakened and glanced over at her. She stood with arms firmly crossed, and a disconcerting, if not reprimanding, scowl on her face. I offered her a surrendering smile.

"You are right. I'll lecture Mister Cadman forcefully about it next time I see him."

"I bet you will," she snarled.

I peered up Central Street. A large carriage carrying tightly bundled bales of cotton now obscured Tim from view. I pondered when I would see Amy again—how I would miss Point Village and the Westport countryside. Even Ezra Hick and his bumptious demeanor would leave a small rift in my heart. How badly I would long for home.

Molly clutched me by the hand and plucked me along. "We don't want to miss the boat, Miss White. We must get going?"

After an uneventful sail to New York on the smaller Fall River Line boat, Zoeth, Molly, and I boarded the 331-foot steam vessel *Vanderbilt* for the ocean voyage to Washington D.C. It was by far the largest moving object I had ever witnessed and the swiftest and most comfortable vessel I had ever sailed on. If it was not for the swishing plash of its enormous side paddlewheels and the distant drone of its powerful steam engine, a girl would barely realize she was crossing open water. Strolling its promenade deck while out of sight of land was as comfortable as a casual walk over hard packed soil of any large city street.

I was fortunate enough to sail on the *Vanderbilt*'s last voyage as a passenger ship. As told to me by the ship's first mate, she will be soon commandeered by the Union Navy and commissioned to hunt Confederate marauders—southern naval ships that were assailing commerce on the high seas. Its first assignment would be to hunt down the Confederate sloop of war *Alabama*, the scourge of northern shipping. Happy to receive the fortuitous information about the *Vanderbilt*, I made certain to write everything down, where it would supplement my wartime journalistic dossier.

We rested on our forearms and pressed our bodies against the gunwale rail, watching as the enormous ship drifted toward the Sixth Street Wharf in Washington. A small steam craft nudged the stern of the *Vanderbilt* over to one side, helping the cumbersome vessel make a final approach as deck hands flung lines down onto the pier.

"Look at all those buildings," marveled Molly.

"Very exciting."

"What is that round building … there, in the distance," she pointed.

"Why, I don't know. Looks like it's under construction."

"That's the new United States Capitol building," said Zoeth. "The Capitol Dome. Work on it has been suspended since the war began."

"The United States Capitol Building. Now that is exciting," I declared.

"And what is that building there to the left, Mister Winslow … the one without windows?"

"That's not really a building, Molly. It's a monument to George Washington. It is going to be a tall obelisk when it's finish. It will be taller than any structure in the world."

"Taller than the pyramids in Egypt?" blurted Molly.

"Taller than all the pyramids. Now I must go and investigate about the luggage. We need to hire a carriage to take us to Alexandria for the locomotive south."

"Can I come with you, Mister Winslow?"

"Come along."

"I'll wait here," I informed them.

Left alone, I studied the waterfront from the lofty deck of the *Vanderbilt* and the assemblage of sailing craft along its wharfs. As one vessel left a pier another immediately filled the vacant berth. Leaning on the mahogany railing, I observed as the steamer *John Brooks* docked beside us. The *Vanderbilt* towered over the lesser ship, giving me a bird's-eye view of activities along its entire deck.

Lined along the pier were numerous Union soldiers, unripe recruits waiting to board the double-stacked paddle ship to be transported south to the battlefront. As they were escorted onto the ship, a set of doors swung open toward the rear of the vessel and a procession of infirmary personnel, dressed in white, trudged down a gangplank and onto the busy wharf. They carried stretchers—canvas platters ferrying injured soldiers home from the battlefield. Wounded enlistees limped among the hospital pallets, some with the help of a comrade supporting them by one arm and buttressed by a wooden crutch beneath the other. All were bandaged or mended to some degree, with blood-soaked gauze wrapped around their heads; some with arms in slings, others hobbling on one leg while the free limb hung swathed in plaster dressing.

Toward the bow of the *John Brooks*, newly enlisted troopers were escorted to the foredeck and ordered to stand in formation, facing away from the anguished wounded that were surreptitiously led away for hospital care. The entire affair appeared well-orchestrated to minimize the exposure that the young recruits would have of the wounded and impaired. I was happy that Molly was not here to witness what was unfolding on the dreary *John Brooks*. It was a dismal revelation of the brutal enterprise at the battlefront and an eye-opener to say the least. Taking out my notebook, I wrote down what I was witnessing: It was a dreadful and grim scene as disabled and beaten infantrymen were shepherded ashore. One after another, they marched—an alarming spectacle of young and once able-bodied boys, some no more than babes, now demolished and disabled.

Two of the injured men looked up and admired the *Vanderbilt*'s elegant paddlewheel. One of them looked no older than fourteen, the other, perhaps sixteen.

"You have chronicled them with well-chosen words," a baritone voice uttered, inches from my ear. I held the notepad close to my chest and turned around.

"Forgive me for spying. It has been a tedious voyage and, in my boredom, I could not avoid the distress on your face as you studied activities on the *John Brooks*. Inquisitiveness got the best of me, I'm afraid." He extended his hand. "I trust you can forgive me."

I ignored his limb and bowed my head in polite salutation, instead.

"That's quite alright, sir. I have a cat at home and am very tolerant of inquisitive curiosity."

"My name is Walter. Friends call me Walt." Timidly, he pulled his hand away.

"Emily," I said.

"Of course, Emily, it was fitting of you to refuse my handshake. After all, a lady traveling alone must be discreet."

I did not correct his inference that I was traveling unaccompanied. I was not trying to be unfriendly. But one must be careful of strangers too eager to be familiar. Walter was a tall man, slender and somewhat commonly dressed. He wore a limp, collared, wool sack-coat over a lackluster canvas shirt, unbuttoned along the upper chest. On his head was a wide-awake, felt chapeau sporting an excessively wide brim that spoke to a bohemian essentiality. His trousers were held up by a richly stitched rawhide belt and embroidered silver buckle. The drab, hessian pants looked out of place, tucked into lavish, black leather boots, sporting harnesses with gold clasps. He appeared a confection of culture and simplicity. With finely cropped beard and hair that was brownish and streaked with blanch strands of white, he was clearly twice my age. Droopy, sensitive cow eyes begged for conversation. What harm could it do? Besides, it was an opportunity to record people I met along the way and practice my journalistic inquiry.

"You mentioned that my words were well chosen. What words do you refer to?"

He walked over to the rail, propped himself on his elbows, and pointed to activities on the *John Brooks* with his bearded chin.

"Specifically, those boys below. Characterizations like shepherded babes and youngsters … some barely fifteen. They are much too young for military duty. … pups who exaggerated their age to wolves who embraced the deception with contemptible authority."

"They're so young, are they not?"

"A defilement of innocence, you see … taking advantage of naiveté and guiltlessness." He shook his head. "This war. It's just the beginning of a long-drawn-out affair. Look. As you have chronicled, Miss Emily. Sheep, boarding a ship of primal babes for a slippery journey down the river Styx and the inescapable anathema of war. There is no way that I can see how it can be avoided."

"I see you understand the spirit in which I write. What you say is seemingly true, if not explicit."

"But, then again, I also say it is good to fall. Battles are lost in the spirit in which they are won. I beat and pound for the dead. I blow through my embouchures, my loudest and gayest for them. Viva to those who have failed. And to those whose war-vessels sank in the sea." He looked over to me with melancholy countenance. "That is why I stress that one must do anything but let it produce joy, not war." He hesitated and smiled. "I ramble on, don't I?"

"I gather you do not approve of this war."

"My endorsement of such matters is not an issue one way or the other. I am but one man."

"But, you must admit, the issue, if one speaks plainly, is one of injustice. And inequity must be met head on and amended. Do you not agree?"

"In that respect, war cannot be avoided. You must remember that victory is never glorious nor defeat devoid of laurels. In both circumstances, no one wins and none defeated. The only achievement is the injustice of bloodshed. My concern are those expected to address such injustice … babes?"

"I suppose you are right."

"And what are your sentiments on the matter?" He asked the question, looking over the side of the rail as if he spoke to the wind.

"If you are an advocate of subjugation, then the north must be defeated. On the other hand, if your heart has been preordained by the Almighty, then slavery and southern sovereignty must be abolished."

"Brave sentiments for one so young," he said. "You are a refreshing free thinker, Emily. God has produced very little of them."

"May I presume, since you brought up the subject, that you are a God-fearing man, Mister Walter?' Or is it not ladylike for me to inquire?"

"One has very little to do with the other. War is a manifestation of man, whereby freedom and serenity the essence of a Creator. But if you are searching for my sentiments on the matter, allegiance is not in words but in deeds. And we lack the time to demonstrate each other's true nature. So, let us speak of more amiable affairs."

"Like?"

"You have traveled from New York. Are you planning on settling here in Washington?"

"Oh no. I'm a journalist on my way to Charleston to cover the war."

It was a broad proclamation on my part to introduce myself as a newspaperwoman. But since Rudolf French considered me as one, my admission was no less than accurate.

"You don't say? A matron of news."

"And yourself?"

"I have come to care for my brother, George. He was injured in battle."

"I'm sorry to hear that. I pray it's not serious."

"Shot in the face. But God has been good to us. He is convalescing nicely and should have a complete recovery. I will live here in Washington until he is well."

"Happy to hear he is doing well."

"Ah, a writer you say. We have much in common. I too am a writer and journalist."

"Oh?"

"Brooklyn's *Daily Times*." And you?"

"New Bedford *Daily Whaler*."

"New Bedford. I know the place well."

"But I'm a journalist, not a writer."

"Of course, you are. All journalists are writers."

"No, I mean I have not published any formal works. Have you?"

"Oh, a few novels."

"That is intriguing. What are the titles of some of your stories? Perhaps I may have heard of them."

"Well, there's one volume of poetry I wrote, which has earned some notoriety. It's called *Leaves of ...*"

Before he could finish, Molly ran over and took me by the hand.

"Come, Emily. The baggage is being taken off the ship. We must hurry."

"This is Molly," I said, as she tugged at my arm. "I am accompanying her to the Carolinas to visit family."

Molly examined the man, giving him capricious inspection and dismissed him, as if someone just served her a bowl of broccoli.

"Hello, Molly," said Walter, stooping to greet her.

"We're in a hurry," she proclaimed haughtily.

"Oh?" He chuckled.

"Come, Emily. We must go and catch the carriage across the river."

"It was nice chatting with you, Walter."

Molly persisted.

"It was engaging, young Emily ..."

"Emily, Emily White. It was my pleasure."

I offered him my hand. With an abiding smile and temperate grip, he shook it. Molly pulled at my arm tearing the handshake apart.

"Walter Whitman," he introduced, as she continued tugging. "Good fortune to you, Emily White."

In stumbling abduction, I was dragged away.

"Goodbye, Mister Whitman. I shall pray for your brother."

Clutching me by a finger, Molly scurried us along the wharf. I looked up toward the ship where Walter Whitman stood by the rail and where I left him. With the wide brim, gypsy hat, he was not difficult to find. He waved as I did. I must admit that it was a pleasure to meet a fellow journalist and to identify myself as one. Unsurprisingly, his familiar name hit a cord with me. I knew I had heard it sometime before.

We slogged through a multitude of dockworkers, soldiers, and their family members, to where Zoeth sat on the travel trunk waiting.

"Ah, Emily, good. I have made arrangements for the carriage to Alexandria," he said. "Once there you will board the train and we will part ways. I will make arrangements for a train home and you will continue onto Charleston."

"I wish you could have accompanied us," I said.

"Yes, Mister Winslow. Please do come."

"I cannot. That would only complicate matters. Besides, there are those who need me in the Underground back at home." He pulled a small map from his pocket displaying the route the train would take. "Now, Emily, you will have to change trains here, in Richmond … then again here, in Wilmington, North Carolina." Folding the topographical guide, he handed it to me. "So, make certain that all your baggage makes the change from train to train."

"I will," I assured him.

"Once you leave Wilmington, it will take you straight to Charleston. From there you must make arrangements to hire a carriage for Dukes Plantations."

"Understood."

"I can't wait, Emily. Can you? I will get to see Mother and Tyler."

"Now, when you change trains in Richmond, there should be a telegraph office there. Notify Dukes Plantation of your intentions. Remember, Emily. As far as anyone in Charleston is to know, you are Molly's governess and nothing more. You were hired by Rudolf French to look after his daughter and your charge is Molly's care and welfare. Any investigation you conduct must be kept secret … between you and no one else. Ultimately, your assignment is to discover the whereabouts of Hannah. Once you do, you are to telegraph home and we shall make arrangements with the authorities. Unfortunately, there is nothing we can do about Malachi. By southern law, Malachi is property."

"But that's unforgiving. What if I do find them both? Perhaps I can help Malachi …"

"No, Emily!" he shouted, before I could finish. "Under no circumstance are you to help Malachi or anyone else of color. If, by chance, you have an encounter with Malachi, don't even let on that you know who he is. By nature of self-preservation, if he sees you, he will not acknowledge you. He knows that there is nothing we can do for him and admitting that you may know one another will just create a hardship for the both of you. We do not want to do that. Do you understand?"

Though I hated to admit it, Zoeth's firm advice was a sound one. Of course, his tone was more one of worry than reprimand, making certain that nothing went wrong and that I understood—it was all in my hands.

"Yes, of course."

"It is likely that Malachi was sold down river."

"Down river?"

"It's a term used when a slave is sold further south. And it is likely since Malachi was a runaway, he has been sold."

"It is all so disconcerting."

"You must have courage. Pray on it. The Lord will help you."

"Don't worry, Zoeth. I will not jeopardize my quest."

"Good. Molly, you understand everything I just said. Do not fraternize with any of the slaves. The family at Dukes Plantation will try and keep you away from the slave folk in the fields. Once there, they will want you to spend most of your time in or around the big house."

"Papa has tutored me over and over about things."

"And do not confide in the house maidservants. Some are very dedicated to their masters. They may share anything you tell them. Don't expose Emily or discuss facts about her. All you know is that Emily was a stranger until she was hired to accompany and care for you. So, it is best you address her as Miss White"

"I know, I know."

"Do you understand everything I just said, young lady?"

"As Papa would say … from the capital letter to the period."

Soon after Zoeth Winslow finished outlining our objectives, the carriage to Alexandria arrived. The jaunt across the Potomac was short and uneventful. Zoeth made certain we boarded the train for Richmond safely. After some departing words, a short prayer, and heartfelt embraces, Molly and I were on our way. The adventure to the fields of rice and cotton had begun in earnest.

Chapter 19:
The Auction of Souls

The train trip between Alexandria, Virginia, and Charleston, South Carolina, was long and tiring. Molly read her illustrated copy of Hawthorne's *The Wonder-Book* and I entertained myself while watching the rural countryside whisk by. The tranquility of grassy fields and bucolic farmland was rudely hampered by the fragmented click-clang of steel wheels. By the second day of travel, it was beginning to drive me delirious.

Since I couldn't enjoy any measure of silence, I rifled through my shoulder bag and retrieved an old letter, one written by Samuel. I brushed my fingers along the ink inscription on the envelope, envisioning the loving hand that addressed it. I decided to read it for the fiftieth time in hopes of inwardly muffling the sounds made by the train's wheels. I could not help but sadly dwell on Samuel's whereabouts or how strange it was that I would arrive at my destination and the exact town where he was seen last. Mournful contemplation was acutely punctuated by the exasperated cries of an infant somewhere toward the rear of the car and amplifying the din beneath my feet. A friendly but boisterous squabble erupted across the aisle where two old gents amused themselves in an aggressive game of checkers—as if such emotions were possible during such a tranquil pastime. Someone in the car sneezed, the wheels beneath us squealed, while Molly let out a giggle. I placed Samuel's letter back in my bag. No distraction, no matter how cherished, could muzzle the noise. I closed my eyes and decided I would try and take a nap instead. Just then, the train conductor came walking by—an iron ring of keys jingling in his hand. He had an announcement. I took solace in the routine notice he conveyed. Charleston was fifteen minutes away and the long train ride would soon be over.

We arrived at the corner of Meeting and Pinckney Streets where Molly's father had made arrangements for us at the Charleston Hotel before we left New England. Standing at the front desk with my rich purse and gifted allowance, while having a courier opening doors and carrying my bags, I felt somewhat mature, if not worldly. I was a modern traveling girl with significant responsibilities and vital commitments, on an urgent assignment to preserve the Union. In truth, I was terribly intimidated, frightened even, entertaining such a summary.

The hotel was situated on the edge of the old French district of town, where conversations in the ancient melodic language could still be heard. Accommodations were lavish and far beyond what I was accustomed to, though I have nothing to compare it to since I never stayed at a hotel before. The polite desk clerk was kind enough to arrange post for my letter to the *Daily Whaler* announcing our safe arrival and an immediate notice to the Dukes Plantation informing them that we were awaiting our next course to an already exhaustive itinerary. Poor Molly was fatigued. I was still alert and somewhat manic. Travel feverishness, some call it. Once in our room, I tried to unwind and rest. Once my head hit the pillow, I realized that the jangling rattle of the train wheels was still sounding in my brain. I sprang to my feet.

"Would you like to take a walk, Molly?"

"Don't we need to wait for the telegram?"

"The desk will keep it for us when it arrives. Besides, it may not come for a day or two."

"Think I'll stay here and take a nap. My feet are still quivering from the train."

"Yes, dear. You take a nap and rest. I'm going for a short stroll. I shouldn't be long."

"Emily."

"Yes?"

"Do you think Mother will be happy to see me?"

"Of course. Why would you ask such a thing?"

"Well, it's just that she has not seen me for such a long time. I'm practically a stranger." She slipped into bed and got under the covers.

"What a silly thing to say. A mother never forgets a loving daughter. You are just anxious. That's to be expected. She'll be elated to see you."

"Think so?"

"Unquestionably. It was the long dreadful train ride. It has made you tired. When you are tired, fears and uncertainty are magnified. You rest. You will feel better." I put on my waistcoat, took a short peek in the mirror, and fluffed my hair. "Now keep the door locked."

"I will."

I flung my handbag over my shoulder and made certain the lock on the door was engaged.

"Emily."

"Yes."

She stared at me, briefly. It was a sentimental if not a gawking gaze. "I love you," she said, timidly throwing the sheet over her head.

Her words sparked warm memories of Grandmamma and the times when I left the house and she would recite them in just that order. I love you. Now they were being repeated once again, not by someone who had guardianship of me but for whom I was given trustworthiness to care for.

"Love you too, Molly," I said with a simper, just before closing the door.

Charleston was truly a metropolis. Not quite as big as Providence or Boston, cities near where I live, however, with the exception of New Orleans, it was the second largest city in the South.

My stroll took me south on Meeting Street. At Saint Philip's Episcopal Church, I turned onto Market Street where my trek took me past Market Hall, on the way toward Concord Street and the Cooper River shore. Suddenly, there they were, in the not too distance—a sea of tethered rigging and lofty spars. I could plainly see sprouting masts soaring high and prodding cumulus clouds hanging low in the deep cobalt sky. As I got closer, the savory scent of salted air was arresting. The fragrance reminded me of Point Village and home.

As I approached the Charleston waterfront, a poster displayed in the window of a brick building snagged my eye. It was an illustrated assortment of chains and binding restraints. At first, I thought the advertisement was for farming hardware, devices used on horses or livestock, until I read the caption below. It appeared the endorsement promoted an assortment of manacles, leg irons, and chained neck shackles, along with a variety of padlocks and keys—fetters and constraints meant for human bondage. On another window was a broadside promoting the marketing of human souls, or slaves as some called them, to be conducted in an open-air public sale.

Auction for the sale of thirteen Slaves
To be held on, June 23rd outside Dixon
Tavern, east of Burden's Causeway on
Johns Island. Experienced gang of rice
hands. Six men, four women, two girls,
and a small boy. Men between twenty
and sixty-one years of age and all able-bodied.
Two girls, ages thirteen and
ten, and small boy of five years but big
for his age. Excellent investment. Sale

authorized by a rice plantation in North Charleston scaling down operations from rice to cotton.

Seller, David Deas

I lost my breath while a sad consciousness of awe washed over me. I pressed my nose against the glass window, cupped my face from the sunlight, and looked inside. A bearded man nursing a cigar smirked and saluted. I jumped back. Above the window, and bolted high up on the building was a twenty-foot-long sign with foot high lettering: *David and John Deas—Slave Dealers.* The bearded man walked out the front door and into the street. He bid me good day and continued up the road. Chagrined, I lowered my head and hurried away. Stepping into the road, I was nearly run down by a horse and his rider. Assessing my bearings and being more careful, I scurried down toward the harbor.

Charleston was the busiest port I had ever visited. Much of the crowding had to do with ships that were hampered by the Northern blockade and detained along the wharfs. Captains had to choose the right moment to break out into open water without being commandeered or sunk by the Union navy. Some ship owners delayed commissions in hopes that the war would end soon.

Once I arrived at the waterfront, I sat by the seawall on a weathered barrel stamped with the word 'nails' and watched traffic in busy Charleston Harbor.

Relaxing by the seaside had the calming effect I expected. Shipwrights hammering and sawing expunged the rhythmic rapping of the rail car that had persisted in my head. Even the squawking of seagulls, which at times can be quite irritating, serenaded me with melodious chants and nearly operatic acoustics. I got up and walked along the edge of the pier. The sound made by the wavelets beneath the pillars supporting the planked structure had a therapeutic quality, which helped mollify the tense muscles along my neck and shoulders. A hooked, beaked seagull propped itself on a piling and looked down on me with stern perception, as if I was an oddity that didn't belong. He screeched. Below him, a mother duck appeared from behind a fishing craft leading her family of ducklings, a parade of billowing balls of fluff, paddling in a chorus of honks and squeaks.

I got up and stretched my legs. Looking down on the water, I slowly circumnavigated the perimeter of the wharf. Nearby, a small fish-shack displayed a sign that read *Boyce's Wharf.* The ship tied there swung a gangplank out onto the gravel yard as I moved out of the way. I started back toward town. Abruptly, I heard a man shout.

"Keep moving, keep moving," he gruffly hollered.

I looked over. Disembarking was a weary and destitute group of black folks. The man with the commanding cry stood gripping a whip, overseeing the black men who shuffled quickly down the ramp in small steps, chains jingling, each man shackled at the ankles and to each other. The women followed in a somber march, heads down, small bundles beneath their arms, carrying their entire worldly possessions. My heart sank when I noticed that one of them was a girl about Molly's age, and another nearly twelve. Trailing toward the back was a boy of five or six years, struggling to keep pace while being led by the hand. Suddenly, my throat was tied in a knot and my stomach dropped to my feet. It was the broadside in the storefront window.

I dashed up the wharf away from it all. I maintained my startled sprint toward town in a shameful attempt at escape, not knowing what I was escaping from. I stopped when I arrived at East Bay Street. Leaning against the wheel of a carriage by the side of the road, my head tucked in the small of my arm, I caught my breath. For a minute, I thought that I might vomit. Suddenly the words of Rudolf French erupted in my head: "You're of the fairer sex and women have a proclivity toward frangible vulnerability, a delicate soul and one much too clement for the news business." I stood up firmly, bit my lip, and tugged at my waistcoat. While walking by, pedestrians stared over with puzzled inquisitiveness. The man sitting in the carriage looked back at me with curiously.

"You alright, Miss?" he asked, in a southern drawl.

"Yes, yes," I sputtered, moving away. His accent made fresh in my mind what part of the world I was in.

With steely resolve, I reflected on the last few minutes and on what Rudolf French had said the day I was hired to work for his newspaper. Suddenly, Charlotte White's voice spoke. The words were not in my ears but in my heart. "Run not from adversity," it said. "Give nothing to pain. Step forward and place your nose in the mire. For the misery and hardship of others may be yours in the morrow." This was prudent advice given to me long ago—guidance of courage and valor. Little understood at the time, it was spoken but very discernible now.

After a short walk up East Bay Street, I discovered a bench by the Charleston Customs House where I sat to think. Why did I allow the shock of the moment to control my emotions? I was so angry with myself. It was fortunate that Rudolf French was not here to witness my disheveled and turbulent behavior. I closed my eyes and threw back my head. *What to do, what to do, Emily?* I asked myself. There was nothing I could do. It was not my world. I retrieved my notebook from my shoulder bag. One thing I could do was rehearse the correspondent within me—practice the craft I had chosen to perform as a journalist and chronicle what I had witnessed at Boyce Wharf.

I finished flushing my memory of the facts and put away the chamois-covered notebook. Just then, two men came walking out of the customs house behind me and stopped by the road. One was tall, distinguished looking, and wearing a felt topper—the other short, bald, and bulbous. The shorter man lobbied his companion to accompany him. I could not help but overhear their brief conversation.

"I'm heading there right now," declared the stout, smartly dressed gentleman.

"I thought the Deas auction was not until next week," said the other, as he casually lit a cigarette.

"It's going on as we speak, man."

"Where?" He flung the match to the ground and stepped on it. Tossing back his head, he blew out some smoke, savoring the virgin puff.

"Three blocks down East Bay … by the Post Office and Exchange Building. It's touted as the largest sale of its kind." The plump fellow unfolded a sheet of paper from his pocket. "See."

His companion glanced down at it and shook his head. "No, no. I'm going home. It's been a long day at the bank."

"Oh, come now."

"Furthermore, I've seen enough of those exhibitions. Quite depressing."

"I find them exceedingly amusing. And there's likely to be a slugfest or two. Come with me, my man. We'll have some ales and cheer the winners. We'll make a jolly time of it."

"Good day, Arthur," sneered the man with the top hat. He then promptly marched away in rebuke of his friend's dubious invitation.

The short fellow called Arthur shrugged his shoulders and tossed the paper into the road. Whistling a cheerful tune, he marched down East Bay Street. I assumed he was on his way to the post office. I waited until he was well away.

I gave chase to the discarded notice as the harbor breeze carried it up the tree-lined avenue and along the furrowed gutter. I sprinted and stepped on the tumbling parchment before it could blow away any farther. I looked around, making certain no one was watching me give chase to idle trash in the street. Across the way, a dark-skinned penniless vagabond scoured the road for discarded cigarettes or withered cigars to salvage unspent tobacco. He glanced over and smiled. With dignity ruffled, I did not. I turned and quickly picked up the paper. It was an augural broadsheet advertising an auction. I read it loudly to myself.

For sale

——Negroes——
Great Bargains to be had.
To be sold at public auction on June 19th and held at Post Office Row at the base of Broad Street and East Bay Street in the city of Charleston S.C. Choice cargo of sixty-nine slaves including rice field and cotton hands, direct from Butler Island, Georgia Plantation. Thirty-eight prime men of assorted ages, including twenty skilled rice women and girls, with some children. All inspected for malaria and Smallpox and deemed in clean health.

Sale conducted by:
David Deas, John Deas,
and Mortimer Calhoun
All sales legal and final

I irritably folded the revolting advert and stashed it into my notebook. What had unexpectedly shocked me just a few moments earlier now was outlandishly unexceptional. I quickly realized that I was not in Westport any longer and decided that I had to experience southern milieu absent of erupting emotion. After all, it was behavior unbecoming of an able-minded correspondent.

I glanced south toward the post office where the auction was being held, and then north in the opposite direction and my hotel. I was uncertain which direction I should take, whether back to the comfort of my room or toward what was assured to be a contentious evening of ill circumstance. Across the avenue, the vagabond continued his wanton search for discarded tobacco butts. With a determined pirouette, and dignity intact, I spun on my heels and trudged off in the direction of the Charleston Post Office and Exchange.

The closer I approached the Exchange Building the slower I walked. In uncompromising deliberation with myself, I became more resolute than ever that I would attend this callous event. If not as a complacent spectator to uncompromising evil, then as a surreptitious journalist and unfailing witness to the unambiguous reasons for why my treasured country was fractionating into war.

I placed my forearm over my eyes and glanced up at the blazing sun. Summer was still a couple of days off and already the southern heat was oppressive. Even with the harbor breeze, perspiration trickled down the side of my face. Yes, summers could be hot in Westport, but not as sweltering this early in the season.

When I arrived at my destination, there was no mistaking the ghastly carnival that was unfolding before my very eyes. I had read about it, been told about it, but never envisioned that I would one day behold the brutal marketing of human souls.

The post office building was a large and elegant Portland stone structure. On its hip roof was a circular steeple, or as I knew them in New England, a widow's walk, consisting of ornamental balustrade, tucked between a series of Greek columns. The lofty edifice complemented the columned pilasters on each side of elongated windows high up on the upper floor.

The auction was being conducted on its north side below some windows. The stage was a series of planks held up by crisscrossed stacks of railroad timbers. The weathered-planked podium stood just under three broad, arched windows along the ground floor. To one side of the podium, two men sat at a table, entertaining transactions by patrons amongst the crowd of exclusively men. The man I saw earlier, with the beard and cigar, behind the poster in the storefront window, was orchestrating the auction. Standing by him, looking stoic and defeated, were two young black men in leg restraints.

I observed the bustle from a safe distance across the street. Surrounding the podium was a group of men dressed in every manner of attire. They cursed, laughed, and debated the merits of the lots as slaves were escorted by an overseer up onto the platform. A group of curious women, both black and white, stood across the street and watched. I noticed two black girls talking and pointing—trembling hands over their mouths. I sauntered over and stood in front of them.

"It's thay weeping time, weeping time all ova agayn," proclaimed one of the girls.

"Hmm, hmm, it sure is," said the older companion.

"Ays remembuur with they done sold my momma ayn' pappy when ay were just a child. I wept for weeks."

"Gud, help us."

"Ay nevur done saw them agayn."

"Hmm, hmm."

"We bes get a-goin and tote thees goods home befawe Massa sells us up thay riv-ah."

"Hmm, hmm, Gud help us."

I looked back for the two slave women. They had suddenly disappeared. Retrieving my notebook, I jotted down the enduring words one of them spoke: *June 19, 1861, auction, Post office, Charleston—The Weeping Times.* I closed with the arresting declaration often recited by Rudolf French, "*De profundis.*" I underlined it twice. Before someone could notice, I stashed the notebook.

"Sold!" came the impaling shout from the podium. Startled, my heart skipped a beat. I crossed the street. All eyes were on me. "What is this girl doing here?" the gawking display asked. Some may have felt that a girl at a slave auction was bad luck or that my presence was a transgression against ladylike civility. After all, the buying and selling of slaves was a man's affair. If that's the way they felt, it did not concern me. I worked my way in and out of the crowd of men while keeping my eyes on the podium. One fellow stepped in front of me and blocked my path.

"Looking for your husband, madam?"

The man clasped a mug of beer, sold by the tavern across the street. His inquiry though inoffensive was somewhat insincere.

"Still looking for a wife, hey Arthur," someone in the crowd trumpeted. His associates broke into laughter.

I noticed he was one of the men I saw earlier from outside the Customs House. I ignored him. Stepping out of the way, I took a place by the table where auction transactions were settled.

"May I help you, young lady," asked one of the men.

I shook my head while at the same time ignoring him. Another walked up and offered me his chair. I smiled, nodded, and sat down, never speaking a word. At the moment, secrecy and stealth was my journalistic virtue.

"Chattel number twenty-two, twenty-three, and twenty-four," roared the bearded auctioneer. "Rice hands. Bid high. They will not go cheap," he cried. "Now, can I have an opening bid?"

The bidding was slow and steady. At twenty-two-hundred dollars it stopped.

"These here Negroes are worth three thousand if they are worth a dime."

The slave dealer walked over and tore the shack-shirt off one of the men, exposing his naked upper body. The black man kept his head down as he was ordered to walk up along the podium.

"As you can see, there are no whipping scars or markings of any kind," proclaimed the auctioneer. "A very obedient gang. This chattel is the strongest lot of the day." He ran his cane along the black man's pectorals. "Invest your eyes on that flesh. Uncompromising muscle. His companions here are nearly as sturdy. Why, he's as strong as a draft horse in any stable."

"Do we feed him grain or will black-eyed peas suffice," someone crudely heckled. The callous crowd broke into laughter.

Still another yelled, "I'll give you a bridle, Morris. You can ride him home."

There was more barnyard laughter.

"Two thousand, nine hundred. No more," came a final bid from an authoritative looking man to my left.

"Sold, to the gracious gentleman from Richmond, Virginia. See the clerk at the desk, sir."

"He stole that merchandise," I heard someone say.

I was taken aback when I realized the man was speaking to me. I looked up. It was Arthur. There was no avoiding the fellow. He held his heavy mug of ale aslant as the brew spilled onto his polished shoes. His beer-dampened shirt was tight fitting and sprung open around a tumid belly, while the bloated appendage drooped over his leather belt like a sagging eyebrow. Judging by the fine material of his clothing and the assortment of rings on his fingers, he was no doubt a man of means and wealth. Clean-shaven, he had rosy cheeks and his head was a wiry bird's nest containing one swollen egg—his nose an infected strawberry. He was probably no older than twenty-five but exhibited the anatomy of a fifty-year-old. It was no secret why Arthur was not married.

The man from Virginia had an imposing stature, including a square jaw and woolly sideburns streaming down his cheek like iron chain-plate strappings on the side of a sailing vessel. He looked familiar. He walked with a slight limp and what looked like an old injury anointed his forehead. Approaching the table while escorting the three chained black slaves, he remedied his account with the auction clerk before leaving. The black men held their heads low as they walked by me. The youngest glanced over, then quickly away, probably wondering what a young girl was doing at a slave auction.

"Good luck with your Negroes," blurted Arthur. "Fine stock. You'll get your money's worth with those three." He bent over and whispered. "A Fine Negro and two strapping sons. Too bad the Virginia gentleman is leaving. I would dawdle a bit longer if I were he. Try and purchase the wife and daughter. Negroes work harder when families are kept together. Of course, some would dispute that theory, but it has been my experience that when …"

"Excuse me," I interrupted. "Did you say wife and daughter?"

"Why, yes." He took an auction catalogue from the table. "You will need one of these to keep track of the sales." He ran his pudgy finger along the brochure. "Here, you see. Chattel number twenty-five and twenty-six. It says, 'Dora a rice gal and her wench.'"

"I don't understand."

"Well, dear lady, they separated them. The woman and daughter will be sold independently of the men. Of course, I think it's a mistake. Not with all sales, you see, but surely with this one."

"Why … who would do such a thing?" My ignorance of the Southern practice of selling human beings must have bewildered him.

"There are many reasons," he explained. "The slave may be unsound or old. Maximizing profit or profession. A carpenter or driver will bring a premium price by himself. Selling them as a chattel of only one makes sense, you see. Maximizes profit. Understand?"

"No, I don't," I replied, in contemptuous annoyance. It was apparent that Arthur could not hold his liquor or the illness behind his ethics. And the more he drank the less he noticed that he was talking to a woman.

"One of those three brutes they just auctioned off has quite a handsome, mongrel wife. A mulatto. She will make an excellent house servant. Slaves like her do not come up very often."

"I wouldn't know," I snarled.

"They must have gone down for her by now."

"What do you mean?"

"The dungeon under the post office—the old jail. That's where they have been keeping the group of slaves today."

I twisted and fidgeted in my chair. I tried to ignore the man and turned my back to him. The incessant beer drinker circled around and faced me.

"You have an accent," he declared. "You are not from around here, are you?"

Agitated and outraged I jumped to my feet. I noticed that I was two or three inches taller than the tiresome little man. "No, I am not."

"Somewhere up north, I would say." His beer spilled onto my boots.

"Missouri," I clamored, storming away.

I moved to the opposite side of the platform and as far away as I could get, making certain that Arthur was not following. I suddenly collided with one of the slaves. I found myself face to face with Chattel number twenty-five … the rice hand Dora. She was beautiful. Wispy, peach colored hair, caramel flushed skin, and carbon, silvery eyes. We looked at one another briefly before she was savagely jerked and flung to the ground. Her young daughter, a girl of approximately nine years of age, rushed to her mother's aid and wrapped her arms around her neck. I leaned over and tried to help Dora by the arm. She hotly pulled herself away just as the crusty overseer took my place and dragged her off.

"Next on the block is Chattel number twenty-five and twenty-six," announced the auctioneer, "a rice hand named Dora and her offspring. Lots of interest with this one."

Dora staggered up onto the platform where she fell to her knees. The overseer placed his whipping cane under her chin urging her to stand up.

"Two hundred," someone yelled.

"Three hundred, five hundred, one thousand dollars!"

The bidding was brisk in coming. I moved closer to the platform. The deck above the scaffolding was just about chin level. I looked up at Dora and her daughter. The youngster stood close to her mother, crying, arms around her waist.

"Do I hear eleven hundred?" yelled the slave agent.

"Eleven hundred," someone hailed.

Though I knew it was forbidden for her to do so, I tried to make eye contact with her. I was not certain why. Perhaps it was my way of telling her that I cared and if there was something I could do I would.

"Twelve hundred," bellowed the high bidder.

"She's quite stunning," said the familiar voice.

I looked down. It was Arthur. He held a freshly poured ale in his hand.

"Would you like a beer?"

"No, I would not."

"No trouble. I'd be more than happy."

The bidding had stopped at twelve hundred. David Deas, the auctioneer, skillfully worked the floor, pointing out all the favorable facets behind the current sale. Just then, a rakishly dressed middle age man appeared on the platform—apparently an honored customer. He wore a silk jacket with tails and felt top hat, set off by a brightly colored red cravat. Ruffles overflowed down his shirt and sprouted from his cuffs. His skin was waxy white, and half-moons shadowed beneath his eyes. The pitch of his voice was high and its cadence musical. His walk had an epicene bounce.

"Can I approach and inspect the merchandise, David," he asked of the auctioneer.

"He's going to steal your wife, Arthur," someone in the audience hollered.

The crowd broke into laughter.

The man with the cravat circled Dora as if he were inspecting a quarter horse at the racetrack. Pushing the slave woman's daughter aside, he cupped Dora's hips and caressed them up and down. He stood a while and studied her, regarding his subject with shear arrogance and pomposity.

"Still room for lots of offspring," he declared with conviction, as if it made a difference to him. Placing white gloves on, he lowered her lip with his thumb and inspected her teeth. Ambling behind, he lifted Dora's blouse along her back and inspected it for welts or proof of punishment, which could speak to a troubled or abnormal slave.

"Yes, yes, I will bid on her," he concluded, as if he was doing the auctioneer a favor. "But I have no interested in the child. You will make much more on her if you separate the two."

My jaw dropped when I overheard his suggestion.

"I think we can arrange that," said the sly auctioneer.

"No!" I yelled.

My voice reverberated across East Bay Street. Everyone glared at me. For a moment it appeared that all of Charleston had come to a halt. The auctioneer lost his peddler's smile and the dapper gentleman with the corpse complexion threw back his head and turned his back to me as if I had intentionally affronted him.

"You heard the lady, David," affirmed Arthur. "We will have none of that. They sell as a lot, mother and daughter, together."

"Sorry," said the auctioneer. "My brother has spoken. We shall sell them as a unit."

"Sixteen hundred!" Echoed from across the street.

Dora finally made eye contact with me but quickly looked away. Her glance brushed me with a pound of acknowledgment if not an ounce of gratefulness. I looked over at Arthur.

"Thank you."

"It's my nature," he said, slurping the suds from his beer. "Families should stay together, white or slave. Besides, that dandy thinks he's privileged."

"Eighteen hundred!" came the new bid.

"Just the same. Thank you … Arthur."

"Twenty-two hundred!"

"No thanks required. After all, they are just slaves. And there's plenty more where those two came from. Good day, my lady," he said before surprisingly walking away.

The auctioneer slammed his foot on the platform and pointed out the new buyer.

"Sold! For twenty-two hundred dollars."

Chapter 20: The Carriage for Dukes Plantation

Molly shook me until I awakened. "Get up, Emily, it's here, it's here," she cheered.

I propped myself up in bed and reclined against the brass headboard. "What's here?" I yawned, stretching.

"The telegram," she waved a slip of paper. "You need to get ready."

I snatched the ink-smudged leaf from her hand.

"I went down to the front desk looking for it. It arrived late yesterday."

"Oh, good. It says we should be ready by noon." I looked at my watch on the nightstand. "It's only eight o'clock?"

"I don't want to miss it."

"There is no way we will miss it. We have plenty of time, Molly. First we need to go down and find a restaurant and have breakfast."

I buried my face in my hands reflecting on the events of the previous day. Cramming my knuckles into my eyes, I kneaded away the night's slumber. A peevish Molly sat quietly in a chair by the side of the bed, arms crossed, with an admonishing stare. Grievous gray blue eyes twinkled with obstinate impatience. I was still half asleep and lacked the constitution to entertain juvenile pouting.

"Yes … what is it Molly?"

"I don't want any breakfast."

"Well, I do. And it's only eight o'clock. We have plenty of time to get ready."

"Papa always says that it's later than you think."

"Well, your father's not here."

She sat humming. I ignored her. The humming became louder. "I'm waiting," she crooned.

"Why don't you go downstairs and wait. There's a bookstore a block up the street if you get bored."

"But I don't want a book. I want to be ready when our ride arrives."

"And we will. Why don't you wait in the lobby and keep a lookout? I'll put on some clothes and be down as soon as I can."

"Oh, alright," she moaned, starting for the door. "You promise to hurry?"

"I promise," I yawned.

Once dressed, I retrieved my notebook and went over the events of the day before, making certain that I had recorded all I witnessed at the Post Office and Exchange Building. After the auction of Dora and her daughter, I remained for three more chattels before I had had enough. As the auction progressed, the cruelty and sorrow became overwhelming. I should have known what to expect, especially after reading Solomon Northup's book. I was certain his accounts were accurate and factual. But at the time I read it, I ingested its content with a distorted mien, one toward fiction, since accounts in the book were so flagrantly inhumane and unthinkable.

Before going to bed the night before, I had written five full pages of events I had witnessed in my little brown notebook, including sentiments and commentary. Hopefully, I would be successful in my telling and make it palatable for New England readers and acceptable to the *Daily Whaler* when I got back home. I called the piece "The Weeping Time"—though it made for distasteful reading on an empty stomach. Having skipped lunch and dinner the day before, a hardy breakfast would surely restore my strength and lack of ambition for the uncharted events ahead. Unfortunately, it did not work out that way.

Arriving at the hotel lobby, I walked over to the desk clerk, checked out, and asked about a place to have breakfast. With the name of a highly recommended restaurant in hand, and my mouth watering with hunger, I stepped outside in search of Molly. I found her around the corner on Pinckney Street talking to man by a lavish carriage. Up on the bench behind the four horses, two black men sat quietly. Molly ran over as soon as she saw me.

"It's here!"

"What's here?"

"Our ride to Dukes Plantation?"

"Are you sure? The telegram said it was not until noon."

"I told you we had to hurry. Papa's always right."

"You will see your mother very soon. You must be very excited."

"Of course, silly."

"I'm so happy for you, Molly."

"Are you not excited, Emily?"

"Yes … yes I suppose I am."

Uncertain about which direction my mission to Dukes Plantation would take me, the affirmation I offered was a skeptical understatement. After what I had experienced at the Charleston slave auction, I could not shake the unsettling air or itchy intuition that something was rotten in the state of Denmark … very rotten.

Molly gripped my hand tightly and yanked me along the uneven walkway toward the carriage.

"Let's hurry, Emily."

"You must call me Miss White from now on," I stammered, floundering behind her. "We don't want to give ourselves away."

"Yes, Miss White."

Once at the carriage, I was introduced to the gentleman who had come to take us to the plantation. He was rather gaunt and tall, with a crouched posture, as if one shoulder was much heavier than the other. Scarecrow hair protruded from beneath the unraveling brim of a straw hat. It was unclear where the hat ended and his hair began. Oily strands of blonde were pasted to his brow, held there by perspiration that glistened. With crinkled attire, he was less than tidy. He sported a scraggly, van dyke beard, giving him a swashbuckling appearance. Detrimentally, the goatskin patch he wore slung over one eye had me asking myself—were there pirates in Denmark?

With a somewhat disingenuous cordiality, he introduced himself as James Wilcox of Dukes Island Plantations. Unbeknown to me, there was more than one farmstead at Dukes Plantation—the main estate growing rice, and Dukes Island growing cotton, some distance away.

I asked our escort to acquaint me with the two black companions that loaded our luggage. He refused—alleging that it was not proper or of any consequence. The two men remained nameless, even when he called out to them, ordering them into the hotel to retrieve our baggage.

Molly and I climbed up and waited inside the coach. I looked down at my watch. It was now 9:45, and the temperature in Charleston was already oppressive. The two helpers strapped the trunk in the rear of the carriage. James Wilcox hauled himself up into the coach and sat beside me. I got up and moved to the opposing bench and took my place by Molly's side. Wilcox smirked.

The horses gave out a spirited neigh and groan as the coach unexpectedly lurched forward. We swayed in our seats while the car wavered on creaking leaf springs, thundering along Charleston's cobbled byways. Finally, we were on our way.

I soon discovered that James Wilcox was a strange and enigmatic individual. We had been traveling for over an hour and he had not uttered a word. Most of the time, he sat napping with hat over his eyes. Molly appeared content reading a book. I took up my time studying the fleeting countryside. The coach negotiated a lumpy patch of ground jarring our usher awake.

"Ho ... watch the road up there," he hollered.

Awake, he took a long, tapered cigar, which he kept tucked into the rawhide band around his hat, jabbed it into his mouth, and put a match to it. The coach soon filled with smoke as scorched tobacco spewed from his nose. Though I had not noticed it earlier, Wilcox carried some sort of bullwhip coiled tightly by his hip. Protruding from his boot was the polished, ebony handle of a large knife. On close inspection, I could make out the pearl handle of a revolver tucked in his waist just under a gauzy shirt.

"I suppose that whip is a necessary instrument of your trade, Mister Wilcox."

He glared at me as if I just accused him of a crime. "It sure is, Madam," he said, taking a long drag of his slim cigar.

"I find the braided leather interlace on the handle quite beautifully done."

He reached back and stroked the whip as if to make certain it was still there. "You have good taste, madam. It's a vital tool for plantation supervisor."

"You mean a plantation overseer, don't you?"

"If it pleases you, madam."

"My name is Emily, remember?"

He ignored me, rolling the cigar between fingers.

"I assume you must use that whip on horses and cattle," I boldly pressed him.

He cackled, though I did not realize any humor. "Yes, horses and cattle. Disorderly ones."

Slipping the long knife from his boot and a peach from his pocket, he carved. He gripped the cutlass with a bit of fruit resting off the tip of the juicy steel blade. With the damp cigar pinched between his fingers, he offered me the slice of peach. Charred ash from the stogy was hurled by the breeze and came to rest on the coral-colored fruit. I turned away. I was feeling uncomfortable confined in close proximity to the man.

"No, thank you, Mister Wilcox. Peaches are bad for you," I said, though I felt starved and lightheaded. He frowned. Molly put down her book.

"Are peaches really bad for you?"

"Continue reading your book, Molly," I croaked.

Wilcox blew off the ash and placed the peach wafer in his mouth.

"Is that a knife or a sword, Mister Wilcox?"

"What, this?" He held the menacing-looking knife in his hand and studied it closely, as if for the first time.

A ray of sunlight bore down through the coach's curtains and flickered off the surface of the mirrored blade. The light glittered in his one hazel eye.

"She's a beauty, isn't she?" he said. Running the blade plumb along his arm, he removed a patch of sun-bleached hair. "Sharp as a razor too. An original Jesse Clift blade … a Bowie."

"You don't say."

He flung the barely eaten peach out the window and held the knife inches from my face. "Keeps a sharp cutting edge like a Negro keeps his manners," he snarled. He wiped both sides of the nine-inch shank on his shirtsleeve and placed the cyclopean, peach slicer back in the sheath stitched to his boot. "Bowie knife," he said. "Best tool a hunter can carry."

"Whether hunting man or beast, I suppose."

He considered what I said with an impish smirk.

"Whether man or beast."

In further conversation with our less than chivalrous escort, I pondered going mad when he informed me that we had another two hours of travel. It was hellish hot. There was no pleasant way to describe it. The scorching breeze that blew in the coach windows did little to elevate the discomfort and only made matters worse. *Should have had breakfast before leaving Charleston,* I thought to myself. I was feeling dazed and woozy. I looked over at James Wilcox. God help me. There were two of him.

"I'm thirsty," pleaded Molly.

Wilcox popped the cork on his canteen, and she took a drink.

"Thank you, Mister Wilcox. That was good."

After handing the tin back to him, Wilcox put the canteen up to his mouth and gulped. Wiping the neck of the steel flask with his shirtsleeve, he held up the canteen and offered me a drink. My mouth was stuffed with cotton and my throat a gritty desert. My stomach felt like an empty infernal, and my lips taut and withered. There was very little at the moment that looked as inviting. Nonetheless, I reluctantly shook my head and waved it away.

"Sure?" he asked. "You look like you need some."

"I'm sure, Mister Wilcox."

With raised eyebrow, he shrugged his shoulders and thrust the cork back on the canteen.

I found the plantation overseer repulsive. After what I had witnessed at the auction, the word overseer had become a four-letter word to me. As a matter of fact, it was two four-letter words. To accept anything from an overseer in the way of sustenance was unsettling. Instead, I frisked through my shoulder bag and retrieved a grape size quartz pebble Grandmamma had given me when I was just a little girl. It was snow white and round and the size of a hummingbird egg. She called them thirst stones. "Keep this stone in your pocket during summer. If you get thirsty place it in your mouth and tumble it with your tongue. The saliva it spawns will ease the thirst."

Thanks Grandmamma.

Luck was with me when I fell asleep during the second half of our trip. The curtains were drawn, and the light was dim. Molly had her head on my shoulder and had fallen asleep.

"Welcome to Dukes Plantations," said James Wilcox, drawing back the curtains. Looking out the window, I noticed that we were riding between two flooded pastures over an elevated road. Slaves were working in the fields. They waved as we drove by.

"Wake up, Molly. We've arrived."

Instantly, she came alert and stuck her head out the window. "Oh, look," she crowed. "They're working the farm."

"This is what a rice field looks like, is it, Mister Wilcox?" I asked.

"They have started draining the fields. The seeds have germinated and it's time to cultivate."

"Is that why they flood the fields? So, the seed will germinate?"

"That … and it holds down the weeds. Once the field is drained, they will hoe and hand pick weeds. That's what they're doing in that section, there," he pointed out. "After they are done weeding, we will flood the field once again to help the rice grow and keep down unwanted vegetation."

"I have never seen anything like it," I said, not certain whether I was appalled or astonished.

"Growing rice is a process. The field to the right was fifty acres of cypress gum forest. Dukes had it cleared two years ago. This is the first year of planting."

"Oh, look," cried Molly. "Those women are walking in all that mud. Looks like fun."

Wilcox gave out a hardy belly laugh. "Oh, it's fun alright."

A group of women was bent over, pulling weeds in ankle deep muck. Their dresses were tied up high and dry around their knees and they donned large straw sombreros that did little to quell the oppressive heat.

"As you can see, we are good to our slaves. They are well clothed, well fed, and happy."

"Are they, Mister Wilcox?"

"What else could they possible need?"

"Perchance Freedom."

He gave me a berated scowl and banged on the coach roof. "Stop the wagon," he yelled to the driver.

The creaking and rumbling of the wheels and squeaking suspension ceased. My ears were humming after almost four hours of thumping from horse's hooves. In a nearby rice field, I could see eight people, six black men and two women, working in a cluster digging weeds—some with a hoe, others with their hands.

"Why have we stopped, Mister Wilcox?"

"Listen, dear lady."

In the distance I could hear singing. The timbre utterances were leisurely but laborious. One had to listen carefully to discern any hope or expectancy the chanting delivered. Wilcox held up a finger and tapped his ear, instructing me to take notice. He gaped, highbrow, a glint in his one good eye, as if proud of enlightening me to what he interpreted as the true nature of the black happy slave.

I brought my ear closer to the coach window and closed my eyes. I preferred the darkness to the loathsome image that sat across from me. Unexpectedly, when my eyes shut, I saw Grandmamma's serene beaming face, cultured ancestry, a heritage of two proud peoples, African and Wampanoag—her gentle nature of seeing the good in all people—even people like James Wilcox, who she would claim warrants pity in place of scorn.

The workers in the field noticed that the carriage had stopped. They sang louder. Whether for us or at us, it didn't make much difference. It was haunting and mournful. I was in no mood to humor James Wilcox's little lesson on the happy slave. Still, I was drawn to the spiritual siren and its melancholy inflection.

He is comin on a cloud
Wit a trumpet soundn' loud
Up da riv'ah Jordon
Up da riv'ah Jordon.

And my Jesus on e'throne
We'll be takin me a'home
Up the riv'ah Jordon
Up the riv'ah Jordon.

In a field of rice I wait
Till'ee leads me to the gate.
Up the riv'ah Jordon
Up the riv'ah Jordon.

To my knees I will wade
In da sun without no shade
Up the riv'ah Jordon
Up the riv'ah Jordon.

En' I hope it won't be long
Till'ee comes I sing da song
Up the riv'ah Jordan
Up the riv'ah Jordan.

I could not help myself. Tears welled in my eyes, whether for memories of Grandmamma, or the reprehensible inequity I just witnessed in the sweltering Carolina sun, I could not tell. Molly snapped my meditative recollection and tapped me on the arm.

"What are they singing about, Miss White?"

I looked across to the overseer. He was smiling as if he were the archetypal cat with the canary in his chops. "They are singing about how kind and good Mister Wilcox treat's them. Is that not right, Mister Wilcox?"

Nurturing silence, he sat, twisting the tip of his scanty mustache between his fingers. Staring out the coach window at the group of singing slaves, his smirk turned into a contorted grimace. Angrily, he rapped his knuckles on the ceiling. The carriage heaved and we rolled once again.

It was not long before the big three-story house came into view. The impressive dwelling was constructed of red brick and of a Georgian Style. Behind the lush gardens that graced the front of the building was a sweeping portico with a series of Corinthian columns. Above the extensive portico was a porch with a classical railing enclosure and crowned with an impressive pediment gable. The most imposing attributes of the house were five lofty, dormer windows protruding from the slate roof and flanked by a uniform, balustrade barrier. The balustrade ran the full length of the roof along the structure's facade and was embellished by tall, carved amphorae at each corner.

The coach encircled the cobbled courtyard, coming to a stop along the front door. Unable to control her elation, Molly tugged at my arm. With every jerk, I felt like passing out. Without saying a word, James Wilcox disembarked and disappeared into the house. While we waited for someone to greet us, I studied the place, notably the porch above the portico. Though my head was starting to swoon, I thought I saw a woman looking down on us from above. I felt fuzzy and my surroundings obscure. The last thing I remembered was Molly standing outside the coach yanking at my arm to hurry. At that very moment, the world of nod came calling and everything went black.

Chapter 21: A Mother's Inexplicable Love

The next thing I saw was a stately, aureate chandelier with no less than thirty candles hung low from a gold leaf garnished ceiling. I was uncertain what I was looking at or how I came to rest on the divan where I lay. Sitting in a chair by my side, Molly held my hand.

"She's waking, she's waking," she cheered joyously.

My surroundings were hazy and my head stifling. I wiped my brow and blinked. Suddenly, a group of shadowed faces in a circle appeared, hovering over me—one of them a very striking, handsome young man. To his left was an older gentleman. On the other side of the sofa, were two black faces, one but a girl.

"You fainted, Miss White, when you stepped off the carriage. How do you feel now?" asked the younger man.

As my vision improved, the room brightened. "Where am I?"

"Dukes Mansion," said the lovely face. "I'm Tyler Dukes."

"Are ya alright, Miss?" asked one of the black women, the older one wearing an apron and holding a silver tray. On the platter was a pitcher of frosty water. The carved crystal vessel was misty, dripping, and inviting.

"It appears you are not accustomed to our Carolina heat," explained Tyler, handing me a glass of cool water. "Take this. You'll feel better."

I sat up, sipped, and studied the room. The older man walked off and sat in a chair with a newspaper. Holding it up, it obscured his face. Molly sat on the edge of her chair; an anxious expression smeared her face. I lovingly fondled her chin.

"I'm alright now, Molly. We shouldn't have skipped breakfast this morning."

"I'm sorry, Miss White. It was all my fault. I was in such a hurry."

"Ya had naw breakfast?" declared the woman with the tray. "Hmm, hmm, not healthy to skip breakfast, Miss."

"We had no dinner last night either," declared Molly.

"Clorina, go to the icebox and make Miss White and Molly a roast beef sandwich," Tyler asked the woman with the tray. "You do like roast beef, do you not?"

"Roast beef. That sounds wonderful."

"Mustard on mine," exclaimed Molly.

"Mustard it is," chuckled Tyler.

"Right away, Massa Ty," said the black servant.

"Betsy, make sure all the linen on the beds in the spare bedroom have been turned down," he instructed the black girl.

"Yez, Massa Ty," she acknowledged, leaving the room.

The older man walked over, carrying his newspaper under his arm.

"You'll feel much better after you have eaten and rested from your long trip. Wilcox should have stopped along the way and bought lunch. I have spoken to him about it. Next time he will know better."

"Oh, this is my father," said Tyler. "Tyrone Dukes."

I looked up at the man and nearly fainted a second time. The water I was drinking gushed down my chin and spurt from my nose. Molly patted me on the back as I coughed and caught my breath.

"You alright, Miss White?" asked the man.

I gave him a good hard look. Yes, it was the man. To my astonishment, standing before me was the gentleman from Virginia, the one I had seen just the day before at the auction. And possibly one of the men I saw on the brigantine back in New Bedford.

"Yes, yes. I must have swallowed wrong."

"Yes, well, I need to go out and make my rounds," said the Virginian. "You rest. Tyler will attend to the needs of you and the young lady. We will talk again at dinner this evening."

"Until then, Clorina will fix you a sandwich," said Tyler. "That should hold you over until dinner. I'll have the houseboy bring up your luggage. After you have eaten, I'll have one of the servant girls show you to your accommodations. Formal dinner is at six."

"Isn't he wonderful, Miss White?" bubbled Molly. "I finally have a brother."

"You have always had a brother," said Tyler.

He kissed her on the forehead.

"Da room is ready," announced Betsy.

The young girl showed us upstairs to our quarters. Molly was given the choice of her own private chamber but preferred to room with me instead. The servant girl was a light-skinned African no more that thirteen. Though well into puberty, the tone of her voice was squeaky and high pitched, enhancing her with an endearing charm. She was what was referred to as mulatto, a term I heard commonly used at the auction in Charleston. I discovered that light skinned slaves were prized by slavers for being adequate house servants. Still others found them hardheaded and difficult to discipline and not worth the trouble. At least that is what I overheard at the auction. Grandmamma, who was referred to by many as mulatto, detested the phrase. She maintained that it was degrading and vulgar since in Spanish it made reference to a mule. Not only was I forbidden to use it, with time, I came to believe the colloquial term just as hurtful as insulting.

"We're almost the same age," said Molly to our escort as we climbed the stairs.

"We isz. But wez not the same," she made plain.

"What do you mean?"

"Why, yous a white gal and a'im a slave."

"Not to me," explained Molly. "I feel that …"

"That's enough Molly," I shrilled.

"I was only going to say …"

"What we feel is our business. Do I make myself clear?"

"Yes, Miss White."

When we entered the bedroom, the servant turned down the sheet on the bed and fluffed the pillows.

"Maybe we can take a walk later," proposed an innocent Molly.

"Ay don't think so, Miss. But if y'all need anythinn, ay ken get it faw y'all."

"Thank you. It is very kind of you," I let her know.

"Ay be downstairs. Juss halla. My name is Betsy." The black girl bowed and left the room.

Molly scurried out after her, stopping at the top of the stairs. She watched the servant make her way. "Thank you, Betsy," she cried.

After she returned to the bedroom, I inspected the foyer before closing the door.

"I'm sorry, Molly, for being so curt. We need to watch what we say and whom we say it to—conduct ourselves with formality."

"I was just going to tell her that to us she wasn't a slave."

"Yes, she is. As long as she lives here in the south. We must hold our beliefs and bite our tongue when it comes to our abolitionist ideology. What we think about such matters is our own affair. If we say the wrong thing it may make this visit very unpleasant … or unpleasant for Betsy."

"For Betsy … why?"

"Well, she has her duties. If we rip her away from them, she may get in trouble … placed in the fields pulling weeds or even whipped."

"I never thought of that."

"Would you want to be out in the fields … sunrise to sunset, in all that heat, pulling weeds, working with a hoe?"

"I suppose not."

"These black people are prisoners, Molly. They can't just get up and walk away."

"I know. I keep forgetting."

"Just be careful. And remember I am your governess."

"Yes, Miss White. Can I ask you something?"

"Yes, dear."

"Do you think we will find Hannah?"

"*Shh*, that's what we are here for. We can only do our best."

She held her head down and sobbed. I embraced her.

"We must be careful, Molly. I love you and want you to be happy. You are like a sister to me."

"Really?" she sniffled.

"Really."

Throwing her arms around my neck, she embraced me tightly.

"Has there been any sight of your mother yet?"

"Tyler said she is sleeping. She has been ill. Oh, Miss White, I hope she's alright."

"I'm sure she is. We should not worry about what we don't know. Now, let's unpack, shall we?"

I was weary from the long trip from Charleston. We unpacked our things and I decided to nap. Molly left her bed and lay in mine, resting her head by my shoulder. Poor girl was starving for someone to commune with, someone her age, to share secrets, talk and dream of future expectations—of pet ponies, ruffled frocks, and jaunts by the ocean. I had to restrict such companionship or conversations between her and the young slave girl and make plain to her that these were tragic beings living in a turbulent world. Betsy's destiny and prospects for a better life and the securement of self-determination were unimaginable to her. It would be cruel to share Molly's innocence and her love of adventure and travel with a poor black girl trapped and restrained by those of Molly's color.

It seemed like five minutes after my head hit the pillow that a knock came to the door. In fact, it had been two hours. The servant Betsy stood by the door, waiting after inviting us down for dinner. Molly got up in an instant and rushed for the door.

"Dinna's is a-bein done served. Oz hea' ta show ya to da dinnin room."

"Take Molly with you, Betsy. I'll be down in a few minutes.

"Yes, Miss."

I changed my clothing and familiarized myself with the room and my surroundings. I couldn't believe I was finally here, in another state, another world. It may as well have been the rice pastures of Pakistan or the cotton fields of India. Our bedchamber was established around the rear of the house. A sizable window overlooked a patio and the finely appointed garden along the back of the house. The room was airy and cool, kept so by a grove of towering live oaks that shrouded the carefully cultured grounds, acting as a natural awning for the terrace below. The window was open wide, and a refreshing breeze streamed in, as the leaves on the trees rustled and fanned the still air, while peculating the oppressive rays of a relentless southern sun.

I stood by the chiffonier mirror and combed my hair. Placing down the brush I examined my face as most young women do when feeling fatigued. I was pleasantly delighted when I placed my nose up to the looking glass and it did not shatter. It should have. I was a horror. My clammy skin was pale and sticky and dusky circles were ripening beneath my eyes. I dipped the corner of a small towel in the basin of water sitting on the washstand and gently dabbed my face. I was in desperate need of a respectable soak and scrub—a proper bath to wash away nearly four hours of road grime.

I became suddenly aware that I was overly concerned about my appearance. I was a plain and simple country girl and proud of it— more accustomed to an oar and dory than a brush and comb. It was so unlike me to regard such corporal matters as having every hair in place. If I were honest with myself, I would confess that it was Tyler Dukes. I wanted to look pleasing and make an impression. He was a dazzling specimen of a boy. I found him not only kind but intriguing and alluring. I know what you're going to say. I am practically spoken for and that I worship Samuel terribly. But a girl can feast without eating. Amy would say that a nibble or nip did not hurt anyone. Though I am not so certain I would go as far as nibbling. What does that even mean? Nonetheless, after all I witnessed in the rice fields today, I told myself that enthrallment and male pulchritude would be an innocence I could feel free to indulge in. I was ready to make an appearance at the dinner table.

I stepped out into the foyer and shut the door. What sounded like the creaking of a door hinge was, in fact, a distant squeal. I stopped and listened. An argument ensued between a man and woman. Though I could not hear what was being said, it was apparent that the man was enraged and the woman loudly dismissive. The voices emanated from behind a wall in the hall and toward the front of the house where the master bedchamber existed. The room was isolated from the bedrooms toward the rear of the house. It was private and fed by a grandiose stairwell that radiated from the receiving antechamber by the front door. I walked in the direction of the din and listened. There was the slam of a door. The heated dispute and loud quarrel appeared to have stopped. I stood quietly with my ear toward the wall.

"Ken ay helps ya, Miss?"

I leapt, my hand to my chest. "Oh, Betsy, it's you … I was looking for the stairwell."

"Ya ken't walk through that there wall, naw matter how hard y'all try, Miss," she said, dumb-faced. "Da staers are this here way."

Abashed, I followed. The passage took a turn down a long corridor that led to the narrow stairwell down to a salon between the kitchen and the rest of the house. The servant-girl kept looking back, making certain I was following.

"Don't ya get lost, now."

We continued our little trek through a sitting parlor, by the library, along the living room, and, finally, the dining room. All eyes were on me once I entered. The men at the table rose to their feet. Molly clapped, happy to see me.

"Come and sit here, Miss White."

The dining table was enormous. I had never seen such large expanse of polished lumber. With a few fasteners, some canvas, and mast, I could sail it to Cuttyhunk Island.

"Delighted you have recovered," said the Virginian.

Tyler rushed over and pulled back my chair. As soon as I was seated, the men did the same.

I had taken a place by Molly. As her governess, it was expected that we sit together. After assisting me to sit, Tyler returned to his side of the table. To my far left, at the head of the table, was the master of the plantation, Tyrone Dukes. Also at the table sat a jowled-face gentleman I was yet to be introduced to. A woman, presumably his wife, sat by him. To my dismay, the overseer, James Wilcox, walked in and took a place across from me.

"Ah, James. Have you taken care of our little problem?" inquired Tyrone.

"She's been delivered successfully. With a new master, the gal won't be causing any more trouble around here," declared Wilcox, gleefully.

Dukes cleared his throat. "Good. I asked you to dinner to discuss some other delicate matters but, having Miss White dining with us, we shall not burden her with plantation business. We will talk about it later."

"Oh, please, don't allow my presence to interrupt a business meal," I said, salivating at what I may learn.

"There's that troublesome group of Nig …"

"Wilcox!" shouted Tyrone. "I said, later."

Undaunted by the reprimand, Wilcox shook his head and lit a cigar.

"I needed another servant," said the jowled stranger. "I would have purchased that troublesome Negro from you Tyrone … if the price had been right."

"Is that so," said Tyrone.

"I have a gift for making slaves obedient and happy, you know."

"I'm sure you do," acknowledged Tyrone. He quickly changed the course of conversation. "Ferguson, you have yet to meet Miss White."

"My pleasure, young lady," said Ferguson. "This here is my wife, Cora."

Mrs. Ferguson looked over, nodded, and then looked away with a somewhat shunning mien. She was a diminutive woman, attired in black as if in mourning—with stern, hollow cheeks, sunken lips, and an unbridled wandering eye.

"I'm happy to know you," I said.

Still looking away, she bobbed her head in reluctant acknowledgment.

"Mister Ferguson and his wife have a tobacco farm across the river on Edisto Island," acknowledged Tyrone.

"Don't forget, Tyrone. And five hundred acres of prime rice land," said the man, proudly.

"Yes, of course."

"Miss White, you have a foreign accent," blurted Ferguson's wife.

"I assure you, Misses Ferguson, I am an American," I said.

"I gather you are not a Carolinian American?"

"No. But not very long ago, pilgrims practically landed in my back yard by the pair of willow trees that grew there," I quipped.

"Miss White is from Massachusetts," replied Tyrone. "She is visiting with Molly here. My wife is Molly's mother."

"Oh, I see," said Cora, although harboring aversive preconceptions.

"Though, I don't see the resemblance," remarked Tyrone, under his breath.

"Are your accommodations to your satisfaction, Miss White?" asked Tyler.

"Satisfactory and more, Mister Dukes."

"Come now. It's Tyler."

"Of course … Tyler," I said, anxiously.

"The prevailing southerlies blowing up the Edisto River keep nights bearable."

"I found it surprisingly cool in my room. There was a pleasant breeze from the trees behind the house."

"If you sleep with the windows open, you must not forget to use the mosquito netting hanging from the ceiling above your bed. It's malaria season and the bugs will eat you alive."

"I'll remember," I said.

"Is mother coming down to eat?" asked Molly.

"She should be down shortly," replied Tyler, looking over his shoulder at the door. "Mother has not been feeling well lately. I'm sure she will be very excited, as you are, when she sees you."

"We can wait for her no longer," proclaimed Tyrone, slapping his hand on the table. He looked over at the servant. "Clorina, start serving the meal."

Dinner was started without the presence of the plantation's matriarch. I found it odd that an overseer would have dinner at the master's table. It was soon made plain to me that Tyrone Dukes was James Wilcox's uncle.

I did not understand the outrage by Tyrone over his wife's illness. I expected that he would express grief, not annoyance, about her absence. Perhaps there was more to it. However, other than the sympathy I had for Molly, how Tyrone handled his relationship with his wife was none of my affair.

A small army of slave girls, captained by Clorina the servant mother, proceeded to set platters of food on the table. With the exception of Clorina, every one of the serving girls was of mixed blood and cocoa-skinned.

The meal was nothing short of a feast. Trays of roast beef and baked ham were placed at the center of the table. There were sweet potatoes, summer squash, and sweet corn. Not surprising, there was also rice—lots and lots of rice, prepared in every conceivable manner. There was buttery southern rice, Hoppin-John rice with black-eyed peas, and, of course, Charleston red rice, with chopped tomatoes, pork sausage, and sprinkled with celery and onion. Platters were passed around and exchanged in a sinfonietta of clanging silverware, porcelain, and glass. We all filled our plates. Shamelessly, Wilcox crowned his dish with a mountain of baked ham and nothing else. Once the main platter of ham was bare, another, filled with slabs of the same, was brought out to take its place. The Charleston red rice looked inviting. I spooned some onto my plate.

"Be careful," warned Tyler. "That red rice is very spicy."

"Can't be any more spicier than shrimp Mozambique," I said.

"Shrimp Mozambique?"

"A dish my Grandmamma use to serve. It's a Portuguese-African dish—very fiery and spicy. When you put some in your mouth, you would swear that the shrimp were still alive and snipping your tongue."

"Well then, that rice shouldn't bridle your taste buds much. Think I'll have some."

He reached over, taking the serving platter of red rice from my hand. His fingers brushed over mine as I passed him the oval plate. He deliberately held it there for a few seconds longer than necessary. A warm tingle surged from my belly inducing a timid grin. His eyes smiled back at me. Quickly, I pulled my hand away.

"So, Miss White, how did you find the slave auction?" sparked Tyrone.

"Auction?" I replied, somewhat wedged between his question and Tyler's charm.

"That was you at the Charleston auction, was it not?"

I hesitated. "It was."

"You attended a slave auction?" blurted Tyler.

"I was just passing … but, yes, I stopped there."

"You sat at the head of the class," said Tyrone, "By dealer David Deas' table. One would think you were officiating."

"I was not, I assure you," I scoffed, blushing.

"Well, it was difficult to sort out what your business was there. Very few women attend such an event, unchaperoned."

"If I remember correctly, the auctioneer addressed you as the gentleman from Richmond."

"He did. And I am originally from Richmond. The Dukes have a long lineage, over a hundred years of Virginians. It is how most Carolinians know me."

"But you live here in South Carolina."

"Have done so for over fifteen years."

"And you purchased three men, yesterday."

"Not men, Miss White, three Negroes … and at a barn bargain. If you must know, in the last two weeks, twenty-two more Negroes have come into my possession. Does that shock you?"

"I suppose you assume that, being from up north, it should. It does not."

"But you do not approve."

"You must be specific, Mister Dukes. Approve of slavery or your particular purchase."

Dukes laughed. "Choose one."

"Not all Northerners oppose slavery. And twenty-nine hundred is a bargain for any three human souls."

"Conciliatory response, Miss White. But it does not speak to the crux of my inquiry."

"You paid almost three thousand for three Negroes?" sneered Ferguson. "I have never paid more than five hundred for a slave."

"You get what you pay for, my good man."

Though I was somewhat ambiguous, I became weary of the bigoted conversation. It was apparent that Tyrone Dukes was quizzing me on the ethics of servitude or, perhaps, probing for the true purpose of my visit, for which I was certain he already knew. I tried my best to keep him in the dark about all aspects of my thinking. To my advantage, the conversation took a detour when Ferguson pressed Dukes about a private matter.

"Have you made a decision on that land that abuts the creek by my place, Tyrone?" asked Ferguson. "I need the water rights on it or I will lose two hundred acres of rice on the upper slope."

"You have managed without it thus far," replied Dukes.

"I have been diverting water from Adam's creek. The land around the creek has been sold. I have been informed that I must abandon my operation and vacate the property. If I could tap the creek on your lot, I could gravity feed my field. I find my offer very generous. Don't see how you can refuse it."

"I will have to think on it some more. I may be using that parcel myself."

"You have over two thousand acres here, Tyrone, and not all of it cultivated. You have owned that acreage for ten years now and have done absolutely nothing with it whatsoever. Besides. You said you were relocating to your new cotton estate down in Port Royal soon."

"I'll let you know later in the week."

"But, Tyrone …"

"I said later in the week, Ferguson."

Ferguson's wife rested her hand on her husband's arm and appeased him. Tyrone Dukes put a bite of roast beef in his mouth and smirked. The exchange between the two men was more than I cared to witness. Fortunately, Tyler conveniently diverted the conversation.

"Are you submitting any contestants for the regatta tomorrow, Mister Ferguson?"

"Bah … foolish waste of labor, my boy."

"Ferguson doesn't have any contestants worth submitting. Not when he only spends five hundred a head," chuckled Tyrone.

"I purchase laborers to work my fields, not participate in an absurd sport."

"I noticed that you have a couple of big boys working for you that you can enter, Mister Ferguson," said Tyler. "The regattas do wonders for field morale. Weeks after the races we find a substantial growth in labor."

"The rest of the year, growth in labor comes from the cracker at the end of my whip," blustered Wilcox.

"Quiet, Wilcox," snarled Tyrone.

Wilcox mollified his displeasure with his relative's castigation by filling his plate with more ham.

"Mister Wilcox helps coordinate some of our races. He can help you get started," suggested Tyler. "We can even lend you a boat if you like."

The conversation about the regatta continued until dinner had ended. I discovered that boat regattas were popular here in the south. Plantation owners would meet once a year to participate in a contest of speed and agility. If you were a slave and a powerful rower, you would be taken out of the fields and placed into training weeks before the event. Steak and potatoes would replace rice and beans. Though all the slaves who participated felt fortunate to be chosen to compete, to the plantation owners, they were no different than thoroughbreds or quarter horses.

Once we were finished eating, there was more food left unconsumed than when we first started. Just as Tyrone was getting up from the table, his finely dressed wife made her appearance.

"I see you have started without me," she said, walking over to the head of the table.

Victoria Dukes was much younger looking than I had envisioned. And though there was much talk about illness, she looked visibly healthy.

"Happy to see you could make it, my dear," admonished Tyrone.

Molly jumped to her feet before the woman had a chance to sit. "Mother?" she cried.

The woman looked at her as if pestered by the girl's presence. "Come over, child, and give me a hug," she slurred.

Molly ran over and threw her arms around Victoria. "Oh, Mother. I'm so happy to see you again."

"How could you remember, child? You were barely an infant last I laid eyes on you. Now, my dear, go sit down so I can eat."

Molly backed away slowly, admiring her, euphoric countenance plainly on her face. She lingered, savoring her proximity to the women.

"Go on, now. Sit down," directed Victoria, taking her place at the table.

I was bewildered by her demeanor toward her daughter. The behavior was uncommonly lofty and haughtily retiring. She didn't appear very happy to see her daughter at all. Molly sat back down. Taking me by the arm she embraced it, as a surrogate for her own mother's limb.

"That's mother," she whispered, gloriously happy.

I caressed her hand and rested my cheek on her head. "She's beautiful," I acknowledged.

Victoria Dukes proceeded to fill her plate with food. Everyone sat silently and watched—everyone except James Wilcox, whose face was entombed in his plate; fork and knife clanging, as he scooped up his meat.

"You didn't have to sell her," alleged Victoria, slurring her language.

Listening to her flawed speech, I thought to myself, *could this be her illness—perhaps an attack of thrombosis or apoplexy?* Though I know very little of such medical occurrences, I am familiar with one or two of their aftereffects—one being a contortion of the face, and another a slurring of speech. Fortunately, Molly did not seem to notice.

"My good wife, the Negro was nothing but trouble. She ran away three times. I could no longer endure the cost of chasing her down."

"If you didn't punish her with a whip, she would not have tried to run away. She was my favorite servant."

"A servant, my dear, precisely," Tyrone reminded her. "I removed her from the fields and allowed her into my house, gave her a warm bed, the lazy duty of a servant, and what does she do? Steals from me."

"Sugar, Tyrone … a pound of sugar. That was all."

"Stealing, my dear, is stealing."

"Allow them to steal sugar today and they will murder you tomorrow," claimed the overseer.

"Quiet, Wilcox," barked Tyrone.

"Err," grunted James Wilcox, jeeringly, a mouth full of ham.

"James, why don't you go down to the Negro cabins by the tidewater swamp and make sure those three men I purchased yesterday are assigned cabins, will you? I don't want any of the three men sheltered in the same cabin quarters. I want them separated."

"I'll make sure of it."

"Best be on your way then."

"A little nourishment for later," he uttered, shamelessly, taking a loaf of bread and gathering slabs of ham from the platter.

"Get on with it, man," snapped Tyrone.

The overseer stomped out the door leaving a trail of breadcrumbs as he went. Clorina followed behind, quickly mopping up.

"I don't know why you keep him. He is boorish and gruesome. The man has no relationship with a bar of soap."

"He's my nephew, Victoria. He keeps order and harmony in the plantation and he's good at it. I didn't hire him for his hygienic practices."

I had heard so much about the culture of southern gentility. I saw none of it at the Dukes table. Clorina started back to the kitchen. Victoria clutched her by the arm and held up her glass. The servant peered over at Tyrone. He nodded. Taking a bottle from a cabinet along the wall, she poured some green colored liquid into Victoria's fancy glass, followed by a measure of water. Victoria dropped in two sugar cubes and mixed the solution with a perforated silver spoon. Bringing the cup to her lips she threw back her head and emptied it. She slammed the empty glass down onto the table. A thud echoed across the room. The servant filled it once more.

"That will be all, Clorina," instructed Tyrone.

"That will be all, Clorina," parroted Victoria, in unmitigated contempt as the servant took the bottle away.

"We have spoken about this," Tyrone reminded her. "Moderation."

"As if I were a child. But then again, children don't indulge in spirits," she mumbled. "Do they?"

"Don't be foolish, Victoria. You've had enough."

"Since you won't drink with me, I have to drink for the both of us," she cried, louder. She held the decorative crystal glass with the tips of her finger as if the pellucid vessel was burning her hand. She took a sip.

I was beginning to understand that Victoria was not ill at all but a modern-day Xanthippe.

"See, Tyrone. As you instruct … moderation."

"Mother, why don't I take you to your room," said Tyler, gently prying the glass from her hand. "You look a little peaked. I'll have Clorina bring you up some dinner."

"I'm trying to set an example for our guests, Victoria," shouted Tyrone. "You may not have noticed, but we do have company."

"Yes, well, we best be going," announced Ferguson, abruptly.

"Won't you have a drink with me, Cora, before you go?" stammered, Victoria. "Help you with those stomach contractions you often get." She laughed, loudly.

"Let's get going, shall we dear," said Cora.

"You will let me know about that plot of land, Tyrone?" inquired her husband.

"Another time, Ferguson," snarled Tyrone, waving him off with his hand. "Show the Fergusons out, will you, Clorina."

Cora Ferguson's wandering eye glared at us as she got up from the table. She eagerly clutched onto her husband's arm and nudged him along. I watched, blushingly, as the two were handed their coats and escorted out the door. Tyrone ignored them and, instead, nibbled on some rice.

"Mother appears very angry," whispered Molly, not quite understanding the state of mind her mother was in. "I hope she doesn't drink too much of her medicine."

"She'll be alright," I told her. I straightened a couple of strands of her hair and kissed her atop her head.

"Come, Mother," implored Tyler.

"I love you, dear," she said, kissing her son then pushing him away. "But I can find my own way."

She stumbled off, just after retrieving the half empty glass of jade liquor. Tyler stood dismayed as she made her way out the room. Abruptly, she stopped and turned.

"Come with me, Molly, won't you?"

I jumped to my feet. "No." I yelled.

Everyone looked at me.

"I mean, Molly and I were … well, going over some schoolwork."

"Coming, Mother."

"Molly, get back here," I cried.

"No! She's my mother and I want to spend some time with her."

"But, Molly."

"Please, Miss White," she pleaded.

I nodded my dubious approval and hoped for the best.

"Did you know this house was built in 1842 by Negroes," lectured Victoria as mother and daughter strolled away hand in hand. Their voices faded as they left the room. "Good craftsmen, those black folks," I heard her say. "As good as you or I."

Tyrone wiped his mouth with the serviette and flung it onto the table.

"I have business to attend to," he said, to no one in particular. He left the room.

Sadly, Victoria French, now Victoria Dukes, was inebriated. I stood in awe, rudderless, wondering what would happen next. Across the room, Tyler was adrift. Poor boy was probably contemplating a defense for what just occurred. Clorina quickly gathered the empty plates from the table and started for the kitchen. For a large older woman, she was swift and nimble on her feet. One could tell by her casual deportment that the events that just ensued were routine in the Dukes household.

"Now, if ya young folks give me a minute, I shall go into thay kitchen an' get ya'll an awful big slice of apple pie and honey oatmeal cookies. Hmm, hmm!"

Chapter 22: Slave Boat Regatta

The following day, Molly and I sat lazing in the rose garden at the rear of the house enjoying breakfast. No matter where we wandered on the Dukes property, there seemed to be an accessible servant always ready to provide for us. We sat in rattan rocking chairs by a wicker table beneath the umbrella of a live oak. Breakfast was no different than any other meal at the Dukes mansion in that there was more food than we could possibly eat. Just as we indulged ourselves in hotcakes and popcorn cereal, Clorina came marching up the stone promenade with a full tray containing poached eggs and pecan sticky buns. Molly sat quietly cherishing her glass of warm milk and honey. I sipped my tea, eager to query the young girl about the time she spent with her mother.

"When I got to the bedroom last night you were sound asleep," I said.

"I was tired."

"Of course, you were. Did you have a pleasant visit with your mother?"

"I think so."

"Oh?"

"Well … Mother is not what I expected."

As I predicted, Molly did not sound enthusiastic about her meeting with her mother. It did not surprise me considering the woman's condition. It was not only her state of mind that must have been disappointing but Victoria's brazen conduct—the neglectful way she greeted her daughter and her obvious lack of affection. Perhaps it was the liquor. A palliative gate one enters to escape from an unhappy life.

Some of the fishermen who worked at Point Village were always intoxicated … drunk, to put it plainly. In my rather short tenure here in this world, I have discovered that there are several wobbly comportments to those who have had too much drink. It was a lesson taught to me by Charlotte White who had a way with those that were three sheets to the wind, as the whalers described it. In general, we can prune it down to three basic species: there's the sad drunk, who wallows in the misfortunes of life and weeps over spilling his drink; there's the angry drunk, a fellow who finds fault with everyone and everything and often wants to know what in the devil's name you're looking at, when it should be obvious it's him; and, finally, the happy drunk, who trumpets shanties while his comrades-in-drink divest him of his hard-earned dime. Victoria Dukes appeared to be an exemplification of all three.

"I'm sorry, Molly."

"Oh, it's not your fault. I'm the one who wanted to come."

"Did she say something hurtful to you?"

"No, not really. It must be an awful illness she has."

Some call it just that, I thought to myself. "An illness?"

"Mother sat on the floor. She talked about how poor she was growing up on Poverty Point in Fairhaven and how terrible life is now … then she fell asleep. I tried waking her up so she could go to bed, but she just lay there. I was afraid for her. I sat with her for the longest time."

"Oh, Molly. It's not her fault. She's not well."

"No, it's not that. She's not happy."

"Some people have demons in their closets that visit them at times and make them unhappy." I said, not certain what to say.

"Demons in their closets?" she repeated, somewhat befuddled.

"Yes, you know, in their hearts and the way they think."

"Oh."

"What else did she say to you?"

"She said that Grandpapa beat her when she was a little girl."

"Did she tell you that?"

"He drank too much. When she sees black people being punished, it reminds her of the whippings she used to get."

"Poor woman."

"I don't think Mister Dukes is very nice to her."

"Married people sometimes quarrel. Did she not ask how you were doing in school or what you wanted to do when you grew up?"

"No. She did ask if Papa was still in the newspaper business and if Hannah was still with us."

"Did you bring up Hannah?" I clamored.

"No. She did."

"What did she say?"

"She asked me how long Hannah had been gone. I asked her how she knew. She just said that people come and go and that she expected that Hannah had probably moved away … back with her people on the Vineyard."

I pondered what Molly had said, unsure what to make of it. I took it as a clear hint that Victoria knew Hannah was missing.

"Look who's here? Hello, Tyler," said Molly.

"We are up early," he said.

"Early? It's nearly eight," I reminded him.

"Well, early for me," he concluded, chuckling. "Are you girls ready for the big regatta race today?"

"I can't wait," chimed Molly. "I love being down by the water."

"We can leave together." He sat by Molly and took a pecan bun from the tray.

"Is it far to the river?" I asked.

"See those trees just there," he pointed. "Just the other side of them is the river. You can already see everyone starting down the road." He took a bite from the sugary brown bun. Dimples breached his cheeks when he chewed. "Owners from plantations all up and down the valley will be there ... from twelve plantations. We are entering three boats this year."

"What sort of boats are they?"

"Dugouts ... like Indians use to build ... constructed from cypress trees on the property ... anywhere between twenty-five to fifty feet long. The latest one we had built is almost sixty feet long."

"I love sailing," said Molly.

"You don't sail these boats, you row them," he laughed.

"Can I help you row?"

He laughed yet again. "Northern girls have very little concept about how we live here in the south."

"As you do about how we live up north," I sparked.

"You've got me there."

"Won't you be rowing one of the boats?" inquired Molly.

"Whites don't row. The boats are slave workboats. The Negroes work them to transport rice and other goods across the river. Once a year we race them. It's a celebration; black and white have great fun. The boatmen do all the rowing. We whites are just the spectators. Of course, there is a wager or two by the owners. The slaves who win get extra rations of beef and pork. They eat like kings for a week. The slaves really enjoy it."

"You really think they enjoy it?" I flared.

"Immensely. Boatmen have the easiest and most prestigious job on the plantation. They are envied and respected by all the other slaves."

"And a boat regatta once a year makes up for a state of servitude, does it?"

He snickered. "Subjugation, servitude ... those are northern terms."

"They are your laws," I noted, objectively.

"I don't want to talk about it."

"I wager Victoria will not be at the regatta."

He got up and wiped the sticky bun from his hand. "Leave my mother out of this," he snarled.

I thought about what I said. He turned his back. I stood and placed my hand on his cold shoulder. He flung it aside. I was impatient in my premature plot to pluck his politics on the topic of slavery. It was unnecessary to bring his mother into it.

"Tyler … I'm sorry. The entire country is at war over such an issue. Let us not do the same. It was cruel of me to mention your mother. Will you forgive me?"

There was silence for a moment. Holding his head down, he nodded.

"I couldn't consider myself a southern gentleman if a boy didn't defend his mother, now could I?"

"No, you could not."

"I have mixed sentiments about such matters."

"Oh?" I was surprised to hear him say that.

Just then, Tyrone Dukes approached on horse from around the side of the house. His appearance suspended our conversation. He was smartly dressed in full Confederate regalia, with sword and a long gray military frock worn down to his knees. The wool jacket was decorated with two gold stars at the collar, a silk-tasseled sash around the waist, and double-breasted gilt buttons. Tyrone loved to move around dressed in his military uniform. Furthermore, the military commission he was bequeathed was but an honorary one. A government decree allowed him to reimburse another recruit to serve in his place. In addition, a supplementary endowment that he provided the military bestowed on him privileges that only money could acquire—a position without service. As a private citizen, Tyrone Dukes financed supplies for Fort Beauregard on Phillip's Island, including ammunition and armament for the gunboats that patrolled Port Royal Sound. This entitled him to accoutrements and the robes of ceremonial vestment to exploit the posture of a titular Major, with little authority and exemption from martial responsibility.

I took notice of Tyrone's uniform and the buttons that embellished it, just as James Wilcox came trotting over. The fasteners were the same as the one I found in Asha Potter's cold hand. However, all the buttons were present on Tyrone's garment. It was formal attire and, as Rudolf had made clear to me, not the sort of garment worn casually, especially if he were up north. My inspection was fruitless.

"Here comes Father," grumbled Tyler. "Playing soldier again."

Tyrone halted his horse, regarding me with dubious air.

"James and I are riding out to the regatta, Tyler. Are you coming?"

"Yes, Father, we all are."

"Good morning, Mister Dukes," said Molly, cheerfully.

Dukes ignored her. Instead, he stared at me. "We have always left the women at home. It's a man's sport, you know."

"There will be other ladies there, Father. They will be with me. I will look after them."

"Very well. Keep them away from the hands in the fields." He tugged at the bit in the horse's mouth and rode off.

James Wilcox lingered and glared down at me. "How are you today, Miss White? I trust you slept well." He took a cigar that he kept tucked into the leather band around his hat. Striking a match on the handle of the bowie knife in his boot he lit the thinly rolled tobacco.

"Like a babe in mother's arms, Mister Wilcox. And you?"

A vacant smile matured on his face as smoke spewed from parted lips.

"Wilcox, come along," yelled Tyrone.

James Wilcox sneered, tipped his hat, and galloped off.

"Something unsavory about that man," I declared.

"He's an overseer. All overseers are unsavory," said Tyler. "It's a requirement for the job. No bother. After today, he's leaving for Dukes Island at Port Royal."

"Dukes Island."

"Yes. He's the overseer at our cotton plantation south of Beaufort. It's where the big house is."

"I heard Mister Ferguson say you were moving there."

"That's right. Mother spoke fondly of the house on Dukes Island until her condition worsened. Now, Father's been putting it off."

"Are we still going to the boat races?" moaned Molly.

"We sure are," said Tyler, ruffling her hair. "Would you like to ride there, or should we walk?"

"It's a nice enough day," I pointed out, "let's walk."

I ran into the house and collected floppy, brimmed hats to protect us from the sun, though the day was turning overcast but dry. The walk down to the river would take us nearly thirty minutes, through flooded rice fields and past a series of canals. Molly appeared to be enjoying herself, skipping along the lane and lingering occasionally to collect wild violets that sprouted by the culverts along the roadway. I stopped at a small arched walking bridge. Resting my elbows on the railing I watched as slaves seated some long timbers in the ground.

"What are they building?"

"They are not building anything. They're placing the lumber boards into a rail across the canal to create a dam. In a few days the field will have dried and the weeding will begin."

A short distance away a group of black men were walking across the lane in an orderly fashion, from one field into another. One of the men who trailed behind carried a walking stick and appeared to be jamming it into the kidneys of the man laboring to walk in front of him. He yelled for him to hurry. The abused man appeared weary. He stumbled over the culvert and fell onto the roadway. His tormentor proceeded to kick at him, hollering for the poor fellow to get up. I was alarmed for both the man on the ground and Molly.

"Why is he doing that?" I cried. "I don't want Molly to witness such cruelty."

Tyler marched over to the group. Wrenching the rod from the man's hand, he broke it over his knee and helped the stricken slave to his feet. After a few words, the group of slaves cheered and ran toward the river. Tyler lumbered back carrying the broken staff.

"Gave them the day off," he announced with conviction, tossing the stick into the field.

"Oh, Tyler. I'm proud of you."

We watched as the group of men sprinted away.

"Doesn't it make you feel good?"

"They deserve much more, I suppose."

"They do, you know."

He bit his lip and nodded. "We best be going. We don't want to miss the festivities."

We continued down the road toward the river. There was a sudden gloom in the air—perhaps it was the scene I just witnessed, or the way the light was smothered by a gray and darkening sky.

"Why was that man hitting his companion?"

"He was just recently assigned driver."

"Driver?"

"Like an overseer. But he doesn't attend to the daily operations of the plantation, just keeps the hands in line. Wilcox must have trained him."

"But he's black."

"Most drivers are. That was old Pip he was pushing around. May have to put that driver back to work in the fields. He wouldn't like that. Reprisal by his peers would be dreadful."

"You sound a bit miffed."

"I liked old Pip. Use to ride me on his back when I was a child. A very gentle sort. Poor Pip. He really shouldn't be working the fields any longer."

"None of them should."

"I am truly my Mother's son. There's something not right about this way of life. I don't know how I feel about things any longer."

"I would think you are on the right track, Tyler."

"Slavery," he remarked, as if the retort were a cuss word.

"Slavery." I cursed.

We walked silently. I did not want to accost him with a lesson in civility or injure any maturing convictions about abolitionist principles or theories. I had the golden fish on the silver hook, and I had to be scrupulous on how I reeled him in.

"Can I ask you something personal?"

"Ask away."

"I can understand why you have taken Tyrone Dukes name. After all, you were but a child when your mother married him. But why do you call him Father?"

"I have never given it much thought. Besides, he raised me."

"You have a birth father, and he loves you. Speaks very proudly of you."

He smiled. A glow bloomed on his face. "Two men … one a father who has become a stranger to me and yet a stranger who is indeed my father. I don't remember much of him. He spent most of his time building up his newspaper company. I do remember the times he took me sailing. I couldn't have been more than four or five. I remember the whaling boats along the shore, the smell of whale oil … yes, that eternal smell. And how could I forget Hannah. How she would sing Wampanoag Indian songs to me until I went to sleep."

I bit my tongue. The topic of Hannah was one that, in time, would arise. But with the regatta ahead of us, now was not the moment. I could see the river over a bluff down the lane and the huddled crowd that had gathered there. We came upon a fallen tree by the side of the road that was hewed into a bench.

"Let's relax a minute," he said, sitting down. Molly sat beside him and embraced him by the arm. "Do you like it here, Molly?"

"So many fields."

"Yes, there is."

"We are almost there. Look. I can see girls my age. Can I go ahead?"

"Be careful," I said.

Molly skipped over the grassy knoll and down to the river. I took a place by Tyler and sat down. He sat with his legs spread, studying the ground between them. Yanking a frond from a small fern that grew beneath the bench, he tore away the leaves one by one and tossed them.

"A penny for your thoughts or a tickle for a nickle."

"What?"

"Oh, just something that I use to say when a child."

"Did your mother teach you that?"

"I never knew my mother."

"I'm sorry to hear that."

"I was raised by the most wonderful lady anyone could have."

"What happened to your real mother, if I am not being too inquisitive?"

"I don't know. I was an orphan."

"You mean like Jane Eyre."

"Yes."

"And she was a governess also."

I was pleasantly surprise with his literary prowess. "Have you read *Jane Eyre*?"

"No, not really, but everyone has heard the story. It is Mother's favorite. I remember her reading bits of it when I was a child."

"I have read it three … no, four times."

"Remind me. How does it go?"

"Well, Jane is orphaned when her parents die of typhus. She then goes to live with her uncle, Mister Reed. Still later she attends Lowood Institute, a school for orphaned girls …"

He stared at me as I spoke, an inquiring expression on his face. It made me uneasy.

"What … what is it? Did I say something wrong?"

"No, please continue."

His eyes swept my face like a silky warm breeze on a cool afternoon. I got up to think.

"Where was I … oh, yes, then Jane leaves the school and gets a job as a governess at Thornfield Hall. Remember? Then she meets Rochester, and saves him from a fire, which I thought was a bit much."

He exhibited a puerile grin.

"Are you listening?"

"Oh, yes," he said, as he stood up and his eyes focused deeply into mine. "It's beautiful."

"As the story unfolds, Jane falls in love with Rochester but he is promised to another, then …"

"Absolutely beautiful," he repeated.

"Think so? Heartwarming … but I wouldn't call it beautiful."

He reached up and gently ran a strand of my hair through his fingers. "You are. You are beautiful, Emily."

"What?"

I reached up to pull his hand away. No one was more astonished than I when I subtly embraced it, guiding his fingers toward my face, where I fondled them along my cheek. I felt a dire need to be held, loved, and adored. It was an insane moment. I closed my eyes to think. What was I doing? Suddenly, a pair of moist lips fell onto mine. A cloak of warmth came over me. Eyes shut, I reached up and ran the back of my hand along the contours of a strong chin. Our mouths parted. I darted my tongue along my lips, which were dry and wanting. He kissed it. I pushed it out further as he nursed me inside his warm mouth. With his arms gingerly around my waist, his hands wandered down my thighs in nefarious conviviality. My blood boiled as my dignity blistered. I thought about Amy's advice. I had gone from window shopping to breaking the glass and pilfering the goods. I pushed him away. Bumbling, I concluded my telling of *Jane Eyre*.

"Where was I? Oh, yes. And through hardship and endeavor, Jane triumphs, becoming Edward Fairfax Rochester's salvation and fulfilling her happiness. The end."

"You tell it seductively."

"I did no such thing."

"My apology, then. Must have been the way my ears heard it."

"With the actual book in hand I could have read it to you and not be interrupted."

"Oh, did I interrupt you?"

"You certainly changed the narrative."

"You appeared to take pleasure in my telling."

"Pleasure is no substitute for salacious conduct, Tyler."

"You think an innocent kiss salacious?"

"It was not the kiss. It was my flagrant behavior."

"Your behavior was endearing. I'm attracted to you, Emily. I thought that perhaps you felt the same about me."

"Whether I did or not it is a practice in betrayal."

"Betrayal?"

"I have a boyfriend. His name is Samuel. He's in the Union army. When the war is over, we are hoping to wed."

"Life sometimes takes us down a different road than the one we had planned. But it is not my intention to sully your reputation or trample your desires."

"Sometimes we trample over our own desires."

"We will think of in no longer."

Tenderly, he took my hand and kissed it.

"Friends?" he asked.

"Friends," I said, careful to reclaim my limb.

The river shore reminded me of the saltmarshes of Horseneck Island in Westport. A patchwork of fleecy cordgrass sprouted from the shallow riverbed, a meandering mesh of sea-hay and fluttering culms were skulking up the sandy coast. Between the clumps of grass was a flotilla of slender riverboats. Not all of them were dugouts. A couple were built with conventional practices, constructed of vertical ribs, hefty stem post, and typical hull planking. They were tributary skiffs—half the beam and over twice the length.

A couple of slaves stood by one of the boats clutching their oars. The slender paddles were twice the height of the boatmen. One pair was nearly thirteen feet long. We arrived just as the first squadron of dugouts was pushed away from shore. Each boat had four to six men. Though all participants were black, it was truly a white man's event. Wages and betting were conducted with the possibility of big winnings. More importantly was the opportunity for bragging rights and the entitlement of having the most efficient boat crew in the plantation river valley. For the slaves, the profit was being away from the drudgery of the fields and possibly a measure of retribution by their masters.

The black men splashed and sprinted by the side of their slinky canoes, laughing and cheering, guiding the vessels into deep water. With synchronized calibration, they jumped into the boat, took hold of the oars, and quickly paddled away. Their companions on shore cheered them on, while others broke into song. The riverbank was overflowing with onlookers, clusters of white and black parties, though none shoulder to shoulder. The whites lined the shore while most blacks watched from a distance. The separation gave the slave spectators the privilege of singing and dancing in groups, depending what plantation they were from. Celebration was conducted away from owners who shunned such frolic. They sang the songs in hobbled poetry of support for their team or good-natured lampooning of their rivals. In dactylic code, even the owners did not escape the japery in their chant.

Skimming along the river at speed, the rowers sung their anthems of salvation and woe. One plantation crew sang louder, striving to drown out the other. The veil of harmony between black and white was a powerful one. The premise of the happy slave was exhibited in clandestine fashion. To the idle northerner, it appeared a joyful life of competition and song. And, for one day of the year, it was. But I would not endure one day of bondage for all the regattas in the world.

We passed by a group of cheering blacks. I noticed that they were the men we saw on the way here. Old Pip rested on a log behind them. Molly sat at a table enjoying a picnic with a group of white girls. Up on the grassy embankment were others sitting on blankets and indulging in food and drink. Tyrone Dukes, dressed in military attire, parleyed with a group of plantation owners. They laughed, exchanged money, and patted each other on the back. Tyler and I sat on a grassy patch of ground close to the river's edge.

"Look … there," blurted Tyler, pointing. "Look how fast they're going. We're ahead."

"How far do they row?"

"They must row up to that mast with the yellow ribbon in the middle of the river, then back the other way until they come to the other pole with the red ribbon. That's the finish line. Put your back into it, Simon!" he yelled, hands cupped to his mouth.

"Which is Simon?"

"The Negro sitting in the back of the white boat. He sets the rhythm and helps steer … mostly, though, he just leads the men in song … drive them, Simon, drive them!" he hollered.

"I sense you like Simon."

"I do. We're winning, Father," he shouted over to Tyrone.

Tyrone Dukes ignored his stepson. He appeared in a heated conversation with a fellow plantation owner.

"It doesn't appear that he cares," I said.

"He has a lot on his mind, with the war, Mother, and the new house at Port Royal."

"Why is he dressed in uniform?"

"Leaving later today for Fort Beauregard at Port Royal Sound for military service."

The news of his leaving was somewhat disheartening. I was hoping to have more time to discover whether Tyrone had anything to do with the disappearance of Hannah or the death of Asha Potter. It was plain to me that he may have been in Fall River the day we were transporting Isaac Sinclair from Andrew Robeson's underground station. Was he one of the men knocked off their horse? After all, he did walk with a limp. Even if I could prove that he killed Asha, what could I possibly do about it? Absolutely nothing. Tyrone lived in a rebel state. With war between North and South it very well could have been another country.

For now, my sacred mission is to discover what happened to Hannah, without becoming a casualty myself. With the current hostilities, I could be easily presumed a spy, disappear, and no one would ever find me. Then what would happen to Molly? I was more aware than ever that I needed to tread lightly. For a New England girl, that will be hard to do.

"We did it, we did it!" shouted Tyler, arms and fists in the air, jumping with jubilation. "We won the first round. Isn't that great, Emily?"

"Yes, great," I said, trying not to unmask my boredom with tournaments. A man's hunger to win was an exercise that always confounded me—a male enterprise that spoke more to ego than to nobleness. The same was true for all the male onlookers at the regatta, especially the black men who would profit nothing from the winnings of their masters. Whether boat racing or horse racing, it is all a ruse where owners are the profiteers, and the spectators the workers—the pawns, divested of their valued time and hard-earned money. It seems to be inbred into the male species, this desire to compete and win. I, for one, will never understand it. For if I did, I may very well understand war and the barbaric sport of slavery.

"Come, Emily. Let's go congratulate Simon."

We ran along the shore to applaud the victors of the race. Tyler clapped as the six men pulled the boat up onto the grassy shore.

"Good job, Simon!"

"We done push her, Massa Ty," said the man, striving for breath and sporting a smile.

The team sat on the gunwale, their feet wading in the water, waiting to race the winner of the next round. I suddenly recognized Simon. He was one of the coach drivers who gathered us up at Charleston. He sat on the spongy grass by the water's edge. Tyler inspected one of the oars.

"These are the new oars we had built. They are just about three feet longer than the ones we used last year."

"Had ta row hard but it done made a difference," declared the slave.

"Are you going to introduce me, Tyler?"

"This is Simon. He and another Negro work this boat up and down the river every day."

"Good job, Simon," I said reaching out to shake his hand.

His eyes bulged. The black man looked at my extended offer with flinching trepidation and bewilderment. He sat on his hands and refused to extend one.

"Don't," growled Tyler. "There are people around. He's not supposed to touch a white woman."

"That's nonsense."

"Emily, understand. There's an order to things here whether we like it or not. If you break that order he will suffer retribution, not you."

I should have known better. Simon kept his head down, pretending I was not even there. I noticed James Wilcox watching us from a short distance away.

"Massa Ty. I don't want no trouble," pleaded Simon.

"They'll be no trouble," assured Tyler.

"Yes, Massa Ty."

"Why don't you push the boat out into deeper water and get ready for the next round."

At that very moment, I noticed something Simon was wearing as he splashed away. It was a wampum band of beads strung around his wrist. I quickly darted into the water after him. I clutched him by the arm. "Where did you get this?"

He quickly tore his limb away. Fearful eyes glared at Tyler.

"What is it, Emily?"

"His wrist," I shouted. "That band he is wearing."

Tyler waded through the water and took Simon's arm, examining the string of lavender-colored beads—small ovate spheres made from the shell of the mollusk quahog. He slipped it off the black man's wrist.

"Those are wampum beads," I declared.

"What did you call them?"

"Wampum beads. Made by a Wampanoag."

"So, they are made by an Indian. There are plenty of Indians up and down these lowlands. Why are you so hysterical about it?"

"I want to know where he got them."

"Where did you get this, Simon?"

"Found it, Massa' Ty. In da boat when I was takin that woman across da riv'ah."

"What woman?"

"What's the trouble here?" asked Wilcox appearing out of nowhere. He carried his knife in his hand, sculpturing a corkscrew from the peel of an apple.

"No trouble," replied Tyler. "Emily just wanted to know Simon's secret to winning races."

"Is that a fact?"

The coiled peel fell to the ground. He stabbed the naked apple with the glimmering blade and cut off a piece.

"I row a skiff back at home," I remarked. "I found his method interesting."

"You're not at home anymore," Wilcox made plain.

"I thought you were leaving for the Dukes Island," said Tyler.

"This afternoon," replied the overseer. "What's that in your hand?"

"Some trinket Emily was showing us."

"It all revolves around Miss White, doesn't it?"

"Sometimes even the sun, Mister Wilcox," I blurted.

Tyler slipped the bracelet around my wrist. "Can I help you with something, James?"

"I will handle it myself," he sneered, walking away. He slithered over to Tyrone Dukes and the two spoke.

Tyrone nodded and glanced over. I watched them with some consternation as they walked off together.

"I don't like that man," I said.

"He's just sticking his nose where it doesn't belong. Thinks the slaves are his property. Whenever a white stranger goes near a black man, he assumes they're planning some grand escape."

"I's sorry Massa' Ty."

"Where did you get those beads, Simon?"

"Like ay say, Massa Ty, I done find it n'da boat. Must of fell from da woman they done took away."

"What woman, Simon?"

"Indi'n woman, with Malachi."

"Malachi!" I cried. "Took away … where, when."

"Easy, Emily. Now Simon. Did you say an Indian woman?"

"Yes'm. They done taken her and Malachi to da road, on da otha side of da river."

"What are you on about, Simon? Malachi ran off. He's been gone for almost three months, now. When did you see him?"

"O'va a week last, Massa Ty."

"I knew it. She's here somewhere, Tyler."

"Who's here?"

"Hannah."

"Hannah!" he chortled. "Why that's ridiculous. What would Hannah be doing here?"

In the distance, someone blew a conch shell. The sound carried, echoing up the river valley. The long boats in the middle of the tributary suddenly stirred as oars were plunged into the water. A roar peppered over the crowd. Hoots and hollers washed down to the shore. A new race had started.

"Come, Emily," commanded Tyler.

"Where we going?"

"Back to the house. I've lost my excitement."

He marched up the lane. I gave chase.

"What about Hannah?"

"We will talk about Hannah later. Come along, Molly."

"Tyler, wait."

Before leaving, I waded through ankle deep water and over to Simon. Slipping the wampum off my wrist I handed it to him. He looked down at my hand and backed away shaking his head. I smiled, hung the wampum on an oar and walked off. Once a good distance away, he picked up the trinket and slipped it onto his wrist. Having so little, I did not feel right taking the ornament away from him. It was probably the most valued thing he possessed. Besides, I was not absolutely certain that the wampum belonged to Hannah. This I knew. The enigmatic wrist beads were not his. However, more notably, they were not mine either.

Chapter 23:
A Hint to a Feather

Tyler and I sat in the kitchen eating.

"Why is ya young folks hangin around n'da kitchen. Ya should be comfortable n'da dinnin room," said the servant.

"It's quiet here. No one is ever fighting," said Tyler

"Ya is rite about tat, Massa Ty." She poured us a glass of milk from the icebox.

"You remind me of Grandmamma, Clorina."

"Come now, I's jus a Negro gal."

"She was kind and generous just like you."

"Ya serious, Miss Emily?" she said, wiping the table.

"I sure am."

"Lordy, lord!" She placed a dish of pudding in front of me.

"Thank you."

"Is notin. It is wat I's hea fa'wa," she said, leaving the room.

I dipped my spoon into the rice pudding. "Where is Dukes Island, Tyler?"

"Port Royal Sound. Just south of here. Closer to Beaufort."

"Is it a big island?"

"Around two thousand acres of prime cotton soil. You should see the main house, Emily. It is twice the size of this one."

"How many slaves work there?"

"Right now, there is probably over a hundred at the island and almost two hundred here. Tyrone claims that it's what makes our slaves so prized. They are experienced in picking cotton and rice."

"Oh, Tyler, it's no wonder your mother feels the way she does. All those captive lives. They are people like you or me. They have families, wishes, and dreams. You speak of them like they're cherished possessions or something."

"I do, don't I?" he muttered somewhat guilt-smacked. But you have to understand. It's the only life people know here … a way of living in the south. Doesn't matter if you are black or white."

"Oh, Tyler, but it does matter, don't you see?"

"What would we do if there were no slaves, what would happen to Dukes Plantations … what would happen to them? We are all tied together."

"And you have done the tying. The rope is in your hands. They are your slaves."

"Miss White," he snapped. "I have no slaves. My mother has no slaves. They belong to Tyrone Dukes. We take little interest in my father's … in Tyrone's affairs."

Clorina walked back into the kitchen. "My, my, da Lord 'as given us a glorious day. I's sure is thankful."

I looked over to the window. It was anything but a glorious day. I presumed she was not talking about the weather but the actual experience of being alive. Even as a slave.

"Thanks for the pudding, Clorina."

"Want mawe?"

"No, that was plenty."

Tyler sat looking disconcerted and ruffled. Perhaps I was too harsh on him with my bold and resolute New England spirit. It was time to change the theme of conversation along the vein of diplomacy.

"What is it you want to do with your life, Tyler?"

"I was planning on being a doctor."

"A noble profession."

"I have one year of doctoral training, enough to practice in the military as a medic. One can attain valuable experience in a theater of war … types of injuries are countless."

"I regularly ask myself whether it was the right thing for Samuel to do … join the military. You remind me of him … kind, gentle, more of a pacifist than an aggressor. You really want to join the military?"

"No. My compulsion is to save life, not take it. Even as a medic, I would not be able to avoid carrying a rifle or engaging in battle."

"Terrible way of gaining medical experience."

"I would like to become a full-fledged doctor. Not just a medic. Most of the good medical schools are up north. Tyrone said that, because of the war, money is scarce. I had to wait a while before returning to school."

"Not really. Perhaps you should move back home. Rudolf would be happy to put you through medical school."

"I can't. Someone must watch after Mother. She's not well."

I finished drinking my milk. Clorina immediately filled my glass. He walked across the room and leaned on the icebox by the window and reflected, a sorrowful past cast across his face. Outside, a slave gardener toiled in the garden swinging a scythe and cropping the grass.

"Tyler?"

"Yes."

"Do you remember Hannah when you lived in New Bedford?"

"I sure do." A mournful look faded. A gentle smile bloomed across his face. "I remember the pow-wow peace dance we use to do together. Of course, she was just trying to entertain a little boy with boundless energy. But she always outlasted me. After a while, I would fall asleep on the floor and she would lift me into bed. In the morning, her smile was the first thing I would see. Mother didn't appreciate having her there for some unknown reason. Hannah was a treasure."

"Sounds lovely."

"Then everything changed. All I remember was Mother and Father fighting. Then Hannah disappeared. I imagine she couldn't take the quarreling. Before I knew it, we were on the boat to Charleston."

"Why didn't she take Molly?"

"Strangely, I don't remember anything about Molly being born or why she stayed behind. I was preoccupied with not ever seeing my chums at school again. I don't even remember her as a baby."

"Why did your mother leave?"

"Don't know. Never asked or gave it much thought. Children rarely do. But, suddenly, I can't avoid ignoring the past. I must consider condition for my future … Mother's and mine. With the war, everything could all change tomorrow."

"I understand your priorities. Mine at the moment is to find Hannah."

"Can I ask you something, Emily?"

"Yes, of course."

"You were surprised this morning when Simon mentioned Malachi."

"Was I?"

"Yes, you were. Your concern seemed to imply that you knew him."

"*Shhh*," I hissed, looking over at Clorina.

She worked quietly by the stove.

I took him by the hand. "Let's go sit by the garden."

"Ya young folk holler if ya need anythin," she bubbled, as we went out the door.

We walked to the back of the property to the stone wall that separated the gardens from the fields. He clutched onto my hand tightly as we went. Tyler was good at clutching, but not very good at letting go.

"Can I have my hand back please?"

Before releasing it, he brought the tip of my fingers to his lips and kissed them. He was a relentless crusader on a wooing campaign. At every accessible opportunity, I was blitzed by an embracing siege of kissy skirmishes. Though endearing incursions were overpowering and exceedingly inviting, my intent was to not surrender under any condition or allow myself to be fervidly conquered. However, I was happy he was not cross with me after the grilling examination I put him through earlier. I felt I could trust him. I needed an ally.

We sat on the wall looking out onto the flooded rice-land. In the distance, field-hands toiled under the muggy air of a cloudy sky. Servitude was the order of the day and every day for black families. Wishes, hopes, and desires were substituted by bondage, retribution, and anguish—freedom a momentary apparition. Futurity was fleeting and manifested by the tip of a hickory cane or lashing whip.

The blazing sun was waning, still, the leaden air was stifling. An oven breeze exhaled from the direction of the swamped, rice meadows even though the sun was hidden. However, it was not all discomfort. The humid, sweet fragrance of herbaceous greenery and germinating rice saturated the air. The nectarous scent emitted from a patch of yellow jasmine that grew below the stone wall purified the senses, leaving one in lethargic splendor. I plucked one of the lemony-colored flowers and examined it.

"I will confide in you, but you must promise not to betray me," I told him, threading the yellow flower in his shirt lapel.

He kissed me. A jolt of bliss rushed up my spine. I whacked him on the arm.

"Can I trust you? And I don't mean to flirt with me."

"You can."

I hesitated, giving thought to how much I should divulge. "Yes, I have met Malachi in New Bedford, at your father's house. His wife and child were there also. He was staying in your father's barn behind the house when he was attacked and kidnapped. Hannah was in the barn at the time, so they took her also."

"Hannah. Kidnapped?"

"Yes."

"Are you sure?"

"Why do you think I came to Charleston, Tyler? Your father sent me."

"Poor Hannah."

"How well did you know Malachi?"

"He was the plantation carpenter. The workshop was in the old Tobacco House on the east side of the property."

"Tobacco House?"

"Yes, where we dry and age tobacco."

"Oh, I see."

"Malachi was the most valuable slave on the central coast of South Carolina … a true craftsman. I was just a tot when we built a hobbyhorse together. I still have the toy soldiers he carved for me … along with a flute."

"You sound as if you really liked him."

"I did."

He got up and walked over to the edge of the wall, staring out to the field and the slaves working there. Depending how the wind was blowing, their haunting ballad was carried across the field and I could make out the stirring and wistful chantey.

"After all," he said. "I helped him escape."

"You what?"

"I helped Malachi escape north. Told him to go to New Bedford. Look up my father. He would find work there."

"Hallelujah!"

"I arranged for Malachi, his daughter, and Ruth to escape north. Finding Ruth and seizing her from another man's plantation was no easy task. If I am found to be responsible, the law calls for an extensive fine, along with imprisonment, of even death for aiding an escapee. You see, Emily. I must trust in you now also."

The disclosure that he helped Malachi escape astonished and gladdened me. I was convinced that I could place my confidence with him now. I truly had an ally in my cause.

"What brought you to help him?"

"Tyrone was making advances toward Malachi's wife and Mother was upset about it. I promised her that I would take care of things."

"I thought Malachi's wife came from another plantation?"

"She did. It's a long story."

"Tell me about it."

"Well, Ruth was Father's wedding gift for mother. She was Mother's personal domestic. Ruth must have been around thirteen at the time. Mother held the bill of sale for her."

"Bill of sale?"

"A deed … proof of ownership. Ruth was Mother's property. She lived at the house and was treated as a daughter. But Father was relentless in his wanton advances and interest toward the slave girl. In time, Mother found out about them … in Mother's wedding bed no less. She was furious with both Tyrone and Ruth—even though the poor girl tried her best to evade Tyrone's advances. A short time later, and in one of her drunken stupors, Mother sold Ruth to Ferguson for a dollar. Father was furious. Mother came to regret the sale terribly. Tyrone tried getting Ruth back, but Ferguson would not sell. He wanted a thousand dollars for her. Tyrone would only pay the dollar, which was what Ferguson had been compensated for the sale."

"Sounds so convoluted, Tyler."

"It is. To make matters worse, when Ruth was sold, her daughter Queenie stayed behind. The child was property of Dukes Plantation. Father did not care to sell the child and Ferguson did not want to buy her. With time, Ferguson needed to acquire some property from Dukes Plantation to retain some water rights that he desperately needed. Father's been holding the land deal above Ferguson's head ever since. Finally, the man offered to throw Ruth in on the deal. Father's yet to agree."

"Are Ruth and Malachi married? Is Queenie Malachi's daughter?"

"Yes, married by one of the slave elders, but the marriage is not recognized by South Carolina law, not that it would make any difference. Though Ruth was Mother's property at the time when the child was born, she officially became property of Dukes Plantation. All children born on Dukes' land are Tyrone's property. And though Queenie was indeed Malachi's, he was not allowed to live with or see her. Last I had heard, plans were being made to sell Queenie separately down river."

"What a tangled existence."

"Now it's all undone.

"We must find Hannah and Malachi. Simon said that he took them across the river in his boat."

"We are not certain that it is Hannah."

"Tyler, I'm sure those wampum wrist beads belong to Hannah … she was brought here. I need to find out where they have taken her."

"Tyrone detests runaways. Disciplined slaves are either sold or exiled."

"Exiled? Where?"

"Exiles are taken to work Dukes Island. Not so tempting to run away from there. The river current runs strong down both sides of the island. You need to be a good swimmer, or you can be swept out to sea. Besides, the island's heavily guarded. Wilcox has stationed drivers and dogs all over it. Some of them make Wilcox look like a monk in their cruelty and betrayal."

"Do you think Hannah and Malachi can be on Dukes Island?"

"I'm afraid they can be anywhere between here and Louisiana."

"Can you show me the Tobacco Barn?"

"If you like."

The Tobacco Barn was a five-minute walk and within full sight of the main house. It was an average looking barn with steep gabled roof and a corral for horses. High above and along the roof line on both sides of the structure was a series of portals covered with swinging, planked shutters.

These were used as vents to air the attic and dry the curing tobacco hung along the barn rafters.

Tyler unlatched the ten-foot-high barn door and slid it aside. Along its steel track, the metal wheels rumbled as it glided off to one side. The smell of cured tobacco flowed out. It was a strong, leafy smell mixed with the aromatic scent of burnt cherrywood or marinated prunes. Along one wall was a workbench. Hung behind it was a series of saws, chisels, and hammers. Stacks of wood and sawdust were everywhere.

"I haven't been in this barn in years," said Tyler.

"Smells great in here."

"Not to me."

I walked around, unsure what I was looking for.

"See those poles up there along the rafters?

"Uh-huh."

"That's where we hang and air the tobacco. Of course, we only grow four or five acres, enough for the local market. This barn has many uses. It also functions as a place for horses and as a carpentry shop."

"It's a huge building."

He watched me carefully. I wandered, searching in every corner.

"What are you looking for?"

"Oh, I don't know. But I may … once I find it."

Toward the back of the barn sat a broken-down buggy and a two-seat buckboard, derelict and crumbling. Along the rear wall was an array of wagon wheels beneath a cluster of leather harnesses and dusty saddles. Just to the right of it was a door.

"Where does that lead to?"

"If I remember correctly, it's a small sunken room used as a root cellar." He unlatched the door.

The space was dark and recessed about four feet into the earth.

"Be careful. This room is essentially one big hole in the ground."

"It's damp down here … really cool."

"It's a root cellar."

"I've never been down in one. In New England we keep perishable goods in the basement under the house."

I ascended some rickety steps into the darkened space. Shelving was anchored along its stone and brick foundation and stacked with pickled goods. There were bins filled with grains, like oats and corn, and others with potatoes, onions, or cabbage greens. But what caught my eye was a pair of chained manacles bolted to the brick footing a couple of feet above the ground. On the dirt floor was a pile of hay. I knelt to inspect it. A mouse scampered by me and writhed beneath the stone foundation.

Shocked by what I discovered I didn't even flinch when the rodent made his appearance.

"What are you looking for?"

"Someone has been kept here?"

"What do you mean?"

"Look, Tyler. They had someone chained here."

"I don't remember Wilcox keeping any slaves here. Tyrone strictly forbids him from locking away slaves anywhere near the house where Mother could see them. Keeping slaves chained in here is unlikely."

"Where do they take them, then?"

"Weeping posts by Cabin Row."

"Cabin Row. What is that?"

"A series of cabins where slaves live. There's about four or five such communities scattered on the property. The nearest one is about a quarter mile from here."

"You said weeping posts?"

"That's what the slaves call it. A pole in the ground where they chain slaves for discipline."

"You mean retribution."

"If you like. They are all over the island. Just the sight of them keeps slaves in line."

"You have witnessed this yourself?"

"No. But I overhear when Wilcox talks to Tyrone about the beatings he deals out."

I got down on one knee and ran my hand along the floor and over the furrow in the stack of hay. "Look, Tyler. You can see a body imprint here … and another there. At least two people were kept here chained to the wall."

Tyler stood silently. I could see that he was dismayed as he confronted the truth of the world around him, since he never gave it the critical appraisal it deserved in the past. It is easy for one to avoid the vicious gospel of slavery when one does not witness its cruel dogma and the perverse foundation on which it stands. Taking little interest in plantation affairs, Tyler kept mainly to himself, complacent to the travesties of plantation life. It was not that he was entirely unaware; instead, he never looked inward and exercised oversight. Rather, he gave little consideration to the dereliction of moral and sacred obligations he had for those in chains. I could feel pity for his ignorance to the evils of the agricultural Bastille before his very eyes. But I don't.

He stared down at the hay with the dim light. I could sense his mind probing the heinous world he lived in and asking himself burdensome questions. Discernment along with culpable remorse was beginning to percolate. For Tyler French, the time for reckoning and acquaintanceship was emerging.

I knocked over a rusty steel bowl along the ground. Beneath it was an eight-inch-long bird feather. I reached down for it.

"What is it, Emily?"

"Looks like a blue jay tail feather."

If I were at home conducting an investigation for the newspaper, I would call such a discovery evidence. For now, it was just stray plumage. I placed it in my pocket, stood up, and brushed off my dress. "Take me away from here, Tyler, will you?"

His hands around my waist, he steadied me up the ladder and out of the cellared room. As he closed the door, I noticed the padlock was crisp and untarnished; the nails that held the latching hasp still exhibited the burnished sheen where the hammer had struck them.

"That lock was placed there recently," I informed him.

He examined it. "Hmm. Yes, it has."

"Who locks a root cellar?"

"To keep slaves out?"

"Or to keep them in."

We walked around the house and to the front door. I looked up to the porch above. Victoria Dukes was standing, watching us. I put my head down and pretended not to see her. At that moment, I realized that she was the woman I saw when I first arrived at Dukes Plantation.

We returned to the kitchen where Clorina greeted us as if we had been gone all day. As always, she pestered us, insisting we have something to eat. Molly sat at a table drawing with her sketching pencils. Rummaging through her satchel, she looked for the right pencil.

"Hello, sweet girl," said Tyler, kissing her on the head.

"I thought you were going to take a nap," I said.

"Too hot. I couldn't sleep."

"What are you drawing?" asked Tyler, peering over her shoulder.

"Clorina."

"That's quite good. I like the way you've drawn her head scarf."

"Uh huh."

Clorina took a peek. "Lordy, Lord, child, I's not tat tubby, is I?"

"That's alright, Clorina," replied Molly. "That's what erasers are for."

"Child all da erasas n'da world can't help Clorina."

The slave servant broke into resounding laughter. The good-natured guffaw nearly shook the dishes off the kitchen shelves. One could not help but be infected by it and laugh along.

"Did you make a new friend at the regatta today, Molly?" I inquired.

"Nah. Those girls were rude."

"Oh?"

"They kept calling the men in the boats terrible names."

"Ya pay tem no mine, child," said Clorina. "We know who we is. Hateful names don break any bones."

"Don't fret, dear. You have plenty of friends at home."

"I was making friends with this girl. Some woman took me away. Said it wasn't allowed."

"Lordy, lord child, ya done placed ya hand in da cookie jar," bellowed Clorina, as she worked some pans along the stove.

"We love you, Molly," I said. "That's all that matters." I pulled up a chair and sat beside her. I took the bird feather from my pocket.

"Here, you can have this."

"Oh, neat," she chimed taking the feather from my hand. "Did Hannah give it to you?"

"You think that feather belong to Hannah?"

"Uh huh."

'Why would you think that?"

"It's just a bird feather," added Tyler "There are blue Jays all over this country."

"Oh no. This one belonged to Hannah, alright."

He took the feather from her and inspected it closely. "It's just a feather, Molly. How could you possibly say that it was Hannah's?"

"Yes, Molly. How?"

She reached up and took the silky blue feather from his hand. "You see these two tiny holes through the shaft at the base?"

"Yes."

"Well Hannah put them there. She showed me how to drill holes in them with a hatpin. You have to be careful not to crack the stem, though."

"Why would she drill holes in the base of a feather?" Tyler asked.

"To put a string through, silly. This way she could hang it from her ceremonial waist belt or from her ear. It's Hannah's feather, alright."

She handed the feather back to me. I inspected it. The revelation that Hannah was barbarically tied to a brick wall in a dark and dank root cellar grieved me. But the discovery of the bird feather was an additional step to finding what happened to the Wampanoag governess.

"Miss White, can I ask you something."

She lowered her eyes glumly and twiddled her pencil on the table. Her skittish demeanor spoke to hidden despair.

"About what, dear?"

"Hannah," she said, looking over to her brother and Clorina with dubious suspicion.

"It's alright, Molly. You can ask me anything you like. Tyler knows that we are looking for Hannah."

She glanced over at him. He smiled and nodded. "Do you think we will ever find her?"

"I pray about it and so should you."

"Emily," said Tyler. He signaled me to follow.

I handed Molly the blue feather. "Here, it's yours."

"Thanks."

"You stay with Clorina and finish your drawing. Tyler and I have some business to attend to."

With a frivolous smile, she held the feather behind one ear. "Clorina, do you have any string?" she asked, as Tyler and I left the kitchen.

"What is it?"

"I was thinking of speaking to Mother. Perhaps she can share something that will help."

"Help?"

"Yes, with Hannah's disappearance or anything else she may know."

"Do you think she will be receptive?"

"You never know with Mother. I can only try."

The next day I was nearly finished with breakfast as I was waiting for Victoria to come down and join us. Little did I realize that having family gatherings for morning meals was a rare occurrence at Dukes Mansion. Victoria almost never came down or would just have breakfast in her bedroom. Nonetheless, Clorina always set out a place at the head of the dining room table in any event.

Molly and I sat patiently and quietly sipping tea. Tyler slouched in his chair, a fretful hand caressing his brow. He drummed his fingers along the table.

"I don't expect Mother to be down for breakfast," Molly speculated. "I stopped expecting anything from her. I don't think she likes me."

Tyler glanced over at her, sympathy on his sleeve.

"Oh Molly, that's not true," I said. "She is ill. She needs help, not scorn."

"Every time I try and talk to her, she's potted."

"Now, now, Molly, it does not help calling names."

"Potted?" inquired Tyler.

"Father said those who have too much hard drink are as useless as a potted plant."

I shook my head and sighed. There was no explaining Victoria's erratic behavior and her dismissive nature of her daughter. Even I had to confess that the woman's capricious conduct and how she has treated Molly was nothing short of feckless. The longer we waited for Victoria the more exasperated Tyler became. Finally, it appeared that he could take no more.

"Excuse me." Wiping his mouth on his napkin he angrily tossed it down and left the room.

"Where are you going?"

He ignored my inquiry. I could hear footsteps in the distance as he climbed the grand marble stairwell at the front of the house. Molly sulked.

"Did I say something wrong?"

"No. I just think Tyler is worried about your mother."

"I'm worried, too."

"Tell you what. You can call me Emily from now on."

"Can I?"

"But not when Mister Dukes or Wilcox are around."

We could hear pounding on a door from upstairs. Teacup to my mouth, I flinched with every battering thud.

"I think he's angry," Molly pointed out.

"Mother. Open the door!" we could hear him yell. The demand echoed throughout the house.

"He's going to break down that door."

The slave servant moseyed over like nothing special was going on and topped Molly's cup with tea.

"My, my, child, ya sure fill tat d'hea tea cup wit lots of milk. Lill room faw tea now."

"Sugar, please. I like my tea with lots and lots of sugar," she declared.

"Here y'all go child." She pushed a bowl of sugar toward the youngster.

"Thea's plenty mawe where dat come from," she laughed.

Off in the distance, the pounding and shouting continued.

"Emily, why do you think Mother is so strange?"

"Well … some grown-ups lead uncertain and complicated lives. When you have a grand dream and things don't go your way it can be quite unsettling. Some try to escape and self-medicate with intoxicating drink. Instead of relief, they create an entirely new set of problems, so they drink more to alleviate those, and it becomes a ceaseless circle. Meanwhile, their dreams drift further and further away until all they have left is to drink some more. Know what I mean?"

"I suppose. But what can we do to help?"

"I'll tell you what we can do," blurted Tyler, as he walked back into the room. "We are going to leave here and take Mother to Dukes Island. It's the only way to get her away from the demon drink."

"Did she say she would go?" I asked.

"She has anesthetized herself to a degree that I cannot awaken her."

Wide eyed, Molly scribbled her drawing and listened.

"What shall we do?"

"I will carry her downstairs and sweep her up into the coach, but I will need your help."

"Are we going to the island?" asked Molly.

"Looks that way," I replied.

"Oh, Emily. Is Mother going to be alright?"

"We will make sure of it."

"Molly. Go to the kitchen and tell Clorina to send one of her boys to find Simon down by the river," instructed Tyler. "We need him right away."

"I will," she cried, rushing off.

"I need you to help me go through some of Mother's clothing and put some things together."

"Now?"

"No time to waste. I'll take you up to her room."

"Will we be gone long?"

"Don't know. But we must be prepared for an extended stay—at least until Mother is better. Find her cat. We need to take it. She loves her cat."

The drive between Dukes Plantation and the island was an epiphany that opened my eyes to the breadth of bondage in the south. We rode by one flooded rice field after another with innocence in a struggle of habitual serfdom—captives subject to the vassals of rice, restrained and imprisoned black humanity with the consecrated sanction of the state. What I had witnessed was an unconscionable industry from birth-of-day to the curtain-of-night—ensnared hostages trudging through swamped pastures amongst the mosquito, snakes, and searing sun. It was a feudalistic complex that enriched plantation barons well beyond any grail that the average alabaster-skinned free man from the north could envision.

We left the plantation before lunchtime and arrived at the river at Dukes Island crossing late that evening. Simon loaded the coach onto the rope-ferry barge with help from one of the plantation boatmen. Victoria slept most of the way. At times Molly expressed concern for her Mother's health, revealing her fear of whether Victoria was even breathing. I must admit that she was in deplorable condition.

The island terrain was a combination of swamp and highlands. Most of the swampland was along the river and bordered most of the estate like a moat. Unlike much of the marshes on the mainland, Dukes Island's swamp was a jungle forest of buttress-rooted cypress trees and wilted live oaks. They sprouted from a bed of aquatic soup, amidst duck weed vegetation and algae.

As we approached the northern end of the island, the countryside became more arid and horticultural, containing rolling meadows and rippling grassland. We were wending across a sandy loam road, a paradoxical landscape from the lower part of the island, that led to this agronomical utopia unfolding before us. I dipped my head out of the coach window. Until this very moment, nothing was more majestic or more imperial than a New England whaling vessel, unfurled and under full sail as it rounded the point at Fort Flats off Fairhaven. What unfolded before me rivaled it. Dukes Plantation house came into view and swiped my breath. It was a Delphic manor, a white Athenian Acropolis in the heart of Confederate America. If one cared to count, there were no less than twenty-eight Tuscan columns encircling the entire two-story architecture. Shuttered windows draped from floor to ceiling. From the second level of the building, hanging mid column, was a veranda that circumnavigated the entire structure. It was corralled by a highly embellished wrought-iron banister and painted white.

"Oh-my-Lord, will you look at that," I uttered, as the majestic residence came into view. Grandmamma would have swatted me with a rolling pin east of Tuesday for using the Creator's name in vain at that moment. But I believe that even He would forgive me any blasphemes asseveration. Even from a quarter mile away, the sight was cosmic in its majesty. What would it possibly look like once we drove up to the front door?

"There it is," announced Tyler, looking out the coach window.

"Wow-wee," gawked Molly. "That is the biggest house I have ever seen."

"Shall I drive up to da front door, Massa Ty?" asked Simon.

"Under the portico, Simon."

"Do you think she's alright?" I inquired, worried about Victoria. "She slept throughout the entire rocky ride."

"Why doesn't she wake up?" asked Molly, sounding distressed.

"Not to worry. It has happened many times. She is up all night with her absinthe and sleeps all the next day."

"Is that what she was drinking?" I asked.

"Tyrone gets it from New Orleans. It's all she drinks. Strangely enough, he won't touch the stuff."

"Absinthe? Why that brew is venomous. I heard stories of whalers who lost their minds drinking it … makes one visualize what's not there and fantasize about what is."

Tyler opened the coach door and climbed out. Simon helped as they carried Victoria into the house.

Once inside, it was evident the house was still under construction. Although it was completely done on the outside, the interior needed finishing touches—woodwork needed shellac and ceilings whitewash. Still, the inside was just as impressive as the exterior. So grandiose were its walls that any attempt at description would do it little justice. When I closed the door behind me, the resounding slam echoed endlessly throughout the stately foyer as the reverberating din spilled into empty rooms.

Simon carried Victoria up the grand staircase, her limp white face cradled on the black man's shoulder. Tyler led the way, carrying his mother's bags as I followed holding a worried Molly by the hand.

"If Massa Dukes find me carryin' 'is wife 'e would have me killed," said the exceedingly frightened slave.

"Well, Simon, Mister Dukes is not here at the moment and you're much stronger than I am. It's a long way up these stairs."

Tyler swung open the eight-foot-tall door. Simon gently deposited Victoria on the bed and quickly retreated.

"We'll let her sleep some," said Tyler.

Molly pulled up a pillow and took a place by her mother.

"I think I will stay with her. You know … so when she wakes up, she's not alone in a strange place."

"It's her bedroom, Molly," explained Tyler. "She'll know where she is."

"Just the same."

"Alright, just the same."

"Can I be goin', Massa Ty? If I'm found inside da house …"

"We'll go together," proposed Tyler, his hand on the nervous man's shoulder. "Back to the house at Charleston for Clorina. I'm getting hungry."

Chapter 24: Emily's Forbidden Wanderings

The lane that led away from the house was a shrouded lair of live oaks. The spiraling branches of the massive trees embroidered the sky, shading the road in a most pleasant fashion. Stalactites of weeping Spanish moss swayed to breezes spewed from the river almost a mile away. The droopy grass webbing melted from the branches above and helped block out the hot mid-day sun. They were venerable and imposing timbers. I recall the whale-men of Point Village spinning tales of ancient oak trees in the south that were so old that they grew bristly beards or long dangling robes suspended from sinuous limbs.

The placid air beneath this enchanting byway was laden with the sweet scent of moist earth or freshly cut grass, which had a whisper of stale lavender. The lane had a magical otherworldly essence where time itself appeared to stand still. It took only two or three minutes to traverse and, though the passage could not be more than six or seven hundred feet long, it seemed to go on forever.

It had been days since our arrival on the island and we have been shut in and confined to the house the entire time. Unexpectedly, Tyrone Dukes had returned to Dukes Island from military duty and made living at the house most uncomfortable—insisting that under no circumstance should Molly and I wander the island. Further complicating matters, Tyler has failed to ask his mother about Hannah, insisting that her condition was improving and he did not want to upset her.

I could not bear being cooped up any longer. Since our arrival, James Wilcox had taken up the obnoxious routine of sitting in the yard, playing nursemaid to his stogy, and staring up at our bedroom window—a barefaced act of intimidation. Early this morning, I tried persuading Simon to saddle a horse so I could take a ride and spend solitary time—just me and a chestnut yearling. He was reluctant to do so in fear of reprisal, until he witnessed me saddling the horse myself. After helping me, I assured him that I would take full responsibility should he be questioned. Nonetheless, he was not pleased. Though I have never owned and rarely rode a horse at home, I was quite familiar with them. Perry Davis, my next-door neighbor, had taught me all the tricks I needed to know to master a strange horse—straightforward, really. All one needs to do is get to know your gallant chaperon, make friends with the animal, and institute the order of preeminence—you are commander … the way a strong girl regards a husband, Amy would say. It's as easy as that. Although to be successful, it takes some resolve, forbearance, and a pocket full of sugar cubes.

Leaving the forested corridor of live oaks behind, I was immediately drenched by the ever-present Carolina sunlight. To each side of me were fertile fields of Sea Island cotton, the best variety in kind. The dense, shrubby landscape was dappled with downy bolls as far as the eye could see. It reminded me of a hay field near home where I once observed a short autumn squall and sudden burst of heavy wet snowfall. The weather event lasted no more than twenty minutes. It was quite beautiful. The pearly, clumped flakes attached themselves to the top of the dried grass in flocculent wads of frosty nuggets. But there was no wintry utopia in these sandy, loomed fields. Instead, I felt an ominous sensitivity—one of dread and despair, especially when I considered that the cotton dress I was wearing was the byproduct of slave labor and could have had its roots in this very soil.

The yearling appeared to know where we were going and, perhaps, happy to have a gallop. Although I enjoyed the breeze against my cheeks, I reduced the sprint to a leisurely canter as we approached a small pond and cluster of trees—just what the shade gods ordered.

After leading the yearling to water, I took my canteen and small knapsack filled with refreshments and made myself comfortable beneath the umbra of the tiny grove. In the carry-bag was a pear, a couple of corn biscuits, and a book, a gift granted me by Zoeth Winslow. The undisclosed volume was still in its brown paper wrapper. I tore it open and was surprise by the title. *North and South* by Elizabeth Gaskell. Opening the cover, I came across Zoeth's short note.

Dear Emily

I thought the title very appropriate to accompany you on your trip south, though it takes place in England and not America. As an admirer of Jane Austen, I am certain you will enjoy it.

Your loving friend,

Zoeth

I thumbed past the embossed green covers of the narrative and discovered that, like Austen and Dickens, the story is spun around the privileged and underprivileged—a theme in which I have always had an interest. Sitting by these slave fields, the book was more appropriate than Zoeth could have realized. After reading some, I fell asleep. The next thing I knew, I was awakened by fitful giggling. A group of slaves, some no older than ten or eleven, were marching by carrying stacks of willow baskets on their heads. Most were women. Two of the young girls appeared to take humor in my impromptu slumber or the prostrated way I came to slump against the tree. Ahead of the party rolled a wagon filled with still more of the woven hampers. I finally discovered that the reason for the laughter had to do with my horse, which wandered away and followed the bunch. I gathered my things and quickly gave chase. One of the girls took hold of the roving animal and led him back to me.

"Thank you." I took the straps. The juvenile displayed a bashful smile and scurried off.

"Wait. What's your name?" I said.

"Summa,' Miss." She turned and smiled.

"Summa'?"

"Yea, ya know, like spring n' summa."

"Oh, Summer. Why that's a beautiful name."

In a fearful shun, the slave girl continued to follow the others. I did the same.

"Can I walk with you?"

"What for?" she replied, somewhat wary.

"I just feel like company."

"With black folk?"

"Is that a problem?"

"No, Miss. I just a slave."

"To me you are just a little girl."

She looked over with doubtful gaze.

"Ya a stranger here."

"Yes, I am."

One of the two men in the group came over and took Summer by the arm, pushing her ahead.

"Sorry, Miss. She won't botha' ya no mo'a."

"She wasn't bothering me. I was bothering her."

"Miss?"

"I said she was not bothering me."

"Ya a stranga' here."

"It appears to be the general consensus."

I noticed that the black man had a rattan whip hanging from his waist.

"Ken ay help ya wit sometin, Miss?"

"My name is Emily," I said, offering him my hand. "What is yours?"

He looked down at my limb as if I was handing him a smoldering fireplace poker. I knew the routine. But it was worth a try.

"Not propa,' Miss. A Negro must never touch a white woman."

I took a pear from my bag and offered it to him.

"You can tell me your name, can you not?"

He nodded the fruit away. "Cyrus, Miss."

"Ah, Cyrus the Great. One anointed by God. Liberator of the Jews."

With a shy shuffle and a nod of the head, he endorsed my declaration with a smile. "We must go ta work now, Miss."

"Go on, then. Just pretend I'm not here."

He trotted off and caught up with the others. Once they all reached the end of the field, one of the black men unloaded the baskets from the back of the wagon and stacked them by the side of the road. Without delay, the group of slaves commenced picking cotton. Cyrus stood at the road instructing and cheering the laborers. I soon became mindful that he was a slave driver. His job was to audit labor and keep his comrades in line and working.

I had been told of such job assignments, of good drivers and bad ones. Some were eager to please their masters and could be just as cruel—still others conducted themselves as covert adjudicators, trying their best to lessen punishment appointed their fellow slaves, while covering up perceived infractions or laziness. Some drivers worked the fields alongside slaves, while a few privileged others just stood by and supervised. Most, if not all, were black and appropriated from the slave roster. In return, they were rewarded with extra food rations or time off. To the master, no driver was any better than a common slave. At any time, a driver could be replaced by the slave he abused the day before.

Cyrus appeared to be one of the equitable drivers Tyler spoke about. Walking up and down the chamfered aisles, he helped collect filled baskets and supplied the slaves with water. The remainder of the time he spent standing at the foot of the aisles singing gospel tunes and looking out over the field.

Along one of the cotton aisles, Summer and another young girl were leaning over, picking away. I walked past Cyrus to the stack of baskets piled by the wagon. With his back to me, the tall slender driver turned his head slightly, keeping a peripheral eye in my direction. He was bewildered when I picked up one of the baskets and paraded into the cotton field. He yelled out, asking where I was going. I ignored him.

Watching me closely, the two girls continued their labor. I stood with the circular basket resting on my hip studying their method of picking. Moving over one aisle I placed the straw hamper down and tore a cotton boll from its stem. The girls giggled. The chuckle was familiar. For every handful I picked they accomplished four. The assembly of slaves stopped and watched me with puzzled amazement. Cyrus hollered and ordered them back to work. Summer came over and started to strip the bush I was working on.

"Like this, here," she said. "Ya grab da cotton, twist, an' pull."

I tried her method.

"No. Ya must leave da burr behind. Only pick da cotton. Tat's da way Massa teach us."

"Like this?" I tore the cotton portion of the plant away from the calyx below the bulb but left some of the fleecy fibers behind.

"Ya, tat's it. Ya done got most av it."

"What are these?" I inquired, extracting small nuggets from the base of the woolly cotton.

"Those there are da seeds. Don't bother with dem. They will be done removed at da gin house."

I tossed the pods to the ground and dropped the supple cotton into my basket. Summer returned to her aisle and commenced picking. Pilous cotton protruded from between virgin fingers as she reached and pulled, reached and pulled.

"What is your friend's name, Summer?" I asked.

"She's not ma friend. She is ma sista.""

"The younger girl looked away, extinguishing a winsome giggle.

"Hello, Sister," I said.

"She shy," declared Summer.

"How long have you been picking cotton?

"Since I waz five."

"How old are you now?"

"Don't rightfully know … eleven … maybe twelve."

"And you do this work every day?"

"Pick cotton ever'day."

Frenzied and without warning, Cyrus marched into the field and ordered his fellow slaves to work faster. Yelling into one girl's face, he poked another with the butt of his whip. Waving the barbed flogger over his head, he intimidated anyone who dared stand idle. Summer and her sister ignored me and continued working as I watched with exasperated incredulity. It was not long before I discovered the reason for Cyrus abrupt aggression—James Wilcox. He had galloped up on his horse with his bullwhip in hand and brutality in his eye. Cyrus ran over to him.

"What's that woman doing here?" he demanded.

"Don't know, Massa Wilcox."

"What do you mean you don't know?"

I picked up my basket and ambled over. "Mister Wilcox. What a pleasure. Come to give us a hand?" I put down my basket and wiped my brow with the back of my arm. "I expect if you help, we can have this sixty-acre field scrubbed before midnight."

"Who told you to leave the house?"

"It was not who but what told me. And, according to you, it was the color of my skin."

"You have been given stringent orders not to leave the property."

"Oh? Is this plot not a portion of the same?"

"Don't be curt with me, young lady."

"I live in a country where I am free to come and go, Mister Wilcox … or has the Confederate constitution restricted the inalienable rights given me by my Creator?"

He struggled to control his horse. It squirmed and waggled, dancing in place—blanched, foamy sweat flowed freely down the animal's shoulders as it languished in the heat. The slaves continued toiling. They ignored the exchange between us. The cotton field setting was an ocular spectacle of colorful turbaned heads, bobbing up and down, as stooped pickers fixated on their work.

"I expect you back at the house within the hour."

"Is that an order, Mister Wilcox?"

Not acquainted with insubordination and unable to sanction my speech, he just glared at me. Having issued his gratuitous edict, he saved face by galloping away.

When the obstinate overseer was out of sight, Summer and her sister ran up to me.

"My, my, he was angry. Ay nev'a done saw anyone talk back ta Massa Wilcox like y'all did."

"I expect no one ever does."

"Not since tat Indin' woman."

My ears instantly perked.

"What did you say?"

"Massa Wilcox done tried ta make her pick cotton, but she just spit on da groun' at his feet."

"What woman, Summer, what woman?"

"Da Indin' woman."

"Do you mean Indian woman?"

"Yeahs'aw. She don't care who she talk ta."

I clutched the girl by the arms. She stiffened. Angst apprehension expressed on her face.

"Where is this Indian woman, Summer?"

"I … I don't know."

"Think, Summer, think!"

"The Swamp House," said a gruff voice. Cyrus stood behind me, arms crossed.

"You know about the Indian woman?"

"Yeah, Miss, I do."

"Where did they take her?"

"Ay can't say. She done worked da fields foe weeks. All sudden she just done stop workin'. Massa Wilcox was right angry with her. He done whip her. She spat at him ayn' he done took her away. Dat all I know."

"You said Swamp House?"

"Yeah, da Swamp House. It is where y'all go when Massa Wilcox wants ta punish ya."

"Where is this place, Cyrus?"

"Da otha' side of da island where da sun rises. It's where Massa Wilcox lives."

"You mean the east side of the island."

"When they done punish ya, they take ya ta da Swamp House."

"Why do they call it the Swamp House?"

"It was built close ta da swamp. Most of da time da floor is flooded. Ya is lucky if da alligators don't get ya."

Cyrus took Summer and her sister by the hand. "We haf'ta go back ta work, Miss."

"Wait." I took my sun hat and handed it to Summer.

"This will help you with the sun. I'm afraid I only have one. You will have to share it with you sister."

A wide grin grew on her face exposing picket white teeth. The tiny tusks gleamed in the puncturing sunlight. Buffed onyx cheeks radiated like two plump eggplants.

"Tank-ya, Miss."

She tore off her turban and placed the hat on her head. It was a little large and came to rest on the bridge of her nose. Sister laughed.

"Wear it over your head wrap, Summer. It will fit better."

"Tank ya, Miss," said Cyrus. "It is kind of ya."

The driver led the two girls back into the cotton field. I climbed up onto my horse, paused, and watched. The assembly of slaves swam in a field of cotton flooded by unrelenting sunlight. And I was helpless to do anything to help them. Cyrus launched his baritone voice over the field and delivered a spiritual chant. The congregation of captives repeated the chorus as he thrummed the melody. Turning the horse around, I wistfully rode back in the direction from which I came.

I tied the horse to the ring hanging from a cast iron hitching post by the back of the house. Victoria Dukes lounged on a thatched rocker on the porch, petting the cat in her lap. To my surprise, she was smoking a long meerschaum ladies' pipe, a male habit made popular in Europe amongst members of the fairer sex. Molly sat at her mother's feet, a bowl of fruit on her lap.

"Look, Emily, strawberries. I picked them myself." She held the bowl up. "Want some?"

I took one of the pulpy berries and sat in one of the rockers along the veranda.

"I see you have been out riding," said Victoria.

"I needed to get away."

"And what do you think of our little Island world?"

"Enlightening."

"Where did you go?" asked Molly.

"Oh, here and there." I reached over and took another strawberry from the bowl. The cat jumped down from Victoria's lap and meandered over. It lay sprawled at my feet. "There are cotton fields all over this island." I leaned over and petted the cat.

"I'm not surprised," said Victoria, puffing her pipe "A couple of years ago there was nothing here—just trees and alligators. A little servitude, a measure of civility, and southern progress has arrived to Dukes Island."

"I sense some misgivings," I said, scratching the tabby's belly.

"Not at all. I love it here. It's quiet and peaceful. Callers don't just show up at your door. I'm quite happy here. I never leave the house. Have no idea what the rest of the island looks like. Don't need to."

"Don't need to or don't want to?"

"Goes against my nature."

"What does?"

"This plantation business."

"You mean slavery."

"Who said anything about slavery?"

"You said it went against your nature … the plantation business. What did you mean?"

I waited, but she never acknowledged my question. It became an awkward moment. Victoria was a sad woman of few words and I expect an unhappy wife. Why else would she spend most of the day locked away in her bedroom? As in Charleston, she took her meals in her self-imposed sanctuary and rarely came out. When she did, she would sit in a rocker on the veranda outside her room just above the front door and stare down the carriage-drive, as if waiting for her liberator to come and set her free. In all the time I've been on the island, this was as close as I had gotten to a sober Victoria. I was surprised she said as much as she did. Unable to engage her in any further conversation, I thought it unwise to ask her about Hannah. Likewise, Tyler felt that we had to wait for the right time to engage his mother and explore what she knew without hampering her recovery.

We sat quietly. Molly rummaged through the bowl seeking the perfect strawberry. The cat pensively stared up at me and purred. Stymied by what to do next, I was abashed by the silence. I got to my feet and wandered along the veranda. Behind Victoria and along the wall was a stockpile of casks and small crates. A pungent, sweet odor spewed from one of the barrels.

"What's in those small barrels?" I asked.

"Some paint spirits or something. The carpenters are using it on the wood fittings and doors."

"I think I'd like some milk with these strawberries," said Molly.

"I'll get you some," I said.

I entered the kitchen and called for Clorina but there was no reply. I took a glass from the shelf and removed a pitcher of milk from the icebox. It felt hardly chilled. Inside the chest there was almost no ice—in the drip pan beneath, a bath of tepid water. I brought the vessel of milk to my nose and sniffed. Suddenly I heard a man's voice approaching. It was Tyrone. Placing the milk down, I panicked and ran into the pantry and drew the curtain.

"I knew that woman would be trouble the moment I set eyes on her," said Tyrone.

"I ordered her to return," explained Wilcox.

"What was she doing out there, in any event?"

"Picking cotton."

"Picking what?"

"Yeah, out in the west field like a ferret with a basket picking cotton with the rest of the Negroes."

"I specifically instructed that girl not to leave the house."

"I tell you, that was the woman in the wagon we were chasing back in New England."

"Quiet, you fool. Someone may hear you."

Tyrone peered out the window just by the pantry door. I hid behind shelving.

"What is it?"

"Just my wife and the child."

"What are we going to do about this Jezebel? Who's to say what the Negroes may have revealed to her."

"It's not the Negroes that I'm worried about, it's my wife. Lately she's developed a benevolence and concern for the welfare of the slave population."

"She's had nothing to drink in almost two weeks. She's like a new woman."

"That's trouble. She knows about the Indian woman. And she's not just any Indian. Victoria has had a history with her."

"How did she find out?"

"I told her."

"Why would you do that?"

"I thought she would be happy about enslaving her."

I moved closer to the doorway and spied past a crack in the curtain. Wilcox poured himself a glass of milk.

"Argh! This milk has turned," he said, wiping his mouth on his sleeve.

"We need her on the riverboat. We'll sell her with those other three slaves as soon as possible."

"What? Your wife?"

"No, you idiot, the Indian slave."

"What about the Yankee girl?"

"Depends on what she knows or uncovers."

"There are plenty of alligators in Mosquito Lagoon. If she insists on wandering the island, she may just have an unfortunate accident."

"Something will need to be done about her soon—but one thing at a time. Until then, I need to keep Victoria quiet."

"And how do you propose to do that."

Tyrone removed a bottle from his pocket. "Straight from the busy docks off Canal Street in the French Quarter of New Orleans."

"What is it?" Wilcox examined it up to the light.

"Victoria's deliverance from reality … emerald goddess in a bottle. The French call it *La fee' Verte*—the green fairy."

Wilcox uncorked the container and brought it to his nose. "Oh, that's disgusting. Smells like licorice and turpentine. What's the proper name for it?"

"Absinthe."

"And she drinks this tonic?"

"Everyone has their poison, my good man. That sour mash hooch you ingest smells no better."

"Why, it's the best Kentucky bourbon you can buy."

With disparaging retroflexion, Tyrone smirked and shook his head.

"That's the trouble with you, Wilcox. You have an untutored palate. You see, you have no insight or appreciation for Ruban blue liquors, such as a fine French one or Provencal brandy."

"So … you silence her with that absinthe. Do you think she has told anyone about the Indian woman?"

"I doubt it. Too much guilt. She hated that Indian. Talked about her until my brain would go numb. And when I delivered the Indian to her on a silver platter, she altogether has a change of mind. Hates me for it … hates me for her own witless guilt." He moved to the window and watched his wife smoke and rock. "For now, I need to do something about it before that Emily White woman does and complicates things."

"So, what next?"

"I'll stop in Beaufort today and make arrangements with the riverboat to stop here on the island and transport the Indian to Savannah. Get her off my hands. From there, I'll place her on a ship to New Orleans. Slave auctions there are strong and no one asks questions."

"Sounds like a plan."

"Well, I'll be on my way. If I hurry, I can make Beaufort before supper."

Tyrone Dukes left while Wilcox wandered the kitchen looking for something to eat. I pulled the curtain back ever so slightly and watched. Rummaging through the icebox, he pulled out a tray of roast meat and sniffed. Breaking a loaf of bread in half, he hollowed the center and stuffed in the meat with grubby hands. Suddenly, someone walked in. I pulled the curtain back and hid.

"Coffee box is empty, cousin. Do we have any more?"

"In the pantry," said the other man. "I'll get you some."

I cowered in the corner as the curtain slid open. It was Tyler.

"Emily?"

I placed a finger to my lips—puckered trepidation wrinkling my face.

"What are you doing in here?" he whispered.

"*Shh*!"

"Did you say something?" asked Wilcox.

Tyler clutched a canvas bag of coffee from the shelf and quickly drew the curtain. "I said, I found a fresh sack."

Wilcox drew the polished Bowie from his boot to cut the sealed coffee bag open. "I'm out of coffee."

"Take the bag with you. We have another."

"Yes. Think I'll do that," he said, slipping the menacing blade back in the boot. He tucked the coffee under his arm. "Thanks," he mumbled, a mouth full as he started for the door.

I watched out the pantry window. Wilcox stepped off the veranda, ignoring Victoria, and headed in the direction of the barn. I winced as the pantry curtain slid open.

"Are you alright?"

"Why, yes."

"Why are you hiding in here?"

"Oh, I don't know. Perhaps because James Wilcox wants to feed me to the alligators down by the swamp."

"Alligators?"

"I was getting myself a glass of milk when I heard him approaching. I did not want to have an encounter with the man, so I hid."

"Can't blame you."

"I find him notorious."

"To say the least … raised by wolves."

"Wolves?"

"His father was a violent drunk and his mother … well, I shouldn't speak ill of the lady."

Still feeling jittery by the close encounter, I nervously straightened my hair and combed the loose strands with my fingers.

Tyler took a cluster of hair from my shoulder and brushed it back. "You're beautiful, you know that?"

Feeling flustered, I smiled.

"Your eyes," he said. "I never noticed … I would have sworn they were brown." He placed the tips of his finger on my cheek and ran them across my face.

"They are brown." I said, my voice quaking.

"They look hazel."

"It's the light. Eyes change color depending on the time of day."

"Do they?"

"I assure you. My eyes are brown."

"Let's have a better look." Nestling my chin, he lifted my face into the light. "No, no, they are hazel, alright."

"I expect I know the color of my eyes, Tyler," I argued, backing away.

He took a step closer, holding me at bay. The small room gave me little conciliatory escape. I was trapped—my back against the wall. I could see Molly playing with the cat out the pantry window. Victoria sat rocking, her face shrouded in smoke from her pipe. Quite sure of himself, he moved even closer, his face inches from mine. I rested my hands on his chest and tried pushing him away.

"Now that we have concluded that my eyes are brown, can you let me by, please?"

"I am certain. They are hazel," he concluded, kissing me on the corner of my mouth.

I avoided eye contact as I rushed to leave. He quickly dodged my escape and I crashed directly into his arms. His strong limbs wrapped around me, roving fingers cradled my ribs; his warm breath fanned my nose and cheek. He studied my face and gazed into my eyes as if searching for veiled treasure.

"I think I'm falling in love with you."

"Don't be silly." I tried pulling away.

"No, really. I feel faint whenever I lay eyes on you … as I do now."

"It's distorted incendiary euphoria caused by deficient oxygenation in this small space. Now let me by."

He laughed. "You say the darnedest things."

"Tyler … We need to go."

"You don't understand. I feel it here," he said, placing his fist over his heart.

"Sounds like angina-pectoris. You should see a doctor."

"See. That's what I love about you. You are so witty."

Great, I thought to myself. *I am loved for the gray matter between my ears. What a girl always wanted to hear*. Taking into account the awkward circumstance at hand, it was something to work with. He was persistent, but I had a plan. If I surrendered, I could gain a momentary reprieve and catch him off guard. Thus, I brandished all my guns. With spiritedness, I squirreled away my true intention and instead assured him with indirect deportment that I was interested.

Wetting my lips, I pushed myself toward him and kissed him passionately. We stumbled while our bodies crashed against the shelving along the wall. Plates and cups crashed to the floor. Peeling back his arms, I laced my fingers with his and squeezed. With duplicitous passion, I kissed him again and again while contriving a maneuver for my escape. I kissed him once—twice. He closed his eyes and waited for another. With nettled conviction, I stomped the heel of my boot down onto his foot as hard as I could. He cried out. Bulging eyes played homage to a gaping mouth. As he groaned in agony, I delighted in an effortless retreat.

"Wait, Emily." He gave chase.

I stopped short and wagged my finger in his face. "Tyler French. We spoke about this behavior. Don't do it again. It's inimical to our friendship."

"I just wanted …"

"I know what you wanted."

"And just what did I want?"

"Audacious conduct only wedlock should entertain."

"Why Emily … are you proposing?"

I stepped on his foot once more for good measure.

Marching through the kitchen, I walked outside. I held the back of my hand to my mouth trying to bridle any sign of whimsy. After all, I was not really angry. Rather, I was somewhat delighted in a peculiar way, considering the boredom of the past few days. And what girl does not relish being told she is beautiful by a handsome boy. My conduct would make for an amusing yarn. My best friend Amy would be proud and happy to hear it.

"What took you so long?"

"Sorry, Molly, I was detained." I plopped myself in the rocker.

"Where's my milk?"

"It's spoiled."

"Ice is like gold way out here," sounded Victoria. "Tyrone will need to appoint a special shipment from Charleston," said Victoria.

Tyler stood by the kitchen entrance, arms crossed, staring over to me with waggish repose. I ignored him.

"I can get you some fresh milk from the barn if you like, Molly," he said.

"You don't have to. Strawberries are almost all gone. Want one, Tyler?" She held a berry up and laughed. "Look, a red, Egyptian pyramid."

He plucked the fruit from her hand.

"Eat too many of those berries, young lady, and you'll get a bellyache," said Victoria.

Tyler walked to the edge of the veranda. The orange tabby followed and rubbed up against his pant leg. I sat quietly as he studied me with ambivalence—and rightfully so. His attention was soon drawn away to Victoria.

"Mother," he snapped. "I told you not to smoke your pipe by these barrels. You may cause an explosion."

"You are like an old maid, Tyler. I should have had a daughter instead of a son."

"You did have a daughter," said Molly.

"So, I did … so I did."

I got up from the chair to investigate.

"What's in those barrels?"

"Pure form of alcohol," he said.

"What in the world for?"

"The carpenters mix it with shellac chips to make a lacquer for sealing doors and woodwork."

"A varnish?"

"Something like it. That solvent is very flammable."

Victoria tapped the pipe against the arm of the chair and emptied it of charred tobacco. "I'm going up to my room," she announced, getting up and walking away.

The cat slithered behind her.

"Can I come?" asked Molly.

"Come along, then," she said, exhibiting little enthusiasm.

I was disheartened by the way Victoria treated her daughter. She displayed little interest in the child, substituting love with tolerance. Though the relation between mother and daughter was not a propitious one, Molly appeared unconcerned and cheerful to be with her.

Tyler sat in her chair. "Sometimes I think that Mother has no concept of affection."

"She's a troubled soul, Tyler.

"I still love her, you know."

"I know."

We sat quietly, rocking. The day was cooling, and a breeze snaked between the stately home's fluted columns. In the distance, the treetops bowed and shuddered to a sailor's blow.

"Must be a lively swell out in the Atlantic," I said.

"Why would you say that?"

"The top of those trees in the distance … they are really rustled."

"Oh." He removed his boot and rubbed his toe.

"How's your foot?"

He glanced over, smiled and shook his head. "It's not my foot that ails me, it's my ego."

"Grandmamma often said that the ego flaunts with failure, while grace nourishes success."

"I'm not very graceful, am I?"

"Perhaps with the right girl. Once you find her you can combine ego and grace and achieve happiness."

"Is that what your Grandmamma said."

"It's what I said."

He gingerly placed his boot back on his foot and resumed rocking.

My earlier encounter with Tyrone Dukes and James Wilcox had not escaped me. I was uncertain about how I should tell Tyler about what I heard. Clorina came strolling across the yard carrying a bunch of flowers that she had picked from the garden. She hummed a blissful tune as she walked by and into the kitchen. A gusty whirlwind suddenly drifted along the yard, carrying random leaves and a cloud of parched soil. The rotating funnel came out of nowhere and dissipated as quick as it arose. There was a saline scent to the air as a transient ocean breeze swept inland. Above our heads, a circling flock of gulls hovered and cawed, sounding a cautionary chorus.

"Bonaparte seagulls," he said. "They are all over the island. I have never seen them over the house."

"There must be a storm brewing offshore."

He looked over and smirked. "You're a wizard now, are you?"

"Seagulls have a pressure indicator in their heads that acts like a barometer. Tells them there's a storm coming and to seek shelter inland."

"Don't tell me. Your Grandmamma taught you that."

"As a matter of fact, she did. So has every fisherman."

"All I can say is that your grandmother must have been quite the woman."

"Charlotte White was a woman for all seasons. She never went to school, but she was the smartest person I have ever known … oh, not in a traditional sense. What she lacked in formal education she more than made up with instinct and wisdom."

"You must miss her."

"Terribly."

I fought back a tear, turning my face. He reached over and patted my hand. I looked up at the dawdling sea birds soaring below a darkening sky. They prompted memories of Charlotte's love and hate relationship with the feathered scroungers. Though she complained about their wailing screeches, they would follow her home on her evening walks, knowing full-well that they would be given a morsel of bread to nosh on.

"Hannah is here," I burped.

"Here?

"On the island."

"Is this what you think?"

"This is what I know."

"You have been talking to Mother, haven't you? She told you something."

"No. I promised you I wouldn't. At least not until you thought she was ready."

"You know something?"

"When I was hiding away in the pantry earlier James Wilcox and Tyrone were talking."

"Father was here?"

"Yes. I heard him say to Wilcox he was leaving for Beaufort."

"You must have gotten an earful from those two."

"Yes … and about Hannah."

"Go on."

"And Victoria."

He rose to his feet and reached for the kitchen door. Clorina's humming voice faded as he shut it.

"What did you hear?"

"It's what I saw that concerned me."

"And?"

"Tyrone took a bottle of liquor from his pocket and showed it off to Wilcox."

"So. They always drink together."

"It was absinthe."

He flung himself back in the rocker. Fingers laced together and elbows resting on his knees, he gazed down at his feet and grappled with what he had just heard. I looked across the yard toward the barn. Wilcox mounted his horse and galloped away.

"Absinthe. Are you certain?"

"Tyrone called it emerald goddess. He was afraid of what your mother may tell us about Hannah. My impression is that he is planning to start Victoria drinking again, to keep her anesthetized ... at least until they take Hannah off the island."

"Tyrone is responsible for Mother's drinking. Ever since his affair with the slave girl Ruth, she started expressing qualms about the occupational practices of plantation life."

"You mean slavery, don't you?"

"Well, yes."

"Tyler. Where is the Swamp House?"

"The what?"

"The Swamp House. One of the hands out in the field said it's where they take slaves when punishment is handed out."

"When were you out in the field?"

"Today. I took a horse and went for a ride."

"Tyrone is not going to like that."

"So I've been told."

"Well, Wilcox administers discipline. If there is such a place called a Swamp House it would be at Mosquito Point where he has his place. A dry patch of ground of perhaps twenty acres in the middle of the swamp."

"How do we get to it?"

"There's a small bridge over a narrow stretch of marsh. Otherwise, you have to go across the swamp into open water overlooking the mainland."

"And Wilcox has his home there?"

"Yes. It is a private peninsula where ... wait. The Swamp House? I know where that is."

"Where?"

"Near the Wilcox place ... by the edge of the wetlands ... an abandoned barn. It was built close to the marsh. When it rains hard, the swamp floods the inside of the place."

"Have you ever been there?"

"No. I heard Tyrone and Wilcox talk about it. They had plans of moving it to higher ground. Not sure if they ever did."

"Can we go out there?"

"It would be easy enough to find. I have never been out to Mosquito Point."

"Let's go, then," I said, jumping to my feet.

"What, now?"

"Yes now!"

"I'll go find Simon. I'll have him take us with the buckboard."

I sat back down, rocked, and looked out onto the yard past the rose gardens. I was feeling somewhat apprehensive—as if I was being watched. I glanced over my shoulder toward the kitchen door. I was quilting newfound fears and horrors in the rarely visited dungeons of my mind. We all have such a dreadful place where we contemplate the foreboding, even death.

As terrible as the thought could be, I framed theoretical contingencies to how I could be seized in broad daylight and, like Hannah, sold abroad to the highest bidder. Wilcox could snatch me with his Bowie and hide me away in the dank hold of a marauding ship, one that would take me to Morocco or the Barbary Coast, to reluctantly serve as a slave to a shadow-skinned master. Or, perhaps, have me transported to Istanbul or the far reaches of the eastern Turkish wilderness to live a venereal existence as a concubine harem girl, obliging an incessant master and his perverse debaucheries. More realistically, I could simply be taken down the road, not far from the house, and bound to a tree in the swamp off Mosquito Point, as fodder for primordial alligators—where my cries could be stifled by the seething mire and brackish vegetation, with ultimately no confirmation that I ever existed. Grandmamma had warned me that reading Edgar Allen Poe would harvest intimidating thoughts and allow the mind to roam the depths of imagination, enhancing dreary insight into the absurd and the implausible. Did I listen?

Suddenly, I heard footsteps. I stopped rocking and perked my ears. They were getting closer—louder. They came up behind me. I jumped from my chair.

"My, my, Miss White. Did I frighten ya?"

"Oh, Clorina. It's you." I clutched my chest and sucked some air.

"Is no one else, child," she said, with a titter.

In her hands was a tray containing two glasses and a tall pitcher of lemonade. She placed the refreshment on the small wicker table between rockers.

"It's a hot one an' just though you an' Massa Ty would like some lemonade."

"That is very sweet of you, Clorina." I sat back down.

"Sweet? Not me child," she laughed. "Da only sweetness around he'ya is da blessing of da Lord, I tell ya." Handing me a glass, she poured some juice. "Not awful cold but sure is wet." She wiped her hands on her apron. "Is dey'a any'thin else I can do faw ya, Miss White?"

"Yes, Clorina. I wish you would call me Emily … just plain Emily. It's my Christian given name, you know."

"Lordy, Lord, Miss White. Can't do tat. It's da white man's law. Just da way it is, child."

She stood quietly looking down at me and waiting for me to issue a request or perhaps administer a demand. She was fixed—anchored in a Caucasian universe where the stars burnt brightly but lacked humanity and righteousness. No one on this island radiated brighter than this lowly servant woman, with innocence and kindness that flickered with radiance brighter than any of her white overlords. With her billowy, ebon cheeks and trustworthy smile, she begged to be of service.

"Sit down, Clorina. Have some lemonade with me."

"Too much ta do, Miss White. Someone done broke some dishes in da pantry. I need go clean it up."

I winced. "Need some help?"

"Help is fo'a da poorly ailing an' da old. I's neither," she declared walking off laughing. "Ya just holler fo'wa Clorina if ya need any'tin."

I took from my shoulder purse, a notebook that I often carried and transcribed the events of the day. I had plenty of free time while here in the south and the memo-book was beginning to read more like a schoolgirl's dairy than a newspaperwoman's journal. Nonetheless, I'm certain, once home, I will have one or two worthy stories to transcribe.

I wrote in very small print. The narrative continued around the margins just inside the notebook's fore-edge. It was the only writing pad I brought with me and I was running out of space. I found writing paper difficult to acquire here in the south. This curtailed any communication or written reports I could post to my employer, or letters to Seabury or Amy.

I took a small pencil-sharpening knife from my bag and whittled. One had to be careful not to break the lead once the tip was honed to a fine tapered point. To scribble in tiny print, the writing instrument had to be slender and sharp. However, I must admit at not being very good with the cutting blade.

I studied Tyler Dukes as he sauntered over from the stables, writing down what I observed—tall, alluring, beguiling, and shamefully desirable. You must understand what I witnessed and what I was thirsty for was completely antithetical. But striving to be a newspaperwoman, my description needed to be accurate and detailed, not simply superficial—

though, with the description I penned of Tyler, you may not be persuaded that I was very successful. As he got closer, I blackened out what I had just written, breaking the acicular tip of an already shortened pencil.

"What are you writing?" he asked, arms crossed and resting a shoulder against one of the porch columns.

"A diary. … the day's events, observations, desires." I took out my pencil-sharpening knife and cut away.

"Desires? You don't say … am I in there?

"Could be."

"Can it be that you are opening doors for me?" His tone was pregnant with salacious curiosity. Leaning over, he peeked at what I had written.

I closed the notebook in his face and placed it in my pocket. "If I am opening a door it's to let you out, not in." I held up the newly carved pencil and examined it.

He grimaced. "Simon will be over shortly." He went back to propping up the column. "He's harnessing the buckboard."

After indulging in some lively exchange over the obvious distinction between overt infatuation and unbridled fidelity, we were on our way.

The buckboard was a three-bencher. Tyler and I sat on the center plank while Simon drove the horses up front. The buckboard was used to transport slaves to distant work sites and ship cotton from the fields. The floor of the wagon was littered with the fleecy white fibers, soil, and dried vegetation. Tyler complained, as wispy mites of cotton streamed in our faces.

"I have never swept out da wagon before, Massa Ty. It is done used for work and slaves, not folk."

The fact that Simon made a distinction between slaves and folk both saddened and perturbed me.

"Oh, leave him alone, Tyler. We should have taken the buggy. Why are you so concerned about such a trivial matter as a dirty carriage?"

"I guess I'm just a little on edge. Picking on a slave is easy around here."

"Well, you should have swept the buckboard out yourself."

"That's not important. I'm just worried about things."

"I know."

Though I did know, his quibbling continued. The wind increased as we doddered along the dusty road. A cloud of baked earth swirled behind us vacuumed by the wagon's progress. Dirt was everywhere. This inspired Tyler to forge even more grievances.

We continued down a gradual slope in the landscape and turned toward a grassy lane. This led to the very eastern tip of the island. Ahead, water from the swamp had migrated across our path and flooded the roadway. Simon brought the wagon to a halt. He looked back at Tyler, wide-eyed and uncertain.

"What is it, Simon?"

"The swamp, Massa Ty."

"Well, drive across it. It's not very deep."

I sensed Simon's concern had more to do with our proximity to the Wilcox place than the depth of the water. What he feared, I could sense. The vistas here were unlike any other part of the island. Bald cypress trees were everywhere with an occasional live oak crowded between. The road ahead negotiated what could only be described as a cypress jungle where sunlight begged but failed. The trees grew out of a lagoon of lichen and moss. By the fringes of the elevated roadway were marshy shallows—soil-less turf supporting broad-leaf cattails and framed by purple loosestrife. All sorts of amphibious creatures sprung along the side of the road. Green frogs, snapping turtles, droning dragonflies—wildlife was everywhere. It was a child-explorer's wonderland—strange, alluring, and beautiful.

I was enchanted by the anomalous scenery and random scents of fermented vegetation. One could almost taste the atmosphere of the place. Even sounds made by birds were mystical. The tweets and chirps of the cotton fields were replaced by shrieks and hoots, as demonic shrills echoed from the trees. At any moment, I envisioned feathered monkeys with wings swooping down from above, or that the motionless, ancient cypresses, with their dredged roots proliferating from the aquatic soil, would walk amongst us.

"It is quite beautiful out here," I said. "Unlike any place I've ever been to. So tranquil and alive."

"It's different country, that's for sure."

"I can sense the diurnal activity of swamp dwellers all around us ... like we're being watched."

"Amazing that I never knew such a place existed."

"I thought everyone on the island knew about the swamps."

"Yes, of course. I knew there were swamps that bordered the island. But unless you witnessed what is really here, you cannot envision the true eeriness of the place."

"I agree. There's a ghoulish element to these surroundings. No doubt. But it is also peaceful."

"Peaceful as a burial ground."

"Clearin' up ahead," said Simon, pleased that the sun was making its appearance once again.

We came to a narrow bridge that led to higher ground. From this vantage point, we could see most of Port Royal Sound and the distant ocean inlet to the northeast. Once across the rickety bridge, we drove through a meadow of hay and were greeted by a chorus of chirping songbirds and a cloaked, scortching sun that hid at times behind darkening clouds. This was the peninsula and domain of James Wilcox. Just beyond the hay field was a culvert embodying the overflow from the swamp. I could plainly see a barn by its banks in the distance. It must have been the swamp house that the slaves spoke of. The wagon suddenly slowed to a crawl as Simon recited a fearful orison under his breath.

"Deliver me, O'Lord, deliver this here broken slave," he chanted repeatedly.

"What is it, Simon?" I inquired.

"Why are you driving so slowly?" said Tyler.

"Massa Ty, I sees wickedness up ahead." He stopped the buckboard stood up and pointed.

"The Weeping post, Massa Ty. A brother in chains."

Tyler stood up and took a look. Abruptly, he ordered Simon to continue driving.

"What is it, Tyler, what do you see?" I asked.

He just sat quietly, looking troubled.

"What did you see?"

"What are you waiting for Simon?" asked Tyler.

"I, I, don't know, Massa Ty. My arms … legs have a cripplin' feelin."

"He's scared," I said.

Tyler jumped over the driver's bench and took a place by the man's side. He clutched the reins from the slave's hand and drove the wagon forward. Ahead was a man slumped on the ground, his arms hanging above his head, wrists chained to the top of a post buried deep into the earth. Some distance behind it stood the Swamp House.

As we approached, two devilish-looking dogs came out of nowhere, growling and barking. They were the largest canines I had ever seen. Simon jumped in the back and sat by me. Whether to protect me or have me protect him was not clear. What was apparent was the terror on his face. Tyler brought the wagon to a halt by the chained man on the ground and dismounted. One of the dogs sniffed at him while the other jumped up on his shoulders, begging kisses. Standing on its hind legs, the hound looked down on him.

"Heel, Samson, heel," commanded Tyler, pushing the canine off.

"Are they friendly?" I asked.

"Not if they don't know you."

"Can I get down?"

"Yes, get behind me and let them sniff you. These wolfhounds can be unpredictable."

"What is the other one's name?"

"Goliath. They are good dogs but they are trained to attack at Wilcox's command."

"Good Samson, Good Goliath," I said, holding clasped hands under a trembling chin. I stood immobile as the wolfhounds sniffed at my boots. Long extended tails were erect though wagging, all awhile my concern was for the wretched black man shackled to the weeping post. He was nearly naked, with remnants of ragged, burlap trousers draped from his waist. His face was beaded with sweat and parched lips were crazed and dripping blood. He was either unconscious or dead. After the dogs were satisfied that we were no threat, they lost interest and went about their business. I rushed over to the slave captive and knelt beside him. I ran my fingers down the jagged welts along the poor man's back. Lifting his head by the chin, I tried talking to him. A blistering wound ran the full length of his fragmented face, lacerations made by a bullwhip. Tyler examined him.

"Sure looks like Wilcox's work," he said. "His whip has iron wire woven to the leather cracker."

"That's terrible."

"I have seen him cut a watermelon in half with it." Tyler lightly slapped the man's cheek.

"Gideon, can you hear me? Gideon!"

I tried to remember where I had heard the name. The black man slowly opened his eyes. Startlingly, he managed a grin.

"Massa Ty. How good to see you again," he uttered.

"What are you doing here? I thought you had escaped up north."

"They found me, Massa Ty … took me."

"How, Gideon, how?"

"Up north. A town … a town, name …"

"Get some water from the wagon, Emily."

Simon sat in the buckboard, frightened. I reached under the bench for the flask. *Gideon, Gideon*, I recited to myself. I was convinced I had heard the name.

I handed the tin canteen to Tyler. He poured water over the man's head and brought the wet orifice to his lips. The chain around his wrists clanged as the thirsty man clutched at the jug and struggled to drink. I took my trusty notebook from my pocket and quickly thumbed through it. Finally, there it was. Written in bold print. I read it out loud. "Who's Gideon? Asha's helper. A Negro from down south."

"What did you say?" asked Tyler.

I stooped down and looked the beaten man in the face.

"New Bedford," I said.

A slight glimmer came to his slotted eyes. He labored a grin. "Yeah, New Bedford. Canaan by da sea."

Tyler looked over at me. "New Bedford. Where I was born!"

"Gideon worked for your father's friend, before the man died."

"He dead?" asked the black man, sounding surprised.

"I'm afraid so, Gideon."

The slave groaned and grimaced as he shifted his body and tried to find comfort. Suddenly his eyes closed, and his head dropped limp.

"We need to free him," I said.

"Can't do anything for him right now," said Tyler. "We require a key or at least a file to cut those chains."

I looked over at the barn.

"Maybe there's something in there we can use."

"Won't hurt to look."

"Gideon. Are there any slaves kept in that barn?" I asked. "Gideon!"

"He's blacked out."

"The barn, Tyler! Hannah may be in there."

"It's five feet under water. Can't see anyone being kept there."

"Let's go look."

"Stop right there," came an unexpected command.

It was James Wilcox. He stood with helicoid bullwhip in hand and flanked by Samson and Goliath. Behind him were two white men I had never seen before. They were sordid and unkempt. One of the men, with scraggly beard and missing teeth, toted a long rifle slung over his shoulder. His colleague, shaven, brandished a pistol tucked into the waist of baggy trousers—a leather sock laced with rawhide was capped firmly around the wrist of one arm, where a hand once grew. The man with the beard caught my eye. He wore nothing above his waist but a confederate wool jacket and army cap. The coat's sleeves had been torn away and he donned it fastened by one button at the neck. It was that precise button and all the others sewn vertically down the breast of the jacket that interested me. My eyes widened when I realized that they were the same military fasteners as the one I discovered in Asha Potter's hand. It probably meant nothing. After all, I was in the South.

The two suspicious men placed themselves between us and the barn. It was obvious that Wilcox did not want us anywhere near it.

"Hold back your hounds, Jim," shouted Tyler.

"They won't attack. Just don't let Miss White make any sudden moves."

Sensing the tone of their master's voice, the two hounds uttered a groaning growl.

"Ask him for the key," I said.

"What's she doing here?"

"I'm showing her around the island," said Tyler.

"That's what you say."

"What has this man done to be punished like this?"

"Get back on the wagon and leave here, immediately. You are trespassing."

"Tyrone and my mother own this island."

"Not here. Tyrone may own the island, but he does not own this track of land. He sold it to me, and I have a deed to prove it. It is my property. I rule here."

I stepped forward. Wilcox uncoiled the whip.

"You must free this man," I demanded.

"The governess," he said, churlishly. "Who are you … really? What did you come to Dukes Plantation for?"

"I don't know what you mean."

"You come south looking for someone, haven't you?"

"We just need the key to free this man," I said, my voice quaking.

"I free no one. And if you don't leave here, I may just tie you to a post."

"Free him," ordered Tyler.

"You can't tell me what to do on my property."

"This soil may indeed be your property, but this man you have shackled is the property of Dukes Plantation. I am a Dukes. And I will take possession of my property."

Wilcox contemplated his authority with good measure. He understood plainly the relevance of proprietorship. To his kind, black people were no different than cattle or a horse. And one must never make claim to another man's horse without lawful standing. And though Wilcox held the deed for the land he stood on, the same was not true about the slave shackled to the post. Categorically, being Tyrone Dukes' nephew, he was family. Nonetheless, collateral relationships did not take privilege over the Dukes name. It was conventionalism he understood well and begrudgingly accepted.

Tyler had used the partisan statute of felonious transgression and human proprietorship to his advantage—to set Gideon free, or at least free from Wilcox's injurious clutches. And though I found such barbaric subjugation and elicit transaction absurd, if it freed Gideon, I had no complaint.

The hawkish overseer reached into his pocket for the key. Crassly, he tossed it to the ground in front of us. I rushed forward to pick it up. The dogs growled. I stopped. Wilcox snickered.

"Go ahead, Miss White, I won't stop you. But I can't speak for the hounds."

Hand extended, I hesitated—the key only feet away. I took a wary step forward. The dogs growled louder—tails extended, the hair on their backs standing on end. Goliath revealed his gashing teeth his upper lip curled. They protected their owner while reflecting his sentiment. I was afraid to move.

"Go on. Pick it up," he coaxed.

The two seedy associates snickered.

Tyler calmly circled around me and took possession of the key. I was relieved. I stepped back, striving not to make a sudden move. Tyler unfastened the studded padlock by Gideon's face and the chain dropped to the ground.

"Go … take him," said Wilcox. "He'll only try to escape again … if he lives."

"Simon, lend me a hand," said Tyler.

The slave just sat quietly, as if he hadn't heard.

"Simon!"

Finally, Simon hurried over and helped lift his stricken comrade.

"And what are you doing here, Simon?" snarled Wilcox.

"Doin' what um told, Massa Wilcox, just doin' what um told."

"You wait until Tyrone finds out about this."

Simon looked up at us, impending despair wept from his eyes.

"Don't worry about him," said Tyler. "I'll deal with Tyrone."

I dropped down the tailgate to the buckboard while Tyler and Simon lifted Gideon into the back of the wagon. Simon's hands trembled. Scarcely alive, Gideon's wounds chafed red. He groaned as he was moved onto the splintered oak bed. I sat in the back with him. Lifting his head, I lent him my lap as a pillow. So deep were his wounds that the presence and odor of congealed blood made me queasy. Taking my pencil-knife, I tore at the hem of my dress and soaked a scrap of cloth with water from the flask. Gently I wiped the lacerations. He had an amiable round face with long eyelashes and curled lips at the corners—as if born with a smile. I carefully dabbed the contusions along his shoulders. Tyler and Simon climbed up onto the buckboard.

"Where are we going to take him?"

"The slave cabins," replied Tyler."

"Tyler Dukes," yelled Wilcox, as we made ready to leave. "You may be family but you ain't blood. Just you remember that, boy. Ya hear me?"

"Let's get going," said Tyler. Ignoring the overseer, he took the horse by the reins and released the brake.

"Remember that," yelled Wilcox, as we made distance. "You ain't blood!"

Samson and Goliath gave chase, barking and biting at the wagon wheels as we went. The air was damp and flowing as strong winds gathered. Whatever was stirring off Port Royal Sound delivered a piquant, salty breeze and welcomed cloud cover. Having no sun helped keep the injured man more comfortable, though the alleviation of pain, not comfort, was the concern that distressed me.

We came upon the small bridge. I was relieved that we would be off Wilcox property. But relief was of little solace. Every bone in my body told me that Hannah was on the Wilcox peninsula and in the barn. To leave there not knowing left a vexing twinge in my chest. But we had freed Gideon and that was something.

The buckboard's wheels rumbled over the lumpy ground, joggling indiscriminate thoughts. I wondered whether Molly was happy, if Westport and Point Village was still there, or whether Grandmamma Charlotte was watching over me from the beyond. Clouds overhead thickened. I felt ambivalent about the road ahead—the immediate and future one. For now, the ever-encompassing swamp awaited us. The horse sped up. I looked behind me—back at Wilcox and the receding image and fading puzzle that was the Swamp House.

Chapter 25: A Hurricane and Flames

The next morning, I was awakened by a cacophony of shouts and barking commands outside my window. I propped myself up onto one elbow and listened. The oyster-gray light of daybreak barely lit the room. I looked over at Molly. She was fast asleep. After reaching for the watch on the bedside table, I realized that it was only four thirty in the morning. I rubbed the sleepies from my eyes. The wind was raging through the trees, while they hissed their displeasure with rustling fury. The growing weather from the day before had intensified. "Morning gusts in shadowed glow, means tempest ashore with blight and blow," I could hear Seabury Cory say. It was an old whaleman's adage—a storm was coming.

A thud was carried by the whistling wind. Then another. Someone shouted orders, quickly followed by the sound of creaking, like rusty nails yanked from wood. I got up and pushed the window curtain aside. A group of men were gathered around a wagon. On the ground, someone had removed the lid from a stout wooden crate. Inside was a stack of rifles. One of the men held one to his eye, gauging the accuracy of the sights.

"Yes, yes, these are excellent. How many?"

"We only have fifty of them, Colonel. They were on the road to Sumter when the delivery was conveniently commandeered … loyal jingoistic highwaymen. Paid dearly for them."

"The ammunition?"

"All there. Over five-thousand rounds. Forty-four caliber rimfire."

The Colonel worked the lever mechanism beneath the trigger on one of the rifles. A group of men carried more boxes from a shed behind the house

"Breech-loader, I see."

"Holds sixteen shots—seventeen if you store one in the chamber."

"Yes, Major, these will do nicely."

As my eyes were accustomed to the light, it was obvious who it was—

the spurious, Major Tyrone Dukes. The man he spoke to was of higher rank. With him were six enlisted boys, dressed in gray wool jackets and confederate muffin caps. I lifted the window a bit more and listened. Directly, the curtains were blown back. Voices were louder.

"And the cannons?" said the officer. The question was carried by the wind in fractured syllables.

"They are older M-1841 models—six-pounder field guns, sir. They can fire round shot or canister."

"Bronze castings, I see."

"Yes, sir. There are two of them."

"We could easily profit from another ten."

"Careful loading them onto the wagon, sir. They weigh over eight hundred pounds."

"Get those cannons on board, men," ordered the colonel. "Of course, you will be coming with us, Major."

"Coming, sir?"

"Time is of the essence. Union Navy is amassing its forces offshore as we speak."

"I have heard."

"We expect a sizeable attack at any moment."

"Yes, sir."

"We need every man we can muster, Major Dukes."

I couldn't believe what I just heard. What could it all mean? Will we be under attack? What will happen to everyone living here?

"I understand, Colonel. If I may add, I think I have fulfilled my duty."

"We shall have none of that," grumbled the colonel. "We are under attack, Major. Every patriot must step up and do their part."

The colonel looked up and studied the house. I stepped back and away from the window.

"You have a nice place here, Major. Hate to see you lose it all."

"Yes, Colonel."

"Now we must get back and prepare for engagement. I expect you to be at the fort, straightaway."

Tyrone saluted as the last cannon was loaded and the heavily laden wagon clambered away. He remained at attention as the soldiers rode into an illuminated horizon. The dawn roused a crowing rooster by the barn. The wind blew in, creating a howling din. I closed the window and sat on the edge of the bed. There was a damp chill in the room. I rubbed my arms and mulled over the events of the previous day. Now came news that the Union Navy was poised for attack just outside Port Royal Sound. I thought of Samuel and wondered where he could be. Was he still missing? If so, missing where? It was such a big country. I refused to entertain that he may no longer be alive. It was all becoming overwhelming.

The room brightened as a murky sun hovered just below the cloudy horizon. It was promising to be a stormy day. I looked at my watch—four-fifty. It was too early for breakfast but too late to go back to bed. I checked on Molly. She was fast asleep.

I picked up the prayer book, which I kept by the side of the bed. Thumbing through it, I hoped to find inspiration for what looked like trying days ahead. And yes, I do read the Good Book every now and then, but not the same passages that you would. My prayer book is cluttered with advice and instruction, scribbled wisdom, and sensibilities—axioms written along the margins of every page. Each one authored by Grandmamma, Charlotte White. There had to be several hundred influential aphorisms and pious dictions. Some were difficult to read—penciled notations smeared with multiple spelling errors and equivocal interpretation. However, even those blemished entries contain a great measure of motivation and insight. With prayer book in hand, I lay back on the bed and stared up at the ceiling, trying to clear my mind of a jumble of thoughts. Unexpectedly, I fell asleep.

There was a discreet knock at the door. It was Molly.

"Oh good, you're awake," she said, entering the room.

"Molly … how long have you been up?"

"Over an hour. I didn't want to wake you."

I glanced at my watch. It was eight thirty. "Oh dear, I overslept, again."

"You must have been tired. Can't be helped, I have heard Father say every time he overslept."

"Have you had breakfast?"

"No. Don't want any." Pouting, she plopped herself slumped on the edge of the bed.

"What's wrong, dear?" I stoked her hair.

"It's Mother."

"Oh no, Molly."

"Uh-huh. She is ill again."

It was not good news and unraveled the purpose as to why we came to Dukes Island in the first place. My powers of divination had failed me; I had not thought that Victoria would be so readily enticed by her husband's temptation. It had been less than twenty-four hours since I discovered Tyrone Dukes' insidious plan. I was hoping that Tyler would have kept his mother safe and away from Tyrone until we could speak to her and improvise a plan to keep her abstinent. Pragmatic reflection told me that there was probably little we could do with someone so obsessive. Furthermore, they were husband and wife, sanctified by obligatory measures of observance and capitulation. Once alone, locked away in the bedroom, there is little outside influence.

"Molly … I'm sorry about your mother."

"It's not your fault. It's not anyone one's fault, I guess. It doesn't change anything."

"Oh … what do you mean?"

"It doesn't matter if she is ill or not. I still love being with her."

"I know you do, dear."

"Now she will lock herself away in her room and I won't get to see her at all. I want to help her."

"Perhaps we can."

I got up from bed and kissed her on the top of the head. Out of the window, the trees were swaying and the wind howling—the sun nowhere in the sky. The curtains on the windows inflated with the draft that found itself past every crevasse around the window sash. I walked over to the dressing chest by the window and picked up a mirror.

"Oh, Emily you think we'll be able to?"

"It may take some time," I said, brushing out my hair. "We can only try."

"Mother is so sad."

"Most people with her illness are. Some don't even know it."

"I think she does. She's especially smart. Did you know that George Washington had slaves or that you can't tell a male or female blue jay apart?"

"Is that right?"

"Or that ancient Egyptians shaved off their eyebrows when their pet cat died."

"Your mother is full of interesting tales."

"So are you."

"Nice of you to think so."

"She has lots of stories. But she doesn't like talking about Papa."

"You didn't talk to her about Hannah, did you?"

"No. I did as you said. Don't talk about Hannah unless she brings her up. But she never does."

"Good girl. Why don't I get dressed and we can both go down for breakfast? It's the most important meal of the day and you should have something to eat."

"Oh, alright," she said, moping. "I'll wait downstairs. Clorina may need me in the kitchen."

After she left, I sat on the edge of the bed, thinking about Gideon and the grievous condition he was in when we left him by the slave cabins and in Simon's care. Things changed after our visit to the Wilcox compound.

Nothing good could come from it. My mission south had taken on a surreal trajectory into an unforeseen and perilous orbit. I tried putting it all out of my mind.

The scene outside the window was one of chaos, as the approaching storm intensified. I got dressed and placed Grandmamma's prayer book in my pocket. I tried not to go anywhere without it. Being the size of a deck of playing cards, both prayer book and news diary fit nicely in my hip pocket. I walked out the door and into the vestibule. Shouting echoed up the spiraling staircase. I stopped at the top of the stairs and listened.

"How could you, Father!" I heard Tyler say.

"It is none of your affair. She is my wife."

"She is my mother! Her blood runs through my heart. That is more than you can say."

"I shall not share blame for your mother's feckless behavior. The bottle was stored in the liquor closet. How was I to think she would find it?"

"You knew she would find it."

"I will hear no more from you."

"You will not have to much longer, Mister Dukes. From now on you may refer to me as Tyler French."

"Have it your way, boy," said Tyrone.

There was the sound of shuffling feet and more arguing. I decided to take the servant's staircase. The narrow steps used by house slaves led directly to a small corridor just off the kitchen. Once there, I found Clorina by the stove and Molly sitting at the worktable eating.

"Emily, you're here. Have some of this rice pudding," said Molly, "It's very sweet."

"Mornin,' Miss White," sang the black cook.

"Good morning, Clorina."

"Ya sit an' Clorina will cook ya up a fine breakfast."

With an egg in each hand, she cracked them into a cast iron pan. Pushing the yokes aside she dropped in a large slab of salted ham.

"Hmm, hmm! I'll dirty some brown suga' and mustaad glaze on tat there ham and ya will think ya is eatin' n'heaven."

I took a chair by Molly, stroking her long hair as she ate. "Are you feeling better, dear?"

"Uh-huh. Mother is outside rocking."

"Outside? In all that wind?"

I walked to a window. Much to my consternation, Victoria Dukes sat smoking her pipe while suckling on an absinthe glass. Though she had moved her rocker away from the barrels of combustibles, she no less stubbornly puffed her tobacco. Somewhat protected by the veranda's ample columns, the wind swept her wavy hair and linen dress into a thrashing frenzy. If polled, my reactionary perceptiveness would find her mad. The absurdity of sitting in a gale rocking with a glass of green fairy and a rangy smoking pipe just suggested unsound behavior. On the other hand, Molly supplied a contrasting point of view.

"I'm going outside to sit by Mother and finish my pudding," she said.

"What? Out in that wind?"

"Mother said it's enjoyable … watching things blow around."

"Enjoyable?"

"Yes. When she was young her and Papa sat in front of a tavern on the waterfront and watched the biggest storm that ever came ashore."

"When was that?"

"Long before I was born. Mother said that it sunk ten whaling ships in harbor as they watched. She' going to tell me more about it."

"Is that what she said?"

"Ah-huh. The wind reminds her of home. She said when she married Papa it was the happiest days of her life. Then she didn't want to talk about Papa anymore."

Happy days and home—such words engendered joyous memories for me. I had missed home. Time away was exhausting, both mentally and spiritually. The more I thought of home, the more I felt like I would never see it again. They were thoughts that I had to purge from my mind.

"Imagine," said Molly. "Ten whaling ships."

"Ten ships," I said, reflection still burning. I suddenly felt a sorrowful empathy for the lonely woman out in the blow and away from home.

I recalled the whale men of Point Village in Westport telling tales about the Great Havana Gale of '46. Perhaps that was the storm Victoria spoke of. Grandmamma told of the time a gale blew the roof off of Perry Davis' barn and deposited a forty-foot-long fishing scalloper in our front yard. I don't remember such a storm since I was only four. Though the storm was well remembered, no one could tell me why it was called the Great Havana Gale. Considering Victoria's happy recollections of New England and her estranged husband, sitting out in a storm suddenly seemed a rational, if not a salubrious, exercise.

I sat eating. Who could predict while traveling in the south I would have been served the most delicious breakfast I had ever enjoyed—prepared by a dutiful servant who was not allowed to indulge in the morning cuisine herself.

"I'm full … cannot eat another bite," I said, pushing back my plate.

"Child ya eat'n like a mouse."

She placed a small bowl of rice pudding in front of me and dripped it with molasses.

"I specially made tis for ya-all. We out'a sugar. I put on some molasses instead. It is bett'a for ya anyhow."

Though I was no longer hungry, I made an effort to eat some. Clorina was so gracious and I had no desire of sinking her dory. Though I knew it was not proper, still, I invited her to sit with me and have some custard.

"Oh, no, Miss White, Massa Dukes say we can't be friendly-like with callers."

"I'll have some of that rice custard," said Tyler, walking into the room. "Good morning."

I looked over his shoulder and to the kitchen door. Skittish anticipation had Tyrone Dukes walking in at any moment. Tyler gave me a courteous smile, pulled up a chair, and sat.

"Man of few words this morning, I see."

"Sorry. It has not been a good one."

"Oh?"

"Private matter."

"I understand."

"Do you?"

He sounded anything but friendly. I failed to tell him that I had heard the conversation he had with Tyrone. I decided to move the chat in another direction.

"I invited Clorina to sit and have some pudding with me, but she wouldn't do it."

"Whites and blacks don't dine together, Emily, I have told you that. We shouldn't even be dining in the kitchen where the servants eat."

He was more belligerent than the first time. After all he has been through, I could very well understand his curtness. Still, I struck back.

"That is your protocol, is it?"

"Massa Ty is tellin' da truth. Ya white folk should be eatin' in da dinnin' room, not in Clorina's kitchen."

"Well?" I said waiting for his retort.

"Lordy-Lord," recited Clorina, shaking her head.

He looked at me as if I were some sort of radical subversive or just plain crazed. I glared back, daring him to give me some sort of valid, if not humane, explanation why we could not all sit and eat together in the kitchen."

"Anyhow, I prefer eating in the kitchen," I declared, giving up.

Looking away, he drummed his fingers on the table—the lucid gears of civility turning in his head. Promptly, he got up and took the servant by the arm and escorted her to the table.

"Sit, Clorina."

Confounded, she sat, quietly watching her master out the corner of raven-colored eyes. Crumpled nose and tight-lipped, she exhibited uneasy bewilderment. Walking over to the cook stove, Tyler took an egg and cracked it on the edge of the iron skillet. The ichorous serum dripped into the sizzling pan carrying with it tiny slivers of eggshell. I snickered as he pinched the fragments of broken shell and tossed them aside while trying not to burn his fingers.

Fidgeting, Clorina dashed up from her chair. "Oh, let me do tat, Massa Ty."

Tyler quickly took her by the arm. "Now, did I say you could get up?"

"No, Massa Ty."

He walked her back to her stool and gingerly sat her down. I laughed as she tried getting up once again.

"Ah, ah, ah," he objected, wagging a finger. He dropped a healthy portion of ham into the pan. The meat fizzled and sputtered in the broiling butter. Clorina sat and watched, the sizzling meat widening her eyes.

"I … am cooking breakfast today," he declared. Once he was finished, he placed the fried meal on the table right under the servant's nose.

"Now eat."

"Ya not done cookin for ya-self?" she asked.

"Nope. I was cooking for you … now eat."

"Lordy-Lord, Massa Ty. What have ya done?"

Tyler sat and grinned. He was amused and satisfied with himself. The puzzled woman looked down at her meal and bit a lip, befuddled about what to do. He took a fork, reached over and dropped it on her plate.

"Well, go on … eat."

"If Massa Dukes find me out sittin …"

"You don't have to worry about Master Dukes. He left for Fort Beauregard." He reached out and patted her on the hand. "Eat Clorina … please. Help me show up this white girl here."

Finally, she ate. Her eyes wandered around the room waiting for someone to walk in and stop her—not so much from eating but for sitting at the table with whites.

"How is it?" I asked.

She nodded as she chewed. "Tis good, Miss White."

Tyler opened a window to help cool the room. A stiff breeze blew in. Suddenly, he realized Victoria sitting outside.

"What in the world is Mother doing out there!"

"Enjoying the wind, I was told."

He peered down at his feet and stroked his brow when he noticed the glass of green venom in her hand. He shook his head. I glanced over his shoulder. Molly sat on the floor of the veranda petting the cat, her sparkling eyes fixed on her mother, listening to the rhetorical diary the older woman funneled. Victoria's uplifted arm swung in the air, wielding her pipe, while using the protracted stem as a pointer to tutor a lesson on her imaginary blackboard of life. She fondled the glass of absinthe, holding it close to her bosom—a poison nostrum that diminished misery and numbed despair—if only for a moment.

"Courage, Tyler, courage," I implored, resting an ancillary hand on his shoulder.

"It's Tyrone's fault."

"It was an evil thing your father did."

"He's not my father."

His admission was for the best. I was happy to hear it. Once my affairs concluded in the south, perhaps he would accompany Molly and me home and into the arms of a loving father. I could not help but dwell on the gloom that circumstances would get much worse before they could possibly get better—if they ever did. Sometimes, destiny delivers an outcome we cannot avert, only sculpt. I remember when Samuel Cory left for his military duty. Old Seabury placed his hand on his son's shoulder and said, "Have faith in yourself, and though destiny will scowl, accept truth on your own terms." Though I did not repeat this advice to Tyler, it was what we all had to do. Or at least try.

"Looks like the weather is getting worse," I said.

"You were right about a storm coming."

"When do you think we could go back and search for Hannah?"

"We must choose the right time, when Wilcox is away."

"Can't we just go at night?"

"Not with the dogs."

"Oh, I forgot about them."

"I don't think Wilcox will do anything until Tyrone returns."

"When is that?"

"I don't know. But I'm not going to sit around here idle."

"What are you going to do?"

"I'm going to Slave Row."

"Slave Row?"

"To see Gideon …"

"I'm coming."

"Let's go, then."

"Perhaps Gideon can tell us something about Hannah?"

"We will walk there. To take a horse or wagon would only peak curiosity. Are you up for a long walk? It's blowing real hard out there."

"I'm ready. I grew up by the ocean. It's nothing but a brisk breeze."

Before we left, I quickly ran up to my room and put on more comfortable walking boots. When I returned, Tyler was clearing the tableware into the wash basin while a begging Clorina shadowed behind.

"Please, Massa Ty, tat is no work for the massa," she pleaded, liberating the dishes from his hands. "Tat is a house gal's labor."

I patiently waited for Tyler by the kitchen door, witnessing the whimsical exchange.

"Alright, Clorina. But not until you sit down and finish your meal," he insisted.

Pouting, the servant flung her portly torso into the chair, and picked up her fork.

"Go on," ordered Tyler. "Eat." He looked at me and simpered as Clorina resumed her breakfast. "Let's go, Emily."

We started down a lane behind the house on our way to see Gideon. Just as we were about to lose sight of the big house, three men could be seen in the distance quickly approaching on horseback. Tyler took me by the hand, and we ran into the cotton field. We stooped and hid amongst the slaves picking cotton as the riders galloped by.

"It's Wilcox and his go-to men," said Tyler, as the three men galloped by us.

"Who are those men?"

"Hannibal and Dweez … two henchmen hired by Wilcox and Tyrone to help transport slaves to market. The fact they are here tells me Tyrone is forging some sort of transaction or sale."

"What shall we do?"

"Carry on. We'll cut through the fields and avoid the road."

The route through the mushy cotton fields was difficult. Since we were running, however, it did not take us long to reach the slave village. When we arrived, we found the village barren. Even in a gale, slaves were expected to work the fields.

Ten small log buildings made up the community. Each building had a door in the center and two windows to each side. A stone chimney jutted out the center of the wood-shanked roofs.

"No one here," I said, clutching my chest and catching my breath.

"There should be someone here … elderly slaves too old to work the fields. When we left yesterday, Simon said he would take Gideon over to Cyrus' cabin."

"Which one is it?"

"I don't know."

"I hear banging … there," I pointed.

On the veranda of one of the buildings was an old man nailing a shutter to a window with a rock. He was thin as a swamp reed, with beef-jerky complexion as course as the crevassed bark of an old oak. Like the rings of a tree, one could almost tell how old he was by counting the folds of skin along the man's face.

"I'm looking for Cyrus," said Tyler to the old man.

He glanced over but neglected to acknowledge us. Instead, he went back to hammering the shutter.

"Perhaps he can't hear you over the wind," I said.

"I'm looking for Cyrus," shouted Tyler,

"No, Cyrus heeya," said the old man, tossing the rock to the ground. "Cyrus in da fields."

"Where does he live," I asked.

The old fellow just gawked as if I were a ghost or a talking tree.

"The girl asked you a question," yelled Tyler. "Are you not listening?"

I placed my hand on Tyler's arm. I shook my head,"Don't."

"Ya young Massa Ty," said the old man. He appeared disheveled.

"That's right."

I stepped forward.

"Can you please tell us where Cyrus lives? We have come to help Gideon."

He lifted his bony arm and pointed with a quivering finger to a cabin across the way.

"Let's go," said Tyler, marching off.

"You didn't have to be so mean." I hurried behind him. "He's just an old man."

"I lost my head. Ill-mannered plantation habit, you can say."

"You scared him."

"Scared? I don't think so! There's nothing I can do that is worse than what he already endured in life. Death to him is just a way to freedom."

"It's no reason to be abrupt."

"I'll remember. The old fellow wasn't happy to see us, was he? Poor sod. Probably thinks we are here to take someone away to the Swamp House. Not a good sign when the master of the plantation shows up at your front door making demands."

As we approached the cabin, an old woman opened the door and emptied a porcelain bowl of bloody water. Unsure, she just stared at us.

"Is this where Cyrus lives?" I shouted over the wind.

She nodded.

"Is Gideon in there?" inquired Tyler.

The old woman waved us over.

We were led into a small space. A large stone fireplace occupied the middle of the floor. The quarried chimney had an open hearth dividing the living quarters into two separate rooms accommodating two distinct groups or families. Compared to my bedroom in the big house, the size of the space was uncompromising and stifling. A young girl occupied the adjoining space on the other side of the chimney. She cared for an infant. The baby lay in a hollowed-out tree stump used for a cradle.

"It's small in here," I said.

"It is. Probably houses ten slaves if not more."

"Ya is Massa Ty," said the old woman.

"Yes, that's right."

"Massa Ty, Gideon is not long fo' tis world," she proclaimed.

We found Gideon lying on the floor behind a curtain of burlap stitched with dry reeds. A log of straw propped his head. I dropped to my knees beside him. Tyler tapped the injured black man on the shoulder.

"Gideon … Gideon, it's me … Tyler."

The man slowly opened his eyes and labored to smile. "Massa Ty. Wa-wat are ya doin here?"

"How do you feel?"

The slave closed his eyes, offering no reply.

"Gideon."

"I don't think he hears you, Tyler."

We sat for nearly an hour before the wounded man opened his eyes once again. The old woman tried feeding him some rice, but he was too weak to eat.

"Massa Ty," he mumbled. "I'm thirsty."

"Can we get some water," Tyler asked.

"From the well outside," said the old woman.

"I'll get it," said Tyler, taking the pail from her.

While Tyler went to get some water, I tried questioning the wounded slave. "How did you get captured, Gideon?"

"Mista Potter say there was spies in New Bedford, workin' fo' Massa Dukes. They was lookin' for Malachi an' found me in da mill."

"Who found you?"

"Massa Wilcox an' two men."

"Wilcox was in New Bedford!"

"Massa Wilcox done took me from dat dere mill."

"Did they hurt Mister Potter, Gideon?"

"One of da men pushed Mista Potter and throw him to da floo'. Then Massa Wilcox an' da two men grab me an' we all go. They done left poo' Mista Potter on the floo'."

"Was Mister Potter hurt, Gideon?"

"He 'ad blood on his nose."

"Mister Potter was alive when you all left?"

He closed his eyes.

"Gideon. Was Mister Potter alive?"

The poor fellow was asleep once again. Tyler walked in and placed the bucket on the floor. He dipped a cloth and dabbed Gideon's fractured lips.

"He's out again," I said.

"Let him rest now."

It appeared that my investigation of events on the day Asha Potter was killed was suddenly askew. This complicated things with what I had anticipated to be the facts behind Asha Potter's demise. If Wilcox and the men who took Gideon did not murder Asha, who did? Or was he murdered at all? Perhaps it was indeed an accident. How could I be so wrong? It led me to believe that I should perfect the skills of a newspaper reporter rather than those of detective.

We sat waiting for Gideon to come around. Outside, the storm had intensified. The sound of the howling wind jousted with the cries of the infant on the opposite side of the cabin.

"We can't spend all our time here," said Tyler.

"But I wanted to ask him about Hannah."

"While we wait here, Wilcox could be moving her. The appearance of Hannibal and Dweez is not good."

"What shall we do?"

"Let me think."

I walked over to the old woman stirring some rice in a pot by the fire.

"I'm Emily, what is your name."

"Esther."

"Do you know Malachi, Esther?"

"Yea, he Massa Dukes' favorite boy."

"Have you seen him?"

"Not fo' long time. They say Malachi is in da Swamp House."

"The Swamp House!"

"Yea. They gonna sell em down in Orleans."

"How do you know?"

"Gideon say it. He done see Malachi."

"He told you that?"

"Yea, they gonna sell Malachi and da Indin woman down in Orleans."

I jumped back, my hands to my mouth. I gave Tyler a frenzied stare.

"We've got to go," he cried.

"Oh, Tyler. We must find her."

"We'll go out to the peninsula and see what's in that barn."

"Can we go now?"

"Yes, now, while Wilcox is away."

We left the slave hamlet and hurriedly started for the Wilcox homestead. The storm had arrived in earnest and was now a fully expanded hurricane. The road was a spinning dust tunnel while frightened slaves, their shirts, and turbans over their mouths, hustled for shelter. It was blowing too hard for picking. Baskets filled with cotton were left in the fields as the savage wind lifted and emptied them, sending cotton flocci steaming in the air.

We scurried in one direction while slaves marched in the other. Several of them were pointing at the sky with a mien of dread and awe on their faces. I turned and looked. The heavens were filled with a black whirlwind of ascending smoke, soaring into an already tenebrous sky. Something very large was on fire.

"Tyler, what is happening there?"

He turned. His eyes billowed. Dread and panic washed across his face.

"My God!"

"What is it, Tyler?"

He gazed at the spectacle. Suddenly, I knew what it was. I desperately tried to substitute the obvious with alternatives. There were none—none but the main house.

Tyler started trotting toward the unfolding event. I followed. Four or five steps into it and he was in a full sprint. As soon as we started running all the slaves ran with us. However, we were stopped in our trek by a considerable explosion. A plume of dark smoke spiraled up over the horizon. I continued to run as fast as I could, my mind piecing together what could possibly be happening. All I could surmise was that the Union Navy had finally attacked. The explosion must have been cannon fire from one of the Union ships of war. But how can that be? The house was much too far from shore and hidden by trees.

With Tyler well ahead, I stopped to catch my breath. Palms of my hands resting on my knees, I bent over and gasped for air. Then I realized—Molly. What of Molly? I ran as fast as my lungs could carry me. Debris in the air battered my face as gusts of wind tossed me from one side of the road to the other. "Molly," I screamed loudly. "Molly, Molly!"

Suddenly, there was another enormous explosion.

The once stately residence came into view. Slaves crowded up and down the tree-lined lane that led to the stately front entrance. They kept their distance and watched in horror as the inferno spread. The entire house was engulfed in a bright yellow-orange radiance. Lapping flames curled from every window as the structural columns that encircled the entire edifice collapsed like fainting, charred dominoes. The blaze fluttered madly out through the roof as strong winds fed its hunger. Tyler ran toward the flames but was stopped. He backed away, his arms shielding his face. The belching heat was intolerable. I shouted out for Molly. Without warning, there was another explosion nearly tossing me off my feet. The alcohol barrels had exploded. A fulvous orb of burgeoning flame rose high into the air. The mushrooming smoke curled in on itself as it grew and swallowed the light around it. I screamed out for Molly. Tears swelled as a dreaded fear billowed in my belly and weakness beset my knees. Tyler ran to the back of the building. I scurried close behind. The worst of the flames were around the back where not much of the structure was left. The eight columns that ran the entire length of the rear of the house were no longer there. I frantically called for Molly.

"Here." I heard someone yell.

Molly stood by some trees with Clorina and Simon, well away from the conflagration. The black man waved, hailing me over.

"Oh, Emily, it's terrible, terrible," cried the young girl.

We embraced as she sobbed uncontrollably.

"What happened here, Clorina?" cried Tyler. "Where is Mother?"

"She gone, Massa Ty, she gone," she cried.

"Gone? What do you mean, gone?"

"Mother went back into the house for the cat," explained Molly, "and she never came out."

Tyler ran toward the back door. There was no door. "Mother … Mother," he wailed.

"She gone, Massa Ty," whimpered Clorina. "She gone ta heaven."

"You sure she went inside, Clorina?"

"Yea, Miss Emily. We saw her. She done run into da kitchen fo' tat cat. She love tat cat. We waited, but she neva' come out."

"What happen Clorina … how did this fire get started? Where are the rest of the servants?" The perplexity of logic had me asking questions as if I were working on a news story.

"I … I don't know, Miss White. Misses Dukes was smokin out back. Left da pipe on da table outside. Massa Ty done warned 'er ove'a an' ove'a about tat thing."

"Is that what happened, Molly?"

"I was sitting with Mother on the porch. She went in the house for some water for her drink. The wind blew her tobacco pipe off the small table and into the barrels. I went to pick it up but there was a fire. I yelled for Clorina then I ran."

"I went to da well fo' some water but it done made it worse," declared the servant.

"I'm afraid, Emily, I'm afraid," cried Molly. "We can't find Mother."

I held her in my arms while watching the spreading blaze. The heat wielded by our faces in spurts like waves on the beach. We moved back. Tyler stood close to the flames, stunned.

"Get away, Massa Ty!" hollered Simon. "That is the fire of da devil."

I worried about how close he stood to the blaze. "Wait here," I said to Molly.

"No, don't go," she cried, clutching at my arm.

"I'm going to get Tyler. I'll be back."

I approached him then had to stop. The heat was singeing my skin. "Tyler … Tyler!"

He stood motionless, staring at the fiery edifice. The outline of his body was as an eclipsing silhouette, poised before the blinding flames. His blonde, curly hair thrashed in the blustering wind, radiating an orange glow, set off by the vibrant, blushing inferno. Holding my arms in front of my face, I shielded myself from the hellish heat and finally got close enough to seize him by the arm and pull him away. His limbs and face were pinkish red, singed from the searing heat—the skin on his brow was blistered.

"Tyler … you burnt yourself."

"She's gone," he said, his voice barely audible. "No one could live through that … no one."

I held his fiery face in my hands, as a tepid tear dripped down my cheek. He stood rigid and benumbed. His arms dangled flaccidly by his side while all emotion drained from his heart. Stunned trauma filled the depleted void.

"I'm sorry, Tyler. We just didn't have enough time. If we did, we could have helped her."

"It is all Tyrone's fault," he said to himself.

Molly came over and hugged her brother. "I'm so sad, Tyler," she said, barely getting out the words before sobbing breathlessly.

Tyler awakened from his horrifying stupor and held her tightly. His nose in her hair, he stroked her head adoringly as he watched the fearsome flames. Not once did he shed a tear. He was stronger than I would have given him credit.

"I'll take care of you, Molly," he promised. "You'll see. I'll make up for things. I'll tell you stories like Mother did and give you all the knowledge she gave me. You'll be happy once again … we both will."

I wiped my tears with my forearm as I stood there watching the inferno. Powerful winds whipped the fire, tossing walls to the ground in cindered rubble. Oddly, James Wilcox flickered into memory. We had seen him ride toward the property earlier when we left for the slave cabins. Now I wondered where he had gone.

"Have you seen Wilcox, Clorina?" I asked.

"No, miss."

"He has gone to da ferry crossing," said Simon.

"For the mainland?"

"Yeah. I heard him say to the white men tat they must hurry and return for da … da merchandise for Orleans."

"Merchandise? They must mean slaves … Hannah!"

"Massa Wilcox said to wait here an' tat I should help'em take da ferry across in the wind."

I turned to Tyler. My heart was a twisted mess. How could I bring up the subject of Hannah at a time like this? I had little choice and abundance of need. I had to find her. It was my mission. It was all I had left. Though the dead have moved on, the living must grapple with their residual lives and deal with the playing cards left in their hand. For some, time took care of such occasions—but not for me. There was nothing I could do here for Tyler or Molly. There was plenty I could try and do for Hannah and Malachi.

"Tyler. Wilcox is making ready to transport some slaves across the river. He's gone to the mainland. Simon said he'd be back."

He stood staring at what was left of the big house. How could I impose on him at a time like this? I would need to go by myself. I started my trek for the Swamp House. I was a good way up the road before he called out to me.

"Emily. Where are you going?" he yelled.

"To Wilcox's place."

"Wilcox's place?"

"I must find Hannah."

Having little means or a constructive idea of what I was undertaking, I continued on my way, far from the fiery ashes.

"Wait," he shouted. "I'm coming." He took one last look at the house. "There's nothing left for me here," he recited to himself. He took Molly by the hand.

"Clorina, can you watch her for me?"

"Yea, Massa Ty, I can watch Miss Molly."

"Take her away from here."

"Where shall we go, Massa?"

"Find Cyrus and take her to his cabin. Wait for me there."

"Where are you going?" asked Molly.

"To find Hannah."

"I want to come!"

"No, you go with Clorina."

"But why?"

He stooped over and lovingly stroked her face. "She needs you, Molly. Look at her. She's crying. And you can't abandon a crying friend at a time of need, now can you?"

Molly looked over at the servant. Clorina wiped her tears with her apron.

"I'll take care of her," she sniffled.

"Good girl."

Tyler took a couple of steps toward the fire and gazed for a moment. I walked over and placed a comforting hand on his shoulder.

"Ready?"

"Ready. Simon. You're coming with us?"

"Anything ya say, Massa Ty."

Chapter 26: The Swamp House

All the horse tack, including saddles and bridles, were lost in the fire as the wind blew the flames in the direction of the barn. Simon fashioned some makeshift bridles with rope that had been used as a barrier around the corral. We each took a horse and started for the Wilcox estate.

I struggled to stay on the saddleless mare, straddling the animal tightly with my legs, as we galloped onward amidst a bludgeoning hurricane. It did not take long until we came upon the flood in the road, the one we had encountered the day before. What was yesterday a twelve-inch-deep brook was now a four-foot rushing river. The three of us sat on our horses surveying the dilemma.

"The swamp is being moved inland," said Tyler.

"It's a storm surge," I told him. "I don't remember having ever witnessed one. But Grandmamma said she remembered a time when the water was so high that it had half of my village under feet of water."

"Grandmamma, huh?"

I shrugged and nodded. "Is there any other way of getting to the other side?"

"No. This is the only road onto Wilcox's peninsula. We need to cross here."

"Let's cross together," I suggested, "all three of us, abreast, keeping close. This way we support one another and there is less chance that one of us is swept away."

"Good idea, Emily. Ready, Simon?"

"Yasa."

With Simon on my right and Tyler on my left, we slowly started across. Simon had the strongest of the animals, a Shire that had been used for plowing. The draught horse's strength and large size acted as a breakwater, making the crossing easier than expected. Once on the other side, we darted forward, wasting little time.

We soon found ourselves at the small bridge that led onto the peninsula. Here the flood was only a couple of feet above the bridge. But the headwaters were rising by the minute.

Finally, the roof of the barn or Swamp House came into view. My heart dropped to my stomach. I was soaked from the waist down.

"Are you alright, Emily?" asked Tyler.

"Yes, I'll be fine."

"You sure?"

I nodded.

"Have you noticed," he said, looking up at the sky.

"Yes, the wind has died down quite a bit."

"Even the sun is breaking through."

"I have never seen a storm end so quickly."

"It's over."

"Too quickly. It must be the Devil's Eye."

"The what?"

"The whalemen at home call it the Devil's Eye. It's the heart or center of the hurricane where there's little or no wind. I'm afraid that it is passing over us at the moment. If true, it will return with a vengeance … and very soon."

"Let's hurry, then."

We cautiously moved onto the property, leading the horses with weary caution as we inspected for any sign of life. Samson and Goliath charged toward us, barking dubious threats, their wiry, long hair fluttering in the vestiges of a snoozing gale. Tyler rode ahead and greeted the hounds since they knew him. The dogs sniffed our feet. Deciding we were no threat, they lost interest and pranced away. We got down from our horses.

"Look!" I shouted. "The Swamp House. It's completely under water."

"Can't be anyone in there," declared Tyler. "Not in that flood."

"We need to look."

We tied off the horses and started for the barn. The building was at the edge of a marshy field and stood a good distance away from the main house. Simon looked back over his shoulder.

"What is it, Simon?" I asked.

"Da dogs. They is mean."

"They won't hurt you," said Tyler. "Not while I'm here."

"I go where you go, Massa Ty."

Tyler gave the man a reassuring pat on the back. "Lead the way. You'll be fine."

As we got nearer to the barn, the water became deeper. Once at the door, the deluge was almost up to my chin. Tyler shook and pulled on the barn door, but it was fastened tightly.

"Must be locked somehow. I can't see through this murky water, but it feels like a padlock," he said.

"Is there another way in?" I asked.

"Let me look," said Simon, submerging himself in the flow.

I pounded on the door, calling out for anyone that may be inside.

"Help, help," came a faint cry.

Tyler and I looked at one another.

"Did you hear that?" I asked.

Simon surfaced.

"Padlock, Massa Ty," he said, catching his breath. "Like da one on Gideon."

"We need to hurry and get inside." I suggested.

"And we will," declared Tyler.

"How?"

He reached into his shirt pocket and produced a gem.

"With this!" he smirked.

"A key?"

"Tyrone's key. It opens every padlock on this plantation."

"Where did you get it?"

"Fell out of his pocket and onto the sofa when we were arguing this morning. I kept it in case we ran into another Gideon."

Tyler handed Simon the key.

"Don't drop it," he said.

"Yasa."

The black man disappeared below the surface of the water once again. Up above, fast-moving clouds were crumbling, exposing patches of blue while the tenacity of the wind almost dissipated. Without warning, the door ruptured open and Simon sprung from the depths with the padlock in his hand.

"Tat was easy, Massa Ty," proclaimed Simon, coughing out some of the brackish water. Tyler took the key from his hand.

"Toss that lock away Simon," he said. "I don't ever want to see one of those again.

"Yasa." With a triumphant grin, Simon tossed the lock into the swamp as far as his arm could fling it.

Tyler slowly pulled the door back against the almost five-foot deluge. Once open, we all waded inside. In the middle of the barn, floating high on the water was a large canoe Wilcox was building. It was like no other canoe on the plantation. Nearly fifty feet long, it had the luxury of a doghouse with port windows and resting bunks. There were rowing stations for eight slaves. The vessel was built with conventional framing and planking, unlike many of the dugouts used by slaves. Tyler pushed the vessel aside. Around us was a sea of floating hay. Lumber and other debris littered the grassy surface.

"There can't be anyone in here," I said.

"Not in over five feet of water," added Tyler.

"But I thought I heard someone"

"Hello! Anybody here?"

Again, I heard a faint call. "Help, in here!"

"That door in the back," I said."

The two men pushed their way through the flood and over to the tack room along a far wall. I struggled to keep my head above water. Tyler sprung the door. When I caught up to them, I discovered Hannah slumped up onto Malachi's shoulders in water up to his neck, as he tried to keep Hannah from drowning. The black man struggled to stay on his feet. Chained, his arms swaddling a post beam in a courageous endeavor to keep Hannah above the torrent that was over her head.

"Hannah. Remember me, Emily, Emily White."

Her glance was expressionless. She was much too exhausted to convey any emotion. "Netop-pauog," she uttered.

"What did she say?" asked Tyler.

"She called me friend."

"You understand Indian?"

"Wampanoag. Grandmamma often used the phrase."

"Grandmamma … I should have guessed." Tyler looked up at the chained woman with a consoling smile. "Remember me, Hannah?"

She looked and nodded. A beaming grin finally came to her tired face. "Little Tyler."

"Nana."

"You are a man, now."

"Hang on. We will get you out of here."

We had to undo the chain before we could let Hannah down. Malachi clutched the padlock tightly in his hand. He wrestled with the studded cast fastener, trying to free the looped shank securing the chain. Tyler tried prying the lock from his hand. The limb was a claw frozen in place.

"Malachi, let go," said Tyler. "I've got the key."

Half dead with fatigue, the slave looked up and shook his head, unable to let the lock free.

"He's been gripping it so long that his fingers are probably frozen to it," I said. "Here, let me try."

Tyler moved aside as I gripped the big man's hand. Carefully, I stroked and rubbed the circulation back into his stiffened fist. Eventually

I was able to pull one of his fingers away, then another, and another. The lock fell and swung from the chain. I kneaded Malachi's hand between mine until every digit was flexible and limber. Big brown watery eyes thanked me.

Tyler unfastened the chain and freed it from the ring on the shackle around his neck and from Hannah's ankle. I reached up, gripped Hannah's hand, and gave her a reassuring smile.

"We'll need to cut the rivets on those shackles," said Tyler. "But we can't do it here."

Simon reached up and took Hannah in his arms. I ran my fingers through her reddish-black hair, whisking it away from her face.

"We have come to take you home, Hannah," I assured her.

She smiled and nodded. Though I knew she believed me, after all that she had endured, I could tell she was uncertain that it would really happen.

Tyler helped Malachi gain the circulation back in his legs as we all wallowed toward the door. We were ready to make a hasty escape, or at least I thought. At that very moment, everything changed. Samson and Goliath started barking.

"Horses," I said. I peered out the barn door. The wind was back, and the sun was now hidden behind fast-moving caliginous clouds. I watched as three men climbed off their horses. I quickly closed the door.

"Who is it?" asked Tyler.

"Hard to make out, the house is a good distance away. Wait! It's Wilcox and his two cohorts."

"Did they see you?"

"No, I don't think so."

"They must know someone is here. Our horses are out there."

I continued surveillance through a narrow slit in the door. Tyler helped Malachi stay on his feet, while Simon cradled an exhausted Hannah in his arms. Battle plans are difficult when one is preoccupied with caring for wounded.

"What do you see, Emily?"

"The man with the beard … he's taking the horses away."

"That must be Hannibal."

"Looks like he's letting them run free in the field behind the house."

"Well, that complicates things, doesn't it?"

"They're all rushing inside, brandishing pistols. They must think someone's inside."

"What to do? What to do?" recited Tyler, rubbing his brow.

We were trapped on an island within an island. It did not take me long to realize that the natural mode of transportation to and from an island was a boat.

"We can use the canoe," I said. "Float it out the door and down through the swamp. Where do the swamp waters lead?"

"Out to open water," said Tyler.

"Unless you have another plan."

"Emily, I'm proud of you. It may just work."

I climbed up onto Tyler's shoulders and into the boat. Water flowed freely off my clothing. I was thrilled to find a stack of oars inside. From the ground, I had not realized how big the canoe really was. It was very similar to the whaleboats of Westport that are used to actually hunt down the whale, only narrower. Along the bilge, the water was above my ankles.

Before the wood planking on the newly built vessel could completely swell, water had permeated and filled the boat. Nonetheless, all fissures between the swollen planking had sealed and she floated nicely. Simon gingerly lifted Hannah up to me. I escorted her to one of the bunks inside the doghouse and made her comfortable. I stroked her face and deeply studied her big brown eyes.

"Hannah, are you alright? Is there anything I can do?"

"My ankle. It hurts."

The shackle around her leg had chafed all the skin above her foot. It was raw and swollen.

"We can't do anything for that right now. We'll have it off soon. Until then I'll make a bandage for your leg."

"I'll be alright."

"We have you now. There is nothing more they can do to you. The law is on our side."

"Law? Not here?" she sighed.

There was nothing I could say. She was right. It was up to us to get away. "It will be all good now, you'll see," I tried assuring her. "I'll never wear another cotton dress for as long as I live."

We laughed.

It was not long before we were all in the boat. After swinging the barn door open, Malachi lifted Tyler by the wrist and onto the vessel. Simon plunged the oars into the blackened water and rowed.

Once outside, we discovered that the wind had quickly accelerated. The storm's eye had passed, and we would soon be in a full gale. Whether the storm was friend or foe, only time would tell.

Chapter 27: A Drift into the Fray

With Malachi and Simon at the oars, we pulled away from the peninsula and into the confines of the swamp in good time. In the distance, Wilcox and his two companions ran over to the Swamp House with weapons drawn. Reluctant to wade into the water himself, Wilcox frantically ordered his two underlings to inspect the building. With their guns over their heads, they wallowed over to the flooded barn, unaware that there was no one there. Good fortune was on our side as we gathered a great distance away from the Wilcox property, even as the hurricane had returned for a repeat performance.

It was not long before the overseer realized that the canoe was missing. Once he established where we were, he rushed over to the edge of the engulfed bridge and watched as we escaped in the distance. He called out to his companions to fire their guns. I could see the flare and smoke from the rifle, shortly followed by the crack of gunpowder. We kept low, crouched in the boat to avoid any random shot. Tyler stood defiantly as gunfire erupted from the Wilcox property.

"Get down, Tyler, "I hollered. "They're shooting at us."

"They'll never hit us. We are too far off. The wind is blowing too hard for a bullet to reach us with any success."

Just as he made his calculated claim, I heard a swoosh as a slug whizzed by.

"Get down, Tyler!" I tugged at his arm.

He plopped down beside me. "They can't follow us without a boat," he said. "The main road goes off in another direction. The terrain this way is marshy. We should make good progress."

"Progress? Where to, Tyler? The house is gone."

Daunted, he slumped on the bench realizing what he had forgotten. "I … I don't know but we must leave the island. Preferably to the estate at Charleston."

"We can use the canoe to get to the mainland."

"No. We're on the wrong side of the island. The crossing to the mainland on this side is too wide to attempt in a storm."

"What shall we do?"

"We will need to get to the ferry crossing. How's Hannah?"

"Half dead with exhaustion."

"She doesn't look any different from what I remember," he said, a sad smile percolated on his lips.

"You called her Nana?"

He laughed. "Always called her Nana. When I was a little boy, I couldn't say Hannah."

"How sweet."

Hannah groaned.

"I'm going to see if she's allright," I said.

I looked ahead to where Malachi and Simon sat and rowed. We were gliding along faster than we could ever run. I moved into the enclosed doghouse and sat by a sleeping Hannah as we continued our drift through the towering cypress swamp. I looked up at the storm. The wind sliced through the top of wavering trees. Along the water's surface, it was placid and inexplicably silent. All that was heard was the distant, wailing howl of the menacing tempest against the gentle rowing of oars. Malachi expressed fear of the eerie ambiance and quietness of the swamp as an alligator dove in front of us. Tyler suggested that he sing one of the spiritual work songs like they often do in the fields. He and Simon sang their baritone chantey as they rowed.

A freshly uprooted tree lay across our path. But with the storm surge, there was plenty of deep water and we successfully rowed around it. Once out of the marshland, damaging gusts hit us with a vengeance. Malachi, who was familiar with the island, pointed out that the slave hamlet where Molly was taken was nearby. We beached the boat onto the muddy banks and hiked across a ravaged cotton field. The farmland was picked clean by the ensuing storm. Malachi had regained his strength and led the way. Hannah and I trudged onward hand in hand. I was concerned for her health. Though alert, she showed signs of excessive fatigue and a battered spirit. I have yet to speak with her about what she had gone through, nor did I feel I ever would. Some hardships are best left in the bleak and dreary past.

We stopped and rested by a grassy knoll. Suddenly, we heard cannon fire rumble in the distance toward the open bay. Over the horizon, Port Royal Sound was obscured by the crests of swaying trees. Sadly, the smoke from the burning mansion was still blowing wildly and could be seen from anywhere on the island. There was more cannon.

"Artillery," said Tyler. "I wonder where it's coming from."

"The Sound," I said. "The Union is attacking the forts."

"Oh, I don't think so … not Port Royal. If they did attack, it would be a stronghold further north, such as Charleston or south at Savannah. There's nothing worth capturing at Port Royal."

"Except a foothold between two major southern ports," I declared. "It's not about capturing a city. It's about starving them into submission … expanding the blockade."

"You think like a military man."

"It's what I learned. My boyfriend's in the army."

"Boyfriend, is that it?"

There was another blast, followed by a couple more. We all stood frozen, listening with misgivings but certain about the truth. Tyler pondered what I had said, that the forts were indeed under attack.

"Who conducts a military attack in a hurricane?" asked Tyler.

"How would anyone know it was coming?"

"I suppose … an attack on Fort Beauregard could makes sense. Tyrone is there."

"I overheard Tyrone talking to a confederate colonel outside the house very early in the morning about an eminent attack by the Union Navy."

"You never told me that."

"I didn't know what to make of it. This war is still an illusion to me. Unless one is in the middle of the fray, it feels like it's not happening … only in news dispatches."

"What is tat gunfire, Massa Ty?" asked Simon.

"Perhaps freedom is coming to South Carolina after all, Simon."

The cannon fire continued uninterrupted. There was no doubt an assault on the forts was under way. Altogether, my illusion had materialized into truth. If war was a theatrical play, we were altogether escorted to the front row.

"Let's move on," said Tyler.

After a slog across a ravished cotton field, we arrived at the slave hamlet. I walked by the old black fellow we had encountered the last time we were here. Strangely, he and another man were digging at the ground. They used planked pickets from a fence to dig as downy bolls of cotton blew by them from the fields across the way. The cabins all looked alike. I had forgotten which one Gideon was in. Malachi took us right to it.

Malachi and Hannah sat on the porch sheltered from the storm. They had cultivated an alliance that blossomed into a strong friendship. Sharing hardships customarily forged an invulnerable bond.

Molly burst through the door of the slave cabin with Clorina close behind.

"Oh Hannah, you're here, you're here," she cried, embracing the Indian woman. "I missed you so much."

The warm encounter rejuvenated Hannah's strength, giving her the resourcefulness to carry on. She kissed and stroked the young girl, embracing her with motherly devotion. Clorina looked over at Tyler while wiping tears. Cyrus stood by her. The slave shook his head.

"What is it, Cyrus?"

"Gideon done died, Massa Ty."

"What did he say?" I asked.

"Gideon has left us."

Words failed me. Most of the slaves from the tiny community congregated around Cyrus' cabin. Even at the height of a hurricane, slaves were dropping by to pay respect. Tyler and I went inside with Cyrus. The burlap cloth that was once used for a curtain now covered a proud man born without prospect and left to die lacking purpose. It seemed like the entire hamlet was inside the cramped quarters. I looked past the shoulders of mourners and over to what was once Gideon. Some of the female folk knelt and wept. An old slave woman praised the Lord that the dead man had finally gained his freedom. At the far end of the cabin, the infant cried for his mother. I was smothered by the anguish of death and heartbreak—of bondage.

Malachi and Simon walked in as I pushed by them. I held my head down to mask tears. Once outside, I took a deep breath and wiped my cheek. I sat by Hannah. Molly had her arms around the French family governess. Finding her had made up for the loss of Victoria, and Molly appeared content at the moment. We watched as the two men digging the ground continued their labor.

"What are they doing?" asked Molly.

"A grave," said Hannah. "Remember Molly, many years ago I traveled to a tiny Indian village on the shores of the Merrimack River to visit my uncle. We had received word that he was critically ill."

"He died, isn't that right, Hannah?"

Hannah tucked her arm tightly around the girl. "Yes. We had arrived too late and my uncle had passed away. Family and friends were making ready to dig a grave."

"I remember this story," said Molly. "You were just a little girl. You helped dig it."

"Yes, I did."

"How old were you?" I asked.

"You were eight years old. Isn't that right, Hannah?"

"And you helped dig a grave?" I asked.

"Helped. I was an only child. And although only men dug graves, the tribe felt it was a necessity of life and good for me to be close to Spirit Earth and learn how we all return to her."

As she told her story, the two men continued digging. I had not given it much thought earlier, but it was obvious. They were excavating a tomb.

"I remember the Indian men preparing the empty trunk," she continued.

"Trunk?"

"Yes, the body. It was brought out to the grave site and the Wampanoag ritual of wesquaubenan was performed—when the body is wrapped in animal skins and the dead man's burial mat. The legs were tied close to the chest with the chin rested upon the knees, as he once was in his mother's womb. Unlike white men, our loved ones are buried seated—an honored position."

Though I was very acquainted with the Algonquin burial ceremony, I listened intently.

"Inside the grave we placed my uncle's farming utensils—a hoe, a toothless rake, along with his bow, and some arrows. I was given the honor of placing his prized wampum armbands and winter deerskin mantle beside him. After he was veiled with earth, the bowl from which he ate his last meal was set on the grave along with his favorite pipe and a pouch of tobacco. We prayed to Washuanks, the ancient god of the Indian settlers to the Vineyard Island. Mourners smeared their faces in black soot and the ritual burial dance was offered to the god of water, earth and sky."

"You were very young to participate in such a ritual," I told her.

"I did not think so at the time. It was an observance of plenty. We all lingered around the grave and ate—then we slept by the moon … awoke and ate again; remaining with the dead as long as we could to help him pass to his new life where he could farm and hunt once more and have plenty."

"It's a fruitful afterlife image, isn't it?" I said.

"There is no such observance here today. Not even a shovel by which to dig the grave—just a break from sorrow to inhume the sorrowful."

"We must be going," cried Tyler, quickly exiting the house. We huddled together and hurried down the road behind him.

"Where are we going?" I asked.

"We must get off the island before Wilcox can find us."

I looked back. Simon had wavered.

"Is Simon not coming, Tyler?"

Tyler looked back at the loyal slave.

"Are you coming, Simon?" he yelled, his voice carried by the howling wind.

"I am not going, Massa Ty."

"Not going?" I cried. "We seek freedom!"

"What is it Simon?" asked Tyler.

"My people are on this here island, Massa Ty. I cannot leave them."

He placed his arm around Clorina. The servant rested her head on his shoulder and wept—wept for Gideon, for Victoria, for the unhappy life that they had led and would continue to lead. Simon tenderly kissed her. She embraced him.

"Do ya see what I mean, Massa Ty?"

"I see, Simon."

Tyler walked up to the black man and shook his hand. "I will never forget you, Simon. Perhaps we will see one another again."

"God willing, Massa Ty. If not, then in His presence."

"Goodbye, my friend."

The slave threw back his shoulders and held his head high. He felt proud and honored. It was probably the first white man whose hand he had ever shaken, and he knew it was a friend. I made certain to wave from a distance as we walked off. Anything more intimate was more than my heart could bear at the moment, even though I knew I would never see any of them again.

Unlike Simon, there was no way Malachi would have stayed behind. His fate was sealed on the Dukes plantation—or anywhere in the south. If he did not escape with us, he would be sold to never see his wife and child again. And having tasted freedom, he preferred the dish served Gideon than to work the fields one day more.

There was no respite from the wind as we trekked in route to the ferry crossing. On the other side of trees, along the horizon, cannon blasts continued. This time, they were accompanied by the blast of rifle fire. I made small talk to distract from the clatter.

"Tyler, did you know about Clorina and Simon?"

"It was a surprise to me," he grinned.

"They make a wonderful couple."

"No chance."

"You don't approve?"

"What I think doesn't matter. Tyrone and Wilcox control relationships between slaves—who gets married and who does not. The major rule is that house servants are not to wed."

"You serious?"

"Just the way it is," he said, hurrying ahead. "Just the way it is."

Hannah and Molly lagged behind. Malachi was well ahead, and I jogged to keep up.

"Wait up. How far are we from the ferry crossing?"

"A little over a mile," said Tyler

"What will we do when we get there?"

"With any luck we can take the ferry across."

I let him walk ahead and waited for Hannah and Molly. We walked arm-in-arm trying to stay on our feet in the blustering gale. Finally, we approached the way that led to the mansion that once stood several hundred feet up the tree-lined lane. All that was left was charred timber, smoldering embers, and disastrous memories. Slaves from fields all over the island loitered in the windstorm, gawking at the vestiges of a once palatial estate. Tyler stopped and considered the country boulevard at his feet. I knew he was drawn to take it, to return to what was no longer there.

"Keep walking, Tyler," I yelled.

Malachi was now well ahead of him. There was no way the black slave was waiting for those who wished to linger. I broke free from Hannah and Molly and ran ahead.

"We must hurry, Tyler," I pleaded, clutching and pulling him by the arm. "There is nothing left back there … only torment and agony. Let's keep moving."

He looked down at my hand then at my face. He shook his head—trying to understand why it all had to happen.

"We must keep moving, Tyler. The Storm! Wilcox!"

He looked up at the sky and back toward the smoldering remains of Dukes Mansion.

"Yes, yes. We must keep moving."

Our arrival at the ferry crossing was a distressing one. Not only were we cold, wet, and exhausted, but the ferry was gone.

"Are you sure this is the ferry crossing?" I asked.

"I'm afraid so." He pulled a very long rope tied to a post out of the water. The line was frayed at the end. "It has broken its mooring lines, see?"

"Where's the ferry?" Molly asked.

"This is the crossing to the mainland," said Hannah. "I remember it."

"It's the narrowest passage across the river and connects directly to the road for Beaufort," said Tyler, tossing the severed line to the ground.

"But there's nothing here. Just a couple of small boats," I said

There was a twenty-foot skiff and two dugouts floating on the river. One of the canoes was inverted in the water. The tree the boats were tied to was now in six feet of water. The boats snaked wildly to the rushing tide whilst the water rushed swiftly beneath them.

Tyler looked fatigued and worried. "In this deluge everything looks different," he declared, walking to the edge of the water. "The ferry should have been right here."

"Look!" Malachi pointed down river. The ferry was drifting toward the Sound.

We all stood poised by the edge of the rushing estuary, aghast by the scene unfolding in the middle of Port Royal Sound in the far distance. Not only could we hear artillery, we observed the bellowing smoke and flash of fire blazing out from the sides of warships. Gunboats and sloops-of-war circled the sound, firing their guns upon the shore.

The wind was letting up and it had started to rain. We rushed for shelter beneath the leafy canopy of a large oak tree. It was but a maneuver of habitual caution and seemed inconsequential since our clothing was already soused. We sat atop tightly bundled bales of cotton stacked under the tree. The cotton was covered with blankets of canvas keeping them dry. Evidently, the storm had foiled their delivery and they had been stored along the shore until the weather had lifted.

I sat and watched my country's civil war unfolding before my very eyes. Recollections of Samuel bled into memory. I felt as if I had deliquesced within the pages of a book and was conducting the action upon them. I was accusable, my behavior diabolical, sitting here, directing the arbitrary violence and repulsive performance between right and wrong, yet removed from the action and exceedingly complacent. I felt I had to take action—plug cannons with my fingers or take all the fighters by the collar and lead them to ignominious corners for a respite and appraisal of their deeds—in battle and in truce. Even if I could, there would be little I could do about their politics. And it would happen all again.

Though I felt strongly about moral principles, I had, in fact, chosen a champion in the fray. How glorious it would be to have triumph without casualties, defeat lacking affliction, and success without scars. Sadly, this was the perception one could employ in fiction, or the unrealistic expectations of a child. However, this was war, not storytelling, and I never envisioned that I would be this close—to behold the misdeeds and depravity of lugging iron through the air against ideals, which only betrayed humanity and one's Maker. I was thankful that I did not have to be up close to the specter of spilled blood and the purging of life. Perhaps I felt all these things because I would willingly step forward and engage in all the lunacy if it meant the freedom of black folk and an end to any measure of subjugation.

We had full view. The mouth to Port Royal Sound was flanked by two military forts and patrolled by a contingency of Confederate gunships. We hunkered beneath the tree in the open air, watching a whirlwind of Union warships circle an abstract stage with guns ablaze. It was truly an amazing sight and one that left me awe-stricken. There were multiple explosions along the combative coast as the bombardment took its toll. The Confederate citadels and supportive gunboats were no match for the Union naval armada. The coast was studded with an enterprise of military steamships and canvased war craft. Nearly twenty sloops-of-war, including naval frigates, circled the mouth of the bay and along an imaginary gyrating carousel. Like hawks circulating their hunting ground, the war ships sailed up one coast and down the other in a relentless amphitheater of hostility, as they unloaded cannon with a flurry of sound and punishing percussion.

Molly appeared unimpressed by the incredible history that was evolving at her very feet. Was the lack of interest due to the trauma caused by the death of her mother, or was it just the callowness of youth? She rested her head on the governess' shoulders, her arms around the Indian woman's waist. She looked detached. Fatigued, Hannah ignored the bloodshed along the distant horizon as she nearly fell asleep. After a while, even I lost interest and became bored with the butchery along the sound. On the other hand, Malachi continued to watch with uninterrupted fascination—a bruised spectator witnessing long-coming freedom as it battered in the proverbial door of inequity with cannon and black powder. He watched with toothed grin and I, for one, could not fault him.

"It will be dark soon, Tyler," I let him know. "What are we going to do?"

"The wind has died down a bit, but the waters are much too choppy. We may need do wait until morning when the swell will have gone down."

"Probably for the best," I agreed. "Hannah is run ragged and Molly also needs a good rest."

"I'm hungry," said Molly.

"So am I, dear," I said. "I'm afraid there is nothing we can do about it at the moment."

"There are some wild apple trees just beyond the ridge," said Tyler. "It's still early in the season, but you may find some ripe ones."

"I'll go look," she said. "Can you come with me Hannah?"

The Indian woman smiled and gladly took the young girl by the hand. It was reassuring to see the two of them together. Hannah supplied Molly with the motherly affection Victoria could never give. She had done so since Molly was born. And, at this time of peril, she was of great comfort and help.

Tyler broke up one of the cotton bales and spread the ginned fibers on the spongy grass, preparing a dry place for us to rest for the night. With his pocketknife, he cut up the coarse canvas cloth that covered the bales and fashioned blankets for each one of us. Not long after, Hannah and Molly came running.

"Horses are coming, horses are coming," cried Molly

"It's the overseer and his two companions," said Hannah.

"Everyone. Follow me," instructed Tyler.

I called out for Malachi who sat by the edge of the water watching the battle. We ran into a small, wooded area on high ground, stooped, and hid. Tyler and I watched from behind a fallen tree as Wilcox and the two men rode up. They stood by the rushing water's edge, pointing to where the ferry was once moored. Wilcox appeared oblivious to the military conflict occurring out at sea. One of the men roamed over to the bales. He studied the cotton along the ground and the cut-up canvas that once covered them. Wilcox was called over and the three men pondered the mystery, searching for any clues. Losing interest, they quickly got back on their horses and rode upriver along a grassy footpath.

"They're leaving," I whispered. "I wonder where they're going?"

"There are some slave cabins about a quarter of a mile upriver. They're probably going there," said Tyler.

"Looking for us."

"And any slaves that may be trying to escape."

"What will we do?"

"We can't stay here. They will be back."

We moved to the water's edge. Tyler studied the conditions of the river, hopelessly trying to determine a place to cross.

"It is me he wants," said Malachi. "He will not stop 'til he finds me."

"Are there places on the island we can hide?" inquired Tyler.

"Many places," replied the slave. "But Massa Wilcox come back with da hounds … they will find us."

"He's right," I said. "Wilcox is not concerned with you or me, it's Malachi and Hannah he's looking for."

"He will stop at nothing," said Tyler, pacing the shore. "Wilcox is a dangerous and unpredictable man."

"Why don't we take one of those?" asked Molly, pointing to the small vessels out on the water.

"Too dangerous right now," Tyler said.

"If I fall in, I can swim, you know,.

"Not in that current. We can't take a chance.

"Wait. Why can't Malachi and Hannah get away and take one of the boats?"

"Too risky."

"Not compared to what can happen to them if they are caught?"

"Even if they make it to the other side, a black man and an Indian woman traveling alone … they will not get very far."

"I got away befo'," said Malachi.

"Then why don't you go with them, Tyler?" I suggested. "Leave Molly and me here. We can stay with Cyrus and get across once the tide goes down."

"Wouldn't work."

"I don't want to stay here," pleaded Molly. "I want to stay with Hannah."

"No, Emily. With all that is happening, I can't take the chance and leave you and Molly here. Knowing Wilcox, he may just have you disappear … claim you died in the house fire."

"Then what shall we do?"

"We must stay together."

He walked into the river and stood in knee-deep water surveying the situation. The water churned and rushed around his legs in a burble of simmering folds while the surging current gushed by him.

"We will try the crossing," he said.

"All of us?" I blurted.

"All of us," he echoed, returning to shore.

"How will you get to those boats?" Hannah asked. They are out in deep rushing water."

"I will tie the severed rope that supported the ferry around my waist and wade out to them. I'll pull them back to shore."

"You cannot hold those boats in that rushing water," Hannah warned. "They will be swept away. Don't do it, Tyler."

"I've got an idea," I said. "Let's make a long line out of the cordage that is wrapped around the bales of cotton. Once Tyler gets out to the boats, he can tie the line to them, and we can haul them ashore. All that time, Tyler will be tied to the old ferry rope and he can safely pull himself to shore."

"Emily. You're an absolute da Vinci," proclaimed Tyler.

"Wasn't he a man," said Molly.

She was precious. I stroked her face. Tyler laughed.

"At least Emily and old Leo had the same hair."

I slapped him on the arm.

The plan was executed simply and smoothly. Two of the upright vessels were salvaged and dragged up partially onto the beach. We tied them to a tree. Tyler and I carefully inspected the two work vessels.

"We will take the skiff," I said.

"But the canoe is ten feet longer," declared Tyler. "And much faster to row."

"Longer yes, but the skiff is almost twice as wide. We need the stability, not speed, in that rushing side current. And you don't want to get broadside to the flow on a canoe."

"Listen to her," advised Hannah. "My people use canoes. They are very unstable."

Tyler looked over at Malachi. The black man shook his head.

"Up ta ya, Massa Ty."

"I've had lots of experience with small dories," I told him. "I've rowed them along a three-foot surf and over breakers and rollers right onto the beach."

"We will take the skiff, then," decided Tyler. "Any other advice, Captain?"

"Yes. Let's take as much line as we can gather along with a very large rock. A flat one if we can find one."

"A rock?"

"We will need a bower in case we can't make it to the other side or if we need to rest."

"A bower?"

"Yes, we will need an anchor. This way we can stop the boat from drifting out to the open Sound if the plan does not go our way."

"We are just going to the other side, Emily. It can't be more than seven or eight-hundred-foot gap across."

"A good sailor never leaves shore without an anchor. One never knows when you may need one."

"Anything you say, Captain." He shrugged his shoulders and rolled his eyes.

Hannah and Molly climbed into the flat-bottomed boat. I handed her the canvas blankets made from the tarpaulins over the bales of cotton. Once we were on the road on the other side, there was no telling how many nights we may spend under the stars, and the tarpaulins would act as blankets to keep us warm. I clambered aboard the skiff.

"To the back of the boat," I said. "It will lighten the load up front and Tyler and Malachi will push us off."

All three of us took a seat on the stern bench as Tyler and Malachi pushed the skiff out into the river. The stern suddenly twisted to the rushing current and the bow pivoted and swung out into deep water. Tyler barely made it into the skiff as it began to swiftly drift downwind. Malachi attempted to jump aboard and fell as the small boat heaved and jerked away from him. The slave plunged into the water and began to swim toward us. Unfortunately, the skiff had picked up speed. We watched hopelessly as he paddled vigorously. There was no possible way he could make it. He panicked as he flayed in the water and we got further and further away. We were being raptured by the current and so was he, but at a much slower rate.

"Swim Malachi, swim!" yelled Molly.

We all watched with fear as he floundered in the frothing surf. Tyler and I grabbed hold of the oars and tried paddling toward him. It was hopeless. There was no stopping the skiff's meandering advance, or the prevailing current as strong winds continued to blow. In the distance, the battle ragged. The warships appeared much closer now—cannon fire much louder. I had to do something if we were to save Malachi. My nautical intuition instinctively engaged. Quickly, I tied off the anchor line we had made to the protruding stem post at the bow.

"Throw in the anchor."

"What?" hollered Tyler.

"The rock … throw it overboard … now!"

He struggled with the large boulder that had the other end of the line tied around it. Finally, he got it up on the gunwale and pushed the large stone into the water. The line paid out quickly before snapping taut as the skiff almost came to a halt. Though we still drifted while the anchor dragged along the bottom, we did so at a much slower pace. Malachi, who could not swim very well, came upon us rapidly. Tyler reached over the side. Just as the man was about to drift by us, he clutched him by the arm. The weaving skiff twisted to the tightly knitted swells as the provisional anchor and line labored to hold us in place. Hannah and I reached overboard to help. Brown muddy water washed into the tiny vessel nearly sinking it as we heaved Malachi onto the skiff. At that moment, the improvised anchor line parted and we were once again carried swiftly down river. Malachi belched, disgorging a lung-full of brackish water. A joyous smile bloomed on his face. It was comforting to be alive.

Tyler took hold of the oars and commenced rowing for the opposite shore. Malachi helped. The skiff had drifted quite a way down river, and the passage across was much wider now. Progress was a crawl, if not all but futile. Suddenly, there was the sound of gunfire from the direction in which we left. Lead shot splintered the skiffs cap rail. We turned in the direction of the sound. A canoe drifted behind us and was picking up speed. It was Wilcox and his two cohorts. They had taken the canoe that was left on shore and given chase. We had little choice but to abandon our slow progress toward the mainland and, instead, direct the skiff down river, away from rifle fire and toward the Union warships and erupting cannon.

"It's Wilcox," yelled Tyler, "row, row!"

"The big ships," Molly cried. "They're getting closer."

"We should not have left the canoe on the shore," said Tyler.

"They are gaining on us," I hollered.

"The canoe's faster," I said. "But no. Let's take the skiff, you said."

"Oh, be quiet, Tyler. Row!"

"They stopped shooting," said Hannah.

"That's because they are catching up with us," I pointed out.

"That's the man, that's the man," cried Molly.

"What man, Molly?" I asked.

"The man I saw at the barn at home. The one with the gray coat."

"Yes, he is one of the men with Tyrone Dukes and Wilcox when they took us from New Bedford," said Hannah.

"They are coming," shouted Malachi.

Exhausted, Tyler stopped rowing. "I'm drained," he exclaimed. "The canoe's too fast."

"That's it," I reasoned, about to introduce a plan.

"Not another of your brilliant ideas."

"Quiet and listen. If they are the hare, we must become the tortoise, don't you see?"

"What?"

"Give me one of your oars."

Tyler handed me the paddle and despairingly threw his head into his hands.

"They are almost upon us," announced Hannah.

"Stop that boat," yelled Wilcox, as if we could pull a lever and engage a brake.

That's just what I'm attempting to do, I said to myself.

"Row toward the canoe, Malachi."

"Toward them, Miss Emily?"

"Yes, row backwards … try and stop the skiff's momentum …"

Malachi did as I commanded. The skiff lost speed as we rowed against the fast-moving current. The canoe continued accelerating toward us.

"What in God's name are you doing," cried Tyler.

"Taking the fight to them," I explained. "I'm going to ram them as they go by. Grab an oar and defend yourself."

"Ram them. Have you lost your mind?"

"Trust me."

"I'm afraid," cried Molly.

"Keep rowing, Malachi," I ordered. "Everyone hold on. I'm going to turn the bow upstream."

Hannah and Molly huddled at the stern bench. The young girl's nails dug into the governess' arms as fear tore at her. I plunged the oar into the rushing water at the stern. Employing the paddle as a rudder, I ordered Malachi to stop rowing. The skiff twisted, beam to the rushing water as its bow began to turn up stream. The canoe approached with astounding quickness. It was no easy task turning the boat as gushing water struggled to wrench the narrow rudder from my hands. Finally, we were pointing in the right direction. We were nearly hove-to when the canoe's beam rammed into our bow. The impact nearly split the narrow vessel in half. Hannibal was immediately tossed overboard. He cried out for help. His desperate yelp drowned in his mouth while the merciless current swept him away. Acting like a dam as it hung off our bow, the canoe began quickly taking on water. Malachi stood up and tussled with Wilcox. The overseer brandished his Bowie as he tried to board our tiny ship. Tyler swung an oar and knocked the knife out of the man's hand. Wilcox fell back and into the water.

Dweez discharged his pistol and a slug hit Malachi on the forearm. Just then, the teetering canoe swung athwart to the curling current. Finally, it turned over as I had expected. After he plunged into the water Wilcox hung onto the scuttled canoe's flat keel, while Dweez dangled onto our skiff's stern with his one good hand. He tried pulling himself aboard, clawing at the gunwale with the stub on his free arm. Molly sunk her teeth into the young man's veiny hand. He shrieked and let go. All three rogues were in the water, wallowing for their lives as I steered the skiff back down wind. Unfortunately, we were well into Port Royal Sound, far from shore, and drifting toward the Naval flotilla.

I watched as the overturned canoe drifted well behind us. Dweez, unable to swim, struggled to stay afloat. Hannibal was nowhere to be found, while Wilcox clung to the narrow, capsized vessel. I pulled the oar out of the water. The evasive maneuver I had taken was successful, even though it did not go as I expected. Perhaps not surprisingly, I became concerned for the three men.

"Should we go back and help them?" I asked.

"Oh, no, we're not," cried Tyler, tearing the oar from my hand and tossing it aside. The paddle tumbled over the side rail and into the water.

"What did you do that for?"

"Now look what you made me do."

"I made you do?"

"Can someone help me," pleaded Hannah, attempting to ease the bleeding on Malachi's arm.

Tyler used a pocketknife and cut a swathe of cloth from Molly's dress so Hannah could bandage Malachi's wound. The hurricane had subsided, and rain stopped falling, though it was quite breezy. But fresh troubles were coming our way. Ordnance fire hit the water around us as we drifted toward the warships—and along the shore, starbursts of soil and stone were flung high into the air as explosions crumbled Fort Walker's walls. The concussion from the ship's guns vibrated the very frames and gussets beneath our feet. We cringed and cowered with every blast. I looked back at the capsized canoe, feeling somewhat lugubrious but relieved. I thought about how peculiar it was that I should be so concerned for the wellbeing of the fiendish James Wilcox, or sorrowful for the scoundrels Hannibal and the boy named Dweez. In retrospect, they had endeavored to harm us and were directly responsible for poor Gideon's death—and possibly their own. Yet, I grappled with bewildering mercy for these agents of calamity whose sole devotion was to enslave and harm others. Though I knew it was for the best, I could not deny the worrisome duty of wanting to turn back and help them.

We had lost two oars. With one sturdy set remaining, Tyler rowed toward shore. The plan was beset by raining lead and cannon shot. To place our little boat between the warships and the forts along the beach was self-immolation. Strangely enough, the safest place to be was the heart of Port Royal Sound, right down the center and in Armageddon's ring of fire. Aerial munitions fell just beyond the skiff. I waved a white cloth as an exercise of surrender. Union war ships circled us in a punishing necklace of naval might, discharging their guns toward the mainland. One of the Union gunships broke rank and sailed over to inspect as we drifted through the center of the fray. It must have realized that two men and three women were no threat and fell back in queue giving no further consideration to our presence.

Dusk was falling rapidly. With Malachi unable to row, Tyler manned the oars and took us past the battlefield and beyond Hilton Head. We were in open waters, finally out of range of fire. There was not much we could have done but escape the encounter between the blue and gray and pursue safety out at sea. Night had fallen upon us. Outside Port Royal Sound, I could just make out a compliment of ships hove-to in the darkness—some with beacons and others without. There were perhaps forty or more of them ghosting along the coast and probably consisting of ammunitions vessels, cargo ships, and troop transports. It was obvious that an invasion of fort Beauregard and Walker was in progress.

I had taken the remnants from the broken anchor rode and tied it around Molly, Hannah, and myself, in the event one of us fell over the side at night. Tyler expressed humor in my nautical security scheme but, without hesitation, tied himself to the skiff also. Exhausted, and with blistered hands, he sat back and rested. We were too far out of range from any of the supply ships along the coast to beg rescue. It was too dark and, having no lantern, they could not see us as we drifted hidden between mountainous crests of migrating waters. The sea was blanketed by an enormous swell left over from the storm. Though I could not see the waves in the darkness, I felt the flutter in my tummy every time the boat rose and plunged. Nonetheless, the waves were not breaking, and it was not as dangerous as one would expect. Every once in a while, we took some water over the side and had to use our boots to bail. It was difficult to stay dry and there was not much we could do until morning, when we would try and row back to shore. We each found a safe corner, wrapped ourselves in canvas, and tried to stay warm and get some rest. Tyler and Malachi kept watch.

I was asleep when Molly shook me by the arm. I thought I had dozed for a minute or two but, in fact, morning had arrived. I jumped up and yawned. My eyes were pasty and dry. Along the horizon, daybreak infused a salmon sky. Below me, the rushing sea foamed and fizzled as we surfed down bellowing swells.

"Emily, I'm cold," she cried, holding the canvas cloaked over her shoulders and shivering. The morning was raw and cold. How I wished for the heat of the cotton fields.

"I know you're cold, dear. We all are."

"I'm afraid … we're so far out in the ocean."

I sat up and looked around. South Carolina and its lowlands were but a smudge across the horizon. I could no longer see any of the warships as the skiff was pushed north. Poor Tyler was fast asleep.

"Tyler, wake up."

"Oh my Lord. How long have I been asleep?"

"We have all been asleep. It's morning." I searched around me. "Where's the other oar?

"What other oar?" he replied, looking around the skiff.

"There are supposed to be two oars. I can only find one."

"Oh, dang! I must have left it tied to the gunwale. It must have fallen overboard."

"Fallen overboard! How could you let such a thing happen?"

"Sorry. I was tired and … I, I was must have passed out."

"What will we do now?" asked Hannah. "How will we get to shore?"

Tyler stood up and scanned the ocean. "We must be ten miles or more from land."

"I can see that," I snapped, angry with myself for not being more vigilant.

"I'm afraid," cried Molly.

"It will be alright, Molly," I said, though I did not care much to lie.

"How will it be alright?" she asked. "Tell me, how?"

I looked over at Hannah with desperate eyes. She pulled the young girl over and held her tightly in her arms.

"It will all work out, my little qunnequawese. God will watch over us."

Malachi was stretched out along the floor, his injured arm resting on the rowing bench. His eyes were closed though he was awake.

"How are you feeling, Malachi?" I asked, though I knew he was in pain.

"Fine, Miss Emily. Any day away from Dukes Plantation is just fine."

"At least you can thank the good Lord that Ruth and Queenie are safe."

"Praise da Lord," he sighed. "I know they was hiding in da barn."

"They are safe now. Probably already in Nova Scotia."

"They is gone north?"

"Yes. It was not safe for them to remain in the States much longer. Mr. French made arrangements for their flight into Nova Scotia. I expect they are there by now. Before long, you will be with them… safe in a new land."

He smiled. It was a mournful smile. He hung his head in silence."

We all sat quietly, listening to the rushing waves and watching a gurgling sun break through a barren seascape. Tyler picked up the solitary oar and used it as a paddle. He wedged himself at the bow and paddled from one side of the skiff down the other. It was hard work and not very productive. He paddled for most of the morning, but land never looked any closer. He extended one arm and shook his hand robustly, as the blisters on his fingers burst and the salt water scalded the wounds. Drained and weary, he tumbled into the skiff feeling defeated and overcome by emotion. I clambered over and took him in my arms.

"Rest, Tyler, rest."

He held his head in his hands feeling guilty about the circumstances that he left us in. "We should have never left the island."

"We all made that choice, Tyler."

He looked over at Molly. "I have failed her."

"Were not conquered yet. I have an idea."

He looked up at me. His eyes brightened. "You do?"

"We can use that one oar as a spar. We wedge it in the middle of the skiff, stand it up, and use the anchor line as stays and shrouds to hold it in place."

"And use one of the canvas blankets as a sail," he enlightened me.

"Yes."

"The wind should push us ashore."

"It should. Not at any great speed but any headway would be a progress."

"How will we steer? There's no rudder."

"We can steer with the sail, by adjusting it. And if that doesn't work, we can dismantle one of the benches and make a rudder … hang it off the stern. And we can use this." I held up the sinister looking Bowie knife.

"Where did you get that?" he asked.

"Must have fallen into the skiff when you hit Wilcox with the oar."

"Think your plan will work?"

"We have plenty of line and the knife. One can accomplish great things with some twine and a blade."

"Let's get started."

An hour later, we had the rig in the air and sailing toward the Carolina coastline. Everyone was joyous. Molly even smiled. The spar was sloppy and shook violently in a stiff southerly breeze. Unfortunately, after an hour the wind shifted and blew out of the wrong direction. We were sailing further away from land.

It was time for plan B. We ripped out one of the benches and built a rudder. After some convoluted carpentry using the Bowie knife, we had the plank hanging off the stern. The skiff had some steerage, and we were able to navigate toward shore. Just as we celebrated our dubious achievement, a rogue wave carried the improvised rudder away. Adding misfortune to injury, the oar we had used for a makeshift mast snapped in two and the sail blew over the side. We all sat stunned and battered, unsure what to do next. Our only salvation was a wind shift out of the east to push the little dory toward dry land.

We huddled beneath the canvas and shielded ourselves from the scorching noon sun. We had gone from a chilled icebox to a blaring oven. It was too hot to think. Thirst preoccupied us. Salt and sunlight out at sea has a somniferous reaction, one that anesthetizes the mind and spirit. It charms us into capitulation and restful abandonment of all our worries, even as it absconds the dreams of the foolish while it eases the uncertainties of the wise. It was how I felt; beguiled by the sea and its simplicity—hypnotized by gentle breakers and the repetitious serenade of breaking surf.

I stretched out on the bench and rested my head upon the gunwale and tried to sleep while praying the wind direction would change or a passing ship would find us. My eyes were level with the sea—at other times, the swells towered ten feet above my head. A sea of sargassum weed carpeted the undulated surface of the ballooning waves. Perhaps Tyler was right. We should never have left the island. We should have remained and taken our chances. But that would mean torment for Malachi. And with Victoria gone and the dissolution of the relationship between Tyler and Tyrone, it would leave the boy with questionable leverage over the faith of slaves or even the well-being of Molly and I. After all, it was an island with nowhere to hide. I reflected on the Union Navy's invasion. If, in fact, they moved ashore, liberation would be won for Dukes Plantation slave hands.

The sun was hot on the side of my face. I pulled the canvas tarp over my head to shield from the swelter. The cloth had a musty smell. I found the odor nauseating and stifling. I tore the heavy fabric away. Fostering no concern, I watched a flock of seagulls circling above as they often did with fishing vessels. I could not help but respect them. Mobility was the ultimate freedom—birds rule the sky with such laxity and volition, with the liberty to come and go, even beyond the sight of land.

A wave slammed the side of the skiff, wetting my face and hair. It soon dried, leaving behind its serum of friable salt on my cracked, efflorescent lips. I listened to the raucous roar of the breaking waves as they mushroomed then deflated only to languish into silence—over and over. At times, this watery desert taunts one's awareness with all sorts of unexpected utterances like the sound of people, places, and things, which are not there at all. I even heard Grandmamma plainly call out my name once and the grinding wheels of a carriage twenty miles off the New England coast.

The only specious relief to thirst was sleep. I dozed off to the illusive and flirtatious sound of slapping sails. The delinquent cloth whipped and fractured the forestalling air then fell into impending silence. I envisioned gleaming canvas standing at attention, tugging wildly until tethered with knobby sheets onto bronze cleats. Its peculiar the way the breeze and our clever minds conspire to deceive persuasive ears into hearing what is not there.

Again… it sounded. This time the wind impersonated a man singing. Or was it a whistle—now laughter. Was it mocking me? I listened carefully to the spanking sound of flogging cloth—this time more emphatic than before. Having sailed on the schooner *Sphinx*, the informal sound of a maneuvering sailing vessel was infused in my brain and, at this very moment, acting out in the deep hollow recesses of my aspirations to be saved. It appeared my ears chose to wallow in buffoonery, perhaps to ease the enigmatic boredom of the moment… I don't know. How beguiling and real it sounded. I knew better. There was nothing there. I tried to doze. A short time later, I was awakened by the same familiar lashing—an exhilarating commotion of delinquent canvas. I listened carefully in the event Grandmamma would speak to me from over the boundless, barren waters. I again tried dozing. It was of no use. The thrashing had migrated from the duplicitous depths of perception to the threshold at my ear's doorstep. But unlike all the other times, this moment sounded absolute and resounding. I lifted my head, widened my eyes, and peered over the skiff's rail. To my amazement I could see it plainly—as sure as foam blistered the top of the bellowing swells. Were my eyes now colluding with my ears to deceive me? I jumped to my feet. There it was on the distant horizon. Considering our dire circumstance, it was the most glorious sight I had ever witnessed.

"A ship, a ship!" I yelled, my finger as far over the rail as I could extend it.

At that very moment, a rogue wave struck the small vessel, knocking me off my feet.

"Where?" cried Tyler, helping me up.

I pointed. "There. See it?"

"I don't see anything."

"I'm sure of it!" I held a shaky finger out in the breeze. "It was there, right there, on the horizon!"

We studied the seascape in the direction of my guiding digit.

"The ocean's playing a trick on you, Emily," he said.

I continued to point. Nothing was there.

"I don't see a ship, dear," said Hannah.

I wistfully lowered my arm. "But I heard the sails flapping… I heard them; I tell you."

"We are all hearing things," explained Tyler.

"I heard Mama call ma' name in da night, Miss Emmie," declared Malachi.

I slumped onto the bench. "I suppose you are right… hearing things."

"No! It's over here!" shouted Molly. "Over here!"

The ship was behind us. I had lost my bearings when the wave twisted the tiny skiff, and I was pointing in the wrong direction.

Tyler began wildly signaling with his arms. "Here, Ho! Here!"

The ship came about and sailed away.

"We are too far off," he sighed. "Ho, ho! Over here!" Deflated, he slumped and threw his head into his hands, running them down his face. "It doesn't see us."

"Try again, Tyler, try again," wailed Molly.

He stood up on the bench, legs spread, as if height made him more discernible, and waved the broken oar frantically. The skiff dipped down deep into a trough between ten-foot swells. We lost sight of the ship.

"Keep hollering, Tyler, keep hollering," implored Molly.

The tiny vessel scaled the crest of the next wave. The distant ship came into view once again.

"Here, Ho, ho, here!"

I watched intently as the vessel tacked and fell onto a new course. In the distance, its fluttering sails filled with air and stiffened as the glistening white hull flickered in the sunlight and gracefully glided away from us.

"They will be coming this way," I said. "I'm sure of it!"

"It is sailing off in another direction," jeered Tyler. "Anyone can see that!"

"No, you don't understand. I heard them come about. They will do it again."

"No, I don't understand."

"You see, they are tacking forty degrees to port, left, then forty degrees to starboard, right… into the wind in a zigzagging track. They will have to tack again… in our direction."

"And?"

"You don't know much about sailing, do you?"

"Can't say I do. Been on a plantation most my life."

"You are right. We are probably too far away to be seen. But she will be sailing in our general direction and likely close enough for us to signal her."

He continued waving his arms in the direction of the schooner.

We watched longingly as the vessel crept across the horizon. Earlier, I was certain that I had heard the sound of flapping sails as the din was delivered on the wind and across the vast ocean. I cannot tell you how that was possible with the ship so far off. Perchance the sounds were a contrived prognostication brought about by a desperate mind or the gift of unexpected clairvoyance. If the schooner had tacked afore, I was certain it would tack anew.

We watched for a very long time. It appeared that the ship would pass us in the distance. Hannah and Molly had given up watch and hid from the blaring sun beneath the canvas tarpaulin. Malachi lay in the bilge nursing his injured arm while Tyler slumped between them, whittling at the broken oar with the Bowie.

"It can't see us, Emily," he declared, "it's sailing on."

Toward the back of the boat, I could hear Molly crying. I lifted the canvas over her and offered some comfort.

"Don't cry, sweet girl. We must have faith."

"I'm so thirsty," she sobbed.

Her cheeks were sun burned and lips cracked and swollen. There was nothing I could do for her and even less I could say. If only I had my thirst stone. We all suffered from the same affliction. But she was just a child and to suffer in such a way was heartbreaking to watch.

"I can read you a prayer if you like."

I pulled my prayer book from my pocket. It had been there since I left Dukes Mansion. The pages were saturated and fused together.

"That's the prayer book you keep by the bedside," she said.

"Yes. It was my Grandmamma's. I'm afraid I need to dry it out."

"That's alright," she said. "You can read to me later."

"Yes, I will," I said, stroking her face. "You'll see."

I looked over at the horizon. The schooner was getting further away. I sat down by Tyler. He glumly carved at the split oar. Coiled shavings littered the aqueous bilge below his feet.

"What are you making," I asked.

"Nothing. Just trying to shed some frustration."

"I was thinking. When we get back home you can resume medical school—attend Brown University in Providence or perhaps Harvard in Boston."

"Right now, I would be happy as a lamplighter or store clerk, anything away from the sea."

"I don't blame you. However, it's not the sea's fault."

"Can't be moe free dan we'a now," chuckled Malachi.

"Sorry I got you into to this, Malachi."

"No'sa, Massa Ty, you give me freedom. An' right now I is as free as you."

"You are right there."

"We need to get out of the sun," I said.

I placed a sheet of canvas over the both of us. A dirty sun shined through the soiled cloth casting a dusky radiance. Tyler looked quiet and forlorn. No one had more right than he had to feel so. After all, it had been only a little more than twenty-four hours since he lost his mother.

Throwing back his head, he closed his eyes. The skin on his face was singed and blistered from the house fire. I ran my fingers over the welting wounds along his face.

"Does it hurt," I asked.

He shook his head. "Burns a little when water splashes in my face."

I let him rest. I shut my eyes and listened to the rushing waves fondling the skiffs planking. Every now and then there was a lashing spank followed by a brisk spray as the playful sea had its way with our tiny ship. Hauntingly, I thought I caught Samuel's voice tossed by the wind.

"Prepare to heave-to, slacken that jib," it said. It was soothingly familiar if not memorable. I smiled. How I missed him. Suddenly there was the trashing of canvas whipping in the wind. My eyes widened. Tyler looked over at me, his mouth dropping open.

"Did you hear that?"

"Prepare to hove-to," the voice said again.

Everyone in the skiff leaped out from beneath the sun shelters. To our amazement, the glimmering ship was sailing toward us less than a quarter mile away. At its stern was the stars and stripes fluttering in full glory. Up in the crosstree, hung a large yellow flag. I jumped to my feet astonished by what I saw and toiling not to fall over the side.

"It's a hospital ship," said an elated Tyler.

We stood clinging to one another.

"How do you know," I asked.

"That yellow flag up in the rigging. They fly those over military hospital installations or field infirmary. Knowledge acquired in my first year of med school. We could not expect a more suitable rescue."

"We're saved!" cheered Molly.

We all watched breathlessly as the hundred-foot vessel maneuvered to rescue us. It was then I noticed the breadth and significance of what I was witnessing. The ship ghosted over slowly as it dropped sail. I noticed two men standing tall and proud in acrobatic pose, poised precariously along the very tip of the ship's bowsprit. One rested his hand on the shoulder of the other. Their deportment appeared very familiar. Instantly a rush of warm tears erupted when I realized who they were—Timothy Cadman and the high-spirited Aaron Kerr. Furthermore, tarrying along the rail, I recognized the abstruse Winton Macartney and the youthful Cuffee brothers—Eli Monroe poised royally at the wheel.

"The *Sphinx*," I shouted.

"The what?" cried Tyler.

I opened my mouth, but words did not come. I gaped at the schooner as it turned several hundred feet from us and hove-to. Finally, the helm came into view.

"My sweet Lord," I blurted. I sat down before I almost fainted. The reward of a simple rescue had just been transformed into a grandiose event, one wrapped in a dream and revealed only in fiction. A shiny new dory was cast over the schooner's rail and into the sea as they prepared to come along side.

"Are you alright, Miss Emily," asked Malachi.

I just nodded as tears poured down my face.

"It's Emily," yelled Timothy, from the schooner sprit. "Emily!"

The captain left the quarterdeck and scampered along the rail for a better look.

"Emily, is that you? Emily!"

I jumped up. "Samuel!"

"I see now," said a smirking Tyler. "So, that is the great Samuel."

"The great, *great*, Samuel," I pronounced.

Chapter 28: Gone Once Again

The *Sphinx*'s anchor rode, clanked, and rattled as it fed out over thirty feet of water to the shell-littered seabed below. We had anchored just north of Joiner Banks at the mouth of Skull Creek. Port Royal Sound had become a metropolis of Union naval craft following the North's decisive victory. When we arrived, transport troop ships were still unloading young recruits, dressed in blue uniforms with their innocence on their sleeves, all with angelic hearts. Dispatched on the heels of a naval victory, I was certain, once inland, they would encounter unholy providence and dissolution adorned in gray and hiding behind every tree.

The *Sphinx* had been unofficially commissioned as a medical transport. Its job was to ferry the more seriously injured soldiers from the battle of Port Royal to the newly built Harewood General Hospital, a state-of-the-art pavilion style facility in Washington, D.C. On shore, troops were heading north and expected to take Beaufort and move on to Saint Helena Sound, knocking on the back door of Charleston itself.

The good fortune behind our rescue was nothing short of a marvel—I dare say a miracle, at least for me. The only explanation I can give is that this was destiny cultivated with divine intervention. How else can I explain Samuel returning into my arms by saving my life? With all the ships in the world, it was the *Sphinx*, a schooner from Point Village that liberated us from a salty demise.

I had discovered that Samuel was never really missing in battle. His disappearance was intentional and executed by design and kept secret. He had been on a clandestine assignment, a confidential flight to reconnoiter and scope out the enemy's strength and positions along Port Royal Sound, before the Union could make an attack. Once his mission was completed, he was sent home to appropriate the *Sphinx* for an entirely new assignment—a quest of mercy.

The interior of the *Sphinx* was completely refurbished. Folding hospital bunks were integrated along the port and starboard sides from bow to stern and deck to overhead. Accommodations were designed for sixty to seventy of the most seriously injured troopers, those who could not return to service. The crew was a familiar one, though Samuel was the only confirmed and endorsed Union servicemen.

The *Sphinx* was not part of the Union navy nor was its crew. The duty assigned to it was unorthodox, to say the least, in a last-minute resolution to fulfill the needs of the Port Royal mission. I've been told that the Union navy would like to purchase, if not expropriate, the schooner for its war effort. Though one of the fastest yachts along the east coast, it was lightly built and not intended for large payloads or military exercises. It was a gentleman's vessel and I hoped after its work was done here that it would return to Point Village in Westport and remain a gentleman's vessel for the duration of hostilities and beyond.

Hannah and Molly were given bunks behind a bulkhead by the galley stove. Malachi and Tyler chose to bunk with the crew up on deck where they were sheltered beneath tents.

Considering the expanse of the attack on Port Royal, in numbers and firepower, it is a wonder that less than ten sailors were killed. Though any quantity of death is a tragic consequence. This meant that the number of wounded was a fraction of what the *Sphinx* came prepared for and there would be much more vacant bunks than filled ones.

The *Sphinx* remained at anchor for two days. In that time, Samuel and Tyler had become good friends. With a year of medical school, Tyler's competence as a medic was both expedient and beneficial. A proper medical doctor was transferred to the schooner from one of the warships to assist Silas Brownell, who I was surprised to see aboard, to make the injured comfortable and ready for the voyage to the hospital in Washington.

With the crew bedded down for the night, Samuel and I sat on the rope locker up on deck savoring a waxing gibbous moon. The silence and tranquility of the bay was disrupted by the reverberating steam engine of a patrolling gunship as it slithered by in the shadowy moonlight. Late night was the only time of day in which we could relish time together. I wished that we could have gone ashore, away from everyone, to walk along the golden Carolina beach—just the two of us. But military decree prescribed that no one was allowed to leave the ship.

Too much time had elapsed between Samuel and me. There was so much for us to reinvestigate in one another—to rehabilitate our courtship, to tangle with sensuality, or delight in the privilege of slapping a wandering hand. At this very moment, my desire is to provoke taboos between scandal and shame and, by doing so, disregard vestal proprieties in lustful exchange of guiltless transgressions. I had missed him so much. Perhaps it was best that we are not left alone. After all, yearning and passion may very well have betrayed me.

"Samuel, must you leave again?" I asked.

"I have little choice."

"But it has been a year. Your enlistment should be over."

"Enlistment contracts no longer apply, I'm afraid. A new conscription mandates that I need to serve at least another year."

"It just doesn't seem fair."

"It's for a righteous cause."

"But I missed you and you missed me. It's not easy to be alone."

"I know," he said. "When I was out in the field, you were all I ever thought of."

He kissed me. The bridled walls of constraint conceded to a craving heart as my lips compressed his with feral impulses. A concupiscent hunger bonded our hearts like rabid lovers, a conduct that left many a lonely girl widowed by treasonous passion and lamenting with corporeal regrets. His firm but tender hand cradled the nape of my neck as I moved and sat in his lap for more. I felt like I was thirteen again—my first kiss with Billy Briggs behind Perry Davis' barn. But instead of the pubescent giggling I uttered that day, my heart labored to breathe while he left me breathless and wanting. I could not get enough of him. There was no road that I would not have traveled to satisfy the affection I felt at that very moment. And while I kissed his sweet brandy lips, the intoxication of the moment became overwhelming. I was swimming too deep. I quickly surfaced for air, breaking the shadows of intimacy and leaping to my feet.

"What's wrong?"

"Nothing."

I walked over to the edge of the ship. Leaning over the cap rail, I stared down into the black waters. He was leaving for the battlefield in the morning. I would miss him. I did not want to torment my heart any longer.

"Then why did you walk away?"

He walked over and stood by me. We both stared out over Port Royal Sound, sorting out contrary puzzles in our heads. Me—how I would miss him. He—why I rudely ended a passionate moment. Men and women perceive intimacy on such contrary levels. Why is it that a man must have affection to engage in love, while a woman, love before engaging in affection? I dare shame myself by confessing that I was ready to think and perform as my male suitor had wished. But not to a lover I may never see again—hold again. It was unthinkable. Even Samuel.

"You are leaving in the morning," I said

"Yes. Tim will captain the schooner home."

"And I will be left alone once more."

"And I also. And while you wait in comfort, I must wait in battle."

I felt that he was positioning me for a stroke of guilt. And he was right. I was being selfish. After all, it was not his fault that military conscription would keep us apart.

"I'm sorry, Samuel. It was uncaring of me."

"No, no, I was being cruel."

He took me in his arms.

"I love you, Emily White. You have become my world."

Our lips came together once again. At that very moment, Professor Winton Macartney came strolling up the deck. With an oily rag in hand, he wiped each finger, one by one. It made little difference to him that Samuel and I were having an intimate moment. His way of thinking was flanked only by scientific and analytic duty. He was oblivious to a tender moment when he saw one, or perhaps held it in little regard. Knowing Winton, it was not flagrantly intentional but rude, no less.

"I'm done oiling the engine, Captain. I have rectified that leaking manhole gasket and rebuilt the combustion chamber safety valve."

"Thank you, Mister Macartney."

"It's Professor Macartney, Captain. As you have your designated title, I have mine."

I could see that Samuel was set aback by Winton's trite adjuration. He stood at attention and facetiously saluted.

"I shall not salute, Captain, since I am a private citizen," declared Winton, continuing to wipe his hands.

Samuel looked over at me and rolled his eyes. It was evident that Winton had no sense of banter. But I already knew that.

"Very well, Professor."

"I shall start her up at six thirty. I assume that we will be steaming out into open waters at seven, Captain?"

"Your assumption is correct, Pro-fess-or."

"Well, I bid you goodnight, then."

We stood watching as Winton marched away, the oil rag sticking out of his back pocket.

"He reminds me of Mister Oliver in the sixth grade," declared Samuel.

I laughed. "Yes, I remember. He had waxy white skin and used to make us stand at attention and salute the flag and pledge a prayer for the country."

"He was a funny fellow."

He smiled as our childhood past filtered through his memory. He put his head down and grimaced.

"He was killed a couple of months ago at the battle of Booneville in Missouri."

"Oh no, Samuel. You're not serious."

"I'm afraid so."

"Poor Mister Oliver."

The Union gunship we saw earlier chugged by and dropped anchor. A man with a lantern walked its decks and announced the time of night as if we were children out late and needed to get ourselves inside.

"Twenty-two hundred hours. Everyone to your berths and all lanterns!" cried the man.

"I'm going to bed," I decided. "I'm tired and sunburned."

"Yes, of course. You have had a couple of terribly trying days."

I walked toward the stern of the ship and my berth below deck.

"Are you not going to walk with me, Samuel?"

"In a couple of minutes. A captain has his duties, even late at night."

Something was disturbing him. On second thought, something was disturbing all of us. Perhaps it was the war. And considering my demeanor just minutes ago, I was hopeful that there was no war between us.

"See you in the morning," I said.

He gave me a wistful, if not troubled, smile.

I was awakened from my bunk by the shuffling of feet. It was early morning and still dark outside. Someone was up and moving about the cabin. I verified that Molly was asleep in the bunk above me and Hannah in the one below. The man on the gunship anchored nearby shouted for his crew to awaken. "Zero five thirty hours. Arise and serve your country," came the call. The footsteps in the cabin got closer. I closed my eyes and pretended to be asleep. A pair of spongy lips brushed a gentle warm kiss on my temple. I opened one eye as the kisser scuffled away.

"Samuel," I whispered.

He didn't hear me. I closed my eyes and soon fell back asleep.

I was awakened an hour and a half later by the rumble of the chugging steam engine deep down in the bilge. The hatch on the floor was lifted and Winton Macartney stood below taming his mechanical beast. Hannah was already up on deck. When I looked in on Molly, she was sleeping like an angel. The cabin was a floating infirmary of no less than twenty or more injured sailors. Hollow groans and whining murmurs softly resonated as Doctor Silas Brownell and Tyler helped save a man's shattered arm. The whining and cries got the best of me. I draped myself with a small blanket and hurried up on deck. My day began with a pleasant encounter with the valiant Aaron Kerr.

"Ah, lassie, ah see ye up."

"Aaron. Good morning."

"How ar'ye?"

"Fine."

"Ah hae some breadfest fur ye," he said, pulling an apple from his pocket. He rubbed the furbish fruit on his shirtsleeve. "Mackintosh fur mah lady. Tis my last one."

"That is sweet of you, Aaron."

"Aaron Kerr, where are you?" yelled Winton from down in the bilge.

"Got tae go, lassie."

Before I could say anything more, he scurried away. I was fortunate that I did not blink when I first saw him. The young Scotsman moved and spoke so rapidly that I would have missed him altogether.

On deck, the crew was making ready for the sail to Washington. Timothy sat by the helm with Hannah while she instructed him on a weave of line and how to lace a hammock. I searched the deck for Samuel. Razor was at the bow with the Cuffee brothers getting the capstan ready to lift the anchor.

"Have you seen Samuel, Admond?"

"He is gone, Miss Emily."

"Gone? What do you mean gone?"

"He left on the Union boat that was anchored just there."

I looked over to where the gunboat with the shouting man was once moored. It was gone. I ran back toward the stern.

"Timothy! Have you seen Samuel?"

"He left early this morning. Gone with the troops to Beaufort."

"What do you mean?"

"Didn't he say goodbye?"

A stroked my temple where he kissed me. "Yes, yes, he did," I said, forlornly, looking down.

"Are you alright, Emily?" A finger beneath my chin, he lifted my face. "Don't worry about Sam. He's a good soldier. I'm sure he'll be fine."

"Safe … yes, yes of course."

"We will be leaving in a half hour. Eli is below. He'll make you something to eat."

"Yes, sure," I mumbled, plopping myself down by the helm.

"Well, if you can excuse me, I need to get us ready for departure," he said.

"Of course."

Timothy went off to attend to ship's duties. Sensing my despondency, Hannah came over and sat by me.

"Captain Samuel Cory's your man, is he?"

"Yes. I was hoping we would marry soon." I sat quietly, looking over the rail to where the gunboat was once moored.

"He seems very capable of taking care of himself," said Hannah. "Don't worry about him, dear. Such doings will only bring hardships on you and on him. My mother had a rhyme which she recited when my brother went fishing overnight in the dangerous waters off the village of Aquinnah on the Vineyard."

"A rhyme?

"Yes, in Wampanoag. I translated it best I could. It went something like: A joyful heart when you awake at dawn, will keep him safe while he is gone."

"Very encouraging words."

"He will come home to you once again. I can feel it."

"Thank you, Hannah. I'll try and adopt your advice."

She patted me on the hand. "I'm going to check in on Molly."

"Yes, of course."

Hannah's words were a gift of comfort. Regrettably, once she left, the offering of reassurance quickly melted away. Perhaps, in time, I will learn to live without Samuel and feel at peace with myself, assured that he will return to me safely someday.

It looked like it would turn out to be a glorious day. Enemy flags that once flew over Fort Walker and Beauregard were replaced with Old Glory. Victorious in battle—half the naval frigates and sloops had sailed on to other missions. The warships that remained behind appeared serene and harmless, akin to slumbering dragons in a hydrous lair. The hurricane was just a bad dream, the island a distant nightmare, and all of it was now in the past. At this very moment, and here on the placid waters of Port Royal, the sea was a pond of glass reflecting a cloudless sky. Molly was safe, Hannah and Malachi were rescued, and Tyler would soon be reunited with his father. That was surely something cheerful for me to hang my heart on.

After clearing with officers aboard the steam frigate *Susquehanna*, *Sphinx* was authorized to depart Port Royal Sound. Winton Macartney stood by the helm helping with the controls for the steam engine as Timothy steered us between the Union Fleet. Headway was remarkably swift considering that winds were almost nonexistent, yet we chugged above the seafloor in a relatively straight course and with no sails helping us along. Soon, we had placed Hilton Head miles behind us—next port of call, Washington D.C.

Chapter 29:
Back to the Free World

I hung my prayer book with some fishing twine from the overhead handhold to dry. Since notations were written in pencil, most of Grandmamma's entries were smudged but readable. I am certain that once dry, the pages will bloat and wrinkle, but those are blemishes I can live with if it meant saving the annotations they contained.

Our voyage to Washington D.C. was delightful. Having been marooned miles from land in a tiny skiff, I thought I would have lost my love for the ocean, but it only enhanced my respect and fondness for it.

Many of the impaired soldiers onboard slept or spent idle time in their bunks. Others, with more manageable injuries, hobbled around, looked out port windows, or sunned themselves in the cockpit behind the helm. Doctor Silas Brownell, with the help of new medic Tyler French, kept the injured as comfortable as possible.

We were miles out at sea. It was a beautiful day and I had planned to spend most of it up on deck. The schooner had all its gaffed canvas in flight, swung low over the port and starboard beams as we sailed swiftly downwind. Sailing in the same direction as the wind is the closest man has come to flying. Now you may argue that you have read in books or witnessed with your own eyes a gas or air balloon in flight. But is it really flying? A balloon is but a floating rock—an inanimate repository of hot air—servant to the whims of Aeolus. Have I mentioned that airships are azoic and lifeless? Whereby a sailing vessel is alive. Its winged canvas fluttering in gust or light air and, unlike ballooning, can do so while cradling a full congregation of souls nestled in its bosom. A sailing craft can master both an assault by a tempest or the kiss of a breeze—and in any direction you wish to go. Can't do that in a balloon. Though I will concede that a sail between Boston and Topeka, Kansas, would be most unlikely.

Though autumn was on its way, the southerlies were still brisk and in the right direction. *Sphinx* flew all its canvas with the exception of the staysail jib, which was used during the hurricane and while the schooner was hove-to off the coast of Cape Fear. The staysail was the only sail used during the storm and its task was to steady the ship and keep its nose into the gale. Though it was heavily reefed during the unexpected blow, an impaling wind split the material along its luff and parted the halyard supporting it. The unexpected hurricane had nearly driven the *Sphinx* toward Frying Pan Shoals, south of Bald Island, where the yacht would have surely grounded and broken up. But thanks to the seafaring experience of helmsman and cook Eli Monroe, a plan was devised by which the ship's drift toward shore was limited and its motion stabilized. His actions allowed the craft to ride out the storm safely, while making a crabbing advance away from danger.

The damaged sail was spread along the cabin top where Aaron Kerr sat, toiling with needle and thread stitching the long tear.

"A sailor with bodkin and spool, a man after my own heart."

"Aye, Emily, will ye nae sit with me and hae a chat?"

"What would you like to chat about?" I asked, sitting by the foremast.

"Whether ye heart is free an' lookin' to snaur a mon."

"My heart is spoken for, Aaron, and snares are for possums and rabbits, not men."

"Ye ur right thaur, lassie. Did ye noo mah last burd was a possum an' she played dead every time I tried tae snaur 'er."

I laughed. "How can a bird be a possum?"

"A burd, lassie … ye noo, a girl."

"Oh, I see what you mean," I laughed some more. "I cannot believe that. I find you an attractive gentleman and a catch for any woman with a snare of her own."

"Ah thenk ye fur th' compliment, lassie. I may be pleasant tae th' eye perhaps, but ah ain't noo gentlemon."

As Aaron and I tossed small talk, Molly and the captain wandered over. Tim was threading a rawhide lariat onto a straw hat so the wind would not take it away.

"There you go," he said, plopping the headpiece onto Molly's head. "You know, that hat is too big for you, but I think it should stay on your head now."

"Perfecto. Thank you, Mister Cadman."

"Perfecto, eh?"

"It's Italian or Greek. Father says it all the time."

"Where did you get the hat, Molly?" I asked.

"There's a couple more below," said Tim. "Amy left them. You know Amy and her love for hats."

"And shoes," I chuckled.

I left Aaron to his stitching and chatted with Tim. We leaned along the cap rail and watched the enfolding waves split by the schooner's bow as they curtsied away from the ship.

"I'm going to show Hannah my new hat," declared Molly, running off.

"Don't run," I shouted, "hold on to the rails."

"You never said what you were doing adrift in the middle of the ocean," said Tim.

"No, I never did."

"Do you not want to talk about it?"

"As I told Samuel, not right now. I'm still absorbing it all."

"It's a miracle we came along. Aaron was the first to spot you. 'Look, a wee ship way it haur,' he said."

I laughed. "He does have a way with words, doesn't he?"

"You can write a book about your adventures."

Tim was right. I would certainly post an account in my news diary with the innocuous title of "How I spent my summer." However, a book would have to be a narrative in fiction, for no one would believe the exploits we had endured—such as sailing through the nucleus of the battle for Port Royal in a tiny skiff, with cannon balls soaring in every direction, while being chased and shot at by plantation villains, and regurgitated from the fiery fray while whisked on the skirts of a hurricane, and all this while abstaining from injury. Then to drift miles from shore with only the slightest hint of dry land and no method or means of ever getting back. And to ultimately be emancipated from the void by a lost lover and his ghost ship sprouting from the seaways to rescue a girl who had herself been lost. Yes, I could write an astonishing, if not hallucinatory, account of places and people I have encountered.

The sail to the nation's capital took all of five days. After the infirmed and injured were removed from the ship, the *Sphinx* spent less than a day in the busy port before we were obliged to leave. There was just enough time for us girls to do a little shopping and find clean clothing. Unfortunately, there was no time for sightseeing. Nonetheless, we felt refreshed and civil once more and ready for the brisk sail back to the free world.

Chapter 30: Revelations Both Fond and Foul

Tiny Gull Town, a small cod fishing village, came into view as we sailed several hundred feet off the shores of Sheep Island. Sheep Island, as Hannah called it, was officially known as Nomans Land and sits less than five miles from the camel-tinted cliffs of Aquinnah on Martha's Vineyard, where Hannah spent her childhood. New Bedford was but a three-hour jaunt. Soon we sailed by the new fort at Clarks Point. Navigating by Butler Flats, we skirted craggy Palmer Island Light and the harbor entrance. Though it was a blessing to see the tiny island, a tinge of mixed feelings blunted the joyous occasion when Hannah revealed to me that it was used as a holding camp for Wampanoag Indians who were captured during King Philip's War and sold into slavery in the West Indies. Though the nefarious event occurred long ago, I felt like the south had followed me home.

News had been sent to New Bedford back in Washington announcing our approximate arrival. I had no doubt that Rudolf French would be vigilantly watching from his office window and waiting for us as soon as we stepped on terra firma.

Soon we were walking off the ship and down the boarding plank together—Molly, Hannah, Tyler, Malachi, and I. Holding hands, we marched enthusiastically up the wharf. When Molly glimpsed a sight of her father, she broke rank and ran ahead directly into his arms. Tyler and I lingered as Hannah and the black slave continued on.

"There he is, Tyler, Rudolf French" I declared.

"Yes … there he is."

"Been a long time."

"Ages."

"What are you thinking?"

"Somehow, he doesn't look as tall as I remembered him."

"He's the tallest man in all New Bedford."

"Who's that with him?"

"Oh, that's Edgar Ryan. He's a typesetter at your father's newspaper."

Rudolf and Hannah embraced, passionately. I was surprised somewhat when he kissed her on the lips and held her tighter than he should have. But the embrace was of little account. It was a fortuitous moment when taking into account all she had been through. Who was I to censure affection?

Rudolf sent Hannah back to the house with Molly and Malachi. He stood motionless, waiting, just staring over as we did the same.

"Well, Tyler French?"

"A new chapter," he said, nervously.

"In a new book."

"A father for a mother."

"You will always carry her in your heart. Go to him, he needs you now."

I stood watching as he trudged over to his father. Timidly, he stopped short and offered the newspaperman his hand. Like a true businessman, Rudolf shook it firmly then immediately drew his son into his arms. The boy broke into tears remembering the mother he left behind and embracing half of what was once a happy childhood. With his arms around his son, Rudolf waved me over.

"*De profundis!*" he bellowed.

"Hello, Mister French."

"Emily, my girl," he threw his plump arms around me, lifting me off my feet.

"I'm happy to be back."

"Of course, you are. There is no place like home."

"Home, sweet home."

Rudolf introduced Edgar Ryan to his son.

"You will be coming to work for the paper, will you not?" said Ryan.

"Well, I …"

"Of course, he will," roared Rudolf. "Unless his wants to finish medical school. And I will wholly support him in that."

"We will talk about it, Father."

"Yes, yes. Edgar, why don't you take Tyler to the house? I'm sure he doesn't remember where it is."

With Edgar Ryan's arm around him, Tyler walked down the wharf toward town. I could only imagine the pressman filling the boy's ears with colloquial small talk consisting of ethnological science or some other quirky and compelling interests of his.

"He'll be making many new friends now that he is back home," said Rudolf. He stood proud and joyful watching as his son walked away.

"Many," I agreed.

"Ah yes. It is splendid to have him back."

"I must tell you something, Mister French."

"Of course. There is much for us to talk about. After all, you had a very uncommon adventure."

"No, this is …"

"But you have successfully completed your mission. Molly and Hannah are back safely, and all is well with the world."

"Mister French … you're not listening."

"And furthermore, I must say …"

"Victoria's dead."

He stopped. There was silence. Showing little emotion, he walked to the edge of the wharf and stared down at the water. It was like the news of Victoria's death always existed in the deep recesses of his mind. And, in some way, it did. All it took was an impromptu reminder.

"I'm sorry, sir."

"When?" he inquired, kicking at the ground, hands deep in his trouser pockets.

"Just before we left Dukes Plantation."

"Did she hurt?"

His question was a difficult one. But Rudolf was a newspaperman. He lived in a world of naked facts—truths void of sentiment. A story had to be gospel with no hidden accord or alliances with empathy. Just the facts. I was a newspaper girl. It was the way I would dispatch it.

"There was a fire, sir. She ran into a burning building to save her cat. She never came out."

Like a true correspondent, he didn't flinch. He thought about it a long while. "You will speak to Edgar. Make a place in the paper for it?"

"Yes, sir."

He walked along the water's edge. Picking up a stone, he examined it and tossed it into the river. Looking down at the rippled water he reminisced about the past. "I did the woman wrong, Emily. Lust was the decoy, you see. It set out a morsel of bait to lure the weak of heart to its trap—a pound of bliss for a ton of bounty. The devil always gets his due. Fate dangled temptation and I reached out for it, almost destroying everything."

"I don't understand, sir."

"Nor do I … how is Dorothea taking it?"

"She's taking it well."

"Good, good."

"Hannah has comforted her like a mother."

"Of course, she has."

"Poor Molly, to lose a mother at such a young age."

He turned and took me by the arms. "Molly has not lost her mother, Emily."

"I understand, Mister French. Her memory will always be with her."

"No, no, you don't understand."

"I don't?"

"Victoria was not Molly's mother."

"What?"

"Hannah is Molly's real mother."

His disclosure washed over me, snatching my breath. The order of things was just plunged into a bath of frigid water. Instantaneously, bewildering events of the past resolved themselves. It explained Victoria's cold reception of Molly and Hannah's desperate concern for the child's welfare—or even the reason Hannah was kidnapped in the first place. I threw my hands up to my face and covered my mouth as words stuck between my teeth and wrapped firmly around my tongue. A discerning smile slowly matured on his face. It spoke to the future not the past. He wrapped his arm around my shoulder, held me, and squeezed.

"Now, let's go home, shall we? We have lots to catch up on."

It had actually taken days before I felt safe and comfortable in my own bed. I had been awakened by nights filled with mares, of Samson and Goliath chasing me through the swamp, of cannon balls crashing through the roof of my cottage. This night I was chained to a post in the Swamp House as the water level rose above my head. I could hear James Wilcox laughing, his image the shape of a Bowie knife with bull whips for arms. I screamed and called out.

Amy came running up the stairs from the rooms below. "Emily, wake up!"

"Oh, it was a dream. Amy? What are you doing here?"

"I knocked but you never answered. I let myself in."

"What time is it?"

"Almost eight. Are you not supposed to be at work?"

"Mister French gave me Monday off."

"Well, my darling, today is Tuesday."

I jolted out of bed and searched for my watch.

"What are you looking for?"

"My watch?"

"No use hurrying. You missed the school bell."

"I remember now. I lost my watch in the fire," I said, propping myself up on the bed.

"Here."

She removed the timepiece from its gold chain around her neck and handed it to me. I sprung open the embossed lid exposing the crystal.

"It says ten o'clock."

"Of course, it does. It's not working."

"What good is a broken watch?"

"It's not broken, Silly. I never wind it. Watches are so confining, always telling a body where you need to be or how old you're getting. You can have it."

"You are giving me this?" I started winding it.

"Sure. I rarely use it."

"Why do you carry it?"

"Fashion you see. It looks elegant on the gold chain around the neck.

"So, how do you know it's almost eight o'clock, then?"

"I was just over at Cory's store. There's a clock on the wall. If you must know, I let others carry time for me."

"Oh, I see."

"I've got Daddy's buggy outside. If you hurry, I can take you to work. Better late than never."

"Give me ten minutes."

"I'll wait downstairs. Wear a sweater. It's cool out."

I climbed up and sat beside her in the buggy.

"Is that not your Tennessee Walker, Biscuit?"

"Don't go anywhere without Biscuit. He's obedient and faithful."

"Like a good husband, huh?"

"Talking about husbands, you didn't tell me how handsome Tyler was."

"Amy! You have a boyfriend. Timothy takes good care of you."

"A girl must keep her options open until a ring is around her finger and another through his nose."

"Oh, Amy. You say the darnedest things."

"It's the consecrated truth."

The ride was an apprenticeship to the merits of being husbandless or wed. Oddly enough, she stumbled upon some consistencies and truths about finding a spouse, but most of them would involve a whip and bridle. Conversation and the company of a good friend made time pass quickly—to say little of a healthy fast horse. With his spirited gait, Amy's Tennessee Walker had the *Daily Whaler* in sight in a little less than an hour.

"Here we are," she announced.

"I hope Mister French is not too cross with me about being late."

"Oh, he's just a big cubby bear. If you use the right words, he'll dance on one leg."

"After all, he's just a man," we said in chorus. We laughed.

"You will find a ride home, won't you?"

"Oh yes, Randy Gifford's father always stops to make certain I need one."

I had barely stepped onto the ground when Amy turned the buggy in a half circle and rode back up the road.

"Don't forget to wind the watch," she yelled.

I stood at the entrance of the *Daily Whaler*, courage staggering. First things first, I thought to myself. Discover success with a sticky door, then, get past Ezra Hick unscathed. I turned the knob and gave it a determined shove.

"Good morning Mister Hick. It is good to see you doing well."

He scrutinized me as he often did over wire-rimmed glasses.

"O bed, O bed, delicious bed. That heaven upon eawth to the weawy head."

"What did you say?"

"Thomas Hood, young lady."

"I see."

"Yo'wa late. This is a newspape'wa, Miss White, not a bank. We have stwict hou'wes."

I never knew whether he was trying to insult, employ his hand at humor, or just plain honest. Nonetheless, his approach and greetings always stung like a bee. My encounter with Hick had further weakened my resolve. I could only hope that my editor wasn't angry.

Rudolf French and Zoeth Winslow were lifting windows and airing out the office when I entered.

"Ah, she's here," said an enthusiastic if not forgiving Rudolf.

"What is everyone doing?"

"Ceiling lantern filled the room with soot. Don't you smell that terrible odor?"

"Yes, what is it."

"Smoldering kerosene. But fear not. We'll have the room aired in no time."

"I'm sorry I'm late, sir."

"It's of no consequence. And stop calling me sir. It's Rudy."

"Edgar calls you Chief"

"Then Chief it is."

"It's been some time, Emily."

"Yes, it has, Zoeth. And it's nice to see you again."

The two men sat and discussed the specifics behind the Stone Fleet.

"Still planning a Stone Fleet?" I asked.

"Our country is at war, my girl. It's all hands to arms," roared Rudolf.

"We will talk more about it at a later time," said Zoeth, looking at his watch. "I'm meeting up with Captain Wood and Swift on the matter. Then it's on to Providence on some Underground Railroad business."

"Very well," conceded Rudolf. He walked Zoeth to the door.

"Happy to have you back, Emily," he said as he left.

Rudolf and I were alone. He rushed over to my desk and removed a pile of newspapers. Pulling out the chair, he dusted the seat off with his hand.

"Sit, my girl, sit."

He placed an inkwell along with a pen and stack of blank paper on the desk. I sat with whimsical cynicism, uncertain what he was up to. He stood looking at me with a vacuous grin.

"Comfortable?" he asked.

"Why … yes."

"Go on, then"

"Go on? Where, Mister French."

"It's Chief, remember?"

"Chief."

"Write."

"Write … what would you like me to write?"

"An article. I would suggest something along abolition, a commentary, or perhaps a biographical chronicle … you know, life in Dixieland. Or just a straight no-nonsense report of life on a southern plantation."

I took my journalist's notebook from my pocket. It had been over a week, yet the pages were damp and musty. I opened it and laid it flat on the desk. Some of the leaves clung to one another while others appeared joined as one.

"I would need to look over my notes. There is so much I could write about."

"Yes, so much indeed. Just come up with something and have it on my desk by the end of the day. We will run it in the morning edition."

"End of the day? I don't know if I can."

"Sure you can. I'm going down to the presses and I leave you to it."

"I suppose."

"Is there anything else you need?"

"Well … I'm not certain."

"Good, good. I'm going downstairs and I'll be right back."

He was about to leave when there was a knock at the door.

"Enter!"

The door slowly creaked open. It was the first time I ever heard it make such a sound. I expected Poe to walk in at any moment.

"Mister French, I'm here to fix the kerosene ceiling lamps?"

It was Paul Bourque, the man I interviewed at the Wamsutta Mills. He had with him a roll of wick material and a new ceiling lantern. A ladder was threaded over one shoulder.

"Yes, come in Mister Bourque. Now, I want you to change all the wicks in the ceiling lamps and the broken lantern above my desk. It smokes terribly."

"I'll get on it right away."

"I won't be long," said Rudolf as he left the room

Paul Bourque gave me a derisive glare while he set up his ladder. He flung his mangy coat over a chair by the side of my desk. The garment was patched in places and torn in others. Half of the buttons did not match. Inside one of the pockets I could make out the neck of a bottle containing the man's poison or liquor of choice. Paul Bourque was a bedraggled individual with bituminous oily hair, oily skin, and an oily disposition. His presence alone interrupted my breathing. I moved to the open window for some air. I noticed Rudolf was in the street talking to a couple of whalemen. Proof that he was a master raconteur, if he could muster a conversation of more than two words with a whaler—most of whom were tight lipped and solitary.

I found it difficult to get any work done while Bourque replaced the cotton wicks on the ceiling lamps and flung kerosene all over. The smell in the room was worse than ever. I walked by Rudolf's desk. A familiar scrap of paper in a wastebasket caught my eye. It was the letter I previously found on Asha Potter. I pulled it from the basket as I was compelled to read it. I was certain Rudolf would not have cared.

Holding it to the light, it revealed some truths that astounded me. Asha Potter and Victoria Dukes were siblings. She had written to warn him that there was an informer—a mole in New Bedford, who had relayed information about two runaway slaves to her husband. It warned Asha to be on the lookout and was signed your loving sister, Victoria. This substantiated what I already knew, and that Gideon and Malachi were kidnapped by Tyrone Dukes. But what of this informer she mentioned? It could be anyone in a city of twenty-two thousand. I glanced out the window to the street below. Rudolf was still engaging conversation with the two men. Placing the letter back in its envelope, I tossed it back in the trash.

The crude Paul Bourque had now climbed up onto my desk and dismantled the lamp above it. He knocked over the small glass inkwell that sat there, spilling ink all over the desktop. Instead of cleaning it, he continued to work, my notepad and writing paper firmly under his heel.

Once he was done, he moved himself to the far end of the room to the lantern just above the entrance door. I immediately rushed to my desk and tidied up. Taking a dust rag I kept in a drawer, I wiped the spilled ink. Blotchy footprints were everywhere. I threw myself back in my chair, frustrated and annoyed by the man's ignorance and ill-judgment. He could have at least removed my belongings before using the desk as a scaffold or just used his ladder. I believed he was mocking me. Perhaps it was an outlandish wage for the way I questioned him back at Wamsutta Mills over Asha Potter's death.

I picked up the stack of writing paper blackened by his feet and besmirched in ink. I was about to toss the entire pile into the trash. Without warning, my eyes sent my heart up to my throat. I was staring down at an ink impression left on the sheet of paper—a heel print. The same heel I had discovered at the French barn embossed in coal dust—the exact impression inscribed in blood at the Wamsutta Mill—and now a precise outline of those two renderings stamped in ink.

Dumb-struck, I looked down to the floor where sullied footsteps stained the grainy hardwood. There were eight distinct square rivets in a horseshoe pattern. I unmistakably remembered the locations of the dints in the coal dust upon the floor at the French barn, especially the first two markings that were closer together than the rest. My hands shook. I dropped the stack of paper. They divorced one another, flying in every direction. Looking down, I picked up the man's jacket from the chair by the desk. A button was missing. The remaining fasteners were sewn on by red knitting thread. I dropped the garment to the floor and backed away. Skeptical, he watched me. I looked up. At that very moment, our eyes meshed—mine in horror and his with suspicion. I opened my mouth. I tried not so say it. Unintentionally, the words splattered without fault and in full measure.

"It was you. You're the informer," I gasped. "You … you killed Asha Potter."

He slithered slowly down the ladder and locked the door. Calmly and threateningly, he lurched toward me. I looked around, realizing I had no escape. I retreated slowly as he came closer. My stomach quivered and I was becoming sick. Just as I was about to scream, he lunged, wrapping his hand over my mouth and another around my throat. Gnarly fingers squeezed until a silent scream became a trickling gurgle. My frantic plea for help was severed at my throat. With his large, callused hands clutched tightly around my neck, he dragged me to an open window. I clawed at the sill in a desperate attempt to stop him from flinging me to the street below. I struggled to be heard. A faint and muffled cry escaped me as he lay me grievously over the windowsill. It was just enough of a warning to draw Rudolf French's curiosity. Paul Bourque had me nearly out the window as

I kicked and scraped at him. I could hear rustling at the office door. Just as I thought I could not hold off any longer, my sentiments were followed by a resounding crash. The editor and two whalemen burst into the room. Bourque released me and I fell to the floor.

"*De profundis*!"

"He … he killed Asha Potter," I uttered, clutching my throat and struggling to fill my lungs.

"I … I didn't mean to do it. It was an accident," he surprisingly confessed.

"Come with us Paul," said Rudolf. "You must turn yourself in."

"No! You don't understand. He was going take my job away … re-replace me with that Negro … a dirty Negro. I couldn't let that happen … don't you see? What … what was I to do?"

"You must come with us, Mister Bourque," commanded Rudolf. "Don't make this any harder."

Bourque picked up a letter opener from the desk. "No, no! I will not go. You're not listening to me. He was going to replace me with that Negro. A Negro! Don't you see? I had to do something. I had to stop him!"

Paul Bourque was not about to surrender peacefully. Clutching the dull letter opener in hand, he backed away slowly. I crawled along the floor to get away from him. Finally, one of the whalemen rushed him. Without warning, Paul Bourque dove out the window where he came to rest sprawled and broken on the busy cobbled street below. I stood up and clung to the windowsill and looked down in horror. The man was not moving. Blood trickled from his ear. An arm and leg were contorted beneath his torso. We stared out the window as a crowd quickly gathered. I collapsed to my knees. Rudolf French placed an arm around me and helped me to my feet.

"Come Emily. I'll take you home."

Chapter 31: My Kind of Journalist

Randy Gifford's father dropped me off at work. Today I would not be late but early. What a difference a good night of sleep can make for starting off a workday. You would think that after all I had been through the day before, including being nearly pushed out a window, that I would have had terribly frightful nightmares or remained home and taken it easy. I did not and would not. Though I must confess, a restful and pleasant sleep, like the one I had the night before, was a nocturnal equation for which I had no reasonable explanation. I have been left to count lucky stars. And count away I did.

I felt good about solving the death of Asha Potter and I held my head high as I marched into the lobby of the *Daily Whaler*.

"Good day, Emily," bellowed Hick, unexpectedly. "You look well-wested today."

"Why, thank you, Mister Hick."

It was the first time I had witnessed the self-righteous clerk actually smile. To my surprise, I discovered that the thin-lipped Ezra Hick in fact had a mouth full of teeth.

I walked up the stairs and into the office. I realized my desk and the floor around it scrubbed clean. I threw my things onto the workstation and sat down behind it.

"What are you doing here?" demanded Rudolf. "I told you to take it easy and stay home today."

"I'm eager to get to work. I missed my time here."

"My kind of journalist," he crowed, leaping from his desk.

As he did the day before, he walked over with a fresh stack of writing paper. I noticed a new pewter inkwell with my name embossed across the lid and a quill pen to match sitting on my desk—beneath them a new notebook wrapped in supple leather. On the cover were the initials *EW* in fancy script. Looking the items over, I quivered with delight. I reached into my bag and yielded a number two pencil.

"You ready?" he asked. "It's your first story since you've been back."

"Yes, it is."

"I'll leave you to it, then."

I dropped the point of the pencil onto the paper and began to write.

Yesterday, on the very floors of the Daily Whaler, *the abeyant mystery behind the death of abolitionist and reformer, Asha Potter of Westport, Massachusetts, was solved.*

Glossary of Boating Terms

Aft-main: On a schooner, having two masts, the aft-main pertains to the mainsail on the mast closer to the rear of the ship.

Backstay: Wire or rope that travels between the top of the mast to the transom of the boat and holds the mast up and from falling forward.

Bark or barque: A sailing ship, typically with three masts, in which the foremast and the mainmast are square-rigged and the mizzenmast is rigged fore-and-aft.

Beam: The width of the ship, from side to side.

Belaying pin: A pin or rod, typically made of metal or wood, usually along the rail of a ship where ropes, lines, and sheets can be tied.

Bilge: The inside belly of a ship where the bottom of the hull curves and meets the side of the ship.

Bow: The very front of the ship.

Bower: A boat anchor.

Bowline: A non-binding knot, one which can be easily untied no matter what load is placed upon it.

Brig or brigantine. A two-masted sailing ship with a square-rigged foremast and a fore-and aft-rigged mainmast.

Bulkhead: Walls inside of a ship that separate compartments and which add strength and rigidity to the hull of the ship.

Cable: On a ship, a cable may refer to wire or rope.

Capstan: A revolving cylinder used on a ship for winding the cable or chain for anchoring a ship.

Chainplate: A strong point or steel plate bolted to the ship's sides, transom, or bow and to which the stays, rope, or wire which hold up the mast(s), are attached.

Cleat: On a boat or dock—a T-shaped metal or wood bit used to tie a boat to a dock or anchor or shore.

Come about: To change the ship's direction.

Companionway: The opening in the cabin deck leading to steps or stairs and the ship's interior.

Crans iron or fitting: An iron ring with eyelets. The ring wraps around the tip of the bowsprit and supports the wire or cables, which hold up the mast and support the bowsprit.

Crosstrees: A pair of horizontal struts attached to the sailing ships mast to spread the rigging or support and hang sails.

Crown and anchor: A simple gambling game of dice, traditionally played by sailors in the Royal Navy or fishing fleet.

Davits: Small crane or superstructure used to suspend or lower small boats.

Deadeye: A circular wooden block with grooves around the circumference to take a lanyard or rope, usually in series, and used to adjust the tension on the shrouds on a ship.

Doghouse: A raised portion of the deck to provide headroom below.

Dory: A small boat with flat bottom, high bow, and flaring sides, usually rowed and used for transport to shore or fishing.

Dry dock: A structure able to contain a ship and to be drained or lifted so as to leave the ship free of water on all parts of the hull including the keel and bottom and used for repairs, painting, etc.

Fairlead: A ring or slot in the side of the ship to guide a rope and keep it from moving about and therefore chaffing.

Flensing: To slice the skin or fat from the carcass of a whale.

Flotilla: A group of small naval vessels, especially a naval unit containing two or more squadrons.

Forecastle: The forward part of a ship below deck, traditionally used as the crew's living quarters.

Fore-main: On a schooner, having two masts, the fore main pertains to the sail on the mast closer to the bow of the ship.

Foremast: The mast of a ship nearest the bow.

Forestay: A stay leading forward and down to support a ship's foremast.

Frigate: A fast naval vessel, generally having a lofty ship rig and armed with guns on one or two decks.

Gaff: A spar or boom rising aft of a main mast and supporting the fore or aft main sail having four sides (gaff sail).

Galley: A kitchen or cooking area on a ship.

Gam: To visit or converse with one another for social or business purposes.

Gangplank: A flat plank or small, movable bridge-like structure for use by persons boarding or leaving a ship at a wharf, dock, or pier.

Gunwale: The upper edge of the side of a vessel at the rail.

Halyard: Any line or tackle for hoisting a spar, sail, or flag.

Hawsepipe: An iron or steel pipe in the stern or bow of a vessel through which an anchor cable passes.

Heave to: To stop a sailing vessel by turning it through the eye of the wind and backfilling the sails without readjusting their sheets or lines.

Helmsman: The person who steers a ship or boat

Hove to: *See* Heave to.

Hull speed: The maximum speed a sailing vessel can attain, for which is determined by the length of the ship at the water line.

In irons: A ship that has lost its wind and forward motion and has come to a stop or left drifting.

Knots: A unit of speed used by nautical vessels, being one nautical mile (about 1.15 statute miles per hour).

Lanyard: A short rope or wire through a deadeye to hold and make taunt standing rigging.

Lead line: A thin line that is dropped off the side of a vessel to determine the depth of the water.

Loggerhead: A rounded post, in the stern of a whaleboat, around which the harpoon line passes and is controlled.

Luff: The side or portion of a sail which is supported by the mast or the rigging wire from which it hangs.

Masthead: The very top of a ship's mast.

Mizzenmast: The mast aft of a ship's main mast.

Monkey fist: A ball fashioned into the end of a line to act as a weight for throwing, usually in a decorative weave.

Mooring: A place where a boat is moored, or anchored—commonly marked by a buoy or float.

Oakum: A twisted fiber used for caulking the seams of a ship.

Port: The left side of a ship (as you face forward toward the bow).

Pram: *See* Skiff.

Quarterdeck: The part of a ship, usually aft of the main mast, or at the stern or rear of a vessel.

Ratline: A series of small ropes across a ship's shrouds to act like rungs to a ladder and used for climbing the rigging.

Reach: A point of sail in which the wind is within a few points of the side or beam of a ship, or either forward of the beam (called a close reach), directly abeam (called a beam reach) or aft-beam (called a broad reach).

Reef: A ridge of rocks, or sand, or coral near or close to the surface of water

Regatta: An organized event of boat races.

Rigging: The ropes, chains, wire, etc., employed to support the mast, sails, etc.

Rockweed: A seaweed growing on rocks and exposed at low tides, usually having egg-shaped air bladders set in series at regular intervals in the fronds of the plant.

Roundup: When a ship is no longer in control and heads up into the wind or into irons, causing the boat to slow down, stall out, or tack. When the wind overpowers the ability of the rudder to maintain a straight course, the ship is said to be rounding up.

Rudder: A post hanging from the rear of a ship and contains some sort of flap or blade used to steer a ship. The rudder is controlled by a tiller or ship's wheel.

Schooner: A sailing ship with two or more masts, typically with the foremast smaller than the main mast, which is closer to the rear of the ship.

Samson post: A strong pillar fixed to a ship's deck to act as a support for a tackle, anchor chain, or line, or other equipment, with most being located at the bow of the ship.

Sheets: These are the lines that control and tie the ends of the sails to a winch or cleat.

Skiff: Any of various types of small boats used for sailing, rowing, or transport of small items or goods.

Shroud: A set of ropes or wire forming part of the standing rigging of a sailing vessel and supporting the mast from the sides.

Sloop: Historically, a small square-rigged warship with two or three masts, but in modern times used to describe a single-masted sailboat with one main sail and a jib.

Sounding: The action or process of measuring the depth of the sea or other body of water.

Spar: A thick long pole such as is used for a mast to support the bottom of a main sail and/or the top of a gaff sail. A bowsprit is sometimes referred to as a spar.

Starboard: The right side of the ship (as you face forward toward the bow).

Stay: A rope, wire, or rod used to support a ship's mast, leading from the masthead to another mast or down to the deck at the bow or stern of the ship. Not to be confused with a shroud that supports the mast from the sides.

Stern: The rear portion of a ship, opposite from the bow.

Tack: To maneuver the head of a sailing ship from one side of the wind, into the wind, and onto the opposite side of the wind.

Topping lift: Wire or rope used to support a spar or boom on a main sail or other sails and usually attached to the top of the mast.

Topside: The upper part of a ship above the waterline.

Transom: The flat or rounded surface forming the stern of a ship.

Trying: The process of obtaining whale oil by boiling strips of blubber harvested from a whale.

Try pot: Large tub, pot, or container used to help extract whale oil from blubber.

Tryworks: Location usually aft of the foremast on a whaling ship containing one or two cast iron pots set into a furnace and where whale oil is extracted and cooked from whale blubber.

Whisker stay: A line, wire, or chain usually attached between the sides of the ship at the bow and to the end of an extended boom, pole, or bowsprit, made to hold the spar in place and where a sail can be attached.

Yankee sail: A triangular jib sail usually flown off the tip of the bow or bowsprit and hung high on its stay.

Acknowledgments

I would like to thank my publisher and editor, Stefani Koorey, for her endless assistance in adapting this narrative into print and express my appreciation for her extraordinary talent in constructing and fashioning the cover design for the book.

Applause to Dennis Binette for his gifted skill in laundering the printed word unto the naked page.

Hats off to David C. for his last-minute saves.

And finally, my praise and friendship to furry Onsloe for his patience and calmness and diligently waiting for his walk.

www.ingramcontent.com/pod-product-compliance
Lightning Source LLC
Chambersburg PA
CBHW030822310726
48980CB00006B/600/J

* 9 7 8 0 9 9 0 8 1 6 1 6 4 *

www.ingramcontent.com/pod-product-compliance
Lightning Source LLC
Chambersburg PA
CBHW030822310726
48980CB00006B/595/J

9780615200750